flash
burned

also by calista fox
burned deep

flash
burned

CALISTA FOX

🦁 st. martin's griffin ♒ new york

This is a work of fiction. All of the characters, organizations, and events portrayed in this novel are either products of the author's imagination or are used fictitiously.

FLASH BURNED. Copyright © 2016 by Calista Fox. All rights reserved. Printed in the United States of America. For information, address St. Martin's Press, 175 Fifth Avenue, New York, N.Y. 10010.

www.stmartins.com

Designed by Anna Gorovoy

The Library of Congress Cataloging-in-Publication Data is available upon request.

ISBN 978-1-250-07252-8 (trade paperback)
ISBN 978-1-4668-8420-5 (e-book)

Our books may be purchased in bulk for promotional, educational, or business use. Please contact your local bookseller or the Macmillan Corporate and Premium Sales Department at 1-800-221-7945, extension 5442, or by e-mail at MacmillanSpecialMarkets@macmillan.com.

First Edition: March 2016

10 9 8 7 6 5 4 3 2 1

For David. I pray you found peace, my brother.

acknowledgments

My deepest gratitude to my fabulous agent, Sarah E. Younger; my wonderful editor, Monique Patterson; and everyone at St. Martin's who has contributed to the development of this trilogy. I couldn't be happier with the process and the support!

For my family and friends, I thank you once again for your love and your patience while I'm inside my head with all these characters.

And to my readers, you are never far from my mind when I'm writing. I greatly appreciate your continued support of my dream career and the kind e-mails that come my way!

prologue

I felt the chill at my ankles, swirling around my calves and thighs, moving upward to my stomach, where it seeped inside and slithered through me, to my heart. A frigid force that gripped me, constricting tightly so that I couldn't breathe properly.

With my hands bound above my head, I partially dangled from the exposed rafter of an entryway into the shell of a room that had no drywalling. I knew I shouldn't panic. I'd be rescued soon. They'd come for me. Dane, Amano. They'd never let anything happen to me. Ever.

Dane because he loved me fiercely. Amano because it was his job. Because he was loyal to Dane. And maybe, too, because he felt protective of me regardless of the paycheck attached to being my bodyguard.

On bare tiptoes, I struggled against the restrictive bindings around my wrists and secured to the beam. I'd kicked off my heels in an attempt to escape the man who'd kidnapped me and brought me to this half-constructed house in a secluded box canyon of

Sedona, Arizona—where the gorgeous striated red-rock formations could unwittingly prove deadly with their lack of cell service. So that even for those brief few moments when I'd had my phone in hand there hadn't been a single fucking bar to put a call through.

I continued to remind myself I'd be free soon. That Vale Hilliard wouldn't do anything more than hold me hostage, bloody my face a bit, and rip my blouse open. That he wouldn't get the chance to do to me the things he'd threatened.

I didn't wait patiently. Couldn't. The mere thought of his hands on my body made me scream and want to kick at him.

But this time, he wasn't on his knees behind me, holding my calves steady, keeping my assault at bay.

He wasn't even there.

Yet I wasn't alone.

As I wrested against his silk tie, slowly working my wrists free, I heard the quick-paced rattle that sounded deceptively like a sprinkler quenching a plush summer lawn. There was a second rattle, not quite moving in time with the other so that it was distinct enough to tell me the first had a friend. Then there was a third. A fourth.

My heart leapt into my throat. Fear seized me. I'd faced a diamondback before. At the moment, it was not something I had the constitution to deal with again.

I shot a look over my shoulder and watched in horror as they lay in wait, coiled and hissing. But they were just the beginning of my worries. Scurrying across the plywood floor, scrambling in my direction, were dozens of scorpions. All of varying sizes. Some fire red. Some opaque. Some black.

"Oh, God," I barely squeaked out. My pulse raged and tears burned my eyes. Insidious words tormented my mind.

. . . if you ruin my negotiations with Dane, I'll not only leave you here alone, tied up, but I'll fill this house with everything that terrifies you.

That would be rattlesnakes and scorpions. I'd encountered both in Phoenix, when I was a kid, then again at 10,000 Lux, where they'd been planted for me. I'd been stung before. There was only one other more excruciatingly agonizing sensation than a baby scorpion pumping venom into my system because it didn't know when to stop—losing Dane, as I once had.

Fuck!

I would attempt to climb the two-by-four in front of me, but scorpions could climb, too.

My breathing was now so erratic, it nearly eclipsed the tails going off more enthusiastically. As though the snakes sensed the panic in their prey and enjoyed my suffering before closing in for the kill.

I was trapped. I had no defense. No shoes on my feet to stomp on the scorpions, no way to flee the rattlers, now uncoiling and slithering toward me.

Fat drops rolled down my flushed cheeks. I choked on a sob. I couldn't even scream anymore; my throat had closed up.

Dane and Amano would be devastated they'd failed me.

Dane.

More tears flowed. I'd promised him I'd do whatever he asked in order to stay safe. I knew this would rip him apart.

But I had absolutely no escape against this particular attack. I couldn't get my hands through the slightly loosened sash that secured me and get the hell out of there. Terror consumed me.

As the danger rushed forward and the revulsion clawed at me, I pushed out one last bloodcurdling scream.

"Dane!"

chapter 1

I woke with a start and sat bolt upright, the chill still holding me hostage, despite the warmth emitted from the blaze in the hearth. I shoved perspiration-dampened, plump dark-brown curls from my face as my heavy breaths echoed in the quiet bedroom.

Heart thundering, pulse raging.

My gaze flashed to the empty side of the California king Dane and I shared. To the tall windows in his creekside house. To the clock on the nightstand next to me.

A little after three in the morning.

I barely had time to process the nightmare I'd just had—the vicious game Vale Hilliard continued to play in my mind—when Dane barreled through the double doors to our room.

"Ari." His emerald eyes were wild and filled with alarm.

"I'm okay," I quickly assured him, though I couldn't slow my breathing.

When he saw I was unharmed, he purposely schooled his hard features into softer angles. I'd witnessed his attempt to calm himself in front of me, to not be so enraged looking over what had happened in that canyon, and to not put me on-edge over the action he'd taken when he'd seen the blood on my face, my wrists bound to the rafters.

There'd been no snakes or scorpions. But I had been in Vale's clutches. That had shredded Dane.

"Ari," he repeated in a low tone. "What happened?"

"Nightmare. I woke myself. I'm all right."

I watched him try to loosen his stone jaw, with no luck. I must have screamed aloud, not just in my sleep. And it haunted him, the way the memory of that day in the half-constructed house did. The way it had torn us apart until we couldn't stand another second of the pain and I'd come to him here, making him swear we'd never be at anyone's mercy again. That we'd never be away from each other.

The latter was a necessity. We were fated, each desperately needing what the other offered. The former wasn't exactly a vow easy to make when the affluent Dane Bax was about to open the most exclusive hotel on the continent—and his former investors still wanted a piece of the pie.

I inhaled deeply, let out a long stream of air. Tried to steady myself, in hopes of wiping that guilt-ridden and tormented expression from his devilishly handsome face. "You just . . . You weren't here."

I'd felt his absence at the onset of the nightmare. Perhaps that was why, this time, I'd been left alone in the house, instead of Vale being there—threatening and sinister, but eventually defeated by Dane.

Not tonight. I'd been on my own, my most menacing fears unleashed. Including a missing Dane, who was supposed to rescue me.

He crossed the room in long strides and sat on the bed. The mattress dipped with his sturdy weight and it caused me to lean toward him. I clasped one of his rock-hard biceps to stable myself. And because he was too damn tempting.

His shirt had been tossed aside long ago, when he'd made love to me before we'd curled together and I'd drifted off to sleep, naked in his arms. I'd discovered from the very first night I'd spent in his bed that nothing compared to having his heat and commanding presence surrounding me. All those muscles. He would envelop me from behind, creating a cocoon of bliss and safety.

So much so that when he slipped away in the middle of the night I sensed it subconsciously.

"You didn't mention you had work," I said as he gently stroked my hair.

"Something occurred to me, and I had to speak with Nikolai. Different time zone in Moscow. It couldn't wait and I didn't want to wake him later on."

I nodded. Dane and his *legitimate* investors were doing everything in their power to bring down the more corrupt members of a poli-econ secret society they belonged to, and I knew that was significant enough to weigh heavily on everyone's mind, day and night. Regardless of time zones.

"I understand." I shifted closer to him and he pulled me into his strong embrace.

"I'm sorry," he whispered.

"No, it's okay. I have to get past all of this, find some way to stop freaking out every time you're not right here with me."

Granted, it wasn't as though I could seek professional help for this particular ailment. I couldn't exactly explain to a shrink that my boyfriend was part of a descendant Bavarian Illuminati faction that had turned dark and dangerous with insatiable greed. And he and some of the others fought desperately to extricate themselves from the oath they'd taken long before things had gone awry. Because, now, the actions of the corrupt members crept toward deadly—as I knew personally. Making time of the essence.

"Ari," he said against my temple. "I love you. There's nothing I want to protect more than you."

My fingers grazed his tight jaw. "I know. But there's something else that's important to remain focused on, Dane. 10,000 Lux. It's your vision, your dream. Everything you've been fighting for—something that means the world to me, too."

With an agitated sigh, he untangled himself and stood. He turned toward the windows and stared out into the inky night, jamming his hands into the pockets of his loose, pewter-colored pants. Frustration and anger rolled off him in waves.

I climbed out of bed and, from behind, wrapped my arms around him. One hand splayed over the corrugated grooves of his abdomen, the other flattened against his hard pectoral ledge. He was too magnificently built not to touch. Six-foot-three, broad shouldered, tanned and toned, with lush, strategically mussed black hair and beautiful, mesmerizing green eyes.

I leaned into him, my bare breasts pressing to his heavily muscled back. I kissed his warm skin as his hands covered mine. The chill abated.

"I know you're doing everything you can to save the Lux," I said. "You, Ethan, Qadir, and Nikolai. Even Amano."

Amano had been head of security for Dane's father. Though Dane's parents had died in a plane crash when he was just a month old, Amano had stayed on at the family estate in Philadelphia where Dane's aunt had raised him.

The others were part of the small, generational secret society Dane had broken sacred rules to tell me about. For my own good, and because I'd insisted on knowing everything he was embroiled in.

Getting involved with a mysterious billionaire had posed a huge risk from the start, but it'd proven inevitable from the moment I'd laid eyes on Dane.

"We're not far from the launch of the Lux," I said. "A little over a month. Everything's going as planned. No more mishaps. Clearly, the botching of Vale's ransom attempt, combined with whatever it is you and the others have done to stand your ground, is working."

It was two days before Thanksgiving. The grand opening of 10,000 Lux was scheduled for New Year's Eve, with a jaw-dropping list of celebrities, global political and financial leaders, and other VIPs who had already RSVP'd to the event of the decade. The Lux was the height of opulence, and memberships were costly and exclusive. In high demand.

It had been seven or so weeks since I'd been kidnapped, a pawn to get Dane to reinstate the original investment team. Since then, we'd been blessed with smooth sailing—with the exception of my occasional nightmares, which left Dane tense with fury and remorseful that I'd been caught in the crossfire.

He said, "We've come to a silent truce. But I won't take any chances."

That meant I still had a bodyguard. The six-foot-six, solidly built, dark-haired, mid-fifties, incredibly formidable Amano. A man wholly dedicated to his charge.

"I know everything will turn out fine, exactly as you want it." Dane was a perfectionist, and powerful enough to get what *he* wanted. "The only thing wrong at the moment is that I'm naked and you're not inside me."

He growled. A low, carnal sound that sent heat ribboning through me in the most alluring way.

He unraveled my arms from him and shoved off his pants. Lacing his fingers with mine, he led us to the bed. He climbed in first and held the covers up as I slipped in beside him.

We snuggled in the luxurious sateen bedding, facing each other. Dane swept a curl from my temple. His touch was tender, though his eyes blazed.

"Believe me," he said in his rich, intimate voice. "It didn't go unnoticed that you were naked."

I smiled. "I know." My fingertips grazed his erection before wrapping around the base. Sliding my hand slowly up and down his thick shaft caused him to let out another seductive, sexy noise. Excitement flared low in my belly.

His lips tangled with mine. Sensuous, tongueless kisses that drew me in, so that I forgot all about snakes and scorpions and scary extortion plots.

I sighed contentedly against Dane's lips. "You make everything fade away, dissolve into the background."

"Good," he murmured as he gently tugged at the corner of my mouth with his.

I pulled in a long breath, loving the smell of him. Male heat, a hint of sandalwood, and the enticing scent I could only describe as raw virility. Maybe that didn't qualify as a fragrance, but it exuded from him, encapsulating his masculinity and power.

I breathed him in, feeling a heady rush from the intoxicating aroma. All that strength and confidence. The dark, intense beauty of him. Everything about this man permeated my senses and left me burning for his talented touch, his stirring kisses.

"Make love to me," I whispered.

"Any way you want it, baby."

Ah, decisions . . .

He had a healthy sexual appetite and a clever repertoire. I was certain that even after several months together he still hadn't done to me everything he wanted.

But as my hand continued to pump, I had a change of plans.

"On your back," I quietly ordered.

He crooked a brow.

Okay, so *he* was the commanding one in the relationship. Dane had never once denied me anything, though. And now was no exception. I released him and he did as I asked.

I straddled his waist, my hands gliding over muscles that flexed beneath my fingertips. He clasped my hips and raised me slightly, easing me back.

"Not yet," I said, resisting him, though every fiber of my being ached to feel him thrusting deep. I had something else in mind. "You know how much I love your body."

"And you know I'm not complaining about that. But once you get me going . . ."

"Yeah," I said, leaning forward and nipping his lower lip. "It gets all hot and sweaty between us."

I kissed him long and leisurely, our tongues twisting. His grip on my hips tightened. Our kiss deepened, turning provocative and passionate. I threaded my fingers through his silken hair and let him take the lead. Until I was restless and returning to my deviated plan.

Dragging my mouth from his, I kissed my way over his jaw and down the thick cords of his neck. My hands continued to caress his chest as I moved lower. He relinquished his hold on me and I licked one of his small nipples. Bit it affectionately, making his hips jerk. Then I ran my tongue along his abs, tasting him, admiring all the ridges and warm flesh.

"Ari," he muttered sexily. His hands plowed through my hair, lifting the strands up and away from my shoulders and face. His cock nudged my opening.

I grinned coyly. "I told you . . . not yet."

Shifting lower, I kissed my way downward, over his pelvis. My lips brushed along him, from base to tip.

"You little tease," he ground out.

"I think you can handle it."

"Don't be so sure. Once you get started like this, it's not easy for me to stop."

I slid my tongue along the grooved underside of his smooth head, then closed my lips over him, suckling softly at first while my fist pumped again, unrushed.

"Christ, Ari." He sighed. "Baby."

Flicking my tongue over the indentation caused a bead of precum to form and I licked it up. Then I took him deep and sucked hard.

His hips bucked. His fingers tightened the strands he held before he caught himself and loosened them. "Ari. You're pushing me to the edge."

I loved how he responded to everything I did to him.

My fingers unfurled and I slid my hand down to gently massage his sac, carefully rolling his balls as I took him in as far as I could again.

"Just like that," he said in a strained voice.

I worked him in the way that made his breath come in sharp pulls. My tongue caressing, my teeth ever so lightly scraping on occasion, my mouth suckling.

"That's it, baby." He groaned. "You do it just right. You could make me come in a heartbeat."

I knew he wouldn't, though. There were times when I'd get him off like this, but since I'd gone on the pill and we didn't need a condom, he preferred to come inside me. It was what I wanted, too. Needing to feel all of him, including his release deep in my core. From the first time I'd experienced the rush of heat and moisture, I'd been forever addicted.

My head bobbed a little faster and I heard the hitch in his breath. His cock pulsed in my mouth and I knew I tested his restraint.

When he was close to the boiling point, his hands shifted to my shoulders. "Don't make me lose it," he insisted. "I want to make love to you." He guided me up his body while I left feathery kisses on his skin.

He kept leading me until his head was positioned between my legs, my knees on the mattress above his shoulders. The low headboard was tufted with distressed brown leather that matched all the chairs and the sofa in the room. A wide wooden ledge held a few expensive, artistic knickknacks and above it were framed sketches of various historic transportation schematics, with lighting to showcase them that was currently turned off. The only illumination came from the embers in the fireplace.

I leaned against the pile of pillows along the headboard and propped my forearms on the ledge as Dane's mouth covered me. A raspy moan fell from my parted lips. My spine arched and my long curls tumbled down my back. Lowering my hips, I pressed myself against him.

"You get so wet for me," he whispered, his warm breath teasing my sensitive flesh.

"Impossible not to. Just thinking about what you might do excites me. Actually, just looking at you does the trick."

"But this is how you like to come. With my mouth on you."

"One of many, many ways." Everything he did was thrilling. I could never get enough of him.

His lips tugged at my slick folds, toying with me as an electric current raced through my veins.

I let out a lusty sigh. Dane got serious.

The tip of his tongue flicked over my clit as the tiny bud pulsed with an erratic beat.

"*Yes.*" My heavy eyelids closed and I concentrated solely on how wonderful it felt to have him licking and suckling, driving me wild. He'd been the first and only man to ever pleasure me this way. Every time he did, I was so relieved he'd issued a *nothing's off-limits* ultimatum when we'd started our secret affair. That I'd accepted his demands.

It hadn't been easy, but now, as I climbed that beautiful peak he always took me to, I had to admit he'd freed me from my intimacy-phobic shackles.

"Dane," I whispered as the scintillating sensations heightened. "I'm so, so close."

He worked me a bit feverishly, his tongue fluttering over my clit.

"Yes," I moaned. "Christ."

I twisted slightly and slipped a finger into my pussy from behind, pumping slowly. Not to be outdone, he eased in two fingers with mine and quickened the pace.

"Oh, fuck," I gasped.

The flutter against the knot of nerves between my legs increased in tempo as well. The tension mounted.

"Come for me," he commanded. "Now."

He suckled deep. I erupted. *"Oh! Dane!"*

He didn't let up, and I quaked from the powerful release that went on and on. My body vibrating, my insides sizzling.

"You taste so fucking good." His words and his hot breath on my quivering skin kept my pulse jumping.

It took some time for me to be able to speak. "You want to be in me now, right?" My pussy throbbed with an incessant need for him.

I certainly wasn't above begging—had done it many times before. But Dane didn't disappoint. He withdrew his fingers and changed positions on the mattress, coming up on his knees behind me.

I returned to my propped-on-forearms position, back still bowed, my ass in the air. His supple yet strong hands cupped my cheeks, kneading almost roughly. I hadn't pinpointed which body part of mine he liked the most, since he devoted equal attention to them all and diligently admired the entire package.

He playfully smacked my ass, jolting me.

"Hey," I tossed over my shoulder. "That was for what, exactly?"

With a devilish grin and fire in his eyes, he said, "For being a bad girl and almost making me come in your mouth."

"You like it when I'm bad."

"And when you're soft and sweet."

"But that's not what you want right now."

"No."

"You want me half out of my mind while you fuck me."

"Hard."

My stomach flipped. The throbbing in my core intensified. "What are you waiting for?"

His fingers slid along my cleft, sweeping back and forth over my pussy lips and then massaging my clit. "I don't think you're wet enough."

"I'm plenty wet. *So* ready for you." Everything about the man lit me up, whether he was touching me or not. I more than wanted him—I *craved* him. Had to have him.

"I don't know, baby." He gazed heatedly at me. "I'm really worked up over you. You do a phenomenal job of sucking my cock."

My cheeks burned, though I should be used to his bedroom talk by now.

"I want you," I simply said.

With the hand he'd used to arouse me, he stroked his erection, coating his shaft with my cream, slickening the skin.

"Now who's the tease?" I asked.

His emerald gaze smoldered. "You know what *I* want."

"Dane, *please*," I finally begged, the way he liked. "Fuck me."

His tip slid along my dewy folds, and I let out a throaty moan. Anticipation mounted as he continued to toy with me. It was wicked, a bit sadistic, and exciting at the same time.

My fingertips pressed into the ledge. My nerve endings ignited. And he wasn't even inside me yet.

He rubbed slowly, tauntingly. So very tempting as his cock massaged with just the right amount of pressure against my clit and then along my damp flesh before returning to that ultra-sensitive spot.

"God, Dane." I could barely breathe.

He pressed into me, just the tiniest bit. A sample of what I desperately longed for.

He stilled. I rocked back, forcing him farther in.

"No." He didn't let me get away with stealing more of what he wasn't ready to give me, easing me forward with a hand at the curve on my waist.

"This is just plain cruel," I whimpered.

"Not when I want to make you come again."

He pulled out, his cock stroking along my folds once more. A bit faster. An exhilarating sensation that sent flames over my skin. He pushed against that throbbing bud between my legs and caressed skillfully.

As much as I wanted him inside me, the sensual rhythm along my hypersensitive flesh ensnared me. My eyelids drifted closed. I moved with him.

"Dane," I murmured encouragingly.

"Changed your tune, I see." Triumph tinged his intimate tone.

"Bed is no place to gloat."

"But sometimes you need a little coaxing to my side."

His very dark and edgy side. His intensely raw and occasionally dangerous side.

The hand that held my waist slipped around to my front and skimmed up to palm my breast. He squeezed enticingly, then pinched and rolled my nipple, pebbling it tight.

"You're trembling," he whispered.

"You're going to make me come."

"That's what I love doing."

A smile curved my lips. "And you're fantastic at it."

The crown of his erection nudged in once more. Dipping into me. Retreating. Dipping again.

My inner walls clenched, wanting to hold on to him, to never let him go. Wanting him to fill me and drive deep.

But then he went back to the erotic stroking along my lips and clit. A bit more forcefully, a heartier pace.

Lust shot through me. The thrumming in my pussy grew; the throbbing of my clit became strong, insistent. I clawed at the ledge as his hand shifted to my other breast, his fingers curling around the full mound, heavy and tender with my desire for him. The pad of his thumb whisked over the puckered nipple.

"I'm going to come," I said on sharp puffs of air. "Oh, Christ. I'm going to come so hard."

"Do it," he demanded.

I was so frenzied, my body shook with the pleasure he brought.

Dane's hand slid from my breast to that pearl between my legs, just as his cock thrust into me. *Deep.*

"Oh, fuck!" I called out. "Dane!" I with a fervent peaking that rocked me to the core of my being and sent scorching waves through every inch of my quaking body. "Christ!"

I clutched him, eliciting another low growl.

"Baby," he said as he buried himself all the way, filling me thickly, stretching me. "Squeeze me tight."

My inner muscles milked his cock.

"Like that," he whispered.

He stroked in a measured pace, almost pulling out before pushing back in. My orgasm still radiated vibrantly, prolonged by this new pleasure.

"Dane," I gasped.

One of his hands clasped my hip. The other still rubbed my clit as he pumped into me. "Nothing feels better than you, than this."

I was as caught up in the passion as he was, torn between needing another soul-stealing release and wanting him to stay sliding and stroking forever.

His hunky body curled around mine and he kissed my shoulder, then nipped at the side of my neck.

I pushed my thighs together, flanked by his. Felt him even fuller and more acutely, every hard inch of him.

I gripped him firmly, and he said in my ear, "You know what that does to me."

"It makes you want to fuck me faster."

"And I'm going to." His hips bucked as he plunged rapidly.

My breath hitched. "Yes . . . That is so good."

He hit that sensational spot within that lit me up. I panted harshly as the pressure built and he thrust quicker.

"Oh, God." My eyelids dipped, my back arched more, keeping my ass in the air, giving him the best access. "Fuck me harder," I muttered. "Make me come."

Greedy, sure. But I couldn't help it. I had an insatiable need for him. And the orgasms he gave me were too electrifying to not demand more.

"Ari," he said in a strained voice, his breath tickling the shell of my ear and sending a delicious shiver down my spine. "You're so damn tight. So wet. So fucking perfect."

I was far from the latter, but I certainly didn't mind that he lusted after me so vehemently.

"I need you to come for me, baby." His desire-roughened voice rumbled against my throat. His hips jerked skillfully as he pushed me closer to that alluring precipice.

"Dane." The humming between my legs and the blaze in my core were too tempting not to give in to. Though I held on a few seconds more. "Right there."

"I know." He stroked confidently, inside and out.

Crazed whimpers fell from my lips.

"Ari. Christ." His breath came in heavy pants with mine. "I have to feel you come."

"It's just so good . . ." But impossible to cling to, despite how much I loved climbing higher and higher. The tension reached the breaking point. "Dane!" I cried out as I shattered.

"Oh, yeah," he said gruffly. "That's it, baby. Come all over my cock."

He slipped easily along my coated inner walls, still rapid and demanding. Keeping my climax hot and pulsating.

I stole a glance at him over my shoulder. His jaw set, his eyes filled with excitement and myriad other emotions. He was darkly beautiful. Mesmerizing.

Mine.

Love swelled within me. So, too, did his cock as he pumped heartily and barreled right to the ragged edge I'd fallen over moments before.

"You are too damn irresistible," he told me, our gazes locked.

I felt the tremor move through his body, and then his cock surged and his body convulsed as he came.

"Fuck, yes." He groaned. "Goddamn, Ari."

His hot seed flooded my pussy, searing and wicked—making me come again.

"Dane." I clenched him.

The igniting deep in my core, the release of his essence into my body, the intimacy we shared was all much more than I'd ever imagined for myself. And now I couldn't fathom not having this in my life—not having Dane.

His sharp breaths mirrored mine, filling the quiet room. My body was limp; I was drained. But he held me to him, supporting me with an arm around my waist. With his free hand, he whisked damp strands of hair from my shoulder. I hadn't even noticed the beads of perspiration that had popped up on my skin.

He kissed the crook of my neck, then the nape, in the spot that made everything inside me tight and tingly. I clutched him again.

"Oh, yeah," he murmured. "Keep doing that."

I slowly worked his cock with my inner muscles. He shuddered.

"Can I make you come again so quickly?" I asked.

"Only you could do this to me."

I continued the tight squeezes, slow and measured at first. Then, as he grew hard, I picked up the pace, tensing around him, loving the feel of him as he stretched me once more.

"Ah, Ari," he whispered against my hair. "So sweet and sexy. Needing me as much as I need you."

More than I needed oxygen in my lungs and solid ground beneath my feet.

"I belong buried in your pussy," he said in his sensual tone. "Surrounded by you. So snug and warm and wet." His hips started to move again. Unhurried. Eliciting a slow burn. Pure heaven.

Though I held a claim over him, Dane Bax owned me. Possessed me. Call it whatever you wished, he had become my world. My lifeblood. Someone and something I couldn't exist without.

We both had our issues, our crosses to bear. We were both embroiled in something ominous. A mysterious, fragile intrigue no one outside our small circle knew about. Even my best friend, Kyle Jenns, had limited knowledge. And I'd not uttered a word of it to my father, beyond telling him of the obvious attraction Dane and I shared.

Perhaps that was what made our bond so fierce. We were entangled in a private, sensuous, twisted, fated affair that left us with little control over our feelings for each other. And certainly no escape from them.

Unfortunately, that did not keep us safe from all the outside forces that threatened to tear us apart again.

I tried not to think of the terrifying aspect of being so consumed by love, so desperate for Dane on every level. Lost myself, instead, in the feel of him gliding along my heat and moisture, steadily increasing the tempo as he fucked me masterfully. I submitted to him, as always.

His lips grazed along my spine. Then his fingers lightly traveled up to my nape. Down to my tailbone, making me tremble. He slipped around to my front and cupped my sex with his large hand, rubbing the pad of his thumb against my clit, coating his skin. Then he returned his attention to my backside.

As he pumped into me, he rimmed that previously forbidden spot with his thumb. I'd given him free reign over my body the very first time we'd made love. I'd not once regretted it. Couldn't. Everything he did turned me inside out.

Tearing my gaze from him, my eyelids closed and I rested my forehead against the top of my hand, splayed over the ledge.

He continued the decadent play and another orgasm built.

"Yes," I muttered. Fire roared through my veins as his free hand returned to the apex of my legs and he massaged my clit. "I'm burning up."

I palmed my breast, caressing it and pinching the nipple as all the sensations escalated.

"Come with me," he commanded in a thick tone. "Now, Ari. Now."

He thrust deep into my pussy, his thumb pressed in, and he exploded inside me. I cried out once more as his climax sparked mine, causing all that heat and tension to burst wide open.

My body shook. My lungs sucked in choppy breaths.

"Holy shit!" I blurted. "You are so fantastic."

I always thought it could never get better or hotter between us.

I was always wrong.

chapter 2

"This is the perfect garland," I said as I draped the four-foot-long fluffy deep-green sample around Dane's neck. Tiny bronze satin bows accented with thin, glittery gold and silver scrolls and just the right amount of clear twinkle lights woven through the plush mass completed the festive look.

My very tall, dark, and devastatingly handsome, though perpetually brooding, boyfriend/boss scowled at me. An expression I drolly (secretly) suspected he'd perfected around the age of thirteen or fourteen, given how comfortable and skilled he was with intimidating people.

And though it worked on others—and turned his chiseled-to-perfection features foreboding—all I had to do was tease his lips with mine, a soft tangling with a few sighs of delirium for good measure, and he was putty in my hands.

Case in point—

"Ari, you don't need my approval on Christmas decorations for the Lux," he said. "I trust you."

"Explicitly, or are you just sick of the previews?"

"Both."

I laughed. Slipping into his lap as he sat at a glass-topped table on our back patio reading the paper over breakfast, I said, "I don't blame you. But everything has to be perfect for the grand opening."

10,000 Lux was already touted as the West's Plaza Hotel, eclipsing the beauty of the Bellagio and Caesars Palace, offering more luxury and exclusivity than one could possibly imagine. The resort, the grounds, and the lobby were stunning, with no expense spared. Crafted specifically to steal breaths and inspire envy.

The first time I'd walked through the double doors, the only thing that had kept me from needing to pick my jaw up off the marbled floor over the opulence of it all was that my focus had been centered wholly on Dane. Owner of the prestigious hotel that also boasted five golf courses, designed by the best of the best.

Even my father, former PGA favorite Bryce DeMille, had been in awe when he'd played the Lux's links with Dane. Getting my dad to admit to being impressed when it came to anything related to Dane was a major feat, the courses included.

My father wasn't exactly onboard with my budding relationship. Nor was Kyle, who also worked at the Lux, in the Marketing department. In fact, he was currently up in arms over learning I'd recently moved in with Dane. But that was nothing new when it came to Kyle and anything concerning Dane and me.

"We'll be taking down all the Thanksgiving decorations over the weekend, following the dinner you want to host for the staff today," I said. "Excellent suggestion to treat them all, by the way. They deserve it. And what a great way to do an initial run-through before we get into the pre-launch festivities."

His dark brow crooked the way it did when he wanted to call me on my bullshit without actually having to say anything.

"Oh-kay," I amended. "It was an excellent suggestion *from me*."

It'd occurred to me that, since everyone on-staff had been going through the motions, learning the ropes, perfecting their positions and the world-class service that would be expected of a hotel of 10,000 Lux's magnitude, it would be great to hold a few parties throughout the day before Thanksgiving. The Banquets employees would take turns serving and enjoying a meal themselves.

Plus, it was an excellent trial for the kitchen staff, working cohesively on several large, back-to-back feasts. I'd also talked Dane into being present at each formal seating, to mingle and bond with everyone and to thank them for their hard work.

Everything had been coming together so beautifully of late. A huge relief, given how questionable the future of the resort had been with all the recent mayhem—a delicate term for what we'd experienced because of the corrupt society members.

I shivered at all that had gone wrong. And how I'd been targeted because of my close association with Dane.

His arms tightened around me. "What's wrong?" he murmured against my neck.

"Nothing. Just thinking that winter's moving in. It's a little chilly." A tiny white lie. I didn't talk to Dane about that day I'd been held hostage, not even following a nightmare.

My lips grazed his and, against them, I said, "You promised flannel sheets to keep me warm."

"No," he said, his emerald eyes holding mine captive. "I promised that *I'd* keep you warm."

"Oh, right." I kissed him again, my fingers combing through his hair and my upper body melding to his. My other hand skimmed over one broad shoulder.

With the outdoor heaters placed around the perimeter of the patio, he was able to have breakfast sans shirt. My preference. If I could convince him to strut around naked at all times, that would be even better. But Dane was the type to always be on high alert, fully cognizant of his surroundings, and prepared for anything. That meant at least having his pants on when he wasn't making love to me. Though I knew he lost himself in our kisses, which was when he fully relied on his state-of-the-art security system that monitored the premises.

It was a little disconcerting being so under lock and key but also comforting to know Dane had the danger contained now. Though, obviously, he remained cautious.

I nipped at the corner of his mouth and said, "It'll be a good two and a half or three weeks before we're done putting up all the Christmas decorations. Just in time for our first few pre-launch events with the press and potential members you want to woo."

"I asked Sales to crunch numbers so that we don't oversell the various levels of memberships. And I don't want anyone to ever be turned away from a suite, the dining room, or the golf courses because of full capacity. We need to leave a little wiggle room."

"It'll help to have all the casitas completed before we get into the grand opening festivities."

He nodded. "Almost there." With a grin, he added, "We're so close, baby."

"I know." I kissed him. "And I'm so thrilled. I'm happy you seduced me into the Event Director position—"

His brow jerked up once more.

"Well, you did," I reminded him. With a ridiculous salary and an outrageous annual budget. With a gorgeous office. With his hotter than hell body—and the promise of no-holds-barred sex.

I'd taken a gigantic bite out of all the offers and he'd reeled me in, hook, line, and sinker.

"Anyway," I said. "I'm just so glad everything's coming together. It's so exciting, Dane. Really."

His lips teased mine for a few sexy moments. "I knew you were the woman for the job. And for me."

"So sweet," I whispered as I kissed his jaw. "And flirty."

"Speaking of . . ." This time, his brows wagged.

"Uh-uh." I slipped from his lap. "We're going to be late."

His gaze narrowed. "You've never once said no to me."

It was sort of an unwritten rule I'd agreed to when we'd gotten together. And because I couldn't resist him.

"I didn't refuse you when you joined me in the shower earlier, now did I?" Granted, I wanted him to take me back to bed now, but added, "Today's crucial, Dane. We have so much to do before the first seating. Everything has to be perfect. And don't forget—I want a champagne toast from you. Heartfelt. Warm and fuzzy, even."

Now he glowered.

I sighed. "Heartfelt and . . . glowing," I amended. "I want everyone to know how much you appreciate the effort they've put into bringing the hotel on-line, their training, hiring of staff, *everything*, when we don't even have guests yet."

"I want them to understand that as well." He stood and added dryly, "I don't have to kiss babies on the cheek and let them pinch my nose, do I?"

With a laugh, I told him, "It's a mock run-through at a hotel, not a campaign trail. And employees only."

I headed toward the tall glass-and-wood-enclosed doors.

"Not that I have a problem with babies." His unexpected words chased after me.

I whirled around and stared at him. The first time we'd made love without a condom had been a risky endeavor, since I hadn't been on the pill long. We'd both been willing to take the chance that night. I didn't really know what to make of his comment though, so I simply said, "Think we have enough to contend with at the moment."

I headed into our bathroom for last-minute touch-ups. Then we drove to the Lux. It didn't matter how many times I'd viewed the perimeter with its stunning decorative black-and-gold-leaf wrought-iron fencing in between elegant ecru columns topped with large gas lanterns that burned even during the day, I would forever be in wonderment at the resort's beauty.

Dane's new limited-edition Mercedes McLaren slowed at the gate and he slid the tinted window down for the guard to ID him.

"Nice to see you, Mr. Bax," John said. Bending at the waist to get a glimpse at me, he added, "And you as well, Miss DeMille."

"Thank you, John. Happy pre-Thanksgiving."

"To you both, too."

"You'll be joining us this evening, right?" I asked.

"Wouldn't miss it," he said with a grin. "In fact, it'll be difficult to concentrate on anything else today. I can only imagine how Chef D'Angelo will elevate a holiday meal to Lux standards."

We'd included John with the executives' dinner, the last event of the evening. Dane held him in high regard, since he'd been the one on-duty when I'd been kidnapped. John had realized, in a split second, that what I had thought was Dane's rare Hennessy Venom F5 was a mirror image, but not the exact one. He'd noted the plate on the back of the sports car I'd gotten in to, was from Nevada, not Arizona. And had immediately contacted Amano and Dane to alert them to the situation. That rapid response had gone far in aiding in my rescue.

Amano had given John a raise. Dane had promptly sold the F5, unable to face it in his garage without wanting to rip someone's head off, as it reminded him of the danger I'd been in.

We passed through the tall double gates and along the winding stone road, edged by lush green grass and full sycamore trees. The grounds were meticulously groomed, and as we entered the circular valet area with the fountains and magnificent waterfalls, immaculate hedges, and fancy topiary I felt exactly the same as I did whenever we arrived at Dane's secluded estate. That I was home.

Awe overcame me, but I was used to it by now. The hotel was too amazing for words, with carefully placed vines climbing up the stone walls and the entire front of the enormous four-story lobby

accented with huge, asymmetrical windows showcasing a spectacular chandelier inside that I'd once joked could wipe out a small
village if it fell, and its accompanying, more reasonably sized chandeliers. Relatively speaking, of course. This was the Lux. The
height of lavishness and superior service.

One of the valets, Brandon, opened my door with his usual
friendly smile. I tried hard not to worry about what speculation
might run rampant over the fact that Dane drove me to and from
the resort these days. The story we'd given was that I'd been in a
car accident, which accounted for my presumably "totaled" SUV,
the scar on my forehead, and the fact that I'd left the Lux for some
time following the incident with Vale, which no one other than
Dane, Kyle, and Amano knew about. Everyone appeared to buy
it, but I wouldn't have been surprised if I offered some watercooler
fodder.

"Good morning, Miss DeMille," Brandon beamed. He'd
dressed in his special-occasion uniform—a tailored cutaway black
tux and white gloves. The casual attire for him and the other valets
was dress pants with an elegant polo shirt, both in black, with the
hotel's elaborate crest in gold on the left chest.

"You look dashing," I told him.

"Yeah, Hollywood's been calling. They want me to be the next
James Bond."

"Come on, now. That's not worth leaving 10,000 Lux."

His grin widened. "Sorry, but having my own Bond girl just
might be enough to lure me away."

I laughed. "I suppose I could see how that might tempt you."

Dane collected me, gesturing for me to precede him toward the
entrance. Two other impeccably dressed valets pulled the tall doors
open as Brandon sped off in the McLaren. We entered the lobby,
all gleaming marble and rich wood. The round table in the center
was a focal point with a bronze, silver, and gold vase standing nearly
six feet and positioned in the middle of the table, below the main

chandelier. It sprouted gorgeous cream-colored flowers and dripped lush green foliage.

Farther back were two curving staircases with more of the decorative black wrought iron and marble that led up to a mezzanine. The entire property was breathtaking, but the lobby really spoke to me. The most minute details had been seen to, making it a fairy tale come to life. I'd take the Lux over any palace, any day.

It wasn't just the sophisticated extravagance that made the resort so near and dear to my heart. It was the fact that it was Dane's dream. His vision. His blood, sweat, and tears. He'd conceptualized the hotel and the grounds, then worked with engineers, architects, and designers to bring it all together. He had every right to be proud of the end result.

We walked to the west-wing bank of elevators. The executive offices were on the floors of this section of the hotel. The east wing was reserved for the guest suites and penthouses. The property was also covered with numerous two- to six-bedroom casitas boasting views of golf courses, babbling brooks, or mirror-surfaced ponds. All of it surrounded by the awe-inspiring red-rock formations of varying shapes and sizes. Rippled sandstone mesas, spires, and canyons. The location couldn't be beat.

We stepped out of the car on the top floor and Dane left me momentarily at my office. Amano awaited us.

I unpacked my laptop and responded to some e-mails; then it was time for the first seating. The weather was nice with our mild autumn, following one of the longest monsoon seasons in Sedona's history. The supplement of tall heaters with pyramid glass tops filled with roaring flames made it possible to host the day's events outside in the grand courtyard. A huge space with the potential to accommodate thousands of guests. There were also event lawns and a conference center with ballrooms on-property.

I'd selected the grounds by the gardens and fountains, however, because I wanted to see how we could work with the spaciousness when it came to an intimate group of roughly seventy-five to a hundred per party.

The first soiree was a lively brunch with a jazz ensemble to provide entertainment. The buffet tables were covered with full-length cloths and elegant silver chafing dishes. There were endless choices of salads and sides, along with four different carving stations, including pork loin, duck, prime rib, and the most gorgeous turkey I'd ever laid eyes on. Chef put his five-star spin on the traditional holiday fare as well as the contemporary offerings.

We'd set the brunch with rounds of eight, fully decorated with dramatic floral centerpieces, votives, and real fall leaves in crimson, orange, and gold. The full-length tablecloths were rich sienna satin and enhanced by shorter organza toppers in shimmering amber.

The china and flatware, as well as all of the serving dishes, had stocked the dining room while resort staff had been hired and had been invited to enjoy the food during their breaks for a very nominal monthly fee. It would all be moved to the employee dining room when the Lux opened, and all of the members-only dining rooms, formal and informal, would be equipped with new tables and chairs, never-before-eaten-off-of plates, and accompaniments, right down to butter knives and napkins.

I made the rounds, checking on everyone and noting on my iPad what worked well and what needed improvement. Dane was a gracious host, a little less boss and a little more personable, even cracking a joke or two, which seemed to take the staff by surprise.

The second seating was a four-course plated lunch. We used a u-shaped setting with six-foot tables to get a feel for that sort of execution. For dinner, we had a smaller crowd, since it was only the department heads and their directors. I didn't have a VP over me— just Dane, per his desire.

In addition to cataloging the pros and cons of this last party, I also mingled and sampled the food. A cocktail reception was set in the rose garden, with numerous high tops, three full premium bars, and a martini bar that was a lit ice sculpture carved into the 10,000 Lux crest and which chilled the martinis as they flowed from the top and drained into glasses at the bottom. There were also various appetizer stations, including a seafood tower, dim sum, and antipasto and charcuterie with imported cheeses and meats, foie gras terrine, pâtés, and more.

Tuxedo-clad servers also roamed the grounds, offering fancy hot and cold hors d'oeuvres and Cristal.

I'd brought in the pianist and harpist I'd hired for my last over-the-top wedding as an independent planner and they sounded lovely in the mostly quiet night, with the hint of fountains in the distance.

"This is pretty incredible," Kyle said as he sidled up next to me. He was a sky-blue eyed Adonis with crazily mussed sandy-brown hair. At twenty-two, he was four years younger than me. "You did an awesome job."

"I have staff, remember? Lots of help." Though I inwardly beamed at his compliment.

"Sure, but you planned it all, right?"

"It's surprisingly not that dissimilar from planning weddings."

"I feel like I'm in a movie. And the food . . ." His beautiful blue eyes seemed to practically roll into the back of his head. "I'm eating my way through the stations." He also snagged a duck confit spoon appetizer from a passing waiter and then a toasted baguette round with the most amazing melt-in-your-mouth beef carpaccio I'd ever tasted.

"Don't forget we're also here for dinner," I said. "Chef will *not* be happy if you don't devour all five courses."

"Yeah, wow." He deposited the empty spoon on a silver-plated cleanup tray that came around and then reached inside his suit jacket to the inner pocket and pulled out the menu card he'd lifted from one of the place settings. "I don't even know what any of this stuff is, aside from the turkey—and even that's too fancy to pronounce."

I laughed. "It's a French dish. Don't worry about it. Believe me when I say it'll rock your world. I've sampled everything over the past couple of weeks and have the too-tight dress on to prove it."

For the evening, I'd changed into an emerald strapless mini. The one I'd bought for my job interview, which had actually been a private dinner with Dane on the terrace of the hotel. It was my favorite dress, because it was close in color to his vibrant eyes.

"You look sensational," Kyle commented as his gaze slid over me, glimmering with adoration.

He knew better than to admire me in Dane's presence, but since Dane was currently preoccupied with a group of execs, I surmised Kyle felt bold enough to steal more than a quick glimpse.

Yet I knew Dane's full concentration was never diverted when I was close by. I glanced his way and found him watching us. Scowling.

"You've been spotted," I told Kyle with a hint of excitement in my voice over Dane's territorial nature. "Keep it clean, or you'll get us both into trouble."

Kyle scoffed. "Serves him right for leaving you on your own."

"He's speaking with his employees. Socializing. It's what one does at a function such as this. And besides, he trusts me."

Kyle gave a half snort. "Well, he shouldn't trust *me*."

"He doesn't." Except when absolutely necessary, like on those rare occasions when Amano wasn't available to shadow me.

"Good," Kyle said.

I smirked. "Stop being so antagonizing."

"He started it."

With a laugh, I told him, "I don't need the two of you fighting over me."

"You want to warn me that I'll lose," he said, a dark edge tingeing his usual light-hearted tone. "But you're forgetting that I know how bad he is for you. I'm just biding my time until he fucks up again."

"Don't say that." I didn't like how convinced Kyle was that

things would go awry again with Dane—and that I'd somehow land in his arms. "You and I are friends. That's all we'll ever be. You need to accept that, because nothing is going to take me away from Dane. And for the record, what happened wasn't his—"

"Don't you dare say it wasn't his fault," Kyle shot back, albeit under his breath. "You were *kidnapped*, Ari. Beaten. I saw how fucked up your face was—how fucked up *you* were."

I sipped my champagne, trying to calm my suddenly frayed nerves. "I have a lot riding on tonight, Kyle. Try not to wreak havoc on it."

I turned to go, but he simply said, "Ari."

I melted a little.

Facing him once more, I gave him a look I knew screamed *ultimatum*. "You either deal with it, or you don't." I didn't have to say the latter meant we couldn't be friends. He already knew that.

I'd never once led him on, had never done anything to encourage him or make him think we'd move beyond this stage. Ever. But Kyle didn't give up.

He was incredibly special to me, one of the many reasons I was careful not to give him any wrong impressions. We'd gotten to know each other in a short amount of time and I had put a hell of a lot of faith in him. He was the only one I confided in about my relationship with Dane. And its perils. *As a friend.*

Kyle knew that, but sometimes—especially when he thought Dane was being too possessive—he came a bit close to crossing the line.

"Look," he said. "I know you made a specific appeal to your boyfriend so that I could attend the executive dinner instead of the lunch with my level of staff. So we could hang together tonight. I appreciate that. I'm not trying to be an asshole here. I'm just . . . you know . . ." His jaw clenched briefly. "I hate what happened to you, Ari. I mean, I'm glad you didn't shut me out, that you told me about it. Really glad. I'm always going to be here for you. You know that. It just gets a little irritating that you don't see the big picture."

In a low voice, though no one but Dane paid much attention to us, I said, "What I have with Dane *is* the big picture, Kyle. For me. I told you that I love him. That's not going to change."

"It's okay to say that now." He shoved his hands in his pockets. "Because I'll still be around when you eventually get over the King of Everything and join us real people in the real world."

I glared at him. "If you don't like working at the Lux—"

"You know I do. I have amazing projects and we get to see each other every day. I'm grateful for the job. That doesn't mean I have to like *him*."

"He's part of me," I reminded Kyle, my mouth set in a hard line. I wouldn't yield on this subject.

With a shake of his head, because he clearly didn't like that summation, he said, "Lighten up and drink your champagne."

I took another sip. He flagged down a waiter and grabbed his own glass.

A few more tense moments passed. Then he added, "I'm not trying to upset you. I'm trying to protect you."

"Get in line."

He grimaced. "Yeah, I can see you still have a bodyguard." Amano patrolled the outskirts of the reception. "But . . . nothing's happened recently, right?"

As much as Kyle wanted to prove me incorrect about Dane—which would entail something going drastically wrong—of course he didn't want to see me hurt. Even my heartbreak had torn him up, because temporarily losing Dane had devastated me.

"All's well on all fronts," I assured him. "And we're about to be asked to sit for dinner."

The arrangements now included one rectangular setting with long and low bouquets so conversations across the table weren't hindered, more candles, and continued music. I'd had place cards made up and put Dane in the middle, rather than at the head of the table. That way, he could converse easily with a larger audience, instead of just those fortunate enough to be at his elbows.

It likely wasn't the smartest thing to situate Kyle next to me, but since we sat across from though a few seats down from Dane, I suspected he'd feel a modicum of relief that I was close by, where he could keep an eye on us.

His jealousy had shocked me from the onset—he hardly seemed the type, given his social and economic status. The fact that he was in a league so very far beyond me. But from the moment I'd inadvertently disrupted his business meeting at a resort in town and Kyle had swooped in to flirt, Dane had wanted to keep me out of his clutches. And any other man's.

I sensed Dane's gaze now and spared another glance toward him. Those mesmerizing green eyes glowed seductively in the candlelight. The look that flashed in them indicated he wasn't thinking of how Kyle monopolized me in conversation and stuck close. He was imagining what he'd do to me when we were alone at home.

Biting back a lusty sigh, I tried to focus on what Kyle was saying about pre-launch invitations, the ones he'd been designing. But a dull ache inside had my mind preoccupied with thoughts of Dane.

I squirmed a little in my seat as flames skated over my skin. I couldn't resist a smile and gave it to Dane. One corner of his mouth lifted in the sexy, secretive grin I loved. My pulse raced.

Returning my attention to Kyle, who hadn't noticed my lapse while he dug into wasabi mashed potatoes and ham, I said, "We're adding a special media night as well. Did someone mention that while I was out? It'll be a pretty big press event."

He paused just long enough to say, "No. Date?"

"I haven't confirmed with Dane, but I'll let you know and get you the details. We're looking for an international turnout, so consider that as you're running ideas through your head on design."

"Got it." He went back to the food. "Damn, this is good."

I was looped into a conversation with the VP and director of PR and let Kyle wolf down the rest of his meal. He was of the strapping variety. A former college football player and frat boy. Regular workouts and mountain-biking Sedona's famed trails kept him in phenomenal shape, post-quarterback days.

We'd met when he was the best man for the same wedding where I'd first encountered Dane. My heart skipped a couple of beats at that crazy night months ago and I shot another look Dane's way. He was engaged in a discussion with the heads of HR and Legal, two women who were extremely efficient, with clipped tones and quick brains. Very *let's get down to brass tacks* types. I'd found them a bit terse and dry in the beginning, but once they'd come to realize Dane trusted and valued my opinion they'd eased up a bit. Would even snicker at one of my sardonic comments from time to time.

True to form all day long, Dane stood during dessert and delivered a well-thought-out and engaging speech.

"The majority of you at this table tonight were the first to come onboard when we started hiring at the Lux," he said. "You've worked through construction noise and dust, and you never lost focus on the task at hand. I recruited and hired you for specific reasons. Because you're the best in the hotel industry in your respective fields. Because you've been committed in your past endeavors— and you remain so with this present one. You understand my vision and have adopted it as your own. More than that, you embrace the importance of what 10,000 Lux stands for . . . not just luxury, opulence, *brilliance*—"

He spared another glance my way, because I was one of few who'd caught on quickly as to the true definition of *10,000 Lux*. It was an audiovisual term that meant "brilliant light."

Continuing, he said, "But a phenomenal level of customer service that speaks to the world." He lifted his Baccarat crystal flute and added, "Because of all that you've done to prepare for our grand opening, our reputation has preceded us."

Excitement rippled through the crowd.

Dane said, "As a result, VIPs global-wide have clamored for a membership at the Lux. And, according to Max Denton"—he gestured to the VP of Memberships with his glass of bubbly—"we are less than a quarter of the way from capping all tiers of membership."

I gasped despite Dane confiding in me earlier about the Lux's grand success.

He grinned triumphantly. "We're *the* resort to own, the one everyone wants to be seen at, be a part of, be included in. I predict that, promptly after the launch, we'll close memberships."

A round of applause resonated soundly in the enormous courtyard. Patricia from HR got to her feet. Margo from Legal followed. A second later, everyone at the table stood, giving an ovation to Dane as much as to their own hard work.

Tears of joy burned the backs of my eyes. This was really happening. We'd overcome all the obstacles, setbacks, and terror. And there wasn't a single person—not even Kyle, for God's sake—who didn't take pride in the accomplishment and show respect and appreciation for Dane.

And to meet his goal so quickly . . . That meant billions just from memberships alone, which only provided the privilege of setting foot on Lux property. Members still had to pay for meals, cocktails, suites/casitas, and greens fees.

My mind reeled. As if Dane's wealth hadn't intimidated me before. . . .

He lifted his glass and concluded his toast. "This is something we've *all* achieved. And I want you to know that it couldn't have come about without you. It couldn't have happened, period. So I hope that you'll accept my sincere gratitude for the hours and the effort you've put in and, as I've mentioned to your staff in our earlier festivities, you will find a bonus in your next paycheck that I hope you'll consider . . . generous."

My eyes popped. *Holy shit.* When it came to Dane, I knew what the word *generous* meant. Like pack up your family and treat them to two weeks in Bora Bora—first class all the way.

Kyle leaned toward me and deadpanned, "Think I'm included in the bonuses?"

Tearing my gaze from Dane, I said, "Don't be an ass."

He chuckled under his breath. "Maybe he's hoping I'll buy a boat and sail far, far away."

"Likely."

"Tempting, but . . . you'd miss me. And I couldn't have you pining. It's not becoming."

I laughed. "I'm not sure where that ego comes from, though . . . I do find you amusing."

"That's something, now isn't it?" His eyes sparkled. He was too charming for his own good.

"You do realize there are upward of a hundred women working here who would rip each other's hair out in order to get to you?"

"Hmm, really? That many?"

"Well, I haven't taken an official poll and weeded out the marrieds and otherwise committed, but let's face it. I get the evil eye when you're chummy with me."

"Ha. Now you know how it feels."

My gaze shifted to Dane. He glowered. Though only slightly.

He was clearly on a Lux high. The excitement dimmed and we all sat.

Mark said, "So with memberships almost covered, I guess I'm out of a job."

Some laughed at his joke. Those sitting close to him offered condolences by way of pats on the back or hand.

Dane said to Mark, "First of all, managing all of the memberships is a huge, ongoing job. Trust me, you'll be plenty busy. Second . . ." He shook his head and let out a surprising chuckle. "Who says this is the only property I'll offer?"

Surprise ran rampant. Patricia said, "You're not suggesting other resorts of this caliber . . . ?"

Dane shrugged noncommittally. Exhilaration permeated the

courtyard, overpowering the surprise. Oh, the career opportunities that abounded with this revelation!

I eyed Dane and he held my stare. If he were any other man, I'd say delusions of grandeur got the best of him. But he wasn't any other man. Not an ordinary one. He thought so freakin' far outside the box, so far over the rainbow, I didn't doubt for a single second that if he wanted another property to rival the Lux's magnificence he could pull it off—easily. Plus, I suspected he'd eventually need another challenge.

The remainder of dessert was spent with enthusiasm over the grand opening and what the success of 10,000 Lux might spawn—and how it could impact the execs who knew their worth, their value, in this environment.

By the time we wrapped up dinner and the valet brought around Dane's McLaren, I was almost dead on my feet from all the event planning and the fervor that had engulfed the dinner crowd.

When we arrived home, Dane quietly said, "Sit tight."

He exited his side of the car and came around to open my door. He unlatched my seat belt and scooped me into his arms.

"My bag," I murmured.

"I'll come back for it." He carried me to the double doors and I used the hidden keypad to gain access. The alarm chimed as we stepped inside and I disengaged it with the code while still in his arms.

He took me to the bedroom and set me on the edge of the mattress.

"Maybe you overdid it," he said as he deftly removed my clothes and then slipped a dark-silver satin nightgown over my head. He'd bought it for me in Paris, because the color and the Tahitian pearl accents on the bodice had reminded him of the outfit I'd been wearing the night we'd met.

It was a full-length, luxurious garment I loved to feel against my skin. But . . . "Are you suggesting we're sleeping?"

"Baby, you can't possibly have anything else in mind. You'll be asleep in two minutes." He discarded my shoes and rubbed my sore feet.

"But I had to spend all day pretending we weren't going to end up in bed together tonight so I didn't give myself away to your employees." I speared him with a look, weary though I was. Perhaps a tiny bit tipsy from the Cristal and a work high, too. "Do you realize how hard it is to be so close to you in public and act as though we're not getting naked in private?"

My fingers grazed his chiseled cheek, his set jaw. Along his neck and to that pulsating point in the hollow of his throat where I could lick and suckle for all of eternity and be one deliriously happy woman.

The errant thought made me giggle. I said, "I could literally eat you up."

He groaned. "You know there's nothing more that I want to do at the moment than make love to you. But, Ari"—he stared into my eyes—"I know exactly how much time and effort you put into today, and there's no way in hell I'm sapping more energy from you because of *my* needs."

"Really, put like that, you think I can resist you?"

With trepidation in his voice, he said, "Sleep now. Tell me how you feel in the morning."

I groaned in protest and pulled away, falling back against the delectable mattress and its thick covers.

"My body is *so* ready. . . ." As always.

Dane chuckled. "And your brain is thoroughly fried."

"Like . . . so much. I've literally forgotten everything outside of work. I haven't even returned the last few calls from my dad. Thank God he knows how busy I've been so he's not freaking out. I've missed a dental cleaning and a hair appointment. If Rosa didn't pick up our dry cleaning for us, we'd be out of clothes by now."

"It'll all get back on-track soon. This has been a really big push the past month. And tonight, you just need to forget about everything and relax."

He disappeared briefly to get our laptop bags and lock up while I rallied the strength to walk to the bathroom and take off my makeup, let down my hair.

Dane returned and he lit a fire in the hearth, then snuggled with me in bed. He reached back to the nightstand on his side and turned off the light. Silvery moonlight streamed through the tall trees filling the property and filtered through the unadorned floor-to-ceiling windows.

Spooning me—my favorite sleeping position—he held me tight to his hard body. I felt his heat . . . and his desire for me.

"Dane."

"Shh."

His embrace was firm and protective. Sweet and seductive. I grew restless by the second, despite how exhausting my day had been. And the weeks leading up to it.

"We didn't really get to talk to each other tonight at the dinner," I said in a sleepy voice.

"You're the one who insisted on the seating placements," he reminded me with a chastising tone. "I wanted you next to me. You—"

"Thought it was too obvious," I said for him.

"And, now, I'm pretty sure everyone's wondering if you're with Kyle."

I smiled, though he couldn't see it. "That's ridiculous. We argue like siblings. And I can't possibly be the only one who sees how you look at me. Even when you think it's just a fleeting glance, it's still wholly possessive."

He was quiet for several moments. His warm breath blew against my neck. I cherished the intimate shelter Dane created with his hunky body curling around mine, tucking me against him.

"You think they all know how I feel about you?" he asked in a contemplative tone.

"No. Definitely not. I think they wonder why you bother by way of giving me rides and whatnot. My guess is, they surmise you're remorseful that I was targeted when it came to the on-site troubles. Maybe they just believe you want to make it all up to me."

Silence enveloped us again.

Honestly, I had no idea what people at the Lux thought of our association. To me, it seemed pretty contained. No easy feat when we naturally gravitated to each other.

I asked, "Does it matter?"

"I feel you're better protected if we're not romantically connected."

"Then you'll have to stop glaring at every man who looks my way."

"Impossible," he mumbled.

"Well, then I don't know what to say, except—"

"Marry me, Ari."

chapter 3

My stomach flipped. My heart launched into my throat.

I wiggled out of Dane's firm embrace and flopped onto my side to face him.

"What did you just say?" I demanded, breathless and wide-eyed.

He smirked. "You heard me." Brushing curls off my shoulder and cheek, he added, "Be my wife."

I gaped. It took a few seconds to recover. "Didn't you just tell me we shouldn't be romantically involved?"

"That's not at all what I said. Yes, I feel you're safer if fewer people know of our romantic connection, but that by no means implies I don't want us to be together."

My eyes squeezed shut for a moment. He never did make things easy. Gazing at him again, I said, "So . . . somehow marriage is okay in your mind?"

"You don't seem to get it. I'm one-hundred percent committed to this. To you. I'm deeply, madly, passionately—*insanely*—in love with you." He grinned. The lazy one that made my insides ignite. "No escaping it. So I want you to officially be mine."

"I am yours. With or without the *I dos*."

"I want the *I dos*," he said emphatically.

"Jesus. Dane." My heart beat much too fast, my chest rising and falling quickly against his. "You really like keeping me from getting my feet underneath me."

"Ari." His fingers grazed my temple, stroking languidly. "I've been blessed with the gift of having a clear vision of the things I want. I don't let them slip through my fingers. Ever."

"But . . . *marriage*? Dane, that's . . . um . . . wow."

I couldn't deny the prospect thrilled me. Amazingly so.

Mrs. Dane Bax.

Officially, formally Dane's. Yeah, the thought pretty much rocked my world.

Yet . . .

My eyes narrowed and my mouth dipped.

"What?" he asked, instantly alarmed.

"Nothing."

His brow furrowed. "Don't try to hide anything from me, Ari. I can see from your expression that—"

"No," I insisted, "you're reading me all wrong."

"You're frowning," he pointed out.

With a soft laugh, I said, "Not for the reason you think. I was waiting for the whole 'I'd love to be his wife; *however* . . .' to hit me." I stared deep into his eyes. "But it didn't."

He studied me carefully.

I cuddled closer to him, skimming my lips over his.

"Technically," he said around me nibbling his bottom lip, "you haven't answered my question."

"Perhaps I'm trying to distract you." I engaged him in slow, sexy kisses.

Dane let out a primal growl and eased me onto my back with his hard body pressing to mine. His tongue slipped inside my mouth, sliding over mine, tangling with it. He gathered up satin with a hand and lifted the side of my nightgown to my waist. While he kissed me heatedly, he sank deep into me.

My hips rose and moved with his gentle, sensual rhythm. I twined my fingers in his hair, returning his fervent kiss.

I was not so spellbound that I was oblivious to the complications of getting pulled further into Dane's dark, mysterious world. It was just that I couldn't break free of the mesmeric force that he was—didn't want to break free.

Every piece of me, every fiber of my being, was wrapped around this man. I felt it in the way I responded so fiercely to his weight on me, his chest melding to mine, his kisses searing and addictive. I felt it in the way we made love, tenderly yet intensely. I saw it in his scorching gaze when he stared at me, cataloging all the emotions reflected in my eyes. He was equally ensnared.

And he was right. There was no escape.

His mouth dragged from mine and grazed my jaw, down my throat, lightly nipping at the places he knew drove me wild. One of his hands slipped around to my backside and cupped an ass cheek, lifting me more firmly against him as he thrust fully and forcefully into me.

"Dane." My pulse raged. My insides burned. I draped a leg over his waist, holding him close. One hand remained buried in his lush locks. The other clasped his bulging biceps.

He was so thick and full inside me, pumping smoothly, the head of his cock rubbing that particularly sensitive spot. Tension gripped me, strong and vibrant, fueled as much by emotion as lust.

Marriage went against all of my personal convictions, but when we were joined like this I couldn't deny how perfectly we fit together, how much we belonged together. Regardless of our vast differences. The worlds between us.

So as Dane's head dipped and his mouth sucked my satin-covered nipple, I let my anti-matrimony principles incinerate with my body.

"Dane," I said again on a sharp moan as the fire flashed through me. "Oh, God." The erotic sensations intensified, flamed brighter, and then erupted. "Oh, Christ!"

I cried out as I came, my breath suspended for several moments as the climax took hold, blocking out everything else.

Then Dane thrust harder. Once, twice, three times. And exploded within me, filling my pussy.

I clenched him tight, never wanting to let him go.

Our heavy breaths were one in the quiet room. Our bodies were one. Even our pounding heartbeats seemed to be one. An ethereal bliss consumed me.

Dane's warm, soft lips skated over my skin, up my neck. He kissed me softly and asked, "Is that a yes?"

My eyelids drifted open and I gazed into his sparkling emerald irises. A smile tugged at my lips as tears of happiness pooled in my eyes.

"Goes without saying, don't you think?"

The smile that had started the previous evening, while Dane was nestled snugly inside me, remained plastered on my face. I even woke with it.

Despite being alone in our bed, I couldn't fight the grin. Or the delirium that flowed through me.

Sparing a glance at the clock on the nightstand made me grimace. Through my smile.

It was almost ten o'clock. I never slept late. And I'd missed tee time with my dad.

Still, I was absurdly giddy as I tossed off the covers and slipped from the bed. Not fully recovered from the whirlwind Lux preparations, Dane's lovemaking, my nonstop excitement . . . but feeling refreshed enough not to spend the rest of the day curled in a ball under the down comforter.

I went into the bathroom and splashed cold water on my face, then brushed my teeth. My hair was a tangled mess I didn't even attempt to straighten. I snatched Dane's discarded dress shirt from the night before and pulled it on, not bothering to button the flap. I crossed the hall and grabbed a black lace thong from the bureau in the dressing room, then traveled the long, wide corridor, following the scent of huevos rancheros and coffee.

Passing the great room, I heard Dane on the phone.

I stepped into the vast space, eclectically decorated with tables, chairs, and sofas scattered everywhere and floor-to-ceiling windows and glass doors that highlighted the dense forest and rushing creek beyond the terrace. The fireplace was lit to keep the morning chill at bay. I was barefoot, but the heated stone floor left me toasty warm.

And then there was Dane. One look at him and my internal temperature skyrocketed.

He stood in the middle of the room, wearing dark-gray lounging pants. Nothing more. My mouth watered at the sight of him, so tall, tan, and gorgeous. His sculpted chest and ridged abs drew my attention before my gaze drifted up to his devilishly handsome face.

Our eyes locked. He said into the phone, "I'll call you back." He disconnected and slid the cell into his pocket. "Interesting look," he told me as he took in my disheveled state. "Damn sexy."

"Like I just rolled out of bed after spending the night with a man I couldn't get enough of?"

"Or he couldn't get enough of you."

"Ah, except that he left me in rumpled sheets this morning, when he should have woken me up and made love to me again."

Dane winked. "As much as I was tempted to do just that, I like you cognizant of me when I'm inside you. As it was this morning . . . Baby," he said as he closed the gap between us. "I'm not sure how to break this to you, but you snore like a buzz saw when you're exhausted."

My head snapped back and I playfully swatted at him. "I do not!"

With a healthy laugh, he said, "I'll be sure to record you next time."

"Dane!"

He gathered me in his strong arms and kissed me senseless. Then told me in a rumbling voice, "I'm to blame. I shouldn't have kept you up, or drained you even more by making love to you."

"Never say that," I begged.

He kissed my forehead. "Why don't you eat something? Rosa was here earlier than usual and left breakfast. I think she's worried you're going to get tired of my limited culinary skills and leave me."

"Not a chance. I could starve and still want you." I kissed him. "But that won't happen, because we have the very brilliant Chef D'Angelo on our side. He gave me a fantastic recipe for this evening." I pulled away and said, "Oh, shit. I forgot to tell you. My dad and I don't eat turkey and ham on Thanksgiving Day. We're going a bit off the beaten path when he comes for dinner."

"That's fine." One dark brow jerked up. "You did notice the massive amount of food I consumed at all three events yesterday? It's a wonder I didn't end up in the ER with my stomach pumped."

"No one said you had to eat *everything*."

"It was just so damn good."

I couldn't argue that point. Nor could Kyle, because he'd pretty much scarfed down everything in sight. As had the rest of the staff. The only reason I hadn't devoured all the mouthwatering food was because I'd been busy assessing the planning my team and I had executed, deflecting Kyle, and trying to placate Dane while I purposely kept him at arm's length so no one would speculate about us.

No wonder I'd slept until ten.

Thinking of that made me jump. "I have to call my dad. We missed a round with him at his golf club—sacrilege in his eyes." And one more detail in my life that I'd accidentally let slip.

"I took care of it," Dane said. "Phoned him a little after seven. I reminded him about all the activities at the hotel yesterday and

how fatigued you were. He completely understood. We rescheduled for noon, if you're up to it."

My heart melted. "You don't miss a beat, and think of everything." I kissed him again, then added, "I'll hop in the shower and
we can go."

I whirled around, but he snaked an arm around my waist and
hauled me up against him, my back to his front. "Not so fast. There's
time for you to eat breakfast, and you'll need the fuel for the course."

"True."

"Plus . . ." He turned me to face him. "I want you to acknowl-
edge what happened between us last night."

I toyed with him. "A really great orgasm?"

He nipped at my lower lip. "Now's not the time to be a smart-
ass."

"Actually, sarcasm and comedy are all about timing."

His eyes smoldered. My body burned.

"You win. As always," I said. "In addition to a great orgasm, I
agreed to marry you."

"Yes, you did." His mouth sealed mine in a tantalizing lip-lock
that made my toes curl and my pussy throb.

He didn't let up and I melted against him, grateful for his strong
arms holding me tight. Mine encircled his neck and I clung to him,
letting him take his time, letting him take the lead.

Until I lost myself in him.

We were a few minutes late for our rescheduled tee time with my
dad. He pretended it was no big deal, but I could tell it irked him,
being the former pro that he was. My game was severely off, which
also concerned him. I didn't give a damn about my score. How was
I supposed to concentrate when all I could think about was Dane—
and the fact that he wanted to someday marry me?

Following an unusually poor showing on my part, but stellar on
Dad's and Dane's, we met up at the house.

"This is for you," my father said as he handed over a lovely autumn centerpiece for our dinner table. It didn't quite scream Thanksgiving, because he wasn't into holidays. Hadn't been since his nasty divorce from my mother, whom I'd rarely ever spoken with after I'd turned eighteen. Until she'd shown up on my doorstep a couple of months ago, trying to extort money from me. Telling me she'd exploit the affairs she'd had when my dad was on his PGA tours with a tell-all book.

Dane had eventually stepped in . . . and that had been that. I'd never had to mention a word to my dad or freak him out in any way, for which I was grateful.

"This floral arrangement is perfect." I gave him a peck on the cheek. "Thanks, Dad."

I left the men to football on the ginormous screen in Dane's theater room while I went into the kitchen. Chef D'Angelo had sworn I couldn't fuck up his extremely detailed instructions for Chicken Saltimbocca and I prayed he was right. Not only did I want my father to enjoy dinner with us, I also wanted to impress Dane with my developing culinary skills.

A small insecurity I couldn't shake. He excelled at everything. Even as he joked about not having much talent with food and saying all he knew about cooking came from Betty Crocker—since he'd grown up having personal chefs at his beck and call—he still made the most amazing omelets and eggs Benedict. Maybe it was crazy to want to do something just slightly better than him. I suspected this was the only arena in which I could compete.

So . . . game on.

I had a couple of hours to prepare, since we'd had a late lunch on the course. Therefore, I pan-seared boneless, skinless chicken breasts and then slow-cooked them in a creamy white-wine-and-asparagus-flavored Alfredo sauce I concocted, with fresh prosciutto, sage, and chunks of mushrooms. I added crisp asparagus spearheads toward the end of the process, along with quarters of cherry tomatoes, so they were warmed but still juicy. Then I sliced the chicken and arranged it on a platter, drizzling the sauce over it.

As a secondary dish I grilled a couple of medium-rare, pepper-corn-encrusted New York Strips.

I set the largest of the tables on the patio so I could place all of the food there with us and no one had to move to enjoy. I served a tossed salad with a zesty Italian dressing. Fettuccine accompanied the chicken; whipped garlic potatoes complemented the steak. I'd also baked sourdough and artisan breads, which I paired with olive oil and balsamic vinegar with rosemary, and a basil aioli.

Dane selected the wines from his vast cellar and also nestled a bottle of private-reserve Dom in a chiller.

"This is quite the feast, sweets," my dad said as he eyed the spread.

"Let's hope it tastes as good as it smells," I quipped.

"It'll be fantastic." He grinned. "I didn't realize you cooked more than spaghetti and fish."

"I've been spending a lot of time with the Food and Beverage people at work—I'm sort of inspired. Really, considering how much I've eaten the past couple of months, it's a wonder I'm still hungry tonight. Or that I have any clothes that fit."

"You look sensational, as always," Dane said with a wink as he offered a glass of bubbly.

My cheeks flushed over his flirtation in front of my father—who cleared his throat and tried not to appear uncomfortable with the way Dane gazed so lustfully at me.

Unfortunately given my mass consumption of food of late, I couldn't block the flash of Dane's childhood friend Mikaela Madsen from my mind. His supertall, superhot, supermodel-like friend, to be exact.

She'd attempted to buddy up to me when she'd seen Dane and me together a few times, but then dropped out of sight when I'd left the Lux. And Dane.

I was certain that once she returned from Italy with her boy-friend and soon-to-be business partner, Fabrizio Catalano, and discovered I was back at the hotel—and back with Dane—that she'd be knocking on my office door with gifts, like before. Keep her enemies close, I suspected was her game.

She had her own security badge for 10,000 Lux, after all. Something no other nonemployee possessed, given Dane's ultra-tight safety and confidentiality measures. They didn't apply to Mikaela. I'm not sure any rules did.

But I didn't want to spoil the evening with thoughts of the Heidi Klum look-alike, so I forced myself to get over it.

When both men had champagne in hand, Dane casually said, "Here's to good company, good food, and good health." Not making a fuss about the holiday. I appreciated that greatly, and I could see that my dad did as well.

We all clinked rims and sipped.

"Mm, the expensive stuff," my father said, impressed.

"We'll break out the scotch and cigars later," Dane tempted him.

"Now we're talking."

I gestured for them to sit and started passing the salad and bread around. Dane graciously opted for my dad to take the head of the table, even though it was Dane's house, his domain. I found that respectful. Clearly, it was one more thing about my boyfriend that my father had to admire, regardless of how he felt about Dane being too old for me at thirty. Really, I thought that was code for Dane being too *mature* and *sophisticated* for me. Not to mention well beyond my tax bracket.

I'd gotten an earful of *Are you sure you know what you're doing, sweets?* when I'd told my father I was moving in with Dane. But maybe now he saw that I hadn't turned into a Stepford or become some sort of concubine.

Actually, I supposed I did serve that last purpose, since we weren't married. And hardly a day went by without us stripping each other bare and going at it like sex-starved addicts.

The smile returned. I just couldn't contain it for long.

After dinner, Dane and my father surprised me by offering to clean up, but I shooed them away for more football and the afore-promised scotch and cigars on the patio off the theater room. I didn't need them throwing my organized kitchen off-balance. I'd rearranged all the cabinets and drawers, since I wanted every-thing in its proper place so I could find even the most minor of accessories.

My OCD made me a successful planner, but it also made me anal-retentive about my workspace. Even Rosa had had to learn where I now kept dishes and flatware and how I wanted the pots and pans arranged on the rack that hung over the large island.

I served chocolate lava cake and coffee during halftime, bypass-ing the traditional pumpkin pie. My father stuck around for the rest of the game, which pleased me. I could tell he'd reluctantly had a good time, even clasping Dane on the shoulder as they shook before he kissed me and climbed into his car.

We went back inside the house once my dad had cleared the gate. I hoped he could find his way out. It was a tricky location, set off back roads in scenic Oak Creek Canyon. But I'd given him de-tailed written directions, so I figured he'd be okay.

"I'm ready for a shower," I said. "After golfing and cooking . . . I must stink pretty bad."

Dane chuckled, low and deep in my ear as his arms slid around me from behind. "You were amazing today. Dinner was incredi-ble."

"Thank you. My game, however, was atrocious."

"You didn't seem to mind while we were on the course."

"That was because I was admiring the view. You have a very powerful swing. There were a couple of tee-offs when I actually thought you'd edge out Dad by a few yards."

"Luckily, I'm not quite as good as him."

"Yes, that is fortunate. He's having enough trouble digesting the fact that we're living in sin."

"Ah, but not for long," Dane reminded me. As if I could forget. "Though . . . you didn't mention it to him."

"First of all, it was challenging enough to have him come for dinner while we all pretended it wasn't a holiday. Thanks for playing along, by the way."

"As much as you've told me about your family situation, I can understand how Thanksgiving might seem . . . sardonic . . . to him."

"That's a very polite way of putting it," I muttered. Then I worked out of Dane's tight embrace and turned to face him. "What were holidays like at the estate in Philadelphia, when you were growing up?"

"Eventful," he said. "My aunt went all out for everything, every year. Even when she wasn't feeling well because of the cancer. Apparently, my mother had been big on decorating the mansion and helping the kitchen staff with the meals, so Aunt Lara stepped into the role—and claimed she adored it. I had no basis of comparison, of course, but I thought she did an exceptional job."

"She must have loved you a lot. To raise you and make sure all of the family traditions stayed intact, were passed along to you. It couldn't have been easy. She must have given up some of her own dreams."

"She once told me she'd never intended to have children. My parents had planned a big family, and Aunt Lara had offered to serve as nanny. She liked kids. She just wasn't interested in having her own brood. Primarily, I think, because she'd had some not so healthy relationships with men when she was young. But then, later on . . ." He grinned coyly. "She found the right one."

I regarded him suspiciously. "Oh? You never mentioned she married."

"She didn't. They tried to keep it covert. But I found out about it."

A twinkle in his eye had me dying of curiosity. "Who?" And then it hit me. "Oh, my God. Amano!"

With a nod, Dane said, "I think they were very happy together.

More than just wanting to stay on to protect me and the estate, I'm pretty sure he kept his job in the mansion to be close to her."

"Wow. That's so romantic. Oh, but . . . tragic, too." Considering Dane's aunt had passed a few years ago.

"Yes, it is. But I'm happy they'd found each other."

I couldn't help but think, once again, of Dane's neighbor and friend. "Did Mikaela spend holidays with you all?"

"Yes, she did. Her mother sometimes, too, when she wasn't otherwise engaged."

I eyed him curiously. "So, while Dad was away being an ambassador, her mom was . . . ?"

"They had an open marriage."

I stared at Dane. "How does that work, exactly?" I shook my head. "I mean, I grasp the concept, but . . . What's the point in even getting married? If you're not committed to each other, want outside relationships, want to sleep with other people, then why bother?"

"I don't know," he told me with a pointed look. "It's not anything I'd ever be interested in or would ever agree to. I'd never let another man touch you." He said this with grave conviction.

The very reason he was so fixated on Kyle's attraction to me, and precisely why I constantly reiterated with my friend where he really stood.

"I suppose," Dane ventured, "it had a lot to do with the fact that Ambassador Madsen was rarely in the country and his wife and Mikaela didn't travel or live with him, as I've mentioned previously. It's not quite like your parents' situation."

"That was just plain screwed up," I lamented. "He gave her *everything*. Those tournaments were meant to provide her with all the material things she wanted—thought she deserved—as much as they were to appease his passion for golf."

"Ari," Dane said. "Baby, you can't think that every marriage is destined for that sort of betrayal, whether the cheating is consciously discussed and agreed upon or done behind someone's back."

I knew he spoke the truth. But it was an extremely sensitive subject for me. I'd witnessed—lived through—the devastation of that sort of deception. For me, that was a red flag with relationships. One of the biggest issues that had precluded me from actually having any . . . until I'd met Dane.

"Hey," he said. "Don't get mired in other people's drama, baby. Focus on what we have."

I smiled up at him. "Right." He was absolutely right.

He took my hand and we strolled down the hallway to the dressing room we shared. It was wall-to-wall rich, polished wood, with a standing three-way mirror and chairs and tables strategically placed. A chandelier hung over the marble-topped bureau in the center of the room. Sconces were mounted between the cutouts that housed the racks and shelves.

"So, what was the second reason you didn't mention our engagement to your dad?" Dane asked, not letting me clear the minefield.

I hauled my golf shirt over my head and tossed it in the laundry bin. My skirt followed. As I toed off my tennis shoes, having changed out of my spikes before we'd left the club, I said, "I guess I'm not certain that's what it was."

My brows knitted. So did his.

"I'm not sure what that means," he told me.

"Yeah, I know. Sorry. It's just that . . . I thought you were asking me sort of generically—like would I marry you *someday*? Down the road."

"Ah." He stripped off his polo. Dropping it on the bureau, he rested his forearms on the marble and pinned me with a serious look. "So when you agreed, you were thinking marriage would be a long time off."

I pulled in a deep breath. A rush of contradictory feelings I'd somehow kept at bay all day long made my nerves jump. "This is going to get complicated," I surmised as I dragged on one of his

Henleys, my favorite sleepwear aside from the nightgown he'd brought from Paris.

"I'm listening," he prompted in a measured tone.

Standing at the opposite end of the dresser that stretched almost the length of the room—and recognizing the safety zone it created for what it was—I said, "We didn't discuss a time frame. I figured you were doing what you always do. Present the issue at hand and give me the space to process it."

Now his brow rose. "The *issue*?"

I sighed. "Call it whatever you want. I'm just saying that you know how I feel about marriage, so it's going to take a little while for me to adjust to the idea of it. But I do want to marry you," I assured him.

"In what . . . four, five, ten years?"

"Now you're just being pissy."

Shoving away from the bureau, he dumped his shirt in the hamper, removed his shoes and socks, and peeled off his Dockers.

"Dane."

"No, you're right," he said as he discarded his briefs and yanked open a drawer for his drawstring pants.

I lost my train of thought as I watched him. He was too sinful, too tempting, by far.

Pulling me from the lust-induced haze clouding my mind, he told me, "I understand that, based on your grandparents' and your parents' volatile marriages and subsequent divorces, you never considered making the commitment yourself. You even told me when we met that you weren't the marrying kind. I know you were jesting at the time, but still . . . I do remember you saying it and I did take the comment to heart."

He tied the strands at his waist and continued. "You also once said that I didn't have to worry about you falling in love with me—though I'd expressed it was something I'd never take exception to. But you *did* fall in love with me."

"So, you're working off the theory that I always come around . . . for you?"

His grin was a tad too cocky. I smirked at him.

Then I said, "I won't deny it. And I didn't balk last night. I accepted what you asked of me, because, well . . . I'll admit, it's what I want, too. I just didn't really think of it as a proposal or that we were currently, as of that moment . . . engaged." That last word sort of tripped off my tongue in an odd hesitation. I rolled my eyes.

This wasn't about to get complicated.

It was about to get downright *messy*.

chapter 4

Crossing his rock-hard arms over his chest, Dane gave me another unyielding look. "You know perfectly well that I wouldn't have asked if I weren't deathly serious."

I cringed. "Let's not use that term."

His jaw worked for a few seconds. Then he said, "That does bring up another point. You were right last night when I made conflicting statements. At the moment, I don't think it's wise or safe for us to go public with our relationship. But I do want to marry you."

I winced inwardly at the question that ironically popped into my head. Not wanting to sound materialistic, because I certainly wasn't, I ventured, "Is that why you proposed without a ring?"

He exhaled slowly. Almost agitatedly. "I asked on impulse. Because it's what I want, but not something I've figured out in my mind how to execute. Except . . ." He shook his head. Dropped his arms. Joining me where I stood, he propped a hip against the dresser and reached for my hand. Holding it to his mouth, he softly swept his lips over my skin. "Ari, I want you to be my wife. There's no reticence on my part. No doubt. But you do bring up some valid concerns, and I now know what we have to do in order to pull this off."

My stomach did a peculiar fluttering mixed with a gentle roiling. Exhilaration tinged by a hint of *uh-oh*.

Swallowing down more nerves, I said, "Do tell."

He kissed my fingers, then flattened my palm to his pecs, over his heart. His hand covered mine.

"I can't give you a ring just yet."

Huh. Hadn't seen that one coming.

"Okay."

He glowered a little. "I mean, I *can*. I just don't think it's a good idea. In fact, the fewer people who know we're married, the better."

"You might want to explain that," I said. "So I'm not confused."

"Ari, I want to marry you sooner rather than later. As in *soon*."

"Like, in a year, not four?"

"Like, tomorrow."

I blanched. *"Tomorrow?"*

"I'll make a call. We can apply for a license in the morning, then get married in the evening. Here at the house."

The roiling in my stomach overpowered the fluttering.

He continued, as though it weren't evident I suffered heart palpitations. "If you trust her, we can have your friend officiate."

"Tamera," I squeaked out.

"Yes. And we'll need a couple of witnesses. Ethan, of course. Amano. My lawyer. There will be a lot of paperwork for you to sign. I'll have to contact him tonight to get started right away."

My mind reeled. "Um . . . I . . . Uh . . ." Christ. I couldn't form a single coherent sentence.

Dane's eyes sparkled, as though this sudden decision was the most brilliant one he'd ever made.

"If you think your dad can handle the news, let's include him as well."

I had no clue what possessed me, but I mumbled, "Kyle, too."

"Not Kyle," Dane countered emphatically.

I snatched my hand from Dane's, cogent thoughts suddenly gelling. "Someone has to stand up for *me*. You get three people. I get three people, Tamera included."

A much too sexy grin split his lips. "I know better than to argue with you. And I will concede that Kyle has kept our secret, despite not liking us being together."

"He won't be happy about this, either," I grumbled. "But he's the closest thing I have to a best friend, so from that standpoint, I know he'll want to be in the loop."

"Plus, he'll want that last-ditch attempt to change your mind."

"I won't change my mind," I said vehemently. Where that conviction came from I wasn't entirely sure. Except that pinning down a date, not dragging out an engagement, and knowing I'd be Dane's wife in twenty-four hours made me absurdly giddy again.

"Then we're on for tomorrow night?" he asked.

I shook out my hands, trying to get the anxiety to abate. No luck there. And yet, somehow, I knew *exactly* what I was doing.

"I'll have to call Tamera, make sure she's available." Given that we were talking about a Friday, I suspected that wouldn't pose a problem.

Something else did, though. A dark thought edged my euphoria, chasing away the certainty I'd experienced moments before. I frowned.

"What is it?" Dane asked.

Dread slithered through me. "I don't get to plan my own wedding."

I shifted away from him, pacing restlessly.

"You never wanted a wedding," he reminded me.

Though he had me on the technicality, I told him, "That was

because I never wanted to get married. But obviously things are different now. And damn it, Dane, if I'm going to throw all caution to the wind and do the direct opposite of what I've been saying from the beginning, just because the idea of being your wife makes my toes curl and my heart nearly burst from my chest, then . . . I want a wedding!"

"Ari—"

"I've been a bridal consultant for *six* years, Dane. I'm an event planner at the Lux. Of course I'm going to want to plan my own wedding."

He folded his arms over his chest once more. Just watching how he ground his teeth told me he searched his brain for the perfect solution.

I waited patiently, though still paced.

Several suspended moments ticked by. Finally, he said, "I don't want to hold off on this, Ari. I want a ceremony tomorrow night."

Drawing up short, I demanded, "What's the rush, Dane?" Granted, I'd invariably fallen in love with this notion and wanted it to happen as quickly as possible, too.

Perhaps before *he* changed his mind? Came to his senses and realized I wasn't the be-all, end-all he deserved? That I was no Mikaela Madsen?

Resisting the urge to gnaw on my manicured nails, I tried to lighten the mood by joking, "Are you pregnant?"

He glared at me, which made me laugh.

"Come on," I coaxed. "That was funny."

Reaching out, he pulled me to him and said, "Stop pacing as though the idea of marrying me makes you nervous."

"But it does," I confessed. "And you know why. I don't believe in marriage. It makes absolutely no sense that we're having this conversation and that I'm consenting to everything that goes against the grain just because I'm head over heels in love and, suddenly, the thought of *not* being your wife is something I can't live with or accept."

My pulse raged a bit too quick and my breath labored. I'd felt this way when I'd broken up with Dane months ago. For my own good and sanity, I'd told myself back then, to justify the split. But my well-being and mental health had taken solid blows because of that spontaneous decision. I'd quickly come to the realization that I couldn't be without him.

A terrifying prospect, because it wasn't exactly smart to hinge your entire existence on one person. Yet this was how it was between us. And he'd struggled with the separation as much as I had.

"Look," he said, as he held me tightly with one arm and cupped the side of my face with his free hand. His thumb whisked over my cheek in a tender, loving way. "I've always said I'll give you whatever you want, whatever your heart desires. I won't let you down, Ari. I'll keep that promise. We *will* have a wedding. The most beautiful one you can dream up—I swear it. Just . . . not right away."

I stared deep into his eyes, seeing the insistence, the need, the pledge to this endeavor. And knew it was a vow he wouldn't break.

He added, "Tomorrow will be just for us. After the Lux is opened and I don't have to worry about Bryn Hilliard—Vale's father—and the others, then we can have a wedding at the resort. Or anywhere else in the world you choose."

"The Lux," I told him. "That's where we should be married. You know it."

"Then that's where we'll do it. With a huge reception. Anything you want. But, Ari—" His head dipped and his lips brushed over mine. "Baby. I want to marry you now. Not wait until the spring. I want you to be mine. Fully committed."

His muscles were rigid, his gaze steely. The raw intensity he exuded captivated me, hooked me.

"For the record, I *am* fully committed." I gave further thought to how tormented I'd been when separated from Dane after Vale's attack, and I knew to the depths of my soul what I really wanted. "We have a lot to do to get ready for tomorrow evening," I found myself saying. "It might be a private, intimate ceremony, but it *has* to be perfect."

"It will be. I have every confidence in your planning skills. And I will find something for us to exchange during our vows. Something that will mean a lot to both of us and be a symbol of our love."

"Okay."

There was no point in telling him not to go overboard. He would. That was his nature.

"Seven o'clock?" he ventured.

"Yes."

"You take care of the ceremony. I'll handle dinner."

"You're going to make Chef D'Angelo work on his day off, aren't you?"

The Lux was closed for Thanksgiving and the day after, though we all intended to be back at it bright and early Saturday morning.

"Chef and I go way back, to my first hotel in Tahoe. But I'm not going to tell him the occasion. Just that we're having a dinner party. I'll ask Rosa to serve."

"She'll be so delighted you haven't run me off with your five-card recipe box."

He tapped my nose with his finger and said, "You have a very smart mouth."

"You like what I do with this mouth."

With a carnal groan, he concurred. "You *are* rather talented. Meet me in the bedroom in half an hour."

We left the dressing room and went in opposite directions. I presumed he headed to his office to contact Ethan, Amano, and his lawyer. I grabbed my phone and went into the bedroom, lit the fire, and curled on the sofa in front of the low flames. My first call, to Tamera, would be the easiest one. The other two . . . not so much.

I was relieved that she was available to officiate. Shocked to the core of her being, if her bewildered tone was any indication, but available. And over-the-moon excited.

"I didn't even know you were dating someone!" she exclaimed in her lovely British accent.

"It all happened quickly. The thing is, he's my boss. So we're under wraps about the whole thing, until the spring. After 10,000 Lux opens. Then we'll do a formal wedding, which I'd like you to officiate as well."

"*Ooh*, so I get to be all top-secret, Jane Bond–like."

I laughed. "I didn't think you'd be this thrilled."

"It's sexy, Ari. You both can't wait to be married. That's *exactly* the sentiment I love to hear from the people I bring together in holy matrimony."

She had me on that one. I'd always felt the same, believing my brides and grooms were as happy every day after they'd shared vows as they were during those special moments.

"So you're cool with the hush-hush, on the QT thing?"

"Absolutely. You know you can count on me. Honestly, Ari, I'm just so relieved you gave up that whole *I'm never going to marry* stance."

"You're one to talk. Still single."

"That's only because Mr. Right's GPS is somewhat skewed at present. He'll be on my doorstep as soon as he figures out all the correct turns."

"Yeah," I said on a dreamy sigh. "Funny how that happens."

"God, you *really* are smitten."

I smiled. She was the only one who'd be this positive and optimistic for me. Good thing I'd spoken with her first. It gave me the extra surge of courage to call Kyle after we hung up.

He answered on the first ring. "One day without me and you're missing me already. See? I told you that you'd come around."

My spirits plummeted. "Uh, not exactly why I'm calling." Needing a few seconds to regroup, I asked, "How was your Thanksgiving?"

"I have no idea how it happened, but I managed to eat two servings of *everything*. I mean, I did spend a couple of hours in the gym this morning to work off yesterday's overindulgence, but still. By some act of God, I was actually hungry today."

I laughed, albeit nervously. "I hear you. I spent the day on the golf course with my dad and then devoured dinner. I should have bypassed the cart and walked the fairways. I'm going to need a whole new wardrobe if I keep this up."

"Doubtful."

We both fell silent for a moment. Eventually, I worked up the gumption to ask, "Any plans for tomorrow night?"

"Meghan and Sean invited me over for drinks at their new pad. Well, beer for Sean. Cranberry juice for Meg. Or whatever's best for pregnant women. You wanna come along?"

The young newlyweds' wedding had been my last before I'd taken the job at the Lux. "I would, except . . . I sort of have my own shindig going on here. I was going to invite you over."

Yikes, Ari. You wuss.

I couldn't come even remotely close to telling him what I had in mind for the evening.

In a hesitant tone, he asked, "You mean . . . at Dane's house?"

"I live here, too," I said slightly irritably. "And we'd both like you to come. It's a very small gathering."

"Huh. Color me surprised."

He didn't know the half of it. I actually debated whether to tell him what I was really up to but didn't quite have the wherewithal for the fallout. I'd contended with enough earlier when it came to Dane, and I still had to deal with my father.

"So, can you reschedule with Meg and Sean?"

"I'll be there. What time?"

"Seven. Wear a suit."

"*What?*" he demanded.

I sighed. "It's formal. A holiday thing."

Fuck. I should have phrased it *special occasion*, because he knew I didn't do holidays. Though, really, what did it matter how I labeled the evening? He'd be incensed either way when he discovered I was getting married.

Kyle had been there for me when I'd needed an extra bodyguard so Amano and Dane could work together on their strategy with the legit members of the poli-econ society to legally bring down the corrupt members. He'd been there after Vale had attacked me and during my lowest of low moments.

Kyle was a tried-and-true friend and I adored him. Unfortunately, everything that occurred in my personal life with Dane cut him deep.

"I'll send a car for you," I amended. "This isn't an easy place to get to, especially at night. And that way you can have some cocktails and not worry about driving." He was going to need a few stiff drinks, I suspected.

"Listen to you, all queen bee–like. Lux royalty."

"Shut up. The car will come around six thirty."

I jotted down his address, since I'd never been to his apartment. Then said good-bye and hit the disconnect button.

Several deep, deep, *deep* breaths later, I made the hardest call of all.

"I'm insulted," was the first thing my dad said, before I'd even uttered a word. "You thought I'd get lost on my way out of that maze to 89A."

A slightly crazed laugh slipped through my lips. "Not totally. But glad to know you didn't have any trouble."

"Well, I did," he lamented.

"Dad . . . that's kind of funny." My laugh was a bit calmer this time.

"You're directionally challenged—how do you manage?"

"Practice." Not exactly a true statement. Dane or Amano always drove. But I did pay close attention. Gathering my nerve, I said, "So tonight was a lot of fun. I was wondering . . . would you mind coming back tomorrow evening? Small get-together. Dinner and drinks. Festive."

"*Festive.*" He seemed to try out that word like a new golf glove. "Hardly your style, sweets."

"I know." I was a planner, not a hostess. "It's just that we're sort of . . . that is . . . Dane and I are kind of . . . um . . ." I blew out a breath. "Getting married."

"You're *what*?!"

Oh, crap. Had I really just said that out loud? To my *father*?

My stomach twisted. "I should have told you today, in person, that he'd asked me. But I needed a little time to get used to the idea. You understand, right?" All things considered.

"Aria Lynne DeMille," he said in his old *you're about to be grounded* tone. It was the only time he used my full name. That was Mother's specialty. Though she was essentially the last person I wanted to think of at the moment. She absolutely could not find out about my impending nuptials. Or she'd be beating down my door with some new scheme to get her hands on Dane's money and further destroy my father's reputation. And break my heart all over again.

My dad demanded, "What the *hell* is going on?"

Geez, everyone was so testy. Not that I hadn't expected that, but still.

"Just come tomorrow night. I'll explain everything."

"Are you kidding me?" he grumbled.

"Not in the least."

"Ari. Shit."

I imagined him stalking about, shoving a hand through his russet hair and shaking his head. The way he had when I'd told him I was letting go of the townhome rental and moving in with my new boyfriend who also happened to be my boss. I'd dropped that bombshell at my father's house. Damn it, I should have told him *this* news to his face.

"Fuck," he muttered.

I cringed. My dad didn't typically swear in front me—or at all, as a rule. But I could see where this revelation would blindside him. Send him over the edge.

"Dad." I struggled for the right words. "Calm down. I know it's kind of a surprise—"

"*Kind of?*" he blurted.

"Well, in our defense, we *are* living together. So obviously, we're serious about each other. Even you can't ignore that fact. It's sort of like a . . . a . . ." I wracked my mind, then said, "A natural progression."

Reasonable, right?

He fell silent. I could feel his tension through the airwaves.

"Dad?" I tentatively prompted. "You will be here tomorrow, right?"

"Jesus, Ari." He let out a long breath. "Marriage is—"

"I know, Dad. Of all people, you don't have to tell me it's difficult, not something to enter into lightly, et cetera. *I* know. Am I scared? Hell, yes. But I also can't breathe without him. I love him enough to face my darkest fears with him." Snakes, scorpions, *and* marriage.

There you go.

My worst nightmares.

And yet . . . I'd survived the snake in the stairwell. The scorpions that had dropped from the terrace onto my plate and shoulder—and stung me.

When it came to surviving wedded bliss . . . well, I couldn't survive without Dane, so there was no point in putting this off. Like everything else about us, it was inevitable.

"Am I calm?" I said into the phone. "No. But do I know what I'm doing?" The smile returned. "Dad, he makes me happy. Isn't that good enough for you?"

He merely grunted.

"It'll be fine. I promise."

"Why aren't the two of you telling me this together? In person?"

Touchy subject. "Yeah, I know." I couldn't say it'd come about so quickly we hadn't had the chance. That would scream *impulsive* and he'd poke holes in my reasoning and lose a little more faith in us. So I said, "Dad, you can't deny that Dane has been nothing but respectful. It's just that . . . well, he doesn't have family. Never knew his parents. And his aunt, who raised him, died years ago. He's not exactly traditional. He makes up his mind about something and that's all he really sees."

My father was quiet for a spell. Then, in a tone that contradicted his reluctance to concede, he said, "We're not exactly traditional, either. I suppose it's a tiny bit hypocritical to want him to be conventional."

I relaxed a little. "Maybe that's just one more thing about us that works. He did have a more family values–type upbringing, but he still had to be independent and fend for himself. When you were on PGA tours . . . Mom wasn't always around. And after the divorce. Well. I could have just gotten my own hotel room at thirteen for all the company and parental supervision I had on the rare occasions she let me visit her."

"You never told me it was that bad."

"Because we don't talk about stuff like that, Dad."

He sighed.

"We just get by," I said. "Do what we have to do and not make a fuss out of it." All of that had changed for me this year. "Now I want more. I *have* more. With Dane. Because of Dane."

"Ah, sweets." His darker, agonized voice tore at me. "I'm so sorry your childhood was shit."

Tears stung my eyes. He wasn't being martyrish. It really had been shit. But . . .

"Dad, it was never, *ever* your fault."

"All I want is for you to be happy."

I perked up. Swiped at the fat drops rolling down my flushed cheeks. "Then come here tomorrow night. Seven o'clock. And don't scowl or skulk about, you know? Act like you're thrilled for me. Because, Dad . . . I *am* happy."

chapter 5

I'd really had no idea what was in store for me when I'd agreed to
marry Dane so quickly. Thank God I had years of wedding planning experience. And tons of connections. I called on many of
them, apologizing profusely since it was Thanksgiving weekend
and lying through my teeth that I was consulting for a society
couple who were marrying privately. This intrigued everyone and,
along with my having such sound relationships with them, made
it infinitely easier to order all the flowers, candles, and accents I
wanted.

Dane's contact at the court allowed for us to apply under oath
for our license first thing in the morning and have it expeditiously
issued, though Dane's lawyer, also present, assured us it wouldn't
currently become public record. I didn't want to know how he
could make that happen. Sometimes, ignorance truly was bliss.

We parted ways outside of City Hall, and Amano drove me to
Tlaquepaque, the upscale complex of boutiques, art galleries, and
restaurants in a traditional Mexican village setting that I loved.

I needed a dress.

The temperature had dipped somewhat and the sky was overcast, but I knew we'd have the heaters on the patio to warm the night, so I didn't limit my search for the perfect gown to something with long sleeves. I found precisely what I was looking for at the same shop where I'd picked up the one-off emerald mini Dane had always admired.

After collecting all of the decorations and loading them into the back of the Escalade, Amano and I returned to the house and he helped me set up, along the bank of the creek.

It was near impossible not to check in on Dane and his dinner preparations. Occupational hazard and plain bride-to-be curiosity. I curbed my innate desire, though, instead taking a glass of champagne into the bathroom and soaking in a warm bubble bath, sprinkling the water with a bit of the frankincense oil from Oman that Dane had given me.

The aroma was rich and sensuous, and I drew it in with long, slow breaths. Conflicting emotions warred within me, but they didn't unnerve me. Getting married was the last thing I'd ever imagined I'd do. Yet here I was, about to tie the knot.

Following the bath, I did my hair, opting to pull the sides up and leave a mass of fat chocolate curls down my back, with a few loose tendrils at my temples. I turned my blue eyes smoky and applied smudge-proof crimson-colored lipstick. My stomach fluttered as the clock on the vanity ticked off the minutes.

Norah Jones's "Thinking About You" flowed from the surround sound. It was a sultry melody, soothing. Although my nerve endings tingled, warmth coursed through my veins. Exhilaration and anxiety were a strange mix, but they electrically charged me and it was all I could do to fight back the excitement bubbling in my throat.

I crossed the hall to the dressing room and pulled out the garment bag with my "wedding" gown. It was really just a ball gown. But the moment I'd seen it, I'd been convinced it fit the bill perfectly. I slipped into the dress. As I struggled with the long hidden zipper along my spine, Tamera's silky British voice filled the room.

"Good heavens, you were serious when you said you were getting married tonight."

I laughed. "Thank God I've been through this numerous times. No need for a rehearsal."

"Let me help you." She finished zipping me and I turned toward her. She gaped. Took a few seconds to recover. "Good Lord, Ari. You look . . . *Oh* . . . " Her hand pressed to her heart as her tawny eyes grew wide. "Stunning."

I swallowed down a lump of emotion. "Thank you. I had strictly off-the-rack options, given the short notice."

Her arms spread as she took me in from head to toe. "Seriously, bridal magazine cover worthy. And then some."

My eyes closed for a moment and I tried to breathe normally. Then I said, "You have seen the groom, right?"

"He directed me this way." Fanning her cheek with a hand, she added, "Wherever did you find him, and does he have a brother?"

A smile tickled my lips. "He broke the mold—and it wasn't put back together thereafter."

"No kidding," Tamera said in a dreamy tone. "How, exactly, do you keep your hands off him?"

"Not easily," I admitted.

"No wonder you've kept him all to yourself." She winked. "Now, what else can I do for you?"

"Light the candles? On the patio and just beyond, along the creek."

"Absolutely." She leaned in and gave me air kisses to both cheeks so she didn't disturb my makeup. "I'll see you at the altar, love."

"Oh, Christ." This time, my stomach flipped. No gentle fluttering to keep me on an even keel. "I'm getting married."

"Indeed." She smiled radiantly. "Now would be a good time to tell yourself all those things you say to your brides and grooms at this crucial point of no return."

"Right." I tried to steady myself. "Inhale. Exhale. If you forget all else, remember those two simple words. *I do.*"

"Perfect."

I employed the breathing exercises. Then said, "The thing is . . ." I embraced the calm suddenly seeping through me. "Despite the fear factor for a woman like me—" marriage and the foreboding surrounding Dane's world—"you won't have to prompt me when the *I do* part comes. In fact, you just might have to slow me down."

"Oh, Ari." She squeezed my hand. "Now *that's* romantic, darling. True love, really."

She left me alone to collect my emotional self.

Luckily, it was a few minutes before my next visitor arrived.

"Dad."

"Wow," he said as he eyed the dress. It was full-length and sparkly silver. Sleeveless, cut-in at the shoulders, with the neckline sitting at my collarbone. The bodice was tight and clingy, the material dipping into my waist and hugging my hips. Mid-thigh a slit in the middle caused the skirt to cascade away into a slight train in the back.

I slipped on the four-inch silver satin and Swarovski crystal–accented shoes while my dad composed himself.

"Not too bad for last minute?" I asked.

"You're just . . . Uh . . ." He blew out a long breath. "So beautiful." Emotion tinged his voice, touched his eyes, misting them a bit. The skin crinkled around the corners, as though he fought to keep himself in check.

It choked me up.

"Dad." I reached for a tissue and dabbed at my own eyes. "Don't make me cry. I spent forever doing my makeup."

"Sorry," he mumbled. Then shook his head as though to clear it. But he still appeared deeply affected as he said, "I'll always think of you as my little girl, sweets, but you aren't. You're a very mature, very gorgeous woman. Guess I chose not to accept you were all grown-up, but . . . here you are. Absolutely breathtaking."

I gave him a careful hug, though I really just wanted to throw my arms around him and hold on tight.

"I learned from you and Mother," I told him. "From Grandma and Grandpa. Dane and I are different. I won't let the ugly part of marriage in, Dad."

He gripped my hands in his and stared into my watery eyes. "You know that if it starts to creep in, you have to talk immediately. Don't let it fester. Don't let it destroy you."

"Dad . . ." I pressed my lips together a moment, trying to compose myself as well. "Anything could come our way. One thing I know for sure is that we'd never betray each other. The rest . . . well, you're right. We have to deal with it every day."

"All right, then." He released my hands and stepped away. "No more lectures."

I smiled through more tears. "Dad. I don't mind. Really."

"You always were a good kid."

"And now I'm a good adult. Who needs to fix her makeup."

"You look fine. Absolutely perfect." He gave me a smile before turning to go. Over his shoulder, he added, "All that matters to me ever, sweets, is that you're happy. And safe."

I sucked in a breath. I was marrying a man who was part of a secret poli-econ society. A man who associated with the world's wealthiest, most influential people. And some of those people had already proven they'd go to any length to protect what was theirs— or what they wanted to be theirs. Including taking out little ol' me.

A shudder ran along my spine. But I lifted my chin and told another tiny white lie, for my father's sake. "You don't have to worry, okay?"

"Okay."

He left me and I experienced a whole different level of wedding planning—the side of the bride. Myriad feelings coursed through me as I paced the dressing room, but I *was* grounded with this decision. I couldn't explain why, except that, with every second now sliding by, I wanted to see Dane. I wanted to meet him standing in front of Tamera and tell him how much I loved him and say those two sacred words.

So I bucked up and entered the hallway, where I found Kyle wandering about.

"Hey," I said.

His jaw slacked.

"Nice reaction," I added. "Apparently, the dress is a hit."

"I . . . um—" He shook his head. "Fuck. You're . . . Fuck."

I laughed. "Well. That pretty much covers it."

"Sure. Except . . ." His gaze narrowed on me. "You said holiday attire. Formal, yes. But that dress is like . . ." He shook his head, looking thoroughly confused. And in awe. "Are we going to be on TV or something?"

He had a natural way of cutting the tension. I adored that. Yet I still had a very uncomfortable conversation with him ahead of me.

"Kyle, there's something I didn't tell you about this little get-together."

I took his hand and dragged him into Dane's office, closing the door behind us.

"I know this is going to take you by surprise"—*hit him like a ton of bricks* was more like it—"but this evening is incredibly special to me."

"Ari." He eyed me skeptically. "What the hell is going on?"

"Don't freak, okay. I know what I'm doing. And I know this is going to throw you for a huge loop, but I needed you to be here tonight. As my best friend. As my best . . . man."

I held my breath as he gaped.

Many, *many* seconds inched by. Before I passed out from lack of oxygen, I pulled in a gulp of air, then blurted, "Say something!"

He *seemed* to try to speak. He just wasn't successful at it.

I told him, "I understand this is a shock. But Dane proposed last night and so here we all are—"

"Last night?" he suddenly demanded, coming around quickly. "As in . . . *last night?*" He shook his head, started to do some pacing of his own.

I'd never seen so much tension from so many people over an impending marriage. Even the Delfinos hadn't worn out the rug when they'd learned twenty-year-old Meg was pregnant and her father, Anthony Delfino, had issued the shotgun-wedding scenario to Sean.

"Take a few deep breaths," I said. "You'll feel better."

He halted abruptly, spun around, and glared at me. "Are you out of your mind?"

"First . . . don't yell at me on my wedding day. Second . . . no, I am not." I grabbed his hand again and said, "I invited you here for a reason. There are only a few people who will know about this, and I want you to be one of them. Dane approved—"

"Oh, he approved, did he? As if you need his permission—"

"He knows you will keep our secret," I insisted.

Ripping his hand from mine, Kyle threw his arms up in the air and, in an exasperated voice, asked, "Aren't you tired yet of all the secrecy, Ari? What is it about him that makes you think it's okay to keep everything about your relationship under wraps? *Normal* people don't do that, you know?"

I remained calm, because he deserved to have this outburst. I'd done favors for Kyle, such as getting him the job at the Lux. He'd done favors for me, like staying with me after I'd been roughed up by Vale.

Kyle and I truly did banter like siblings, even though he took it in a different light—more of a flirtation. I'd always been clear on my intentions. He knew Dane was it for me. End of story.

And Kyle had chosen to stay friends, to stay my closest friend. As much as I'd suffer if he walked away, the choice had always been—and always would be—up to him.

"I want you here," I said. "It means the world to me. If you don't want to be on my side with this, I'll totally understand. But I always fight for you, Kyle. Because that's what best friends do."

He grunted. "Fuck it all, Ari. I swear, I will never figure out what the hell goes on inside your head."

His pacing resumed. I knew this would be difficult for him to reconcile. And he'd never, ever get a real handle on it. Not as long as he held out hope that I might someday "come to my senses" and choose him instead.

That would never happen. I knew exactly what I wanted—*who* I wanted.

"Kyle, I'm getting married whether you stick around or not. Though I'd really prefer that you stay."

He glowered at me.

I gave him a smile. Crooked a suggestive brow at him, and said, "There's food and champagne. . . ." Hoping to tempt him.

With a shake of his head, he said, "I noticed your dad's car out front. He's onboard with this . . . insanity?"

"Took some doing to get him there," I confessed. "He worries incessantly, even though he pretends he doesn't. Still . . . Kyle, he likes Dane, despite not wanting to because he thinks he's too extravagant, too . . . *advanced* . . . for me." I rolled my eyes. I couldn't exactly dispute the logic and said, "I don't blame him. I don't blame you for thinking the same. It's just that—"

"Wait," he interjected, holding up a hand. "That's not what I think. I'm concerned about what happened to you just a couple of months ago, Ari. You were kidnapped and got the shit beat out of you. How am I supposed to condone that?"

"You're not," I said matter-of-factly. "And I appreciate that you were offended for me, upset, all that. But don't, for a second, believe that *Dane* condoned it or that he wasn't devastated by it. You saw him afterward, Kyle. You know he was as wrecked as I was. You can't deny it. You *saw* him!"

Kyle's teeth ground for a moment.

"Kyle. I'm not telling you anything you don't already know."

He combed a hand through his hair, the short strands falling back into their tousled place.

"You're right," he reluctantly said. "I just keep hoping you'll get a little smarter about this."

"I swear I'm of sound mind."

He took a bit more time to pull himself together, then sarcastically said, "Think he's worried I'm actually talking you out of this harebrained idea?"

I smiled again. "He anticipated the attempt on your part."

"And still invited me."

"He's that confident."

"Arrogant," Kyle corrected with a scowl.

"Yes. I'll give you that one. But I do love him. And I want to marry him. Sometime this evening would be preferable."

Kyle gave me a long look. "Why can't I resist you—refuse you anything?"

"Because you want me to be happy."

"That still doesn't mean I'll give up."

I sighed. "You are just too much."

We stared at each other, at an impasse of sorts, though he didn't let me down. Eventually, he offered his arm and asked, "Shall we?"

Returning to the great room, I gestured toward the doors that led to the patio. "The ceremony's just beyond the terrace."

"Can't believe I have to stomach all of this," he said as he took in the enormous room and everything surrounding it. I knew he thought beyond the house to having to *stomach me* marrying Dane.

"You'll get used to it," I assured him.

My dad waited for us just outside, away from the others. Kyle squeezed my hand and said, "At least you didn't keep this from me."

"Still best friends?"

He nodded. "Doesn't mean I agree with what you're doing." That razor edge to his voice, from two days before, emphasized his words and his disgruntlement. He paused contemplatively and asked once more, "You sure you know what you're doing? This is a pretty serious step, Ari."

"I'm sure of how I feel about Dane. How he feels about me. I want us legitimately bound to each other. It's something I can't escape."

"It could be a huge mistake."

"It won't be."

My insides churned a bit at how personally Kyle took all this—how disappointed he looked. Slightly infuriated, too. But he was here. And I meant what I'd said. I wanted this.

He traveled the candlelit path as my dad and I lingered in the shadows and the coverage of trees.

I hadn't set out chairs—it would be a quick ceremony and I wanted Kyle and my father standing up for me on my side at the altar. Dane's friends on his.

Turning to my dad, I took a couple more deep breaths. Then said, "Thanks for doing this. I know you're not thrilled it came about so fast. But the fact that you're here . . . That means so much to me."

I hadn't even had to ask him to walk me down the aisle. He'd just known.

"Well," he mused, though not lightly, "maybe you'll break the pattern. Be the new normal in our family."

I tamped down an ironic laugh. As Kyle had expressed there was nothing normal about my relationship with Dane. Or the man himself. Still. I heard what my father was telling me, what he wished for when it came to his only daughter.

A new family tradition devoid of throwing things at walls and screaming at the top of our lungs.

"It'd be a nice change of pace," I concurred.

"Very nice."

Kyle must have cued Tamera, because the programmed music changed and beautiful sounds from the harpist I adored wafted on the gentle breeze that rustled the leaves. The creek ran rapidly.

Moonlight streaked the sky and tinted the forest a lovely silver color. Cascading arrangements of white roses and lush green foliage trimmed the makeshift altar I'd created from an antique stand in Dane's office. Dozens of candles burned in large hurricanes, from holders of varying heights and along the pathway Rosa had helped me clear.

Had I moved past my dream of wanting a huge, extravagant ceremony so that every person I knew and worked with would know I was marrying Dane Bax? No. Would he still be conflicted that we'd had to do it this way? Yes.

But the setting was exquisite and the key people in our lives were present. And when it came right down to it, what I would cherish the most was the fact that we belonged to each other.

My father and I rounded the thicket and stepped into the small opening along the creek. I carried a single red rose as my dad escorted me.

I was cognizant of Tamera and the others, but my gaze homed in on Dane, looking insanely gorgeous in his black tuxedo. To my surprise, a traditional one with a bow tie. I suspected my dad would have no choice but to appreciate that tiny bit of conventionality. Take it where he could get it, as it were.

Dane was devastatingly handsome. So perfect. I couldn't take my gaze from him, couldn't get to him fast enough. Yet my dad kept us strolling at a slow, measured pace that matched the flow of the music.

My heart beat wildly and butterflies took flight, low in my belly. Not out of uncertainty, but because of what I walked toward. Dane.

When I reached him, the corners of my mouth quivered from the huge smile threatening to take over and my chest rose and fell rapidly. My dad unraveled my arm from his and offered my hand to Dane. Then he stepped away, joining Kyle to my left.

Dane's gaze was riveting, locked on me. I had no idea how much time passed before he finally leaned forward and whispered, "You take my breath away."

The smile broke through. Tears misted my eyes. "I did the best I could with the short time frame."

"You can't even begin to imagine—" He swallowed hard. His gaze smoldered. "How stunning you are."

I tried to pull in a bit more air. No go. I prayed I wouldn't pass out. The heat and love in his emerald irises mesmerized me.

Tamera gave us several more seconds to admire each other, stay lost in each other's eyes.

Then she gently cleared her throat and asked, "Shall we begin?"

"Sure," I murmured, not even glancing her way.

With a soft laugh, she said, "All righty, then." I barely heard her words until she came to the vows. Then she graciously asked, "Do you have something prepared, or would you like me to continue?"

Dane said, "I have something for Ari."

Amano handed him a square box with *Cartier* in elegant script across the top.

"Dane." I'd known he'd go overboard.

With a grin, he said, "I don't intend to let you down. Ever."

He carefully folded back the lid and I gasped. Nestled in black satin was a wide diamond chevron tennis bracelet in white gold. As he lifted the sensational piece of jewelry from its perch, candle-light caught the angled diamonds and they sparkled brilliantly. Like nothing I'd ever seen before.

"It's thirty carats," he told me. "Flown in from Beverly Hills with two guards this afternoon."

My heart nearly stopped. "Dane," I repeated. Breathless. A feather could have knocked me over, and I was sure my eyes bulged. "Good grief."

He slipped the flexible bangle on my left wrist while staring into my eyes. "I will always love you, Aria Lynne DeMille. My heart has never belonged to anyone else—and it never will."

Tears pooled in my eyes, crested the rims. The fat drops rolled down my cheeks. I was still breathless. Speechless.

The bracelet was mind-boggling. But Dane's vow to me was all that registered at the moment.

I was vaguely aware of our guests, of Tamera. However, I couldn't get my brain to shift from stalled out to proper functioning.

Eventually, Tamera prompted me again. "Ari, do you have something for Dane?"

"*Oh.* Um . . ."

"She does," he hastily said. Amano handed over another box. Inside was a platinum ID bracelet with thick links. I encircled Dane's wrist with it, my fingers trembling as I tried to work the clasp. He had to help me.

Then I gazed up at him and asked, "How'd I get so lucky?"

Tamera sighed dreamily, as though she were deliriously happy I'd fallen apart for this man. Kyle snickered his displeasure.

"It's actually the other way around," Dane said. "I'm the lucky one."

I got a little caught up in his intense expression but eventually said, "I will always love you, Dane Bradley Bax. My heart has never belonged to anyone else—and never will."

His mouth sealed mine in an impassioned kiss that left my knees weak and my pulse racing.

"We're a wee bit out of order here," Tamera quietly said. "There is the matter of *I do* and *I now pronounce you* . . ."

Ethan and Amano chuckled. I imagined my father rolled his eyes.

Dragging my mouth from Dane's, I said, "I do. How about you?"

"Ari!" Tamera scolded me. "Behave."

"Fine," I grumbled. "But please try to quickly get us to the *you can now kiss the bride* part."

Dane grinned. My heart beat a bit faster.

Tamera efficiently wrapped up the ceremony, and then I was in Dane's arms again, swept away by a searing, soul-stealing kiss that, in my mind, went on and on. Forever.

When we finally came up for air, Tamera said to our guests—who'd waited patiently—"Gentlemen, may I present Mr. and Mrs. Dane Bax."

There it was. I was married.

The hottest man on the planet was officially mine.

The smile on my face had to shine brighter than the diamonds on my wrist. Dane appeared equally pleased. Handshakes and hugs ensued. We signed the marriage license—clumsily on my part because my fingers still shook.

Rosa directed our small party to the terrace for champagne and hors d'oeuvres that she served. Dane's lawyer lingered behind with the two of us. On the makeshift altar he placed a portfolio he'd been holding on to and flipped it open.

"I've made this as simple as possible for the moment," Jackson Conaway said. He was in his mid-sixties, with a headful of white hair, and he wore studious-looking specs. Like Amano, Mr. Conaway had been in the senior Bax's employ, and had remained with the family to oversee all of Dane's legal affairs, of which there were many, I was sure, given the size of his estate. Mr. Conaway had moved from Philadelphia to Sedona in order to be on-hand at all times.

"Essentially, Aria," he said, "I've consolidated the signing pages for you. I'll explain everything in full detail at a convenient time, but for all intents and purposes this evening, half of Dane's accounts, assets, and investments—10,000 Lux included—are yours, and you're now the sole beneficiary of his insurance and retirement policies, his IRAs, et cetera. I'll need your signature on several documents."

I stared blankly at him. "Oh. Um . . . h-h-uh," I stammered. "I wasn't expecting . . ." My gaze shifted to Dane. "I figured there'd be exclusionary clauses, waivers, and such to sign. A pre-nup, even though we've already . . . nupped . . . but you know, like—" I shook my head. My mind reeled.

Dane said, "Ari, you're my wife now. Everything I have, everything I acquire in the future, is yours. Sign the papers."

"Jesus. Dane." I couldn't quite process what he was saying.

I owned the Lux along with him?

Whoa.

I needed to sit down. Damn me for not setting out chairs.

Even more unnerving was that it fully hit me why Dane was so massively paranoid about my safety. The reason for all the secrecy, most important as it related to our marriage.

Now that I owned half of everything, I was an even greater bargaining chip for his axed investors. A much more invaluable pawn. If anything were to happen to Dane—

I anxiously glanced about. Found Amano standing off to the side, rather than joining the others on the terrace.

He watched me carefully. I realized he didn't think of himself as a guest at mine and Dane's wedding. He was on-duty. As always.

Were we going to convert one of the spare bedrooms for him?

I let out a borderline-hysterical half laugh. Knowing Amano, he'd prefer to stake out the house from his SUV, monitoring every square foot on his laptop, iPad, and phone.

I suddenly felt a bit claustrophobic, imagining they insist I start wearing a suit of armor for added protection.

Beyond all that, I couldn't fathom the sudden and extreme hike in my monetary worth.

I'd married a billionaire.

"Ari." Said billionaire nudged me gently. "Sign the papers," he repeated. So calmly, so steadily. "Our guests are waiting."

I stole another glance at Amano. Clearly, he saw the struggle in my eyes. He gave me a shadow of a grin, then nodded slightly.

I took the pen Mr. Conaway offered. He gave me the abbreviated version of what I had committed to on-paper. Dane signed as well. Then Amano, as our witness.

My heart palpitations continued, but Dane wrapped an arm

around my waist and dipped his head to mine. "If you ever need anything, and for some reason you can't come to me, Jack will help you. Don't ever forget that."

The grave expression on Dane's face sent a chill down my spine. "Like . . . if something ever happened to you?"

"Yes."

"Dane," I gasped.

"Shh." He kissed me tenderly. Then said, "Just promise you'll remember."

"I promise."

He led me to the terrace while I agonized over this aspect of marriage I'd obviously not put enough thought into. Any, really.

I'd wanted to be Dane's wife so that I'd never lose him. But I'd only been thinking in terms of him walking away from me—not being *taken* away.

It dawned on me that he'd desperately wanted me to be his wife—to be *his*. So much so that he'd take the risk of marrying me during a volatile time. And cover his bases with people like Amano, Kyle, and Mr. Conaway close at hand to help me if anything ever happened to him.

There was a somewhat selfish angle to us marrying this evening. Yet I couldn't say it was all on Dane's shoulders. I could have told him we needed to wait—I could have insisted and he would have allowed it, because he always gave me whatever I wanted. But I'd agreed to this because it was something I wanted just as badly.

Did love justify being just a little bit reckless?

In this case . . . yes.

I just needed for all of the random variables to make up a smart conclusion.

"Shake it off," he whispered. "You're much too tense."

"Right." I tried to relax, loosen my bunched shoulders.

He carefully maneuvered me through the grove and the light underbrush to the patio. Elegant, lively music played. Rosa graciously kept champagne in everyone's glasses and food in their hands. I thanked her profusely.

She said in her thick Hispanic accent, "I am so happy for you, *chica*. And you are so very beautiful."

"Shall I take photos?" Tamera offered.

Dane and I exchanged a look. Neither of us was the sort to collect pictures. Pretty much a result of our broken-home upbringings and long-suffering loner existences. But tonight the idea was an appealing one.

"I'd like that," I said to him. "If you're okay with it."

"Just a few," he told Tamera as he handed over his phone. "They stay with us."

Dane had a thing about photos or information featuring him hitting the Internet. Part of the secret-society security he'd adopted.

We all posed together and then Rosa took one that included Tamera. The others were just of me and Dane, and I was sure I wore a love-struck expression.

My dad kissed my cheek and congratulated me again. Ethan followed suit.

Kyle said, "Only you could pull all of this off in one day."

"Dane handled the reception."

I wasn't surprised he'd added tons of candles to the gas lanterns and heaters we kept out back. He could be very romantic. Rosa and Tamera disappeared for a few moments, then brought the floral arrangements from the altar to the dinner setting. We enjoyed more bubbly until Rosa announced the first course was ready.

My best guess was that Chef D'Angelo had prepped everything at the Lux, finished it here, then slipped out, since Dane didn't want even him to know about the wedding.

The chilled salads came out minutes later. Then the creamiest lobster bisque I'd ever tasted, with a huge chunk of succulent meat in the center and a sherry crème fraîche drizzle. It was a wonder my eyes didn't roll into the back of my head.

Our main course was Filet Oscar, accented with more decadent, buttery lobster and crab and paired with grilled asparagus.

There was no wedding cake. How could there be, really? This was sort of the wedding that never happened.

A tinge of disappointment crept in on me, but the trio of berry-topped, café au lait, and chocolate crème brûlée was sinfully delicious.

"That was Chef all the way, wasn't it?" Kyle asked as he unbuttoned his jacket, as though needing a little extra room. Not that the calories wouldn't dissolve in a heartbeat. Kyle was nothing short of studly, and I caught Tamera shooting glances his way. I bit back a smile.

"Poor guy," I said of Chef D'Angelo. "Dane made him work on his day off."

With a hearty laugh—I suspected the cocktails had mellowed Kyle out as much as the sinfully delicious dinner—he commented, "You know he loved it. I heard his family isn't allowed in his kitchen at home. If he hasn't prepped meals between his work shifts, they have to order in or dine out."

"That's probably a good rule. I'd need some salads or just plain vegetable broth to counter the decadence or I'd be the size of this house. He literally has hands that work culinary magic."

"And you really think he doesn't have a clue about why he whipped up dinner for eight tonight?"

I shrugged. "It's a holiday weekend. He dealt with Rosa, not Dane. He doesn't even know I live here. Probably just thought Dane had family or friends coming over."

"True. Still . . ." He leaned in and whispered, "Doesn't it suck that you can't tell anyone?"

I smirked good-naturedly. "You can't spoil this for me. It's done, Kyle."

The fact that I was now of billionaire status myself, however, was still unsettling. Made me a little queasy, truth be told. But I didn't mention that to my cynical friend.

"I realize it's not ideal," I conceded, "but not everything that's meant to be comes about in a neat and tidy package with a bow on top. Maybe having to work a bit harder at bringing it all together is what makes it so much more worthwhile."

He regarded me a few moments while everyone else was engaged in animated conversation. I knew my new husband had one eye on us. But Kyle wasn't attempting to make any sort of move on me. He had something else in mind.

"Does it keep him up at night?" he quietly challenged. "Knowing what happened to you? What could happen to you?"

I sighed. "You can't even begin to imagine how anything that happens to me, no matter how minor, tears him up. I know the side you see of him is territorial and, yes, he's had flashes of a violent temper. *Never* directed at me. He's protective, Kyle. Just like you are."

"Only with me, there wouldn't be anything out of the ordinary to protect you from. With him . . . it seems like every shadow holds a threat."

It did. But I couldn't tell Kyle that. What purpose would it serve but to solidify in *his* mind I'd made the wrong choice—and to worry him more?

Trying to lighten the mood, I suggested, "Why don't you ask Tamera to dance? It's a wedding, after all. Didn't you once declare them to be the perfect places to meet new women?"

He grinned. "I'd rather dance with you and piss your husband off."

"I think that *unwise*, my friend."

"Fine." He sipped more champagne, draining the glass. Then he set it aside and shoved back his chair. "I'm only doing this to make you jealous," he whispered in my ear.

I laughed softly. "I'll try to keep from ripping her hair out."

He shot a wry look my way, then rounded the table and interrupted the conversation to offer Tamera his hand for a dance.

They looked quite striking together. Though as Tamera stared up at Kyle, appearing a bit awestruck by his handsome face and hulking build, he shot a glimpse my way, over the top of her blonde head.

I cringed and diverted my gaze. He needed to accept the reality of the situation. Move on from it . . . from me.

I slid a glance toward Dane, who lifted his flute, as though to say, *Well played.*

It helped to cut some of the tension.

As eleven o'clock approached, the party wound down. When Dane and I were alone on the patio—which Rosa had cleaned, though she'd left all the decorations as is—my new husband took me into his arms and held me tight as we swayed to a sexy jazz tune.

"You always leave me momentarily speechless when I look at you," he murmured. "But tonight, as soon as you came into the clearing . . . Jesus, Ari. I couldn't see or think of anything but you."

"I felt the same." Tugging on the end of his bow tie made it unravel. I worked the first three buttons of his shirt, brushing my fingertips over his warm skin. I inhaled deeply, drawing in that unique, scintillating scent of his.

It'd been pure torture wanting to be alone and naked with him all evening but also enjoying the others' company and not minding that we'd had a long dinner with everyone. But this was truly what I longed for—to be wrapped in his embrace, our bodies melded together.

I said, "You got a little crazy with the bracelet."

He lifted my hand from his chest and swept his lips over my fingers. "Not at all. I wanted you to have something extraordinary. But I will buy you a ring," he assured me with conviction in his eyes. "When the time's right."

Meaning when the danger had passed.

So as much as Dane wanted to contend there was a silent truce with the ousted Lux owners, he clearly wasn't certain we were out of the woods.

He flattened my palm against his pecs again and covered my

hand with his. "I know this is all a bit overwhelming." His lips grazed my temple as he spoke. "But you're handling it beautifully."

"All I wanted was you. Everything else . . . the diamonds, the money . . . that's just not my thing, and—"

He kissed me. Likely to shut me up. I didn't mind.

His tongue slipped inside, gliding over mine. I eased the remaining buttons on his shirt through their holes and, in between his teasing kisses, said, "We're wearing entirely too many clothes."

chapter 6

Dane swept me into his arms and carried me through the patio doors and the great room, down the long hallway, and into our bedroom.

He set me on my feet and said, "I'll never forget how you look tonight." His gaze slid over me, slowly, appreciatively. "You're absolutely gorgeous. Heart-stopping."

"Dane." The way his eyes glowed with love made my own heart swell. "You say the sweetest things."

His fingertips skimmed over my jaw. Brushed against my lips. "Thank you for marrying me."

I stared up at him. "You're thanking *me*? I'm the one who won the lottery."

His head lowered and he kissed me. Softly, at first, but then passionately, until my body was pressed to his and I burned with desire.

He eased the zipper down the back of my dress and carefully removed it, laying the garment along the sofa. A ribbon of warmth wound through me at the great care he took when it came to something that meant so much to me. My wedding dress.

It didn't even bother me that I couldn't have a designer one-of-a-kind like most of my brides. I'd found something beautiful that had spoken to me. And Dane's reaction when he'd seen me coming down the aisle had convinced me I'd made the right choice.

Not just with the dress, but in agreeing to marry him. I still wanted a big wedding and always would. But our private ceremony had been wonderful, and the intimacy of it made our union even more special.

I slipped out of my lingerie, then said, "I need to take all this makeup off."

I left him, dressed in my satin robe, and brushed my teeth before scrubbing my face. My heartbeats had yet to return to normal. Same with my breathing.

Dane came in and wrapped his arms around me from behind.

I smiled at him in the reflection we created. "Everything was so fantastic tonight. Dinner was amazing. I might have to start using your weight room if I keep this up."

His nose nuzzled the base of my neck, the crook of my shoulder seemingly distracting him. "With all the work you still have leading up to the pre-launch activities, I'll be insisting you continue eating."

"You don't mind a few extra pounds?"

"Ari." He groaned. "I've told you before and I'll tell you again. You're insanely beautiful. And I am hopelessly hooked on you."

"Let's hope I'm more refreshed looking for you in a couple of months."

"You're perfect." His lips grazed my throat. "You've worked so hard, baby. You've put in so many hours. Immediately following the launch, I want you to relax. Sit back and enjoy the fruits of your labor. Put your toes in the sand and just . . . chill out."

"Like, a honeymoon?"

"Yes," he murmured against my throat. "We definitely need a honeymoon. In February. Over Valentine's Day."

My heart melted. "Dane. That's so romantic."

I caught his grin in the mirror. "I'll take care of everything. Find a remote, private, beautiful location. Someplace where you'll be waited on hand and foot. You won't have to move a muscle if you don't want to. Just soak up the sun, shop, swim . . . whatever you want."

Heat flashed through me. "You know what I want."

His grin turned seductive. "There'll be plenty of that." He kissed his way up to my ear, his tongue pressing to that sensitive spot just below and behind the lobe that always set me on fire.

A soft moan escaped my parted lips. "You're too good to me."

"All I want is for you to be happy."

"Mission accomplished," I assured him. "I am deliriously happy. Ridiculously so. If Tamera weren't all about happily ever afters, she would have been disgusted by my exuberance tonight." I laughed softly. "Instead, she was beyond excited. So was I."

"We belong together. Always."

I squeezed my eyes shut for a moment. Then said, "Dane, you could have married any wo—"

"You're all I want, Ari. It hit me *so* hard, from the first second I saw you. I just *knew* you were the one. Nothing's ever going to take me away from you. I am forever yours."

Tears prickled my eyes. "I just want to be perfect for you. Really and truly."

"You are." His gaze in the mirror didn't waver. "You're everything to me. Every breath I take. So much more than I'd ever imagined I'd find. More than I'd ever dreamed of."

He gently clasped my elbow and led me into the bedroom. Pulling on the ends of the sash at my waist, he untied my robe and divested me of it. I watched with mounting desire as he discarded his own clothes. My pulse raced. His fingers twined with mine and he guided me to the bed. I sat on the ledge as he knelt before me. He lifted my leg and placed my foot on the mattress, spreading my legs wide.

His head dipped and his lips skated along my inner thigh, making the flesh quiver. He kissed and nipped, eliciting anticipation that had me squirming on the bed.

"Dane." I threaded my fingers through his silken hair. "You're teasing me."

"Just warming you up."

"I'm plenty warm. On-fire, actually."

His index and middle fingers glided along my outer folds, spreading them as he moved in, his head between my legs. With the lightest of touches, his tongue licked along my sensitive skin. Such a titillating feeling.

"I crave your taste," he whispered, his breath gentle against my skin, arousing me further. "I crave every inch of you."

His mouth pressed to me. My other hand curled around the bedding as nerve endings jumped.

Then the soft licking started. Slow and sexy. My head fell back on my shoulders, the plump curls falling between my shoulder blades. My eyelids drifted closed.

The tip of his tongue fluttered against my clit. Magma oozed through my body.

"I love when you do this to me. I'd never considered how incredible it would feel, and now I can't live without it."

His lips tugged on my slick folds, jolting me. Then his thumb rubbed my clit in stimulating circles as his tongue dipped into my opening.

Excitement shot down my spine. I ached for him, deep in my core. Especially as he resumed the flicking of his tongue over that swollen knot of nerves between my legs. He slipped two fingers inside me, pumping vigorously.

"Yes," I murmured, the pressure and heat building. "God, that's just . . . so good."

He always took me to soaring heights. No exception tonight,

but I was fairly certain the intensity of the pleasure that currently gripped me had more to do with the fact that I was now his wife.

For all the fear I'd had of marriage, all I could focus on was the beauty of it. The fact that we belonged solely to each other.

As that thought settled enticingly in my mind, Dane gently suckled my clit, his fingers pumped quicker, and I came apart at the seams, crying out his name as the fiery sensations raged through me.

I clung to the rush, the high, as he remained wedged between my parted thighs. He kissed my inner leg again, then worked his way up, over my stomach and rib cage, to my breasts. His tongue curled around my hard nipple, toying with it. Then he drew the pebbled peak into his mouth. I gasped, the sensation sizzling, keeping my blood simmering. Exhilaration echoed through me—I was convinced I experienced the longest orgasm imaginable as my inner walls still clutched his fingers, savoring the last vestiges of a release that went on and on.

Despite the vibrant climax, I still wanted more. Still needed more. As though I hadn't relinquished even half of the delicious tension he evoked.

My head fell forward. "Dane," I whispered against his hair as he continued to tease my nipple. Then the other. I writhed restlessly against him. "I want you inside me."

He kissed the tops of my breasts, my neck. "Whatever you want, baby."

I tried really hard to keep my nails from biting into his skin as I gripped his bulging biceps and hauled him up. His hands clasped my waist and he moved me toward the center of the bed. His eyes shimmered with lust and a dark yearning that made my pussy throb.

"I need to feel you," I told him. "All of you. Fuck me. Hard."

"My sexy, sinful Ari." He kissed me in his searing way, commanding all of my senses, making me burn for him.

Hooking his powerful forearm along the underside of my knee, he lifted my leg so that the back pressed to his chest. The tip of his cock teased my opening for several tantalizing seconds before he sank into me, making me cry out once more.

He only partially hovered over me, propped on one elbow. Mostly, his weight bore down on me, and it felt heavenly. His heat and scent surrounded me. My leg remained sandwiched between his chest and mine, my knee crooking over his broad shoulder. The position opened me fully to him and he moved inside me with long, full strokes that pushed deep.

All hot and bothered now, I said, "Do this to me every night."

He chuckled, though it came out a bit strained from the effort he exerted in getting me off. "You're insatiable."

"Who would have thought? I just needed the right partner."

Another scorching kiss had me climbing quickly to that pinnacle I so loved. He palmed my ass cheek and lifted me slightly off the mattress as he plunged deeper.

"Yes," I moaned. "Oh, God, yes. Fuck me, Dane. Make me come."

He worked me fervently, and my raised hips met his smooth, solid thrusts. Our breathing escalated, filling the quiet room. My heart thundered. My skin tingled.

I loved how he possessed me, owned every inch of me. He knew instinctively what I needed and gave it to me. Over and over.

Staring into my eyes, he said, "You'll always belong only to me."

"Yes."

"You are *everything* to me, Ari."

Emotion welled in my throat. Desire surged through me. He pumped faster, harder, and all the feelings inside me collided and erupted.

One word fell from my lips as I came.

"Dane!"

As I shattered so, too, did he.

It was perfect.

chapter 7

I found it impossible to hide my wedding bracelet at work, even with long sleeves from a blouse or suit jacket. The diamonds sparkled vibrantly with just the tiniest hint of light. It caught everyone's eye. So I had to lie and tell them I'd splurged with my impending bonus and that they weren't real diamonds. I wasn't wholly convinced the fabrication flew, because it only caused people to inspect the bracelet more closely and mutter, "Hmm."

While I wasn't keen on the scrutiny, I only took the gorgeous piece of jewelry off in the shower and before bed, so I didn't scratch the hell out of Dane with it—my nails did that plenty when he made love to me.

Following the success of the Thanksgiving events, everyone at the hotel put their heart and soul into the transformation of the Lux from fall to Christmas decorations. Enormous crates filled with wreaths, lights, garland, and ornaments were scattered everywhere, transported around the property via forklifts and extended-bed golf and other carts. I scrambled to stay on top of the placement of every single item. Studied each decoration hung to make sure it was perfect—the right location, the right angle, the right look.

The Engineering/Electrical staff grumbled over my insistence that they check each strand of twinkle lights—that meant jiggling every single bulb to make sure it wasn't loose—before they were wrapped around the thick trunks of the sycamores and aspens lining the drive into the hotel, the pines near the entrance, the various optimal objects in the courtyard and gardens out back, and the rounded second-story terrace that overlooked them.

But above the tedious, an air of excitement permeated the hotel and the grounds.

There was much to do in the three weeks before our first pre-launch event, which was to be our hosted media night. The days flew by in exhaustive blocks of fourteen or sixteen hours at the Lux, and not much sleep in between.

Dane urged me to take the pace a bit slower, but that was impossible, not just because my to-do list was still a mile long but also because I was beyond excited. It was difficult to shut down my mind. I reverted to the wedding planner's curse of waking up ten times a night to run through mental checklists. Typically, Dane was lying in bed next to me, his fingers clicking softly on the keyboard of his laptop.

Not so a week prior to our first big event.

I found him on the sofa in front of the fireplace in our bedroom, speaking quietly into his phone. I only caught a few seconds of his conversation before he disconnected the call and dropped the cell on the end table next to him.

Curling on the cushion beside him, I asked, "Talking with Nikolai in Russia again?"

"No, Mikaela," he said. "She's back from Italy. Her zoning issues have been cleared up and she's ready to open shop in Old Town."

"Thanks to you?"

"And Anthony Delfino. He has friends in all the right places in Scottsdale."

My mind worked quick on this one. "That was what the meeting was all about at the second wedding reception for Meg and Sean? The one Mr. Delfino hosted at his home in Scottsdale when they returned from their honeymoon?" I recalled that evening, when Dane's mentor and business partner, Ethan Evans, had whisked Dane away to wrap up some mysterious business with Anthony Delfino.

"Yes," Dane said. "I cashed in a few favors to help her out."

"Do you always help her out?" I couldn't resist asking.

He slid a glance my way. "She's been a friend since I've had a memory, Ari. If she needs me—"

"Yeah, but . . . her father is an ambassador. Can't Daddy take care of her roadblocks?"

Dane's head dipped and he kissed the tip of my nose. "Baby, this is no big deal. And besides . . . wouldn't you want me to help someone in need, if I could?"

Another technicality he had me on. He'd given Kyle a job, after all. Had written a huge check to get my mother off my back—and save my dad's reputation. I could only imagine the other countless times Dane had come to someone's aid. Hell, he'd rescued me from numerous threats that went well beyond my mother.

"I concede," I said on a yawn.

"When it comes to Mikaela," he whispered against my hair, "you have nothing to worry about, Mrs. Bax." He kissed the top of my head.

I grinned. And fell asleep while snuggled alongside him.

Unfortunately, my contentment wasn't meant to be.

As I double-checked invoices to sign off on before sending them to Accounting for payment processing, there was a knock on my opened office door.

"Season's Greetings!"

The very distinct, sensual Italian accent made my head snap up from my laptop.

There, in my doorway, stood Heidi Klum.

Well, Mikaela Madsen, but whatever. Same, same.

She smiled brightly, all pearly white teeth and just so striking from head to toe, I could see why every man in her life fell so easily at her feet, eager to do her bidding. I'd probably fall, too, if I possessed the right equipment and the little head/big head mentality.

"Hey," I said as I closed the top of my computer and gestured with my fingers for her to enter. "Nice to see you."

"It's been much too long, darling."

I was thrown by the accent—Mikaela was American. I surmised all the time she spent with Fabrizio in his village outside of Florence lent to her international mystique. Still, the accent seemed so out of place. Yet chances were good I was the only one who noticed.

She crossed the vast space I occupied on the fourth floor of 10,000 Lux and set an elegant, elaborately designed gift bag on my desk.

I stood and came around to meet her for the double-cheek air-kiss thing she liked to do.

She studied me a moment, then said, "You look fabulous. Did you do something different with your hair?"

"Just pulled it up," I commented. It was all meticulously styled, every strand in its proper place. While Mikaela's was the perfectly mussed high ponytail only some women could achieve. That back-combed look that made it seem as though she'd merely rolled out of bed and wrapped a few strands of long hair around the thick mass to contain it, but which likely took a good hour to get just the right tousled look. A style I could never pull off.

"So, you're back from Italy," I mused, hoping my tone sounded neutral. Not bitchy. Not too nice. Just . . . indifferent. Like hers. "I hear you're good to go on the shop in Old Town."

"Everything's being delivered in the next few weeks to set up, and our first shipment is due any day after that. Every variety of gourmet olives, meats and cheeses, oils, and the absolute best-of-the-best Italian wines—all imported from Brizio's village. Italy on Your Doorstep . . . That's our name."

"Very nice."

"I brought you samples," she said, indicating the bag with one slender, beautifully manicured hand. "I'm dying to get a review from you. Dane says you're a fantastic cook."

I gave her a curious look. Had he told her about us? Did she know we were married?

I mentally shook my head. No. He'd been specific about the small circle we kept our secret within. I couldn't believe he'd spill to Mikaela without telling me.

So I merely played along.

"I've been learning from the chefs downstairs."

"Smart girl. They're very talented. And you know what they say about the way to a man's heart. . . ." She gave me a coy look, then added, "You do know Dane's favorite dish is duck with glazed carrots and zucchini salad, right? I picked up a great recipe in Paris while I was at Le Cordon Bleu for a time."

I fought the *of course you did* bubbling up in my throat. Not only was she way too touchy-feely when with Dane, but she had mad skills in the kitchen as well? *And* knew his preferred meal—while I did not.

"I'm sure Chef D'Angelo has it perfected for Dane," I merely commented.

"Without a doubt. They've been together forever. Dane only shares tidbits like that with people who've been in his life for a long time. In my case, since we were toddlers. Amano drove the both of us to and from the private schools we attended and all the activities, like dances. Even the prom."

I assured myself it didn't matter that this woman had shared all the classic adolescent rites of passion with my husband. Because he was mine now.

But her words still stung. Maybe if she weren't so statuesque, worldly, and sophisticated I might not be so bothered that she remained a permanent fixture in Dane's life. Yet she *was* all those things—and more—and that set me on-edge.

"Well, it was nice to see you again," I told her as I walked toward my door, hoping she'd follow. "Thanks so much for the treats. I look forward to sampling them."

"And you must stop by the tasting room when we're open," she insisted.

I caught on very quickly that she specifically said *you*, not *you and Dane*.

Interesting.

Still not wanting to give anything away, I nodded in agreement, refraining from mentioning that my husband and I would certainly do that. Plus, I wasn't the petty type. Not horribly insecure when it came to Dane's affection, either. He'd married *me*, after all.

Perhaps it was just that she seemed to have some sort of claim over him, since they'd grown up together, and she always turned to him when she needed something.

Thankfully, she got the hint and finally whirled around on her ridiculously tall stilettos and strolled out the door, with a chic, "Ciao!" and a waggle of her long fingers.

It did not go unnoticed by me that she headed in the opposite direction of the bank of elevators—toward Dane's office suite.

I seethed.

So, okay. Maybe I *was* a tad jealous. . . .

Preparations at the Lux progressed nicely. Though Dane's anticipation and enthusiasm over the launch escalated, I sensed his tension around the periphery. Understandable, but I tried to assure him that everything had fallen beautifully into place, as I did one more time at two in the morning the day of our media gala.

"Look through the windows," I said as I cuddled against his shoulder while he worked. "It's even snowing."

He spared a glance outdoors. The solar lights he'd added around the copse on the other side of the tall glass panes captured the lightly falling, glittery flakes.

"We'll have a gorgeous dusting on the mesas surrounding the Lux." As I'd imagined from the onset. "Dane, this is exactly what we've both envisioned. And tonight will go off without a hitch, because I have planned this whole thing down to the smallest of details."

Sure, I was nervous, given the significance of the evening ahead of us. But I knew what I was doing when it came to pulling off a five-star event. And the staff at the Lux had been so well trained, their skills so honed, they wouldn't miss a beat. I had every confidence in them. In us . . . as a team.

"This will be a night long talked about," I told Dane. "And the start of an incredible, *memorable* grand opening."

Tingles ran rampant through me. It was no wonder I couldn't sleep.

He gave me a sexy grin. "You have no idea how grateful I am for all that you've done, baby. I knew from the beginning that I could trust you. And you've done nothing but exceed my expectations, over and over."

Shutting the lid of his laptop and setting it on the low ledge of the headboard, he burrowed deep in the thick covers, pulling me closer to him.

"I've never seen such a stunning property," I told him. "Not on film, on TV, in magazines, on the Internet. When people come through those massive gates, they're going to be absolutely breathless. Astonished. And so thrilled to get a glimpse at another wonder of the world."

"No more talk of the Lux," he whispered. "You're awake. I'm awake. Let's make love. . . ."

Despite multiple orgasms, my nerves were shot to hell several hours later.

Dane had relaxed me with his special brand of magic, helping me to sleep for a spell, yet I sprang from bed at six o'clock and went into full-on planner mode. Breakfast barely registered as Rosa served it.

She'd volunteered to shift from working part-time at the house to being here first thing in the morning until evening. Her son was grown and halfway across the country. She said she liked being needed, and quite frankly, I wasn't sure how I would have survived the past couple of months without her to look after the household chores and errands.

I also suspected that, given how well Dane paid her, she was building a nice retirement nest egg.

We spent the day at the hotel. I surveyed every inch of the lobby and courtyard, double-checking the decorations, fluffing, adjusting, having bulbs replaced if they made even the slightest twitch when I inspected them.

Mid-afternoon, I went up to my office and did my hair and makeup and changed into the dress I'd worn the night I'd married Dane. This was a formal function, and it just seemed apropos that I wear something striking and meaningful for each event, starting now.

Dane wore the tux from that evening as well, and it felt right, I thought. Sort of symbolic.

We'd invited my dad to talk up the golf courses, since he had fame and credibility under his belt. Kyle was on-hand, too, as part of the joint Marketing-PR team that would promote the resort.

It was a good hour before anyone was due to arrive as I went over instructions with the tuxedo-clad servers, designating some for the entrance so they could offer champagne as guests arrived and then discussing how the shifts of passed hot and cold hors d'oeuvres were to be managed. There were also seven appetizer stations and premium liquor, margarita and martini bars strategically placed, similar to the arrangements I'd made for the Thanksgiving reception, since that had worked so well.

Dane pulled me aside at one point and said, "You need to take a deep breath and have a drink."

"We're so close to pulling this all off," I whispered, too thrilled for anything to register other than the astonished faces that would soon come through our doors.

Dane's deep-green irises sparkled brilliantly as he said in a low tone so no one else heard, "Baby, everything is just right. *Beyond my wildest dreams* right. I owe you so much for that, Ari. And this is just the beginning for us."

Love burned in his eyes. Tears misted mine. He tried to keep the moment intimate, and I hoped it appeared as though we were just discussing last-minute top-secret details. I didn't steal any glances. Really, everyone was so busy with final preparations, I couldn't imagine they even noticed us. We stood on the far side of the lobby, close to the sweeping staircases.

I said, "You gave me a beautiful dream with this hotel, Dane. And with our life to—"

I got no further.

The lights went out.

Gasps and a few groans ensued. Other than that, everyone fell quiet. Perplexed or in suspense.

"Oh, shit!" My nerves jumped. "I blew the fuses with all my twinkle lights!"

Dane reached for my hand and squeezed it tight. "We'll fix this. And there's a backup generator that'll kick on in a second if we blew the grid."

Oh, my God! I'd pulled a Clark Griswold on one of the most important nights of Dane's and the Lux's existence!

"Dane, I'm so sorry." I felt wretched. "I'd never even considered this. I—"

"Ari, it's okay, baby."

But the generator didn't spring to life. We remained bathed in darkness.

"Dane. Shouldn't the lights be on by now?"

"I'm on it!" I heard Chris Monroe, from the Engineering/Electrical staff, call out. We'd wanted him on-hand for any emergencies, but this certainly wasn't one I'd written into my crisis management plan.

Fuck! How could I have *not* considered frying fuses?

But then . . . I seriously hadn't gone overboard with the lights. I'd been tactical and judicious, striking the right balance. And Chris's team had been with me the whole time, running tests.

"Dane," I said, uncertainty slithering down my spine.

"Shh," he silenced me. "Do you hear that?" His tone remained low but now much more ominous.

"Hear what?"

A breath later, a calculated, deliberate, *distinct* clicking noise filled the deathly quiet air.

No. Not a clicking noise.

A ticking one . . .

And a sharp dripping sound accompanied it.

"Oh, Jesus," I hissed out. "Dane."

He gripped my arm and guided me farther into the lobby, where the ticking echoed louder.

We weren't the only ones to hear it now, and the ripple of, "What is that?" made the rounds. The electricians had flashlights on their tool belts, and beams of light swept the cavernous room.

Dane called out for my dad, and both and he and Kyle suddenly appeared at my elbow.

So, too, did Amano. "Dane." The bodyguard pointed to the enormous table in the center of the lobby. The one situated below the to-die-for chandelier I admired every single morning when I came through the doors of 10,000 Lux.

At the table's base, a little red light blinked.

My stomach dropped to my knees. "Oh, Lord," I whispered. "Is that . . . ?" I couldn't even say the word.

"Bomb," Dane ground out urgently. "And whatever's spilling from the base . . . My guess is, it's flammable. Somehow they shoved something up there. A pipe bomb? I don't fucking know." He thrust me toward Kyle. "Get her out of here. *Now!*"

"What?" I cried out, instantly distressed. "Dane, no!"

"Ari, just do as I tell—"

"I'm not leaving without you!"

"Fuck!" he roared. Then to my dad and Kyle, he demanded, "Get her out of here! *Right this very minute!* All of you"—he announced to the crowd in an urgent voice—"get as far away from the building as possible! Across the grounds!"

He shouted more orders for everyone to evacuate the lobby. Amano raced toward the bank of elevators and pulled the fire alarm. Then he was on his cell, issuing strict instructions to whoever was on the other end of the line to get out.

I was rooted where I stood, paralyzed by fear. Kyle's arm shot around my waist and he yanked at me. My dad had my forearm. They started to pull me away from Dane.

"No!" I cried out as I gripped a fistful of his jacket. "I'm not leaving without you!" I yelled, fear seizing my soul. "You have to come with us!" My heart thundered. My pulse raced. Terror tore through me. "Dane!"

"Ari!" Kyle snapped. "Do as he says! Go with me!"

"No, I—"

Wrenching my hand free of his sleeve, Dane insisted, "Go!" Then he turned away, rushing about, getting the employees hustling toward the doors.

A mass exodus ensued. I struggled every step of the way, thrashing in Kyle's strong embrace, screaming at him and my father to let me go. My arms flailed and I kicked at Kyle's shins as he lifted me slightly off the ground to make a hasty retreat.

"I can't leave him!" I cried. "Put me down!"

"Shut the hell up, Ari!" Kyle bit back.

I craned my neck to get a glimpse of Dane and Amano ushering out the kitchen staff as the flashlights provided just enough illumination for everyone to find their way.

"Dane!" I called out again just as we passed through the twenty-foot double doors of the lobby.

There were panicked and confused hollers above the eerily piercing fire alarm as we burst into the resort's valet area, the outdoor lights from the decorations and fountains edging the glow of twilight. We were some of the last people out—making it well past the entrance and the circular drive and to the grounds and waterfalls beyond. I screamed bloody murder all the way as I tried to free myself of Kyle's vise grip.

Then a thunderous roar filled the quiet night, simultaneous with a massive explosion that propelled those of us closest to the lobby off our feet and hurled us toward the marble-trimmed waterfalls, along with shattered glass and wooden splinters.

I hit the side of one of those short marble encasements, with Kyle's body sprawled heavily on top of mine. The ground shook beneath us.

I screamed again as searing pain ripped through me. Tears flooded my eyes. Above the ringing in my ears, I heard—all around me—the others yelling, sobbing, screeching. The debris rained down, mostly landing in thick treetops or the water so that it splashed everywhere.

"Kyle!"

"Just stay put," he growled. He was still mostly on top of me.

"My dad!"

"Right here!" he called out, though I couldn't tell from which direction or how far away, I was so disoriented.

I heard the pieces of 10,000 Lux pelt the stone driveway.

When I stole a glance through a peephole Kyle's propped-up arm created, I saw chunks of concrete and wood tear through branches that only slightly slowed their descent enough for the few who hadn't found refuge on the opposite side of the circular drive to be able to dodge the massive destruction. We were all mostly a significant distance from the hotel but some of us too close to fully escape the damage. Several employees stumbled about, bleeding and half hysterical.

The blood flowing down the side of my own face barely registered. I had no idea where the burst of energy came from, but I shoved Kyle away and started to crawl toward them, along the glass-covered lawn.

"Goddamn it, Ari!" My dad was instantly beside me, hauling me to my feet.

I stared up at the four-story lobby of 10,000 Lux, a wide, gaping hole of tall blazing flames and billowing smoke.

"Jesus," Kyle breathed as he took in the same scene. Then turned his attention to me. "You're bleeding all over the place."

My hands stung from the shards lodged in my skin, but the agony couldn't compete with the throbbing in my head. Or the instant horror that my wedding bracelet was missing from my wrist.

"Oh, God, Kyle," I said on a sharp breath. "My bracelet's gone."

But that was really the least of my worries at the moment. My gaze swept the crowd of thirty or so behind us, mostly out of harm's way, and away from the burning Lux. Only a handful had been as close to the building as the three of us.

Of those unfortunate souls I said to my dad and Kyle, "Help them, please."

We were all breathing hard; all wore the same stunned and pained expression. The others had scrapes and quickly developing bumps and bruises, but I appeared to be the only one in this small, immediate conglomeration with a crimson river flowing down my cheek and dripping from my chin, staining my dress. My dad was already on the phone to 911.

Very gently, Kyle held me. "You're seriously hurt," he said. "You need to sit down."

"No." Anxiety gripped me. So, too, did my sense of duty. I scanned the crowd. "They're freaked out and we have to calm them." My attention shifted as I noted each familiar face. Instantly realizing two very important people were missing. My anxiety turned to heart-wrenching, blood-chilling fear. "Dane," I whispered. He and Amano were nowhere in sight. "Dane!" I started toward the hotel.

Kyle wouldn't release me. "Ari, no."

"He's not here." My chest heaved. The tears streamed, mixing with the blood. I swiped at the sticky mess clouding my vision. "Kyle," I choked out. "He's not *here*. Neither is Amano." The panic made bile burn my throat. "Dane!"

I struggled against Kyle's caging arms, my horror mounting.

Chef D'Angelo hurried toward us, hobbling slightly. His black pants were shredded at the knees, obviously from a rough fall. "Ari, are you all right?"

"Are you?" I implored.

"Yes, yes. Amano called the kitchen. Dane helped everyone out. Everyone got out, Ari, because of them. *Everyone*." Chef's dark-brown eyes danced wildly in the sockets. His cheeks were sullied and he had a small cut on his chin. He clasped my hands, then suddenly realized they were covered in blood. "Oh! I'm so sorry!"

I winced at his quick grip—he'd let go instantly.

"Not your fault," I eeped out. The pain and the blood made me queasy. My mind turned a bit hazy. I suspected I had a concussion from the blow.

"Anyway," I said. "Thank God everyone escaped." Though relief couldn't fully register. There were too many petrified and wounded people. And no Dane and Amano. "Chef," I insisted, my own eyes as wide and wild, "where is he? Where are they?"

"Ari." He stared at me a few agonizing moments, then slowly

shook his head. "They were the last ones inside. Still in the lobby when—"

"No," I said on a broken breath. My eyes squeezed shut.

Kyle handed me off to my father while he still had his cell to his ear.

"Where are you going?" I demanded in a hoarse voice as I slumped against my dad's side.

"I can't just stand here and do nothing," Kyle shot back. He gave me a full-on tormented look, taking in my injuries, which were apparently quite bad, because he raked a hand through his hair and added, "But damn it, I can't leave you."

"Then don't," I urged. Regardless of my foggy brain, I knew exactly what my best friend had in mind. "Just stay here. Help the people who are out here."

He gave me a long look, our eyes locked. I saw his internal tug-of-war. He hated to leave me. Was torn by it. But Kyle was the stuff of which heroes were made. He'd proven it to me more than once.

Before I could get another word of protest out, he whirled around and ran toward the roaring inferno.

I screamed, yelling out for him. More pain sliced through my heart. My dad held me even tighter.

Chef also called out for Kyle to come back. But he didn't return.

Chef's attention zeroed in on me again, though it barely registered. In a tight voice, he said, "I'm so sorry. Dane and Amano wouldn't leave until everyone was safe."

The throbbing and the haze in my head intensified. A raging pulse beat in my ears. Fury and heartbreak ripped through me, as hot and bright as the mammoth flames engulfing the night.

It couldn't be true.

It was impossible.

There was no way Dane and Amano could have been trapped inside, couldn't have made it out in time.

No. Way.

And now Kyle was chasing after them to do what? Charge into a burning building and try to rescue them?

I could hardly fathom the nightmare suddenly seizing me. My legs shook and my heart felt as though it were being beaten to a bloody pulp with a bat.

Someone—Chef or my dad—dabbed at the crimson river mixed with tears covering my face. I couldn't make out who, because the sticky mess was blinding, along with the pounding in my head.

I struggled again. My dad gently held me. "Ari, just stop."

"Don't let Kyle go in there."

I felt my body slip from my dad's grip. Slowly crinkling. Everything was slipping away.

"Dane!" I cried once more, weakly.

"Ari. Stay with me, sweets. Come on now." My dad's tone was frantic as he eased to the ground with me.

He started talking, but I couldn't latch on to his words. All I heard were the shocked cries, the snapping and crackling of mile-high flames, the popping of whatever continued to explode inside what was left of 10,000 Lux, and the sirens in the distance. So very, very far away. Nowhere near close enough to save the hotel or anything—*anyone*—inside it.

And what about Kyle, so determined to risk life and limb for . . . Dane and Amano?

Oh, God.

He really was a hero.

All three of them were.

I cried harder. I tried to lurch forward once more in my dazed state. But I was weightless and floating.

Then there was nothing but darkness.

I woke to more voices. Not necessarily calm ones. More like insistent and under-the-breath ones. As though they didn't want me to hear.

"Completely incinerated . . . Acres scorched . . ."

"Ammonium nitrate . . . explosion . . ."

"Needed volunteer firefighters from Oak Creek and Flagstaff . . ."

"Search and rescue team onsite . . ."

"Others released from the ER . . . Just Ari under observation . . ."

"Police have questions . . . FBI has been called in . . . Criminal investigation . . ."

My eyes remained closed and I drifted back into darkness.

I came to from time to time, surmising I was in a hospital room. But the pain was so excruciating, I didn't move or bother to open my eyes. Why didn't they give me something more potent?

My best guess was that if I had a concussion they'd prefer I be awake as much as possible the first twenty-four hours.

Impossible.

It wasn't so much that I slept . . . I was pretty sure I blacked out from the throbbing, the haze, and the sheer torment of it all.

It took a while for coherent thoughts to gel in my mind. I had no idea how long, but eventually I was a bit clearer in the head. I licked my lips, only to discover they were coated with a vanilla-flavored balm that my dad or one of the nurses must have brought from the gift shop. My mouth, however, was bone-dry.

I noted that my breathing wasn't quite normal, coming in heavy pulls. And I was nauseous.

Finally mustering some strength, I forced my lids open. Stared across the room at where Kyle sat in a chair, flipping agitatedly through a magazine, not even stopping to read the articles or view the pictures.

I jerked awake at the sight of him. Worse for wear, what with some bandages and burns, but sitting right there beside me.

"Oh, thank God you're alive!" The enthusiasm echoed in my head, not my voice. It was a mere wisp of air.

Kyle tossed aside the magazine. My dad, who'd paced along-side him, came to an immediate halt. They'd changed clothes, but they both had fresh scrapes and bruises that told me I hadn't been out too long. Maybe no more than a day or so.

They both closed in on me. I tried to remain focused. Funny, with all the napping, I should feel refreshed and alert. Instead, I was thoroughly exhausted. Like I could sleep away the rest of the month.

Dane would never let me get away with that.

Dane.

I sat bolt upright at the thought of him. Then promptly let out an ear-piercing wail at the pain that shot through me. I dropped back to the bed.

"Ari," my dad said, his voice thick with worry.

I couldn't concentrate on him, what with the blinding agony and the sudden reminder of what Chef D'Angelo had said.

"Dad." I reached out for him, groping the air. He helped out, clasping my wrist. I realized my hands were wrapped in bandages.

During my drifting in and out, in another conversation I'd heard someone mentioning I had nearly twenty stitches along my hairline. Yet another scar, compliments of the corrupt members of the secret society. And I'd needed a dozen more stitches on my palms from the cuts I'd collected when trying to help the others who'd escaped the hotel.

But that was really of little concern at the moment.

"Where's Dane?" I demanded. "Why isn't he here?"

Because what Chef D'Angelo had told me could *not* be true.

The door flew open and a nurse rushed in—clearly, she'd heard my scream.

My dad told her, "She's in a lot of pain. Can't you give her something stronger?"

"Dr. Lindsey's orders," she told him, a bit exasperated, as though she'd reiterated that a thousand times before. Had I been whimpering or groaning in my sleep? "You can speak with the doctor again when she returns this afternoon."

I wasn't quite following the exchange. To the nurse, I pleaded, "I need a painkiller."

"You're being administered a low dosage of acetaminophen. It's perfectly safe, I assure you."

My brows knitted. "*Safe?*"

Kyle swore under his breath and moved away from the bed. My dad's jaw clenched. I cataloged all the responses, but my mind wasn't functioning well enough for me to process all of this.

Catching on to that, my dad gently rested his hand on my shoulder and tentatively said, "Ari . . ." He shook his head. Tried again. "Did you know . . . ?"

I stared quizzically at him for several suspended seconds.

What the hell was going on?

"Ari," Kyle broke the silence with a clipped, anguished tone. "You're pregnant."

chapter 8

"I'm *what?*"

I stared blankly. Gaping. Reeling. Wanting desperately to sit up again but knowing the agony that would ensue.

"Guess that answers that question," my father grumbled.

I very carefully rolled my head on the pillow to look back at the nurse. She nodded in confirmation.

"I'm Claudia," she introduced herself. "Let me know if there's anything else I can do. For now, I'm sorry about the pain. But you can speak with Dr. Lindsey about it."

Claudia jotted down my vitals on a chart while I fought my way through emotions that were nearly impossible to dissect.

I was pregnant?

For God's sake, I was on the pill. So how on earth . . . ?

I groaned inwardly. "Of course," I muttered.

"What?" Kyle asked.

I fought the natural compulsion to shake my head. It'd only cause more pain. But I did roll my eyes at my own irresponsibility.

"I've been so absorbed with everything happening at the Lux that I forgot about routine appointments, skipped taking my allergy pills from time to time, and . . ."

"And what?" my dad demanded, a deeply concerned edge to his voice. "Skipped your birth control pills, too?"

"Not *skipped*," I assured him. Then cringed. Really, this was something I had to discuss with my father? It was bad enough that Kyle glared at me as though I were the biggest fool on the planet. Now I had to admit the truth to my dad?

Ugh.

The agony of my injuries didn't eclipse my humiliation. "Okay, yes," I simply said.

What else was there to tell them? I hadn't been cognizant of missing my nightly doses . . . but now that I seriously thought about it . . . I couldn't remember taking a pill the night of the Thanksgiving dinner at the Lux or on Thanksgiving Day when Dane had proposed. The night of our wedding . . . nope. A few nights when I'd been so wrapped around the schematics of Christmas decoration placement at the hotel that I'd fallen asleep without having the slightest bit of energy left over for taking off my makeup—or even popping a pill.

Holy Christ.

Honestly, birth control and allergy medicine had been the last things on my mind!

But I had even bigger concerns to work through.

My gaze slid back to my dad. "Dane . . . ?"

The expression on his face said it all. My heart wrenched and I let out a small cry. "It can't be true!" A fresh batch of tears flooded my eyes. "It can't be true!"

"Sweets," he said. "Dane did everything he could to get his staff out of the hotel. He saved a lot of lives. In fact, you were the only one who was significantly hurt. The rest were released from the ER. Like, ten or twelve of them. Mostly injuries caused from the inertia of the explosion, and some struck by debris because they were still too close to the building."

"And Kyle's burns?" I quietly demanded.

My best friend returned to my side. In a solemn voice, he said, "They're not bad at all. I couldn't get into the lobby. The fire was too intense. Those of us who got out . . . we were all really lucky, Ari. It could have been so much worse. But I'm—I *am* sorry. About Dane. Him and Amano," he amended. "They saved everyone, Ari."

I choked on a sob. Couldn't stop myself from crying.

"Maybe you gentlemen should take a break," Claudia suggested. "You've been here the majority of the time. Ari needs her rest. And I really can't have her blood pressure and pulse elevated higher. It's not good for her or the baby."

I wept harder, burying my face in the side of the pillow. My body shook, but I tried not to thrash on the bed, to not disturb the IV they'd obviously had to put in the crook of my arm, since my hands were wrapped. I surmised they'd detected my pregnancy when they'd drawn blood for labs.

I was completely torn, lost without Dane. Shredded to the core.

Looping over and over was the harrowing reality that everything in my life had been destroyed.

Dane—my husband.

My wedding band—because I had no idea how I'd ever get my bracelet back. The symbol of our marriage might be lost forever . . . along with the only person I would ever love.

10,000 Lux was gone as well—decimated.

It'd all been stripped away from me, so quickly. Like that entire chapter of my life had been erased in one horrific nightmare. As though it never existed.

Yet there was a voice inside my head screaming at me to pull myself together, to concentrate on the fact that I carried Dane's child. That a part of him lived on . . . inside me.

All that did was make me cry more, perhaps because there

wasn't tangible proof. In my mind, it was still hearsay. People telling me I was pregnant.

And me still in denial because I hadn't missed *too* many pills. . . .

I winced. Fuck, what did I know about how many were conceivably acceptable to miss? And if this was all true and not some deranged nightmare . . . exactly how pregnant was I?

The guys left, but Claudia stayed, pulling up a chair and very gingerly rubbing my shoulder, stroking my arm. Compassionately saying how sorry she was, but that everything would be okay. Dr. Lindsey had ordered an ultrasound. They closely monitored my recovery. On and on Claudia went, trying to soothe me while I gaped and couldn't even form words to get my endless questions answered.

I couldn't separate the good news from the ghastly. Especially with the terrified voice gaining strength and volume in my head. I'd tried surviving, existing, without Dane once before. It hadn't worked.

How would it this time?

The days passed with investigators stopping by to quiz me, though I couldn't tell them anything more than Kyle and my father had at this point. I didn't mention the suspicions I had about the axed investors being involved in the blast. I had to speak with Ethan Evans first, and I waited anxiously for him to visit me.

In the meantime, I succumbed to follow-up tests, some poking and prodding, lengthy discussions with medical professionals, a determination that my exposure to and the inhalation of the ammonium nitrate didn't pose a health threat to the baby.

A peculiar numbness settled in when Dr. Lindsey confirmed all was well on that front. Without the fetus to worry so much about at the moment, the dark cloud of utter devastation consumed me.

I cooperated fully, of course. I'd never do anything to harm

Dane's child. But I really just reacted to circumstances, my environment, instructions given. It was easier than thinking on my own, since that led to more despair.

Especially since my deepest concerns currently lay elsewhere. I continually asked about Dane.

Had the search and rescue team started their work? Was there anything they'd found, any evidence Dane didn't escape—or that possibly he did?

The questions were tolerated with a lot of sympathetic smiles and commiseration. Until frustration set in because of lack of information and one day I demanded of Kyle, "Have they found *anything*?"

"Like what?" he shot back, tormented on my behalf. "Teeth? Is that what you want to hear?"

"Ari." My dad tried to reason with me. "It was an explosion. That means . . ."

I crooked a brow at him. It was completely masochistic of me, but I wanted him to say the words I simply couldn't form in my own mind.

His lips pressed together and he shook his head.

Kyle spoke up again, because he never sugarcoated things for me. Something I'd always appreciated and admired. He simply said, "Body parts."

My eyes squeezed shut.

My father added, "Everything burned, Ari. The lobby, the vast majority of the main building. Right down to the ground. *Including* some of the grounds."

Likely those body parts Kyle had mentioned as well.

I couldn't fathom any of it. I'd seen the flames, the destruction. Yet it seemed surreal to believe the Lux had been blown to bits. That stunning lobby, all that opulence, Dane's hard work.

Naturally, I still couldn't latch on to him being dead. But if he were alive . . . he would have tracked me down. It would have been the first thing he'd do, and I was easy to find in the hospital.

Even my mother found me.

I let out a hearty sigh of frustration as she swept into the room the next afternoon, filling it with such an overwhelming citrusy scent it puckered my cheeks.

"Aria Lynne," she said in a feigned maternal tone. "Oh, darling. I have been *so* worried. Ever since I heard about the explosion at the hotel."

"That was several days ago, Mother." And she was only *now* showing up, when she lived just an hour and a half away, in Scottsdale?

"Yes, well, I've had my hands full. This time of year is always so busy with fund-raisers to attend and—oh, but what I am saying. Of course I came as soon as I could."

My stomach roiled. I didn't want her anywhere near me, especially when I was so vulnerable, so emotionally and physically wrecked. I knew everything my mother did was anchored to some sort of demonic need to better her own situation. Whatever she was doing in my hospital room had nothing to do with the fact that I'd been injured in a hellish bombing.

That reality—because I knew it wasn't me she ever worried over but how everything under the sun impacted *her*—made all my aches and pains worse.

It was incredibly unfortunate that I had plenty of evidence to prove how distressingly right I was about her devious intentions.

"I thought we agreed to not see or speak to each other ever again," I reminded her.

Actually, she'd called me in a dither one day to say she'd kill the tell-all book she'd threatened to write about her affairs while my dad was on PGA tours—and would leave me alone. That had come after Dane had paid her off and, I suspected, though he'd never confirmed, had threatened her. He'd said he'd *handled* it. I didn't doubt that meant he'd put the fear of God into her.

But Dane was dead now.

That torment stole my breath. Except . . .

Damn it. Was that why she'd come back?

He'd scared her off. But now that he was gone . . . ?

"What do you want?" I asked in as steady a voice as I could manage. Which really was a crock. I sounded hideous. Pathetic, weak, and hideous, to be exact. Particularly as I fought back tears.

"Aria Lynne," she breathed in her refined, pseudo-socialite tone. "I read all the news stories, saw all the footage on TV. Why, you could have died, darling. And I just . . . well . . ." She sank into the chair beside me and gripped my hand. Which I immediately yanked away.

"Mother, I have stitches in my palms."

"Oh, I didn't realize." She shifted uncomfortably in her seat. "Anyway, Aria Lynne, I spoke with a lawyer and he says there's a valid lawsuit to pursue on your behalf, and I—"

My mouth opened and I was fairly sure some incredibly scathing words were about to spew forth. But Kyle had come into the room at the same time and he stared at my mother with murder in his eyes.

"You have *got* to be kidding me!" he blurted. He knew all about her extortion attempt, including the five grand I'd given her initially.

"Meet Kathryn DeMille," I reluctantly said. "Mother, this is my friend Kyle."

"Pleasure." She barely gazed at him. Dismissed him promptly, likely because he didn't wear designer clothes, just a pair of jeans and a T-shirt that strained against all of his rock-hard muscles. "Now, Aria Lynne, as I was saying, my lawyer—"

"Stop," I said.

She was here to file a lawsuit against Dane and the Lux?

My mind reeled. My stomach churned.

Granted, she had no idea she'd be filing a lawsuit against *me*, since I was married to Dane. Something else I wanted her to have no clue about.

But above all of that . . . Jesus. Just . . . *ugh!*

My eyes squeezed shut briefly. I did a mental rewind from the moment she'd entered the room. She hadn't even asked how I was doing. She didn't even care about that. I knew it. I knew *her*.

She'd found a self-serving angle because of a horrific tragedy. A way to get her hands on more money.

I was instantly sick to my stomach.

Before I could even react, though, Kyle grabbed the handles of the Louis Vuitton bag my mother had placed at her feet and hefted it up. "Get out," he simply said, his tone tight, his gaze unwavering, as he glared at her.

"I—what? Who *are* you?"

"A very close friend of Ari's. Weren't you listening? She's hurt, laid up in the hospital, and you're here to try to collect on the fact that she could have died?"

I wasn't sure I'd ever seen him so furious. Not even the night I'd told him I was marrying Dane.

"Get. The. Hell. Out." He thrust the handbag at my mother. I almost chastised him for being so brash—that wasn't Kyle's nature. But . . . he was right. And I was grateful he'd come so immediately and vehemently to my defense.

Obviously, I didn't currently possess the wherewithal to deal with Mommie Dearest. I appreciated that he was there to come to my rescue. Again.

My mother, however, wasn't the least bit thrilled. She glared at him a moment, attempting to stare him down with her high-society, snooty gaze.

It didn't work. Kyle couldn't be deterred.

Finally, she dragged her gaze away and glanced at me.

I bucked up. Because I knew giving an inch with this woman could be detrimental. She wasn't my mother, not in any other way than by notation on my birth certificate. A painful admission but the truth nonetheless.

"You heard him," I said. "All you want is some way to use me for money. Something insidious happened at 10,000 Lux, Mother.

I was hurt. So were others. Kyle could have—" My breath caught. "Two people died." Tears stung my eyes. "It's tragic and sinister and here you are . . . not giving a damn about anything or anyone but yourself. You should be ashamed. But you're not, are you?"

My mother shot to her feet and ripped her bag from Kyle's hand. "I do not understand who you've become, Aria Lynne."

"It's Ari," I ground out, hating how haughtily she said my name. "Just *Ari*, Mother."

"And remember me," Kyle told her. "I'm the guy who's going to be hanging out here making sure you don't come back. Making sure you get nowhere near her."

My mother's jaw fell slack. My new bodyguard crossed his thick arms over his expansive chest and stared her down.

A flicker of fear flashed in Kathryn DeMille's eyes. She tore her gaze from Kyle once more and demanded of me, "Where do you find these people that you associate with?"

"There's absolutely nothing wrong with the people in my life," I told her, forcing my voice not to crack as I thought of the two who were no longer alive. I wouldn't give her the satisfaction of seeing me crumble. "The only reason you can't identify with them is because they genuinely care about me."

Her attention returned to Kyle. "Don't ever touch my purse again."

I could see he fought to contain his fury yet still said, "Take your goddamn designer bag out of here and don't come back. I won't let you near her."

My mother huffed, her expensive surgically enhanced chest heaving. Then she spun around on her dainty shoes and stalked out.

I slumped back against the pile of pillows, every ounce of false bravado quickly draining. I was exhausted by the standoff.

But I said to Kyle, "Thank you. Like so, so, *so* much. Perfect timing and—" Tears suddenly flowed down my cheeks. The ones I'd held in check so my mother couldn't see them.

"Ari, just . . . don't think about it. Forget her. That is absolute bullshit and, holy crap, were you right about her."

"I know." I started to cry. Violently. Kyle sank carefully onto the edge of the mattress and very gingerly comforted me. "Hey, it's okay. Don't sweat it, Ari. We all have family drama. Or in your case, *trauma*. I'll keep her away from you. I promise."

If only he knew how persistent Maleficent could be. And she wasn't the only reason for the painful wails.

I didn't have the heart or energy to say more. Just gave in to my sobfest, so grateful my tears didn't run Kyle off.

Ethan visited the next day, with Qadir Hakim and Nikolai Vasil.

Dane's legitimate society and business partners came bearing an enormous bouquet to accompany the others that had been delivered—note, my mother hadn't even bothered with flowers. This one took up the most space in my private room. My dad and Kyle stepped out.

Ethan gave me a compassionate smile. "I'm so sorry for your loss, Ari."

My eyes burned with more tears. Would this never end? "For yours, too. I know how close the two of you were—how long you knew each other."

"Yes. It's all a bit shocking."

I cut right to the chase, because I couldn't dwell on Dane's death. "How are the police or FBI going to figure out who's behind the bomb? Did you tell them?"

With a slight shake of his head, Ethan said, "It's complicated at the moment, Ari. As it stands . . ." He blew out a long breath. Tension oozed from him, as it did the others. "We're even. It's over. There's no more 10,000 Lux to want to be a part of, and—"

"No more Dane." A fresh batch of fat drops spilled down my cheeks.

"Miss DeMille," Qadir said in his rich Arabic accent—his use of my maiden name made me question whether he knew I'd married Dane or if Ethan had kept the secret. Qadir and Nikolai knew me from the Lux and Dane's house. But did they know the full extent of our association? "You have my deepest condolences. If there is anything I can do, I would be more than honored to assist in any way."

I resisted the urge to ask for another search and rescue team. But it'd been days since the explosion. If Ethan had given up hope that Dane was alive, I'd simply—*foolishly*—be postponing the inevitable reality. One I needed to accept, despite it being near impossible. I just couldn't give up the notion that I'd never see Dane again.

"Thank you, Sultan Hakim." I mustered a little strength. "That's very kind."

"I share his sentiment," Nikolai said. "If I can do anything at all . . . Do not hesitate to contact me. Dane was very special. A vital part of our work."

"Your visit is much appreciated," I assured him. They'd made a hell of a trek to see me, the sultan coming from the Persian Gulf and Nikolai flying in from Russia. They had demonstrated a thousand times more effort in sharing their condolences and concern for me than my own mother had. An extremely painful reality.

"Well," Ethan said. "I'm sure you need your rest. Take care of yourself, Ari."

"I will. Thank you for visiting."

They headed to the door.

I impulsively called out, "Ethan."

He turned back toward the bed. "Yes?"

I opened my mouth, about to tell him I was pregnant. But I'd kept so much of my life with Dane a secret, instinct told me to hold this news close to the chest as well. For now. I smiled as best as I could and said, "The flowers are beautiful."

"Be well, Ari."

Right.

I sighed.

They left and I stared at the ceiling, wondering how in hell I'd ever be *well* again.

Without Dane.

More flowers arrived that afternoon, brought in by Jackson Conaway, Dane's lawyer. His visit was equally brief. Deepest sympathies, lots of paperwork to complete that I would need to sign when I was up to it, accounts to go over, et cetera. I was the sole benefactor of Dane's entire estate. I even owned all that now-useless land the Lux sat on.

The magnitude of the dangerous game nine men had played, and my entanglement, boggled the mind. They'd put everything on the line. A luxury hotel with no rival in the Western Hemisphere. And for five of them, they'd been willing to sacrifice forty or so lives, Dane's and Amano's included. All for money, prestige, power.

A chill ran through me. I understood how billionaire status could put people in a league of such extreme authority that they might deem themselves untouchable. In complete control of social, economic, political, and even environmental climates. I'd read enough about the sway the broader conglomerate considered the "Billionaires Club" reportedly had so that I knew a more focused, more potent Illuminati faction could be even more influential. And this particular group had clearly thought themselves invincible.

I fumed over Dane being that arrogant. But I couldn't really be mad at him when I knew he'd been the one in the right. He'd tried so hard to change the direction of the poli-econ society when it had taken a wayward turn. He'd tried to protect the Lux and the people who worked there, including me. And had made the ultimate sacrifice for the sake of others.

Still, my feelings, my emotions, were painfully conflicted. I wasn't sure who to trust, and that made me feel very alone . . . and wary. Because my most important job now was to protect what was *mine*. The baby growing inside me.

Before Mr. Conaway left, I inquired about Lux insurance and how we could cover the medical expenses of those who'd had to come to the ER following the explosion. And I wanted anyone dealing with post-traumatic stress to be offered help.

"We'll pay for everything," I insisted. "In whatever manner we need to, whatever arrangements have to be made."

"I'll take care of it, Ari. Don't worry for a second. Just get better. And call if there's anything you need. Anything at all."

I breathed a little easier, knowing I could trust him to help Lux employees through this catastrophe.

But a peculiar sensation burned deep inside me. The only word I could attribute it to was . . . *revenge*. I wanted it. I needed it.

How was someone like me going to get it?

While I still stewed internally, I also considered the one visitor I'd anticipated, who had yet to make an appearance. Though Mikaela Madsen had sent flowers, she hadn't come to the hospital. I wasn't sure why I'd expected her to. We certainly weren't friends. Just acquaintances because of Dane. Somehow, though, I kept myself primed and steeled for her to breeze in and make this more her tragedy than it was mine.

Though it occurred to me that perhaps she was too devastated herself to face this and to speak of Dane.

I couldn't fault her and was actually happy she didn't visit. I did feel obligated, however, to send my own bouquet, which Kyle helped me with on his iPhone, since mine was part of the 10,000 Lux rubble.

A couple days later, when Dr. Lindsey deemed it appropriate, she stopped in with a discharge packet.

"We'll go to my house," my father said as I settled in the wheelchair and Claudia rolled me into the hallway. "You can rest there."

"No." I shook my head ever so slightly, since it still ached. "I want to go home, Dad."

"What's the point?" he countered. "Ari, Dane won't be there." He didn't say this cruelly, just realistically. That was Dad's way.

He'd never been particularly affectionate or demonstrative—whatever little bit might have existed years ago had been obliterated with my mother's cheating.

I said, "I just want to be there."

He conceded, albeit reluctantly. Kyle went with us, carrying my dress and shoes from the night at the Lux in the clear plastic bag issued by the hospital. I didn't think about the aftermath of the explosion in terms of the grand opening that would have been days away from my release.

According to Kyle, PR had covered all the media inquiries and issued statements about the bombing, along with heartfelt apologies to those who'd been on-site. They'd also canceled all events and assured members their money would be returned in full.

I wasn't certain what sort of hit Dane's portfolio would take, but Mr. Conaway had been convincing when he'd told me everything would be resolved and I didn't need to worry financially. Ever.

I felt compelled to issue some sort of statement myself regarding the Lux, particularly to the staff who'd been there that evening. But it wouldn't have much bearing coming from Ari DeMille. And I knew better than to reveal my new identity as Mrs. Dane Bax.

I gave my father the code for the security gate when we approached it and slipped back into wrecked mode. Perhaps coming to the house wasn't such a grand idea after all. I stared at the enormous structure and realized my dad had been right. All I wanted was for Dane to be there. Waiting for me.

My breathing escalated. My stomach knotted.

Kyle slipped from the backseat and opened my door. He helped me to the patio and I used the keypad to gain access. We entered the foyer and he reached for the light switch.

"Leave them off, please," I said. Hazy streaks from the overcast day streamed through the unadorned windows, providing a bit of shimmery illumination.

"Where do you want this?" Kyle asked, holding up the bag.

Whoever had packed it had taken great care to fold the dress so no blood showed through the sides.

"Just put it on the chair." I gestured to one of them in the entryway. Then I asked, "Would you mind getting my nightgown and robe from my bathroom? Last room at the back of the house. My makeup and hairbrushes, too. There's a tote under the sink that they all go in."

I didn't have the spirit to step into the bedroom I'd shared with Dane. It was wholly representative of him, decorated to exude his personal style, his strength. I didn't even want to enter the dressing room adjacent to it—with all of Dane's clothes neatly arranged—which was why I'd had Kyle leave the bag here.

My dad said, "How about I make some tea?"

"You'll never find it. You know how OCD I am about the placement of everything." It wasn't as though he could open the pantry and it'd jump out at him.

"I'll take my chances," he muttered, then wandered off. I could tell I broke his heart. That pained me as well, but I couldn't help it.

Nor could I avoid thinking that if I hadn't let my anal, everything-has-its-own-place mentality cause me to tuck away my allergy and birth control pills in a nightstand table—rather than having them right out in the open, next to my glass of water—I wouldn't have spaced on taking them.

But that was all moot now, wasn't it?

Kyle returned with my things and I went into the full bath outside the dining room and changed from the outfit my dad had brought to the hospital, which I figured he'd picked up at the golf shop at his club. I winced as I caught sight of myself in the mirror. Decided it'd be best to take a shower, which was possible since the bandages covering my palms and forehead were sealed, waterproof ones. Unfortunately, freshening up did nothing to alleviate the dark circles under my eyes and the vacant look in them.

Plus, I'd lost weight. More than one might imagine for being in the hospital for a week. My cheeks were a bit sunken and my skin had a sallow tinge to it. Precisely the same as after Vale had kidnapped me and bloodied my face.

Dane would go through the roof again were he to see me like this. And there was no doubt in my mind he'd want to kill someone—and this time, he probably wouldn't be able to stop because I screamed for him to do so.

That, too, was neither here nor there. Leaving me with an empty sensation burning in my stomach.

After fixing myself up, though my hair remained damp and loose about my shoulders, I walked the corridor toward the great room. My dad followed me with a cup of hot tea.

An odd numbness settled deep in my bones. I felt a little lost in the house in which I'd lived the past two months. It was foreign without Dane. Just a building that held no warmth, no hospitality, no sense of family.

As I stood in the oversized doorway, I surveyed the space. Dimly lit and cast in bluish-gray tones. Eerily striking despite the lack of intimacy it held. Much too quiet, without the doors against the far wall opened to let in the sound of the rapid creek water, the whistle of wind through the trees, and the crunch of leaves under the feet of forest inhabitants.

The room itself was perfection personified. Everything had its special, specific place. Flawlessly arranged.

Most of the furniture and accents were items Dane had picked up on his world travels. Nothing I'd necessarily consider personal effects. Unlike the carefully selected artwork and decorations in our bedroom, these were acquisitions. Expensive and sought-after ones that had gone to the highest bidder—Dane.

They didn't really mean anything sentimental. Just that he could afford them.

As I passed by the tall art niche, my fingertips grazed the glass pitcher I'd once admired. I tipped it over. The heavy carafe hit the heated stone floor with a loud crash that echoed in the silence. I quickly stepped out of the way of flying shards.

"Jesus, Ari," Kyle said from behind me.

Drifting toward the wall of built-in bookshelves that spanned fifteen feet high and needed a ladder that slid along a metal rail for accessing the top shelves, I dragged my fingers over the titles of first-edition works and other prestigious volumes. Again, the ones Dane admired the most were all stored in our bedroom.

These were possessions of the privileged. Since I no longer thought of Dane that way—the privileged didn't die in villainous death plots was my thinking—I pulled novels from their perches and let them fall, sprawled open at my feet.

"Sweets . . . ?" Dad ventured in a trepid tone. A very don't-make-any-sudden-movements-or-you'll-set-off-the-crazy kind of voice.

"Everything's just a little too perfect in here, don't you think?" I slid a palm over the shiny black grand piano and jerked the piece that propped the top open. It slammed shut with a resounding thud that echoed through the room with the haunting rattle of strings.

Then I crossed to the doors. One of the tables before them held a glass chess set. I toppled the pieces. Turning away, I spied the pièce de résistance. The gorgeous floral arrangement in the middle of a sofa table that ran the length of a plush couch positioned in front of the tall fireplace.

Rosa replaced the buds every week with fresh ones. Perfect sterling silver and white roses in velvety, verdant foliage. A long and low bouquet that stretched across most of the glass top and peaked in the center. The base was a lovely porcelain number, quite delicate, exquisite. A German or French antique, I'd always assumed.

I hooked two fingers in the fragile pottery and tugged until it crested the edge of the table and smashed against the stone as I walked away.

"Okay," my dad said as he set my tea aside. "This isn't right. Ari, what are you—"

"Not the pictures!" Kyle yelped just a second before I swept my arm over the mantel and sent crystal frames flying. "Fuck!" He swooped in and knelt to start picking up the photos of mine and Dane's wedding night.

"Don't," I said, a strange, evocative despair moving through me. What was the point of them, anyway? A reminder of what I no longer had? Would never have again? "Leave them just like that. Leave everything . . . shattered."

More tears burned.

"Ari, sit," my dad commanded in a stern tone uncharacteristic of him. I'd sufficiently freaked him out.

Because I was feeling rather drained, I collapsed on the sofa, curling against the pile of pillows in one corner. He brought my tea and I sipped as he spread the throw over my bare feet and legs. I wore the long nightgown and robe, so I didn't feel much of a chill. I didn't feel much of anything.

Kyle searched for the switch on the gas fireplace anyway. He found it, but before he flipped it on, I said, "No flames."

This time, neither of them could call my reasoning crazy. They'd witnessed the mile-high flames at the Lux, too.

"I'm warm enough," I assured them. "The tea helps. Thanks, Dad."

"Sure." He was back to that tentative voice. Not certain what to make of me. I'd never been the destructive type. That had been my mother's role. Maybe I'd inherited some of her irrational, violent tendencies after all.

Though I didn't feel irrational. I felt justified to be this hollow inside while I buried my rage, my pain.

"Are you hungry?" Kyle asked, also a bit hesitant.

"Not really."

He gave me a slightly exasperated sigh. "You do have to eat, Ari. I mean, think of the—" He groaned, apparently not the least bit happy with where his train of thought led him. "Think of the baby."

That was the ultimate in reticence.

"Don't hate the innocent," I snapped.

"I'm not a hater," he insisted, his blue eyes clouding. "I'm thinking of the kid as much as I am of you."

"Thank you." I tried a smile, despite the sudden turmoil making my stomach twist at the mention of what grew inside it. My gaze narrowed and I asked, "Do you really cook?"

He scoffed. Leaving the room, I presumed he was off to explore the gourmet kitchen.

My dad sat on the couch with me, at my feet. "How do you feel?"

"Empty." I sighed. "Which is weird, because I'm clearly not. There is actually another human being sharing this body."

"Yes. There is." He grinned the tiniest grin that almost warmed my cold heart.

"You're a total sucker, aren't you?" I asked.

"Well, it's just that . . . I know how hard things were on you growing up. Because of your mother and me. And then at the end of this summer, suddenly—out of the blue—you were dating Dane, moving in with him, marrying him, and now you're having his child. Not ideally . . . ," my father added, his logical side getting the best of him. "It's really unfortunate the kid will never know—"

"God, more genetics," I grumbled miserably. "Dane never knew his parents. They died a month after he was born. His aunt raised him."

My dad grimaced. "Sometimes, it's difficult to dislike him."

"You did your best. He's just sort of . . . infectious." My eyes squeezed shut and I mumbled, "Was."

"Ah, sweets." He rested a hand on my leg, stroked soothingly. "I really am sorry."

"I know." I choked on a sob. "And I appreciate that. Just let me adjust on my own time, Dad. Don't expect too much. Don't expect anything."

"I'd say yes to that, Ari, and let you hide under the covers for the next month, but . . ." He shifted on the cushion and pinned me with a serious look. "This isn't just about you. It's not even about your grief anymore. It's about that baby you both conceived, which you are now committed to—for its sake, and for yours and Dane's. He might not be here, sweets, but you know you have to be extremely careful, attentive, *healthy*, as though it were the best-case scenario. Just because it's not . . . Well, that's no reason to—"

"I hear you, Dad." The tears spilled. "I understand. It's just a little strange right now. I'm not hungry. I'm not . . . anything." I rubbed my stomach. It was concave, not exactly a good thing. "I guess the problem is that I don't *feel* anything. I don't feel different. I don't feel pregnant. I feel anesthetized. Which we both know isn't a reality, since the doctor was so concerned about giving me too much by way of pain meds."

My father grunted. "I wasn't pleased about that."

"I'm okay," I was quick to say. Regardless of the stitches, the most poignant pain ripped through my heart.

"What can I do?" he asked.

"Just sit here with me and don't push too hard. I have a lot to reconcile. A lot to figure out. Not so easy when I feel so lifeless."

He did as I asked, not speaking too much. Kyle served meatloaf and mashed potatoes. Nothing too pungent or spicy. Simple and soft, easily digestible. I eyed him curiously over a forkful of fluffy potatoes.

With a noncommittal shrug, he said, "I have a little sister who was *clearly* an accident, because she's nine years younger than me. I dealt with a pregnant mom with a sensitive stomach and a dad who couldn't cook. Well, he's pretty much in denial about that, but I can attest." He chuckled.

"I haven't met Shelley yet," I reminded him. "We were all going to meet up at Little America in Flagstaff for the holiday lights covering the wooded property."

"Yeah." He gave me a solemn look.

"Yeah," I agreed, thankful he didn't point out the obvious reason why that idea was now shot to hell. I tried not to think of all that Dane would miss out on with his child, and vice versa. What I'd miss out on.

Damn those tears that wouldn't leave me be.

"We can still get together with Shelley, though," Kyle offered.

"Sure. Sometime."

I wasn't in any hurry to make plans—for anything. Luckily, I had eight months before I had to put thought and effort into converting one of the spare bedrooms into a nursery.

I only picked at my meal, taking a few bites to partially satisfy Kyle and my father. Then I claimed I was too exhausted for extensive company and my dad left. Kyle wouldn't budge, of course. I sensed he had found a new duty in taking care of me in Dane's stead. I was too wiped out physically and emotionally to battle Kyle on that front.

Returning to the sofa, I curled up again and was asleep minutes later.

The void inside me vanished the next morning.

Only to be replaced with the very real and finite fact that I was pregnant. My eyes flew open at the crack of dawn. I tossed off the blanket, leapt from the sofa, and raced across the stone floor to the bathroom. Where I promptly heaved the previous evening's dinner. And then some.

As I huddled around the porcelain, afraid to move just yet, Kyle came in, dampened a washcloth, and handed it to me. I pressed it against my mouth for several seconds, finding relief from the chill of the material.

The numbness I felt because of losing Dane abated. I pulled away the cloth and stared up at Kyle. "Okay, *now* I feel pregnant."

That sentiment triggered some sort of defense mechanism that made me even more powerfully aware of what it was I needed to protect—my child, who was also a part of Dane's legacy.

I told Kyle, "I have to eat again."

"I agree. It's going to be hard to keep it down, though."

"Then I just keep eating." I'd need to go online and learn all about morning sickness.

In the meantime, I felt a curious survival instinct kick in. As much as I wanted to disappear into thin air because Dane was no longer with me, he was still a *part* of me—a living, breathing one. I owed it to the three of us to pull myself together. To find some strength to go on without Dane. To take care of his child no matter how devastated I was.

"How about scrambled eggs?" I suggested to Kyle. "No seasoning, superbland."

"And more tea."

"Yes, that might help." Dr. Lindsey had told me that I'd have to find an OB-GYN soon and start on pre-natal vitamins and such. It was time I jumped on that.

The upside of my mental breakthrough was getting past that dazed and shredded state so I could focus on what I'd gained, rather than what I'd lost. The downside was that I was violently sick three days in a row. Queasy in the afternoons and well into the evenings.

"You're really pale," Kyle finally commented with notable concern. "Like this is getting worse, not better."

"And I feel as though I'm marathon eating."

"I think it's time we seek professional help."

"I called three OB-GYNs. I can't get in to see any of them until the middle of next week."

His teeth ground together as tension gripped him. "There's not going to be anything left of you next week, Ari."

He exaggerated, of course, but I was equally concerned that the scale had moved in the wrong direction. The weight I'd gained from the Thanksgiving and pre-launch festivities at the Lux had melted right off, along with several additional pounds.

"Maybe I should try someone in Phoenix?" I wondered aloud.

"Actually, I have a better idea." He polished off his portion of the steel-cut oatmeal he'd made for us and then said, "My aunt's an M.D. She used to work at the hospital, but left to open a private practice, of sorts."

My brow rose as I glanced at him across the table in the kitchen. "*Of sorts?*"

He scowled. "Don't look at me like that. It's legitimate. She really considers it more of an inpatient rehabilitation retreat. Four bedrooms—all with private bathrooms—so it's quiet and conducive to individual care. She has nurses on-staff twenty-four-seven and contracts with physical and occupational therapists. Those are mostly the types of patients she deals with, though she takes on others. And has specialists to treat them. Currently, she only has three patients who live on-property. If she hasn't filled it, that leaves one bedroom available."

"You mean . . . I'd move in?"

"Yeah. It's a fully accredited, certified facility. Although that word doesn't do it justice—sounds too clinical. It's really a beautiful place," he insisted. "About as big as this house, but bright. Cheery. Less . . . Gotham."

My gaze narrowed.

"Just sayin'," he muttered.

"I don't want to leave here."

"What's the big deal?" he demanded with a serious expression. "You won't go toward the back of the house. You won't go into your dressing room or bedroom or even your bathroom. You sleep on the sofa, and to tell you the truth, I'm getting all kinds of bent out of shape and kinked up from crashing in a chair in there."

"No one said you had to stay with me," I reminded him. "You know where the door is."

His scowl deepened. My gut clenched. I didn't want him to leave, honestly. I didn't want to be alone. My dad had gone back to work after taking the week off to be at the hospital. He still came by at night for dinner, but Kyle had packed a bag and designated himself my new shadow.

I was grateful. Deeply comforted, even. But I didn't like him criticizing the fact that I preferred he leave most of the lights off. And I forbade his cleaning the glass in the living room. He'd swept the shards into small piles but resisted the urge I knew he had to remove them.

"Why don't you just drive out with me?" he suggested. "Give it a chance before you shoot it down. It's peaceful, surrounded by red-rock canyons. You'd have people around you who know what the hell they're doing and can help you through this."

My stomach took the opportunity to clench tightly—a now-familiar sign of what was to come next. I shoved back my chair and hurried into the bathroom, giving up my oatmeal before I'd digested it.

After brushing my teeth, I returned to the kitchen. Kyle was doing the dishes. I'd given Rosa an extra two weeks of paid vacation while I adjusted to my more delicate condition and still assessed who I could tell about the baby. I hadn't even mentioned it to Mr. Conaway, and he was one of the people Dane had assured me I could trust. After the bombing of the Lux, I had the very distinct and terrifying view that *anyone* was capable of *anything*, if properly motivated.

So mum was currently the word.

"I guess it wouldn't hurt to check it out," I said of Kyle's aunt's medical retreat. "Especially if she can help me with the morning sickness or get me an appointment with an OB-GYN a bit faster."

"My immediate concern is how ghostly you look."

I couldn't combat that without lying. And the torment in his eyes broke my heart further. So I forced myself to finally go into the dressing room, thinking I might as well pack a suitcase in the event Kyle's aunt still had space available to take me on and I opted to stay.

When I was finished, I stood outside the door of mine and Dane's bedroom, not overwhelmingly compelled to enter, but I wanted one last peek before I left indefinitely. Just to keep the memory of it in my mind and to soak up a little of his essence that permeated the space most reflective of him.

From an end table I collected the last book he'd been reading, Dickens's *Great Expectations*. Pressing it to my chest, I felt a razor-sharp pain slice through me. Dane's voice filled my head as I thought of us stretched out on the sofa in front of the fireplace while he read his favorite novels to me.

Fat drops pooled in my eyes and my knees felt a bit wobbly. I sank onto the edge of the bed and pulled in deep breaths. I ran a hand over the soft, bronze duvet, the ecru sheets.

I frowned. Took a closer look.

Flannel.

My brow furrowed.

I'd told Dane I liked them in the winter. But these were not the sheets we'd slept in the night before the media event at 10,000 Lux.

He must have changed them that morning while I was in the shower. Or maybe he'd had Rosa switch out the sateen ones.

I shook my head. Maybe, at the moment—in the beginning stages of my mourning—I really shouldn't be surrounded by all of these memories and enveloped in a life that no longer existed. Maybe clinging to yesterday wasn't the healthiest thing to do while I tried to move forward—toward tomorrow, with a baby.

Losing Dane was all too new, too fresh, too raw, to think about, anyway. And I feared I just might snuggle under these warm sheets and cry myself to sleep . . . stay here for the next several months.

An appealing, alluring notion. One so strong and palpable, I actually considered it quite seriously. I was exhausted after all. Wrecked.

But I had an obligation to Dane. To our baby.

So I hauled myself up and closed one door behind me while Kyle opened another.

chapter 9

The rehabilitation retreat was set back in a secluded canyon and surrounded by full trees and vibrant flowers, spanning several acres. A detached garage sat outside the elegantly walled property and there was a security gate just off the stone pathway that led from the red-dirt drive. There were a couple other houses in the area, about a half mile or so away in all directions.

Kyle plugged in the code at the gate but still had to wait for verification before the lock released. He gestured me through the opening and I took in the gorgeous grounds, with a few private courtyards, a stream, small fountains that trickled water in a soothing way. Wind chimes hung in the trees and added a soft trill as a gentle breeze wafted through them.

We wound our way to the front double doors. Benches and chairs were scattered all over the patio, a welcoming respite, silently inviting guests to sit and relax. Chill out. Hang and heal.

I liked the atmosphere immediately. Perhaps I had been a little too wrapped up in my bleak world, not turning on lights while I hid from reality.

I inhaled deeply, the fragrant flowers filling my senses. I felt a little calmer. Though my stomach was still a tight pretzel and the nausea lingered on the fringes.

We were greeted by a lanky man in his forties, wearing tan Dockers and a hunter-green polo shirt with a shield embroidered on his left chest, below the name Parker.

Kyle said to him, "Adam, this is Ari DeMille. We're here to see my aunt."

"Adam Parker." He held his hand out to me. "Head of security. Please, come in."

The house was warmly decorated with a lot of comfy-looking furniture, interesting knickknacks, books, and whatnot. In the back of the house was a large solarium. The tall windows and the wood-and-glass-enclosed doors looked out on another cozy patio and gardens beyond.

"What a wonderful surprise," said a petite woman with a soft, youthful face, cornflower-blue eyes, and a smart strawberry blonde bob. She smiled prettily at Kyle. "I wasn't expecting you."

He gave her a gentle squeeze, then told her, "Sorry I haven't been by in a while."

"I was just so relieved to hear from your mother that you were okay after the explosion at 10,000 Lux." She placed her hand over her heart. "What a harrowing experience it must have been."

"This is Ari DeMille—she was there as well," Kyle said. "Since then, things have gotten a little . . . complicated. She needs your help."

"Nice preamble," I muttered. To Macy, I said, "It's a pleasure to meet you, Dr.—" I suddenly realized I hadn't asked Kyle her last name on the drive over.

"Stevens," she politely offered.

Extending my hand, I simply said, "Ari."

"Very lovely to meet you. Now, why don't we step into an exam room and you can tell me why you're here."

We left Kyle in the solarium and returned to the front of the house. When the door closed behind us and we had some privacy, I told her, "I'm pregnant. Four weeks."

It instantly dawned on me, as I considered the date, that we'd missed Christmas. At least, my dad and I had. Which didn't really matter in the grand scheme of things, since we weren't holiday oriented and there was no way in hell I could ever have mustered Christmas cheer when all I could think of was the fact that Dane was—

I shook the thought from my head. I couldn't dwell on that currently, though it would forever fester in the back of my mind. If I could trap it in those shadowy parts where I also kept memories of my parents' venomous arguments and all the volatile smashing of glass and slamming of doors, I might maintain my sanity.

Maybe.

"Well," Dr. Stevens said as she eyed me from head to toe. Then gingerly lifted a few wispy strands of my hair to inspect my stitches. When she stepped back, I raised my arms, palms up, to show her the stitches there as well.

"All of these injuries are from the night of the explosion?" she asked.

"Yes."

She made a soft *tsk*ing sound. "You took quite a hit."

"I was lucky," I assured her, our gazes locked.

With a slow nod, she said, "You were. I understand the owner of the hotel didn't—"

"I'm having a bit of trouble with morning sickness," I interjected, not able to hear the words that were about to come out of her mouth regarding Dane. "I can't keep anything down and I'm losing weight, not gaining."

"That's not a pleasant pallor you have, either."

"I sleep, but . . . not really. I wake up constantly and then I just lay there, stressing about everything." I didn't tell her about the nightmares, which were no longer of scorpions and rattlesnakes but of the blast at the Lux and all that bomb had destroyed— much more than just a building.

"That's not good. For you or the baby." She patted the exam table and said, "Why don't you have a seat and we'll see what's what. Do you have your records from the ER?"

"Yes. And from my stay at the hospital."

She crooked a brow. "How long were you there?"

"A week. I was pretty out of it at first. And they wanted to monitor the baby."

"But they cleared you to leave."

"Dr. Lindsey said everything's fine. And it was at first. But then I started vomiting. It lasts into the day. Sometimes happens at night, after I've eaten. I'm afraid I'm not getting the right nutrients to the baby, but I can't get in to see someone until next week. I don't want to wait that long."

With a delicate smile, she said, "You won't have to. I have contracts with a number of specialists. One happens to be a fantastic OB-GYN in Scottsdale. I can arrange to have her come up routinely. I can also treat the morning sickness."

"I'm nonstop nauseous."

"We'll do something about that. I have several natural remedies, herbs, teas. I believe in a holistic approach to healing. Including the mind and spirit. Helps to keep the body strong."

I cringed. She was one of the New Agers. She didn't want to know how damaged my mind and my spirit were. But I'd come willingly to her, so I'd try to be open to her skill set, the tools and teas in her medical bag.

She recorded my vitals and noted my blood pressure was low. I told her that was a change from when I was in the hospital. She wasn't happy with my weight but kept the optimistic smile on her face. Then she showed me around the house, telling me there were always at least two chefs in the kitchen from five in the morning until ten at night. There were two TV rooms and a study. Plus physical rehabilitation facilities.

On the west side of the house were the empty accommodations for me. A lovely space with lots of windows that overlooked a secluded courtyard.

"Security is of utmost importance," Dr. Stevens told me. "There's one guard inside at all times, and others patrol the grounds and monitor the electronic surveillance of the perimeter."

I thought of the people who'd decimated the Lux and wondered if they took an interest in my whereabouts. I doubted they could find me here, yet was relieved I'd be behind monitored gates and walls.

Dr. Stevens further explained that only the security guards answered the front door. I was safer here than at the house, I surmised, even with Dane's state-of-the-art system. His property wasn't patrolled or manned. Not without Amano.

Then again, 10,000 Lux had been well protected and someone had been able to fuck things up there, not to mention kidnap me.

I shuddered. It was no wonder I remained tense. I hadn't exactly been leading a normal life as of late.

Still . . . I'd give anything to get it back—my life with Dane, that was.

I collected my belongings from Kyle and settled in. There were forms to fill out and, despite my being Kyle's friend, Security performed a background check. I contacted Mr. Conaway to have Dane's accountant set up wire transfers to Dr. Stevens's practice, under my maiden name. I had no intention of spilling the beans now on my marriage to Dane.

Then I drank some tea and slept.

My first week at the retreat was more about observation of the environment and trying to keep food down than anything else. One of the other patients, Gretchen Lang, had breast cancer and was recovering from a double mastectomy, she told me. As a side note, she sadly reported that the surgery left her feeling inhuman. And certainly not the least bit feminine. She wore yoga suits every day, as I did, and vibrantly colored silk scarves on her bald head. She was into meditating—for hours on end—as well as yoga and Pilates.

Another patient, Hannah Olden, was in her thirties and in a wheelchair following knee surgery that came right after a hip replacement—all from a degenerative disease she suffered. She had her doubts that she'd ever walk normally again, and I could see the toll it took on her, similar to Gretchen's battle with feeling useless and alien in her own body. Hannah spent her time painting gorgeous floral arrangements when she wasn't in physical therapy.

I knew very little about the youngest of Dr. Stevens's patients, Chelsea Brooks. She was a tiny girl with blonde, springy curls and big, amber-colored eyes. She kept to herself, in the corner of the solarium where she sat at a four-foot-long table.

One day, I asked Kyle, "Is she building a mini Eiffel Tower out of an Erector Set?"

"Yeah," he said with a grin. "She's amazing. Give her a picture of just about any structure and she can replicate it."

I started to take a couple of steps forward, to get a better look, but Kyle gently gripped my arm. "She doesn't like strangers in her space. She's autistic. Change throws her. She needs to stick to a routine—new people upset her."

"Oh." I felt bad about that. I didn't want to alarm or distress her.

"Don't worry. She'll eventually get used to you. Just stick to the periphery, you know?"

"Sure."

I didn't have a whole lot to do at the retreat, so I asked Gretchen if I could join her yoga and Pilates workouts, since I'd learned she was a certified instructor of both, with pre-natal experience. She seemed grateful for the company.

The kitchen staff allowed me to watch them prep and cook,

which was a nice learning experience and occupied more time. The tea and very delicate biscuits Dr. Stevens recommended for me did wonders for the morning sickness and I was actually sleeping a bit better.

I still woke in the middle of the night, crying softly, trying to contain the heart-wrenching sobs that threatened to shatter the tranquility at the retreat.

New Year's Eve and Day came and went, and I spent both in bed, reading and blocking all thoughts of a Lux grand opening that would never happen.

Slowly, I started to gain weight and look a little healthier than when I'd arrived. Dr. Stevens suggested calming scents to help me relax and keep my stomach from churning. We started with vanilla, moved on to chamomile, then lavender. I gave lilac a shot, but my currently delicate senses were having none of it, and I continued to spend time close to the bathroom.

Sifting through my cosmetics bag, I hoped there was a little bit of Carmex left over, since that had always been a soothing aroma and balm. From the bottom of the deep pouch I dug out a small container. It wasn't the Carmex. In fact, I'd never seen the generic glass vial.

Curious, I twisted the lid off and held the vial to my nose. I inhaled tentatively, then with gusto. Wave after wave of serenity washed over me.

The oil was frankincense. *The* frankincense that Dane had given me, with the enticing orange tinge that seeped pleasantly through me.

Despite my sudden euphoria, the corner of my mouth dipped. I'd never poured any from the bottle into a vial. And I certainly hadn't slipped it in with my toiletries.

Thinking back to that last day I'd been at the house—before coming here—I contemplated the flannel sheets. Such an inconsequential thing for most people. Yet, for me, they held significance. I broke my recently established rule of keeping Dane's voice out of

my head, recalling the morning we'd sat on our patio while I'd tried
to get him excited over garland for the hotel.

You promised flannel sheets to keep me warm.

His eyes had bored into me. *No. I promised that* I'd *keep you
warm.*

Oh, right. I'd kissed him.

Everything had been perfect that morning.

I brushed away tears as I stared at the vial a few seconds more.
Then I dabbed a little of the oil on the insides of my wrists before
carrying it into the bedroom and dotting the pillowcases with it.
The flannel ones. I'd stripped the bed in mine and Dane's room
and brought the sheets with me.

As I drew in more of the rich, enticing aroma, an ominous
thought occurred to me.

Had Dane changed the sheet set to flannel and put a vial of
frankincense in my bag because he'd known something would go
wrong at 10,000 Lux? Had he predicted something horrific would
happen?

He'd even gone to the length of telling me—insisting,
actually—at our wedding that I contact Mr. Conaway if I ever
needed anything . . . and couldn't turn to him for help.

I settled in a chair and stared at the bed, those sheets.

Had he feared all this time that he wouldn't win this game?

It took a while to get moving again. I'd spent another two days
under the covers, telling Dr. Stevens I was okay, just tired. She
brought more tea and biscuits, the latter a bit heartier than previously, and I dutifully ate. And waited for the fallout.

Feeling somewhat stable, I eventually left the room.

Gretchen caught me in the hallway. "Are you okay? You're pale
again."

"I'm fine, thanks. Just a bad week." A shitty-ass start to the New
Year, actually.

With a nod, she said, "I can relate. Say, have you tried meditation? It's been helping me so much. You might like it."

I seriously could not be in my head that intensely for five minutes and definitely not for two or three hours. "I'm gonna pass on that. It's not really my thing."

She gave me her pearl-white smile that quivered at the corners. As though she was trying really hard to project a positive, healthy image but struggled around the edges. I wondered who she attempted to be so strong for—no one ever came to visit Gretchen. She didn't wear a ring, didn't speak of family or friends. A significant other.

Maybe that was why we'd bonded so quickly. The same could be said for me with the exception of visitation, since my dad stopped by regularly and Kyle was always here.

Gretchen went into the solarium for her daily meditation. I followed her. Chelsea let me come a step or two closer to see her current masterpiece, the Chrysler Building. A photo of it—clearly an Internet printout someone had given her—lay on the table beside her neatly arranged Erector pieces.

She didn't seem to mind the audience, so I thought it was more of a personal space issue, as Kyle had noted. He, however, was able to swoop in and chat animatedly to her, though it was always a one-sided conversation. The only people she spoke with, in very low tones so no one else could hear, were Dr. Stevens and the two rotating certified autism specialists who stayed close to her.

Kyle was at the retreat daily. Not just for me. His aunt offered him a maintenance and landscaping job, since he no longer had work at the Lux.

On a Saturday afternoon near the end of January, he lugged in a large box and placed it at Chelsea's feet while she sat ceremoniously in her usual chair at the table. The logo on the side made me smile. Legos.

She had a small set, but from the size of Kyle's delivery I'd say she could build a Chrysler Building taller than she was.

Maybe it was the parent-to-be side of me that found her so fascinating. I watched her carefully, so that I didn't disturb or confuse her. Stealing glances, really, while I read articles on naming babies, caring for babies, keeping babies healthy and happy. The OB-GYN Dr. Stevens had hooked me up with not only was renowned in her field but also had two kids now in college. She was an excellent resource for my gazillion questions on how not to fuck up my own kid's life.

Interestingly, no one inquired as to whom the father was, and I was relieved by that. I would tell my child all about Dane, but I couldn't speak of him to anyone else. Not even Kyle.

With regard to him, I suspected my fellow retreat dwellers and the staff wondered if Kyle might be the father, given how close he stuck to me and how well we got along. I didn't bother setting any records straight. But I did smile more when he was around, could breathe a bit easier.

And, as Chelsea clapped enthusiastically while Kyle dumped heaps of Legos on her table, I got the distinct impression he'd be a huge help when my baby was born. My father would be as well. He actually liked that I was in a round-the-clock care facility. I think he worried I'd gone a bit mental. He had good cause for the concern.

Despite my being a bit messed up all the way around, I did tell Dr. Stevens I'd vacate immediately if someone else applied for the room. She seemed to see, from my eyes, all the shit I dealt with internally, privately. The war I waged between wanting to slip into some sort of mind-numbing coma and desperately trying to be a sound, stable person for the sake of my child.

Thus, she repeatedly told me she felt this was the place for me currently and that I was not unnecessarily taking up space. That was usually right about the time my sickness acted up and I made a beeline for a bathroom. She'd bring me a wet washcloth and give me a knowing—and somewhat *see, I'm right*—look.

While Chelsea started to touch and inspect each and every one of the Lego pieces—a task that might take her a good week to complete, but which likely occupied her mind—Kyle joined me on the sofa.

"You're really good with her," I said, my admiration for him increasing by leaps and bounds since that night of the Lux tragedy, when Kyle had demonstrated he would hero-up for any cause.

"She's incredible," he said of Chelsea. "And so adorable."

"I feel bad for her mother. I met her when she came for a visit. Single mom working two jobs. And they've been through several specialists on their own who couldn't help Chelsea, but she's connected well with Tabitha and Lisa. And Dr. Stevens. You."

"She doesn't seem to mind you much anymore, either."

"This is the closest she lets me get to her, but that's okay. I just like to watch her work. She's so meticulous." My OCD nature responded to Chelsea's impeccable style.

"Yeah. I think she'll be here indefinitely, but she seems to enjoy it. This place is good spiritually as much as it is physically."

"I agree." Though I wasn't convinced I'd ever be whole again. Not without Dane.

Kyle was quiet a few moments, prompting me to say, "I wouldn't take you for the Zen type."

"I'm not. Except . . ." He shrugged, clearly feigning nonchalance. I knew, because his jaw clenched ever so briefly. Then he told me, "I had my own stint here. That's one of the main reasons I suggested you check in, aside from Macy being my aunt and knowing you can trust her."

I stared quizzically at him. "What are you talking about?"

"Patient confidentiality. She won't give up any of your secrets, Ari."

"What does that have to do with your *stint*?"

"She didn't give up any of mine, either."

"Kyle. You're being way too vague."

With a frustrated sigh, he explained, "Since I was a kid playing Pop Warner, I wanted a football career. I wanted to play pro and I put everything I had into making it happen. I was good enough to earn a full-ride scholarship to Arizona State University and broke a few records. All I wanted was to be the best damn quarterback I could be."

Over six feet and solid muscle, I guessed he wasn't too off the mark size-wise, and obviously not talent-wise, since he'd landed a scholarship to ASU.

"So what happened?" I asked. This was not a topic we'd broached before and my curiosity suddenly burned to know more about his past.

"Got hurt." He seemed to grind over this a few moments. I didn't press. Eventually, he told me, "We had a shitty first season and my offensive line couldn't protect me well enough to not take a number of sacks. My left knee seemed to be the biggest target. Finally blew the fucker out on a play where I ran the ball for thirty yards before getting tackled."

"Wow, thirty yards. That's amazing for a quarterback." Then I said, "But damn. Your knee."

"Yeah. I spent the summer here in rehab. Quietly. No one knew. By the time I made it back for the start of practice my second year, I was feeling pretty good. Moving like nothing had ever happened."

"Oh, God," I said, a dismal feeling sweeping through me. "You got hit again."

"Same goddamn knee."

"Christ, Kyle. I'm so sorry." I patted his jean-clad thigh.

"Bad news was that I couldn't come up here during the season to work on it. Man, it sucks to blow out a knee. I had a boatload of cortisone injections, rehab in the off-seasons, knee braces year-round, just to protect it as best as I could. I pretended it didn't hurt like hell. I . . ." He shook his head as his thought trailed off.

"You, what?"

"Nothing. Look, the thing is, when I could be here, it helped immensely."

I was interested in all that he clearly wasn't telling me but didn't pry. Just said, "I don't doubt it. And I'm sure your entire family rallied around you and—"

"No." His jaw set again. There was definitely a lot of angst built around his college football career. "Mom was busy with Shell, and Dad . . . Well. When you have a road-warrior, salesman father whose sole excitement when he returns home is reliving his glory days by challenging his son on the front lawn for the neighbors to see—and said son being superprotective of his knee so that he doesn't do any further damage, thereby not really bringing his A game . . . Dad always thought I was mocking him by holding back."

I winced. "That must have made for some pretty tense times."

"By a lot." He shrugged again. "Whatever. Anyway, point being, this is a great place to recover and readjust. I had a couple of awesome seasons following the first two crappy ones. Because of Aunt Macy and her staff."

"So, then you could have gone pro?"

"I was part of the draft. Put serious thought into what I really wanted to do at that juncture in my life."

I didn't miss the pain that tinged his voice as he added, "But really, I had to face facts. I could play without telling anyone how agonizing it was when I just tweaked my knee the wrong way. But I knew in the back of my mind that I could be out for an entire season if I got hit hard enough in the right spot. I was twenty-one and thinking I should be invincible. I wasn't. And what would I be like when I was thirty if I kept taking blow after blow? Crippled?"

I stared at him, seeing the disappointment in his decision—or in himself. For being human. Fallible. Breakable.

"Kyle." I covered his hand with mine as we sat on the sofa, no one else paying attention. "You think you sold yourself short? Took the easy way out?"

He didn't speak for a while, and I didn't push.

A few minutes ticked by. Then he finally said, "I didn't want to end up like my dad. He wasn't good enough for pro for no reason other than he didn't possess enough talent. He was good, but not worthy of a team picking him up. It pissed him off. Stayed with him. Made him pretty damn bitter." Kyle shook his head. "To this day, I think one of the reasons he's so into his job is because he's a rock-star salesman, making some serious coin. But he takes every trip he can to avoid being at home, especially when there are family events—and you know, all the relatives get a little tipsy and start making comparisons about who's the better football player of the family."

I wasn't exactly knowledgeable when it came to this testosterone-riddled behavior, but I could at least empathize because of the fact that my father had suffered greatly with a bad shoulder that had jacked his own professional career.

"So," I ventured, "the Jennses aren't akin to the Brady Bunch?"

"Not in the least."

"I can relate."

He nodded. Then changed the subject—probably for both our sakes. "What do you think about a night out? A movie in town?"

I considered his request, still careful not to lead him on in any way. As much time as we spent together at the retreat, I had to continue the *we're just friends* stance. But that wasn't really the issue at present.

"I'm still in that stage where I need to stay close to a bathroom. I breathe wrong and start to spew."

With a chuckle, he said, "That's pretty gross, Ari."

"Tell me about it. I walk slowly. I don't move my head much. I avoid loud noises, strong scents, and spicy food. And yet I could be ultra-cautious and *bam*. The stomach revolts."

One of the chefs had been concocting milkshakes for me to coat my stomach, add some calories. They were as soothing as the tea and helped to keep the queasiness to a moderate level, rather than the roller coaster I'd been on previously.

"At least your color has come back," Kyle noted. "And you've got a little meat on the bones. Not much, but . . . better."

"Taking it one day at a time. But, hey. You don't have to hang out here with me. Go out with Meg and Sean. Your other friends. Have a life."

"Yeah, I should get together with the newlyweds. They've been calling me anti-social. But there's been a lot of work to do here at the retreat. My aunt gets so wrapped up in her patients that she doesn't pay attention to what she calls the 'trivial.'"

"It's nice to have you around," I said. "But don't feel obligated for my sake. You've gone so far above and beyond best friend. I really appreciate everything you've done for me."

"I'm worried about you," he said, his expression turning serious.

"I'll survive. Somehow. Rome wasn't built in a day, right?" I glanced around him and found Chelsea watching us as curiously as I usually studied her. I smiled. "Well, if we're talking about the Colosseum, Chelsea could probably build the replica in a day."

He laughed. "Without doubt." Jumping to his feet, he disappeared for five or ten minutes, then returned.

Kyle placed a sheet of paper on Chelsea's table and they shared a private grin.

I actually found myself a bit envious. Though I couldn't explain why, other than missing my own private moments with Dane?

When Kyle returned to the sofa, I asked, "What'd you do?"

"Printed out a photo of the Colosseum."

"Wow. I really had no idea you were so good with kids."

He winked and said in a suggestive tone, "I have many, *many* talents, babe."

chapter 10

The beginning of February brought with it another beautiful dusting of snow on the plateaus of the canyon. And the reminder of
everything I fought to forget for sanity's sake . . .

I'd taken to tending the gardens with Kyle and clipping flowers
for arrangements I could create for Hannah to paint. February was
our pruning season, and since the weather had been mild for most
of the winter, we still had gorgeous blooms. But they needed to be
cut back, especially with the occasional dip in temperature that led
to snow, though it never stuck for more than a day. Mostly just a
few fleeting hours.

I channeled the energy not expended with yoga and Pilates into
the bouquets. That was in between my still-sometimes debilitat-
ing morning sickness.

Dehydration was my current nemesis. I'd suffered three times,
thus far, and it wasn't pretty. Yet despite the complications with my
pregnancy, I'd latched on to this baby like a life preserver. I read

out loud to it, talked to it, played a variety of music, and generally spent an exorbitant amount of my time rubbing my belly.

I contemplated how many months after the baby was born before I could go back to wedding planning. But bridal consulting left a sour taste in my mouth, following my own devastating nuptial experience. So I considered general event planning for other resorts.

I understood I didn't have to work—ever. And while I could take advantage of being a full-time mom, I wasn't sure how I felt about that, either. I weighed the options and even spoke with Chelsea's mother, Abby, about the fact that she had to work. To my surprise, she confessed that even if she had financial freedom she'd feel worthless in trying to be everything Chelsea needed, because she didn't possess the required skill set.

That was when I decided two things. I needed a bigger worldview of parenthood, since mine was ridiculously limited. And I wanted to help Abby so that she didn't have to work two jobs to afford living expenses and Chelsea's care, especially since the latter seemed to be making an improvement in the child's life.

From there spawned the idea of possibly establishing an autistic children's foundation or even one for low-income single mothers. Though I didn't know the first thing about setting up something like that—or managing it. So I retrieved the slip of paper with Mr. Conaway's number jotted down and called him on Dr. Stevens's landline, since I hadn't replaced my cell that was but a remnant at the Lux, along with my diamond bracelet.

He met with me right away to get the ball rolling. Following that discussion, he offered a recap of my investments. His endless reports demonstrated sum totals in each account, percentages of overall capital, return on investments, and so on. As he wrapped up, he pointed out two accounts, showing zero balances.

"What are these?" I asked.

"One is for Dane's life insurance policy; the other is the policy on 10,000 Lux. We're still in the paperwork stage. But don't worry. You have more than enough funds to—"

"I'm not worried," I said. I'd been broke before and it sucked, but I had money saved from my job at the Lux, in addition to all of Dane's vast fortune. "I just wanted to know how everything was segregated."

"Well, I've divided the investments into silos that are held by trusts a couple layers deep before they get to your name. Now, you're perfectly capable of accessing capital immediately," he was quick to say. "But I don't want—and neither did Dane—for anyone to easily track the owner of the trusts. There's some substantial digging to be done in order to connect his money to you."

"Thank you." That was a huge relief. I was tempted to request he create another trust with an impenetrable layer for the baby. But I couldn't bring myself to fully confide in him.

Mr. Conaway did not know why I was at Macy's retreat. I figured he could easily deduce mental instability. Likely the reason he didn't even try to pry.

He said in a very firm, solid voice, "I'll take care of everything on my end. You needn't worry about a thing, my dear." He patted my hand. "Everything's in perfect order; it always will be." He smiled and it was actually kind of sweet.

I nodded, fighting a few tears. "I know Dane trusted you explicitly."

He started to pack up his briefcase.

I said, "Just one more thing, if you don't mind." As we walked toward the entrance, I continued. "I lost my bracelet that night, at the Lux. The one Dane gave me at our wedding. I'd like to offer a reward to anyone who might have found it or if they come across it while they're still sifting through the . . . debris."

It took a hell of a lot to block my dad's and Kyle's voices at the hospital as they'd made me face the gritty reality of what might be all that was left of my husband—teeth.

My stomach lurched. I tried to calm myself.

"I'll see to it," Mr. Conaway assured me.

He gave me a fatherly kiss on the cheek before departing. Very unexpected. But heartwarming.

After my lawyer left, it dawned on me that there had been no memorial service for Dane. I wasn't sure what to do about that. How odd would it appear if I was the one to orchestrate it?

Amano would have taken care of everything, I was sure. I had no idea if someone had planned a service for him, either. I didn't know if he had family or even a girlfriend, since Lara had passed.

Much as I was loath to do so, I decided to take a trip south to Scottsdale to discuss this with the only person other than Amano and myself who had been close enough to Dane to weigh in on the subject.

Unfortunately, I didn't have a vehicle at my disposal. So I had to ask Kyle for use of his Rubicon—though, naturally, he wanted to drive me. I didn't mind and felt a hint of security that he'd be close by.

The trip to the Valley was only an hour and a half, but it felt so much longer. Likely because I was on pins and needles, not necessarily wanting to see Mikaela Madsen but knowing it was the right thing to do, like sending her flowers had been. She'd known Dane her entire life, after all. I was certain she was shredded by his death as well.

We found a parking spot in trendy, Western-themed Old Town, the streets lined with galleries, boutiques, and restaurants. Italy on Your Doorstep was tucked into a lovely space between a renowned barbecue eatery and a classy imitation speakeasy.

The tasting room/market was stylish in decor and atmosphere, with burnt-sienna brick walls and dark polished woods. Mikaela was behind the bar, describing the bouquet and flavors of a Sangiovese as she poured. If I wasn't mistaken, her Italian accent was thicker. I suspected no one in this chic town knew she hailed from Philly, but likely had been told she'd been imported from Milan or Venice along with the finest of cheeses and most expensive of proseccos.

I'm sure she sold the hell of out her wines and antipasto from just her looks alone.

When she spotted me, she cheerfully called out, "Ciao, *bella!*" and set aside the bottle of red. She rounded the end of the bar and rushed toward me, arms spread wide. As though we were besties.

After an actual hug—not the air kisses—she clasped my hands and declared, "Ari, darling! It's so sensational to see you!" She rattled off something in Italian that went over my head, though I doubted it mattered. I had a feeling this was all for effect—for her patrons, aka her audience.

"It's good to see you, Mikaela," I told her. "You look wonderful, as always."

"Business is good," she said. "Come, let me show you around."

I introduced her to Kyle first, then let her play tour guide of the neatly, artistically arranged place. Impressive, to say the least, and I was certain Scottsdale society didn't bat an eye at the lofty price tags attached to everything.

We made our way back to the bar and she said, "Sit. I'll uncork something special for you."

"Thanks, but I'm driving," I lied, so as not to raise any sort of suspicion. I didn't need her speculating as to whether or not I was pregnant. Not that she would have any reason to jump to that conclusion, but I preferred precautionary measures. "Besides, we can't stay long. I just wondered . . . Is there someplace a little more private where we can talk?"

The tasting room was hopping for the middle of the afternoon. I could only imagine how packed it was when happy hour rolled around.

"*Sì, sì.* Of course." She led us to a small office in the back.

We all filed in and I got down to business. "I wanted to offer my condolences in person. I should have come sooner, but I've been . . . recovering."

It took less than a nanosecond for tears to flood her eyes, and I instantly felt the tinge of guilt. This was why she'd played all easy-breezy and cheery out front. Because seeing me obviously brought on a rush of pain.

"I'm so sorry," I said. "I have no intention of tormenting you. I just—"

"I understand, Ari." With a nod, she said, "When I saw from the news reports that you were hospitalized after the explosion, I felt so bad for you. I wanted to come see you. But, of course . . . I was just so devastated."

Kyle leapt up and snatched a couple of tissues from a box on the credenza and handed one to each of us.

"How considerate," Mikaela mumbled as she dabbed at the corners of her eyes.

I said, "The flowers you sent me were beautiful. And greatly appreciated."

"As were yours." She gave me a solemn look and told me, "I still can't believe the Lux is gone. And Dane . . . Well, that's just too distressing to think about. He was always so larger-than-life, so indestructible. I keep thinking he's on an extended business trip, and will be walking through the front door any day now."

I fought the emotion that swelled in my throat. But I couldn't stop the tears from burning the backs of my eyes. "I know it's difficult. And, that I'm aware of, there was no service."

"Nor an obituary—other than the press release from the Lux's PR people. I didn't have the heart to submit one. Dane was such a private person. What would I have said about him? And he didn't have family other than Amano. On top of all of that, I simply haven't accepted the finality yet."

I could understand that sentiment, commiserate. Yet I said, "It seems as though there should be a public recognition of his life. He had friends, business associates, employees."

Mikaela sniffled as her eyes continued to mist. "You're right. It's just so painful to even think of him being—"

"I know," I interjected before she said that one word that would make me fall apart in front of her. "But he deserves to be honored."

She nodded again. "I'll take care of it and let you know the details. Why don't you give me your cell number?"

"I don't have one. It was at the Lux that night."

Handing over a business card, she said, "Then call me early next week. I'll come up and we can have lunch."

"That would be nice." *Weird* was the more appropriate term, but . . . whatever.

We stood and hugged once more. Her gaze lingered on Kyle as he politely told her it was nice to meet her. I didn't know if Fabrizio was still her boyfriend, but she practically devoured Kyle with a hungry gaze.

He didn't seem to notice. His hand flattened against the small of my back and he guided me out.

The drive to Sedona was a quiet one at first. I could tell Kyle had found the exchange with Mikaela as awkward as I had. Eventually, he put a voice to the thoughts we both seemed mired in.

He said, "It doesn't seem right that Mikaela would hold a memorial service, instead of Dane's wife."

I shot him a look. "People don't know I'm Dane's wife, Kyle. No one would question her pulling it all together. They grew up with each other."

He sighed. "I'm not trying to rub it in here. I'm just . . . I don't know. I'm so damn sorry you have to go through all of this, Ari. It's—" He shook his head.

I swallowed down a lump of emotion "You don't have to say anything, Kyle. You can be angry and you can hate the choices I made. I don't regret them. I'm not happy that they upset you—"

"I'm not just upset, Ari." His hands gripped the wheel tightly. "I'm . . . I'm . . . Fuck." Anguish tinged his deep tone, but he finally said, "I'm heartbroken. For you. This really shitty thing happened to you, not me, and yet . . . I'm all torn up—for you."

More tears sprang to my eyes. I should be used to the waterworks by now, but this time I was distraught over how my life so greatly affected Kyle's.

"I appreciate how you feel about me," I said, hoping for an accurate explanation. "I'd be heartbroken for you, too. Having you as a friend, Kyle . . . that helps a lot. More than you'll ever know." I smiled at him. Brushed away my tears—for his sake.

"Just seems like this isn't getting any better for you, Ari."

On the one hand, there was no denying the situation with Mikaela stung. On the other hand, I was still in too fragile a state of mind to plan a service myself. The finality, the closure, was not something I looked forward to. I didn't want it. I liked that I could continue to cling to the bizarre—and, yes, highly improbable— fantasy that somehow Dane had escaped that night.

Even though I knew I was only fooling myself.

I regretted my decision to seek out Mikaela every day after we'd visited her.

Remaining a bit delusional when it came to still fantasizing about Dane miraculously walking through my bedroom door, I faced the fact that I really and truly did not want a service for him. And God forbid she should write an obit to submit to the *Republic*. I couldn't handle that. I didn't want the finality I'd thought of on the drive home with Kyle.

But how did I call it off? Knowing Mikaela, she'd likely find it a fantastic way to plug her business and add more mystery and drama to her image by touting Dane Bax as one of her close personal friends.

Though I did not doubt she was hurting over losing him, I'd gotten enough glimpses of the true Mikaela Madsen to know she used every opportunity to her advantage.

But that really wasn't what had me worked up. I didn't give a rip if she found a PR golden nugget in orchestrating Dane's memorial service.

I didn't want closure.

At all.

I did a lot of pacing and ran a multitude of scenarios through my head as to how I could stop what I'd put into motion. My anxiety didn't help my constantly unsettled stomach, and I returned to that previous state of not being able to keep anything down. Both of my doctors threatened me with IV feeding if I didn't get it together.

So I fought for some calm. Spent more time with Kyle, because he was good at distracting me, diverting my attention. Over the weekend, we were in the solarium, poring over landscaping books at one of the round tables and debating what to do about the bald spot in the east courtyard that was a result of him having ripped out several dead plants and a couple of bushes.

Gretchen had CNN on the flat screen mounted in the far corner. Hannah braved the chill in the air to paint outdoors. She considered the patio her studio rather than the solarium. Chelsea put the Legos to brilliant use, as always.

Dr. Stevens and her staff were building the business by adding outpatient services for a limited number of athletes interested in her holistic approach to physical therapy and healing. They were seen in the detached rehab facility but came into the house from time to time with their specialists for exams. The moderate activity helped to sidetrack most of my wayward thoughts.

Though not all of them. . . .

Kyle ticked off the merits of installing a small pond of koi in the courtyard instead of replacing the greenery. I let him rattle on as he built momentum. But my brain came to a grinding halt when one word penetrated his diatribe.

Hilliard.

My blood ran cold as memories of Vale Hilliard instantly assaulted my mind. I whipped around in the chair and stared at the TV. The breaking news was the sudden indictment of billionaire Bryn Hilliard—Vale's father—accompanied by video footage of him being led from a building, surrounded by what I presumed was his huge team of lawyers.

"Gretchen," I said, breathless. "Could you please turn that up?"

She gave me a little more volume as I stood and walked toward the TV.

The reporter said, "Hilliard is believed to be part of the 'Billionaires Club' and is allegedly responsible for doling out hundreds of millions of dollars to politicians in order to push his own agenda. Until recently, the mostly cash contributions had gone undetected or reported to accountants and the IRS as gambling debts. Other sizable donations were funneled through various companies, as were noneligible expenses."

You almost have it right.

Except that Bryn Hilliard wasn't part of the broader spectrum of the billionaire network—he was one of the select nine who comprised the poli-econ society of which Dane had been a part.

Chelsea rapped a hand on her table and made a disapproving noise. I glanced at her over my shoulder. She glared at me with big eyes.

"Sorry," I told her. To Gretchen, I said, "You can lower the sound. But I still need to hear—"

The reporter continued, saying, "Hilliard's indictment is the second one this week of this magnitude. Billionaire real estate and investments mogul Lennox Avril faces similar charges of criminal corruption, tax evasion, fraud . . . as well as possible murder charges."

He droned on about legalities as my head buzzed and my ears rang. I sank onto the sofa next to Gretchen.

My stomach churned, and I felt the bile rise in my throat but tamped it down. Fought back the green around the gills sensation I'd become all too familiar with since I'd left the hospital. But this had nothing to do with the baby. And everything to do with Dane.

A heartbeat later, I was on my feet without even fully realizing it. A whirlwind of activity in my head propelled me forward. I grabbed Kyle's arm as he stared at me, perplexed and concerned.

"What is it?" he demanded in a low tone, likely so as to not disturb Chelsea further. She didn't like raised voices any more than I did. Though for different reasons.

"Can you take me home?" I asked.

His brow furrowed. "Why? I thought you were happy here. You're feeling much better and—"

"Kyle, I just need another ride. Yes or no?"

Time was suddenly of the essence. I needed to get back to the house while the thoughts in my mind were fresh and held *so* much potential.

"Of course," he reluctantly agreed as he fished his keys out of the front pocket of his jeans.

I rushed through the house with Kyle hot on my heels. We cleared the security gate and I climbed into the passenger side of his Rubicon. Tension gripped me. So did a curious exhilaration. He couldn't drive fast enough for me, and my leg bounced anxiously as we made our way through Sedona, headed north, then wove along Oak Creek Canyon to the turnoff on to the back roads that led to the house I'd shared with Dane.

I was out of the Jeep and racing around to the front door before Kyle had even slipped from his seat.

Punching in the code, I barreled through the double doors and ran down the hallway to Dane's office. Kyle rushed in behind me as I yanked drawers open and tore through file folders. It was a needle in the haystack mission. I had no idea what the hell I was searching for, but somehow—*somehow*—I knew I'd figure it out when I found it.

"Ari, what the fuck?" Kyle asked in a tight tone. "Are you totally losing it?"

"Maybe. Possibly. Likely." I even sounded a bit hysterical. My pulse echoed in my ears and my heart beat way too fast. Still, I rifled through folders and paperwork, tossing everything that didn't strike me as pertinent onto the hardwood floor. Kyle started scooping it all up as I ransacked the first, then the second credenza.

Halfway through, I whipped out a thick black leather portfolio and slammed it onto the blotter on Dane's desk. I flipped it open and shuffled through contracts and amendments, forms, legal documents I really couldn't make heads or tails of, though that was irrelevant. I suddenly knew what I wanted to find.

Toward the back of the folio was another contract, the word DRAFT stamped across the front in bloodred. For good measure, each page held a background watermark declaring the same thing.

A quarter of the way in, I eyed the list of names, neatly centered and all in caps.

I ripped the sheet from the folio and pushed the leather folder aside, focusing solely on that one page. My heart rate doubled. I hadn't thought it possible. Felt a tinge of fear, in fact, at how rapidly it thundered in my chest. Not exactly healthy, but I couldn't slow the erratic beats.

Kyle dropped into a chair across from me. "What's up?"

I reached for one of Dane's favorite Montblanc fountain pens and circled four names: Mr. Dane Bax, Sultan Qadir Hakim, Mr. Ethan Evans, Mr. Nikolai Vasil.

I drew a line through the Honorable Bryn Hilliard's name. And stifled the laugh at the irony of his title.

I scanned further down the list. Put a thick slash through Dr. Lennox Avril's name as well.

Lifting my gaze, I stared at Kyle, hope racing through me.

One thought burned in my mind.

One very distinct and now-plausible reality resonated deep within me.

I couldn't fight the grin as I simply said, "He's alive."

chapter 11

Kyle stared back. "*He* who?"

Spreading my arms wide, I told him, "Dane, of course." Emotion and excitement flooded my veins.

"Oh, fuck." Kyle got to his feet, started to pace. "Okay. I should have seen this coming. I am such an idiot," he rambled. I watched with a raised brow. "I probably should have warned my aunt, so she could keep an eye out for this. Get you professional help. Like from a mental health thera—"

"I have professional help." I crossed my arms over my chest. "I see a counselor twice a week. She comes to the retreat. We talk about death—not so much Dane's, just in general. How to accept it, things like that. Mostly we talk about the baby. How to raise it on my own, what to expect."

He drew up short. "You're not on your own."

"Come on, Kyle. You've been great. No doubt. But you have a life, too. You've all but abandoned it to be with me."

"No, I haven't," he insisted. "I have a job. It just happens to be at the retreat where you're living."

"You've been *so* helpful," I reiterated. "Serious, life-saving helpful. But . . . I don't like to talk much about the baby with you because I know it pisses you off that I'm pregnant."

He slumped back into the chair, disgruntled. "Couldn't you have waited? I mean, you got engaged one night, married two nights later, and then a month goes by and we find out you're having a baby? Jesus Christ, Ari. Take a few breaths in between."

"It was an accident, like your sister, Shell." I smirked. "Water under the bridge, anyway. Well, except that . . . I'm totally right about Dane." I shoved the paper Kyle's way. "The names I circled? Good guys. The ones with the lines through them? Bad guys. Corrupt members of a secret society Dane belonged to."

His jaw fell slack. "A *what?*"

I groaned. This was about to get complicated for him. "A political-economic society that tracks, trends, and analyzes markets and financial shit I can't even begin to understand. Suffice it to say, the goal was to effect positive change by influencing leaders and others with power. But five of the nine members, instead, used the information for personal gain. *These* guys," I said as I waved the sheet in my hand.

There was a distinct edge to my voice and fury no doubt reflected in my eyes, riveting Kyle.

I told him, "Dane just brought down the first two—"

"Whoa, whoa, *whoa!*" Kyle leapt to his feet again. "First of all, Miss Conspiracy Theorist, how the fuck is there some sort of *secret society?*"

"An Illuminati faction, to be exact."

"Like in *Tomb Raider?*"

I laughed. I'd said something similar, with the same amount of disbelief, when Dane had told me about his dual life.

"Kinda sorta, but not really. Anyway, it's been around for generations. Dane is the only one recruited who wasn't born of a founding member, from my understanding."

"And why is this list important *now?*"

With an agitated sigh, because I'd expected him to keep up, I said, "They're the original investors in 10,000 Lux. Long before Dane realized they'd used the think-tank intellectual property of the society to line their own coffers, while others suffered the economic downfall. Dane, Ethan, and those I've circled did everything they could to put a stop to it. But they weren't wholly successful, so they've tried to extricate themselves."

Kyle shook his head once more, this time quite sharply. "Of course he'd be part of a secret society. Was there *anything* normal about the guy?"

"Not that I'm aware of," I conceded.

"Jesus."

Rushing on, I said, "Remember that, after I'd been kidnapped, I told you Dane had cut out the corrupt members from the Lux before construction was underway? That's what all the trouble was about. The sabotage, the explosion, everything. They're responsible."

"Goddamn, Ari. You know, your life would have been much less disastrous—and a hell of a lot safer—if you had just stuck with me the night of Sean and Meg's wedding. But no, you had to get wrapped up with Dark and Dangerous." Kyle's tone was harsh, his voice thick with anger. Even his sky-blue eyes burned with rage.

This was a side of him I'd slowly seen emerging when it came to all the things he disapproved of in my life. And now it radiated from him.

Trying to diffuse his anger, I said, "Now's hardly the time for a lecture, Kyle."

"Oh, I beg to differ!" he erupted. " 'Cause I'm thinking I've given you *way* too much of the kid-glove treatment, when what you clearly need is a healthy dose of reality. For fuck's sake, Ari! People could have died!"

I jumped to my feet and slammed my palms against the desktop. "People *did* die, Kyle! At least—" The angst drained quickly. I plopped back into my chair. "That's what we were led to believe."

"Oh, Christ." He rolled his eyes and paced again, hands on his waist.

"Just listen, okay?" I was breathy once more, my chest heaving. "After the kidnapping, Dane promised me he'd find a legitimate way to bring these guys down. He was putting the squeeze on them, one way or the other. I have no idea what his plan was. But he obviously pushed them over the edge, because they planted a bomb inside the Lux. A *bomb!*"

"That killed your husband," Kyle said acridly.

I glared at him.

He added, "I'm not trying to be cruel, Ari. I'm trying to get you to see the very cut-and-dried facts."

"There aren't any," I told him. "There's nothing cut-and-dried about this Illuminati bloc, Dane's involvement, or the shady members. Nothing about this scenario is black and white, Kyle. It's all gray area. Smoke and mirrors. Incredibly powerful people who have the resources to do whatever they please for their own personal gain. Except . . ."

I inhaled deeply, slowing myself down because I was jabbering a mile a minute. "Dane knew things. Enough to piece together evidence to prove these guys are corrupt—enough to warrant indictments. And even though a murder charge won't stick, because he's alive and Amano might be as well, they could still be charged with attempted murder, I'm sure. After all, there were about forty people inside that building they blew up. That has to equate to some serious prison time, in addition to all the other charges. Fucking with the IRS . . . you're just asking for a lengthy sentence there."

Kyle paced some more. Swore under his breath. Then he faced me and demanded, "Are these . . . *shady members* . . . so powerful they thought they could get away with bombing a hotel? That it wouldn't be traced back to them? Were they banking on Dane surrendering, letting them win rather than evening the score?"

"I don't know. I don't know how these people operate—other than on a level that defies comprehension. They have billions of dollars to throw at something like this, a network of powerful resources. If Dane, Ethan, and the others opted to not come forward, the bad guys would get off scot-free, because no way would the police be able to peg the culprits. Likely not even the FBI. They don't know Dane's connection to Hilliard and his group. What lead would they have to work with, aside from trying to pinpoint who placed explosives in the lobby of 10,000 Lux?"

Though I suddenly had a very good idea of who that might be—the one person who'd had access to security systems, facilities, IT, and the grounds, because he'd been a self-proclaimed jack-of-all-trades. And a weasel in disguise.

Wayne Horton.

The son of a bitch who'd helped to set *me* up when Vale had kidnapped and roughed me up.

My blood boiled. I took several deep breaths, trying to steady myself.

Gripping the back of the chair, Kyle said, "What makes you so sure Dane is alive and he's the one feeding the Feds or whoever information for indictments?"

"Because he told me he'd nail them legally."

Kyle's brow jerked up. "As opposed to . . . ?"

"Beating the living shit of each of them with his bare hands."

As much as it had horrified me that Dane had attacked Vale, the idea of him throttling these men was now an appealing one. Not exactly a settling notion, since I'd personally witnessed what he was capable of—how far he'd go to protect me.

"Dane knew things about these guys," I said, my belief still strong that he was offering evidence, despite Kyle's whole *this cannot be happening* expression. "What an excellent opportunity for him to push that evidence in the right direction, when everyone thinks he's dead. The supershady would never see it coming. Dane's totally blindsiding them."

"Ari . . ." Kyle gave me a compelling look. Actually, it was more of blatant pity, but whatever. "If he'd made it out of the lobby, we would have seen him."

"Unless he and Amano escaped out the back, toward the court-yards."

"And what?" Kyle all but growled, angry again. "You honestly believe he'd allow you to think, all this time, that he was dead? To grieve for him and—"

"No. Of course not. I can't explain the mechanics of this. I only know what my gut is telling me. Dane found a way to make his final push with the corrupt members. He'd never want me to suf-fer in the process, so I have to believe there's a reasonable explana-tion. I know it in my heart, Kyle. Everything he's doing is to protect what's his—that includes *me*."

Dane wouldn't leave me to suffer. But at the same time . . . He'd do anything to keep me safe. If this was his only way, what choice would he have than to disappear, no matter how emotionally de-stroyed it made me? Because if he actually could pull this off, it'd all boil down to a couple of months out of our lives that were sheer horror—well, in addition to the other period of horror following the kidnapping, when I'd broken up with him.

The blast at the Lux could have unwittingly provided the per-fect chance to do what he needed to do, so all of this could end. Once he'd learned no one had died in the explosion and everyone had been released from the ER except me—and he'd know my dad and Kyle would be there to take care of me—Dane would be free to take this course of action handed to him.

As I contemplated all of this, finding huge relief in my logic and completely ignoring any probability that I was way the fuck off my rocker, I stared at the leather blotter in front of me.

Something was missing.

A grin spread over my lips.

"Oh, Christ," Kyle mumbled. "You are so far out there. Seriously, Ari, we need to get back to my aunt's and have your counselor come for a *very* long visit."

I snickered. "I'm not crazy, Kyle." *Maybe.* "I just noticed that Dane's laptop is gone."

"So, it's probably in his office at the Lux. Or what used to be his office."

I shivered at the thought of what the once opulent and pristine 10,000 Lux must look like today. Squeezing my eyes shut for a moment, I fought to compose myself. Then I opened my lids and speared him with a look. "Dane didn't take his computer to work that day. We had too much to do downstairs. He only had his phone with him."

Clearly, Kyle wanted to argue the point, come up with another reason. I didn't let him.

"My guess is, there's a shitload of evidence he's kept on his hard drive and he came back here for it. A clue that escaped me because I'd refused to step foot in here until now."

And I had one more thing to add to the mounting list that tipped the scales of my theory.

Standing, I snatched the sheet of paper again and said, "Can you take me somewhere else?"

"The closest insane asylum?"

"Asshole." I laughed softly. "You'll regret treating me like a loon when I prove I'm right."

"And Dane comes back?" he challenged.

"Yes."

The notion warmed my heart and brought tears of relief to my eyes. Interestingly, my stomach settled. My breathing was almost normal.

As we drove off, I thought I caught a flash of metal in the dense woods—perhaps from a car? I frowned. I really wasn't aware of my surroundings these days. That would have to change so that Dane didn't have to worry about me.

Suddenly giddy, I all but vibrated in my seat as we headed into Sedona. But then Kyle shot a broody look my way and I stilled. Though, on the inside, I was almost absolutely convinced my powers of deduction had served me well. I knew precisely where to turn for that remaining bit of certainty.

I still had Mr. Conaway's unlisted contact details with me. We mapped out his home address using Kyle's iPhone. Turned out to be a tough place to find, and I suspected that was on purpose.

When we finally reached the gated property and were buzzed through, it was all I could do not to knock down his front door in my hyperactive state. His very pert and pretty wife, Eleanor, answered. She informed us in her delicate Georgian accent that Mr. Conaway was always available for a visit from me. Very southern hospitality–like, with the offer of coffee or tea, which we both declined. Though Kyle hedged at the mention of mango iced tea, while I forced myself to contain my excitement.

Eleanor escorted us to her husband's office, toward the back of the house. He greeted us in his polite, professional manner, though I could see his concern over my unexpected appearance in his dark-brown eyes.

"I'm so sorry to barge in like this, without an appointment," I told him.

"It's fine, Ari. Always nice to see you, my dear. You're welcome here anytime."

"Thank you." I tried to dial down my exhilaration. "You remember Kyle Jenns?" I asked as I indicated my friend.

"Of course." They shook. "From the wedding and I also saw you at the retreat."

"Yes. Dr. Stevens—Macy—is my aunt."

"Well, I'm quite happy she's given Ari so much help."

I beamed. "I'm sure you're not the only one."

He eyed me quizzically, then said, "Please, won't you both have a seat?" We took the chairs in front of his desk. "Now, to what do I owe the pleasure?" The quizzical expression turned skeptical, suspicious.

Did he think I was here for a divorce so I could marry Kyle?

I blanched. I'd never be anyone other than Mrs. Dane Bax from here on out, whether he was dead or alive. Though I already knew the answer to that mystery.

Quickly diffusing any sort of speculation, I said, "I was just curious about some of the account information we reviewed previously. Would you mind showing me an updated status?"

"Not at all. I work very closely with Dane's—*your*—accountant to keep everything as current as possible."

His fingertips skated over the keyboard, and then his printer began churning out paperwork. He handed the bundle to me and I scanned the pages that looked familiar, once again not certain what I searched for but hoping it would jump out at me.

Sure enough, when I reached the last sheet I stared at the two very glaring pieces to the puzzle.

Lifting my gaze, I asked Mr. Conaway, "Shouldn't Dane's life insurance policy have paid out by now? I'm the sole beneficiary, so there shouldn't be any disputes or complications. No one to contest it."

He shuffled some papers on his desk as he said, "Given the amount we're dealing with, it can take a bit longer than under normal circumstances." His gaze didn't quite meet mine.

"But you did send the claim in . . . on my behalf? Or wouldn't I need to sign something? For that matter, I haven't even seen a death certificate. Wouldn't the insurance carrier require that?"

His hands stilled. This time he speared me with a solid gaze. A knowing look flickered in his eyes.

Jackson Conaway couldn't lie to me.

I smiled, my heart soaring. More tears built. "I know Dane's alive. I figured it out. I should have figured it out sooner. That's what he expected, I'm sure. What he hoped for from the beginning." Though he wouldn't have known I was pregnant and struggling with all that entailed.

Mr. Conaway sat back in his chair, neither confirming nor denying.

His longtime loyalty to Dane warred with his new loyalty to me. Dane would win out, I had no doubt. So I made it easy for our attorney.

"Tell Dane his wife needs to see him. It's urgent."

We left the office and drove back to the retreat. Mostly in silence until we turned onto the rugged road that led to the rustic area.

Kyle asked, "What if you're wrong? What if you're *way* wrong?"

"I'm not."

"Ari."

I sighed. "Come on, Kyle. It's Dane. In what universe would he be defeated?"

Sliding a glance toward me, he said, "If you really believed that, you never would have accepted he was dead in the first place."

"It was a terrifying time, Kyle. The most beautiful building I'd ever seen had just been blown to bits. People were screaming, injured. I was bleeding all over the place. Dane was missing. All of our hard work was destroyed and employees could have been killed. I'd lost my wedding bracelet. I was in complete despair—and thoroughly wrecked without Dane."

I still had a ton of questions about his disappearance but no one to ask. My theory, of course, hinged on Mr. Conaway getting my message to Dane and him following through on my request to see him.

The waiting game would not be an easy one. But my certainty that he'd survived the Lux explosion brought me a huge amount of peace.

For now.

chapter 12

The *Arizona Republic* not only picked up the obituary Mikaela submitted but also ran a nice piece on the memorial service scheduled for the following week.

Guilt tripped through me.

Oh, boy.

This was a different conundrum to face. An ethical one I'd not factored into my euphoria over coming to the realization that Dane was alive.

A part of me wanted to tell Mikaela of my suspicion and have her call off the event. But that could be detrimental to Dane's efforts, when we needed to perpetuate the myth of his death.

Still, it was difficult to let Mikaela go through with a service when I knew it was a farce. Emotionally, she'd suffer. Financially, too, though I could easily compensate her. I couldn't, however, make it up to her that I let her believe Dane had never made it out of the Lux.

Yes, it was odd that I was so obsessed over this woman's

feelings—after all, I'd feared what her true intentions were when it had come to my husband. But I wasn't like my mother, whose sole focus was herself. I wasn't cold and callous. Which almost made me reach for the phone.

But no. I couldn't tip off Mikaela, even if she was Dane's life-long friend. She had to help me carry on the lie, albeit unbeknownst to her.

And I had to accept that this was all for the greater good. What Dane did was dangerous yet meaningful. I couldn't let my conscience undermine his efforts.

However, I did worry a little about my mother picking up a paper and having a renewed sense of *let's sue the Lux conglomerate*. In fact, I wouldn't be surprised if she'd already tried to take up a class action suit and Mr. Conaway hadn't wanted to concern me with it.

She couldn't reach me by phone, nor did she know where I currently resided. But *out of sight, out of mind* was never a clever tactic to take when it came to Kathryn DeMille, so I stewed over how to stay on top of that potential dilemma.

A few days later, Mr. Conaway came to the retreat. Handing over a padded envelope, he simply said, "This arrived for you earlier."

I eyed him curiously. There was no mailing label with my name on it or his address. No return label, either.

"How do I know this is safe to open?" I asked.

"Trust me."

"Right." I tugged on the sealed flap and dumped the contents onto the table we sat at in the visitors' lounge. A slim Samsung flip phone lay before me. Looked to be of the disposable variety. Pre-paid minutes, no contract, not easily traceable.

My breath suddenly came in heavier pulls. I reached for the phone and flicked it open with my thumb. It was fully charged and had a decent signal, despite our being in a canyon. I pressed the button for text messages, but there were none. I selected the contacts' list, but it, too, was empty.

My gaze returned to Mr. Conaway. "I don't understand."

He was already on his feet, prepared to leave. "You will."

I watched him go, wondering if he thrived on all this cloak-and-dagger stuff when it came to Dane.

All it really did for me was wear on my nerves. I had a phone now, but I still couldn't call Dane. I had to wait for him to call me. And that was pure torture.

I didn't bother programming the Samsung or adding my dad's or Kyle's number. I suspected it was meant strictly for one line of communication—from Dane to me.

Anxiety rippled down my spine, and I found myself staring at the damn thing more often than not, willing it to ring. I even checked the volume numerous times, to make sure it was cranked up. And I never went anywhere without the cell, even leaving it close at hand on the vanity when I showered.

The phone became a bit of a nemesis, but it convinced me further that I was right about Dane being alive.

Kyle asked where it had come from, and I told him the truth. He rolled his eyes and went back to pruning the shrubs.

I met with my OB-GYN and my counselor, as usual. The latter was a bit trickier to deal with because I had to contain my excitement when I was normally very reserved.

"You're showing excellent signs of improvement, Ari," she commented with a smile.

I'd barely spoken to her when we'd first started the sessions, since I could hardly function, let alone carry on a conversation. She'd been extremely patient, commiserating yet encouraging me to work through the stages of grief with her. Not the grief of losing a husband and the father of my baby—she had no idea about that. As far as she was concerned, I was upset over losing my boss. Someone I'd worked so closely with, and of course there was the trauma of what I'd been through. Not to mention the prospect of being a single mother.

I felt a little deceptive now that I fabricated more mourning, but it was necessary, as was the case with Mikaela. I couldn't do any-thing that would jeopardize Dane's covert work.

Kyle and I attended the service for Dane in Scottsdale. A har-rowing experience, despite clutching the cell in my hand and believing it would ring at the right time. Mikaela looked fabulous, even as she got choked up while delivering the eulogy. It tugged at my heartstrings, too, because I had to outwardly share the belief of the masses that Dane was no longer with us.

I was emotionally drained by the time we returned to the re-treat. Kyle took pity on me and didn't harp over the fact that Dane still had not called. *I* mentally harped enough in that vein.

We had dinner and watched TV. That very evening, another indictment was announced. I crossed the name off the list I hid under my mattress. As I wandered aimlessly about my room, a sense of foreboding and a dangerous air encroached on my optimism.

The third indictment would no doubt have the remaining two members on-edge. Although they would have heard Dane hadn't survived the blast, surely they'd find it suspicious that Hilliard, Avril, and now Anthony Casterelli had been targeted by the FBI and the IRS.

Did they wonder now if Dane really was dead?

Technically, in my mind, he'd only been missing, since his body hadn't yet been found. But I'd learned that all news reports—from the very beginning—claimed he was dead. As my mother had picked up on, which had motivated her to come to the hospital to jump on the lawsuit bandwagon. Not just *presumed* dead. Did the FBI have something to do with that?

If the others started to ponder this and pick it all apart, the way I had . . . That would not bode well for Dane.

Or me.

I sat on the bed, an ominous sensation moving through me, like snakes slithering under my skin. I shivered.

What if they came looking for me?

But no—I shook off the thought. How the hell would they find me?

I was pretty much off the grid at this point. I'd only been back to the house once since Kyle had told me about the rehab retreat. And though the reminder of metal flashing in the sunlight, through the trees, crept into my brain, no vehicle had pulled out when we'd left the house before visiting Mr. Conaway.

Plus, the retreat had oodles of high-end security. Dr. Stevens was a stickler for both patient confidentiality and safety. In fact, she'd mentioned the requirements were stringent for her to maintain her accreditations.

I tried to latch on to that, find a comfort level that didn't have me freaking out too much. Even Mr. Conaway had said I was safe here.

Hmm. How would he know that for sure?

I shook my head. Now the cloak-and-dagger was getting to *me*.

My panic escalated as I returned to the living room and watched more breaking news. In Casterelli's case, the reporter actually mentioned a potential connection to the bombing of 10,000 Lux.

Was that some sort of FBI squeeze play? Or was my mind running ridiculously rampant?

"Shit," I murmured.

"Oh, Ari," Gretchen said as she sat next to me. "Honey, I'm so sorry. I should know better than to have this on when they're talking about the hotel."

She was aware that both Kyle and I had worked at the Lux. Naturally, she had no idea of my association with Dane, but I had told her my injuries were a result of the explosion.

"It's okay. I'm interested in how this all pans out. Who's behind it and what's going to be done about it."

For mention of the Lux to come about now . . . I could only speculate that perhaps Dane and whoever he'd partnered with—it had to be the FBI—were closing in on the remaining two corrupt members.

Anticipation gripped me so that I had to spend extra time on the treadmill later to burn off nervous energy. Then I showered in my private bathroom and headed toward the door, wanting to join Gretchen, Hannah, and Kyle for dinner.

Then it finally happened.

The cell rang.

I started. Nearly dropped the damn thing.

My hand suddenly shook, but I flipped the phone open.

"Yes?" I simply said, not sure I should give my name, say it was me on the line—or ask if it was Dane calling.

"Have your friend drive you to the house."

Amano!

I couldn't breathe.

He said, "Eight o'clock."

The line went dead.

I stared at the phone, my heart pounding.

Amano was alive, too!

Or perhaps he was the only one. And Mr. Conaway wanted me to hear the truth from my former, trusted bodyguard.

Fuck.

I was too keyed up to eat but didn't want to draw anyone's attention. Or skip a meal now that I was back to keeping food down and had returned to my normal weight.

While the ladies engaged in a rousing game of Scrabble, I once again asked Kyle to take me home.

His gaze narrowed. "Why?"

"Please?" I asked anxiously.

His blue eyes clouded. "You heard from him."

"No. Amano."

Kyle seethed. "This could all blow up in your face, Ari."

My stomach knotted. "Bad choice of words, Kyle."

With a miserable sigh, he said, "Yeah, I know. Sorry. It's just . . . Okay, Amano is alive. That doesn't mean Dane is. This might be where you get the confirmation you've fought so hard to accept."

I'd already considered that myself. Still.

"I'll take my chances." Though Kyle's warning would not go un-heeded. It was entirely possible that he was right and I would be devastated all over again.

Fear mingled with my unease. I wrung my hands, wondering if I was being masochistic. Setting myself up for a really hard fall.

I wasn't sure I could make it through a second time around. Were it not for Dane's baby growing inside me, I would have been the walking dead.

But I had to find out the truth. I had to know one way or the other. It was time to see if there was a silver lining somewhere on my horizon.

I remained positive as we headed to Oak Creek Canyon, despite Kyle's dour mood.

"I swear, if this is a setup or if you find out he really is gone . . . Jesus, Ari."

"Lighten up on the steering wheel," I said. "You're going to rip it from the dash."

"You do realize how fucked up this all is?"

"I realized that a long time ago," I conceded. "But this isn't your everyday intrigue we're dealing with here."

"It never is with Dane Bax."

I smiled, the hope building within me.

We reached the gate and I perked up in my seat as Kyle punched in the code. One of the stall doors of the detached garage opened.

"Pull in," I said.

"Do we really have to get all *Mission Impossible?*"

Revenge was more like it, I suspected. "Just do it."

The door lowered behind us. Kyle cut the engine.

I said, "You know how much I appreciate this, right?"

"You know how pissed off I'm going to be if he breaks your heart again. Right?"

Leaning over, I gave him a quick kiss on the cheek. "You're a great friend. I think I'll be okay. You, too."

He scowled. "Let's go."

Regardless of the reassurance I'd given us both, my nerves jumped as I reached for the handle.

I'd walked into a very easy trap once before. Considering the people we were dealing with, it could happen again. Even though it had definitely been Amano's voice on the line, there could have been a gun to his head when he'd called me.

I suddenly regretted involving Kyle. I should have asked to borrow his Rubicon, not have him drive me.

Why hadn't I thought of that before?

Yet . . . Once again, my gut told me otherwise. Instinct and everything I'd recently unearthed made me confident of what I would find here.

Kyle took me gently by the forearm and led me through the garage to the main exit. We passed a black SUV—not the Escalade Dane drove—as well as Dane's McLaren and high-performance motorcycle.

We made our way up to the house and I bypassed the keypad and tried the lever. It was unlocked. Stepping inside, I found the entryway and the space beyond as dimly lit as when we'd arrived here after I'd been in the hospital. I didn't bother turning on any lights. Instead, I led Kyle to the great room. The silvery-blue hues of this portion of the house provided just enough illumination because of the tall windows and doors that let in the streaks of moonlight.

I pulled up short just past the oversized entrance, my heart stammering. Kyle instantly let go of my wrist.

Air rushed from my lungs as the figure at the windows turned. "Dane!"

I raced across the stone floor and launched myself into his arms.

"Well, fuck me," I heard Kyle mutter, nonplussed. And astonished.

Dane held me firmly. Everything ceased to exist except the two of us.

Tears began to flow, which quickly turned into body-wracking sobs. My face was buried in the crook of his neck and his embrace tightened.

Relief and joy echoed through every inch of me. Every fiber of my being screamed with the need to get closer to him, even though we were completely melded together from head to toe.

I was overwrought with emotion. All of the positive energy I'd channeled into my belief that Dane was alive could not prepare me for the reality of it. For the feeling of his hard body against my curves, his soft lips at my temple, his warm breath on my skin as he murmured apologies and "I love you" in a tormented voice.

I clung to him, not sure I'd ever be able to let go.

This wasn't a dream. It was real. He was alive and I was in his arms.

Somehow, he'd survived the explosion. And I knew he had to be as wrecked as I'd been, not being able to tell me, to talk to me, to touch me.

"I'm so happy to see you," I sobbed. "I've *never* been happier than right this very moment."

"Baby, I'm so sorry," he whispered. "For all you've been through."

"Nothing matters, Dane. Except that you're here with me."

I couldn't let him go. Clung endlessly to him. Continued to cry.

He kept one arm solidly around my waist and smoothed my hair with the other hand.

In the background, over my soft wails, I heard Amano explaining what had happened after they'd discovered the bomb planted in the table below that massive chandelier I'd always admired.

"Dane was the last one out," he said in his deep, stoic tone. "He went into the kitchen, just to be sure everyone escaped. He wasn't far out of the doors to the courtyard when the building blew. I found him under a pile of stone, glass, and wood. He was unconscious. Barely breathing."

My crying jag ensued, but I tried to concentrate on what Amano said as Dane stroked my hair and kissed my temple.

"I had to get him out of there, fast. He wouldn't have survived. So I carried him over my shoulder to the back lot where the hotel Escalades are and left through the service entrance before the ambulances and fire trucks were even on their way."

"He took me to the physician who helped Vale," Dane told me in a quiet voice. "A private facility—a friend. Part of my network."

So nothing would be reported. Everything kept hush-hush. Including his existence.

Amano said, "I went back for you, Ari, but by then you'd been taken to the hospital. I followed the story on TV, learned your injuries weren't life threatening. I had to trust that Kyle and your father would take care of you, and I had to do the same with Dane."

I'd known there would be a sound reason for all the secrecy.

Continuing, Amano told us, "Dane was in a coma. Responsive in some respects, but clearly in need of healing. I didn't know if he would live, so I didn't do anything—I didn't let anyone see me, not even Jack Conaway, so I could avoid answering questions. I didn't tell anyone Dane made it out alive. And I didn't visit you because Dr. Forrester did not believe Dane was going to survive. I had to wait it all out. . . ."

"Ari," Dane said. "Amano realized from the beginning the opportunity presented, if I pulled through. I could really go after the others if the media reported me dead."

So I'd been right.

Dane added, "I only recently started to make a recovery. I couldn't contact you because . . ." He gave a slight shake of his head. "It's complicated and fucked up. *I* was badly fucked up. Amano had to do all my work for me. He handed over all of the evidence I'd collected to the FBI. They started the investigations without me. I couldn't get any sort of word to you in my state. And because we weren't sure how this would go down. We had to keep you safe. And I needed to recover in order to finish my work."

I heard him swallow hard, telling me it was just as agonizing for him to suffer through his injuries as it'd been to not be able to contact me. Hell, for all I knew, he had no idea where to find me. If Amano hadn't alerted Mr. Conaway until recently that they were alive, then chances were good Amano had no idea where I'd disappeared to after leaving the creek house. No way would he have been able to covertly track me down in Sedona . . . until Kyle and I had come here for the list of society members.

It must have been Amano's vehicle I'd spotted in the woods, since the timing seemed about right.

"I take full responsibility, Ari," Amano said. "And I'm terribly sorry you had to believe Dane was dead. But the FBI latched on to that particular angle from the onset, and I couldn't do anything but follow their lead. For all our sakes. I hope that maybe, someday, you can understand that. Forgive me."

"This is so jacked," Kyle hissed angrily.

"Yes," Amano admitted. "I'm to blame. I chose this direction for Dane. He was in a coma and I took action. This is on me. But . . . it's working."

"I know," I gasped. "I've watched the news." My face was still pressed to the side of Dane's neck, so my voice was muffled. I breathed him in, having missed his heated scent so much.

Amano further explained, "Dane collected a hell of a lot of evidence before the explosion."

"On your laptop?" I asked my husband. "It's missing from your office."

"I came for it," Amano told us. "Not long ago. A day or two after Dane came out of the coma. Ari—"

"No, Amano," I said, still unable to relinquish my hold on Dane. "I know you'd never intentionally hurt me. The society hit us hard—you saw the opportunity to hit back. I already reconciled that in my mind, when the indictments started. You both have an important job to do. I get that."

Nor could I blame anyone but myself for the disaster that had become my life. I'd committed to being involved in this danger when I'd married Dane. Even before that. I had to be strong, so that he could do what was necessary without having to worry incessantly about me.

I also needed to tell him I was pregnant. But if I did . . . Wouldn't that just give him one more thing to obsess over?

Would it make him stand down from what he was trying to accomplish if he feared not just for my safety but also for our child's?

I didn't have any answers, so I opted to remain silent, even quieting the sobs. Though my tears still flowed.

I had to be strategic, the way Dane was—for all our sakes.

"I understand what you're doing," I told him. "It has to be done. I support this, Dane. I just . . . I want you to be okay."

"Don't think about me," he said. "I want you to be careful and stay at the retreat."

"Mr. Conaway told you?" I asked.

"You went to his office not long after Amano had, to tell him we were alive. So it all fell into place."

Dane finally released me and Kyle swooped in with some tissues from the box on a shelf. I wiped my wet cheeks and blew my nose. I could probably cry a few hours more, but it'd be a waste of time when I didn't have much of it to spend with Dane.

He said to Kyle, "Thanks for looking after her."

My friend huffed a bit, then flapped his arms agitatedly in the air before they hit the sides of his thighs. "What else was I going to do? She thought she'd lost everything."

"Not everything," I corrected. Though, sure, at first that had been my thinking. "I still have a best friend." I gave him a smile, then stared up at Dane. "I did lose my wedding bracelet. During the explosion. I don't know where. I've offered a reward, but so far . . . Nothing."

His fingers swept over my cheek and his emerald irises glowed warmly. "I'll buy you another one. It's okay."

"Is it?" I found myself asking as more tears crested the rims of my eyes.

"Ari." He pulled me to him again. I squeezed him a bit tighter than before. He winced. Apparently, I hadn't noticed his discomfort the first time around, when I'd thrown myself at him.

I jerked away and got a good look at him.

"Jesus, Dane."

There were enough glittery rays filtering into the room for me to see the scar over his right eyebrow. I reached for the line of buttons on his shirt and slowly undid them, my fingers trembling. As the material fell open, I gasped.

He had more scars. Angry, long ones that ran over his right pec and across the left side of his rib cage. Nasty slashes I wasn't sure were from glass or surgery.

"There are a few more on my back," he confided. "You'll have to get used to them."

I covered my mouth with my hand as the corners of my lips quivered and a sobfest threatened again.

"I'll be all right," he tried to assure me.

My gaze dropped, falling on the sleek black cane resting against a table. I hadn't seen it with my previous tunnel vision.

"Are you having trouble walking?" I asked, my voice full of agony—for him.

"Wrought iron from the terrace caught me in the leg. Lodged in my hamstring." He said it nonchalantly. My gaze snapped up to meet his. With his set jaw and an intense look on his face, he was anything but nonchalant.

"He's lucky to be walking," Amano set the record straight. "Hell, he's lucky to be alive." I heard the pain in his tone.

Turning to my bodyguard, I told him, "You saved his life. I can't thank you enough."

"This is a very . . . *tenuous* . . . time. I know you understand that—"

"I do," I assured Amano, Dane, all of us. "That's why I'm doing everything I can. Why I'll do whatever you ask."

"This all has to remain a secret, baby," Dane said. "I know it's hard, not fair, but—"

"It's okay," I hastily offered. "I get it. I'll play my part. Just . . . don't totally disappear again. I have to see you." I gripped Dane's arm. "I can't *not* be with you . . . for so long." I turned weepy again. I couldn't help it.

He gathered me close. "We'll figure it out, sweetheart."

I believed him. Put my trust in him, as always.

Amano said, "I'll come by in the morning and pick you up Ari."

I slid a glance over my shoulder at Kyle.

His teeth clenched for a moment. He pinned me with a hard look. "You're just getting sucked in deeper and deeper."

I knew that already. But I wouldn't walk away from this. I *couldn't* walk away. Dane was alive. He was here. With me.

"Thank you for driving me," I told Kyle. Knowing I was hurting him further. But I'd been honest from day one. Dane was my lifeblood.

"I'm just saying," Kyle continued, unable to drop the issue. His gaze shifted to Dane. "This is the second time she's been torn apart because of you."

"I'm aware of that," Dane said. I felt his muscles tense. "And I'm not happy about it, Kyle. But I do appreciate that you're such a good friend to Ari. That you've helped her through."

"I told you I'd be there the next time things got bad. *I* won't let her down."

"Kyle," I pleaded. "Now's not really the time for this. We'll talk tomorrow."

"Yeah," he said with a confident tone and the hitch of his chin. "Because I'll still be around." Then he stalked off.

Amano followed him out.

I slumped against Dane, my heart sinking when it came to Kyle. Yet conversely soaring because I was in Dane's arms again. "This doesn't get any easier."

"I'm so sorry." He kissed the top of my head.

"I don't blame you. I understand what you have to do, what you've been trying to do even before we got involved with each other."

"Yes, but . . . Now you've married into the problem. Because I couldn't go another day without you being my wife."

"I could have said I wanted to wait and you wouldn't have pushed me. But the truth is, I wanted this as much as you did."

"Except that now you're suffering the repercussions."

I did not miss the agony or the anguish in his tone.

"I'm not suffering at the moment." I gingerly held him, my arms around his midsection, feeling a thin line of raised skin beneath my fingertips at his back. Another scar.

"What happened?" I asked.

"Broken ribs. Dislocated shoulder. A lot of glass. A large chunk of stone or marble hit me in the head. That's what knocked me out for so long."

I shuddered. "This is so evil, Dane. The lengths they'll go. People were hurt—they could have died. And to blow up 10,000 Lux . . . My God."

He let out a long breath, laced with pain. Emotional as much as physical, I suspected. "I had no idea they'd go to this extreme. If they couldn't own a piece of the Lux, there'd be no Lux at all."

Glancing up at him, I said, "They have to know by now that you're alive. Right?"

"The FBI is handling it appropriately. Going after them with my evidence, but as far as anyone is concerned, it's information they collected on their own."

"But won't you have to testify?"

"Baby, don't worry about that right now." His fingers tenderly grazed my cheek. "The agents have a shitload of documentation I collected, from a number of sources. The tax evasion issues are substantial enough, but the criminal corruption and murder attempts are the key to bringing these assholes down. They'll be locked up for some time, I assure you. Conspiring to bomb the Lux . . . Fuck. It was bold: *Too* bold. And they'll pay for the revenge they sought."

More of the wicked game in which even I had become a player. A pawn, yes. But still a part of the game.

"I'll fix this," he whispered against my hair. "I'll make it so that you're safe, so that you're not scared."

"I just want to be with you, Dane."

He groaned. "I want that, too. Never doubt that."

He held me close to him again, though I was sure it hurt him to do so, with all the injuries obviously still requiring full recovery. In a perfect world—a world other than the sinister one in which we lived because of his secret society—I would take him back to the retreat. Let Dr. Stevens and her team rehabilitate Dane.

I'd experienced myself their healing powers, both medical and herbal. Spiritual. Even Hannah, whom I'd initially caught crying on occasion when she thought no one was around, had a healthier outlook on her physical therapy and had graduated to a walker, her gait slowly evening out.

I was convinced the rehab specialists could help Dane, too. But that wasn't a possibility at the moment. We couldn't risk him un-wittingly inviting trouble at the retreat, and clearly he still had more work to do with the FBI.

"It'd probably be better if we weren't standing," I mentioned.

"I'm fine."

"You don't have to be macho for me."

He grinned. It brought tears to my eyes. I'd missed seeing the quirk of his mouth, that sexy smile that I loved.

"You can't imagine the hell I've been in, not being with you," he told me.

"Yes," I said, staring up at him. "I can."

A heartbeat later, he swept me into his arms.

chapter 13

"Dane," I instantly protested. "Put me down."

"Ari." His beautiful emerald eyes bored into mine. "Let me be your husband."

Emotion choked me up. I stroked my fingers over his set jaw. "You'll always be my husband. No matter what. Just you—always and forever you. Whether you're here or not. Whether you can pick me up or not. You don't have anything to prove to me."

"Sure I do." He carried me out of the room and down the hallway, with a hint of a limp that I thought he fought to hide.

I understood his feelings, his need to be strong and virile in my presence, the way he'd been before the explosion. Triple Crown Thoroughbreds were put out to pasture for lameness—Dane clearly refused to be one of them. I'd experienced this with Hannah as well. She wouldn't date and shied away from social interactions because of her uneven walk and the havoc it wreaked on her psyche.

Dane wasn't one to shy away from anything. He'd power through just to demonstrate his confidence hadn't taken a hit, to show that he was as capable as ever.

While I could comprehend and deeply empathize with Hannah's hesitancy, I admired Dane's resiliency.

Still, I muttered in his ear, "Don't overdo it, Tarzan."

"Do you know how desperately I've wanted to be with you? But Amano's plan yielded results. At one point, I did yank out the IV, unhooked my leg from its holster, and tried to get out of bed. Landed flat on my face."

My chest pulled tight, my heart constricting. "I wish I could have been there to help you."

"So you know how I feel. A hundred times over. A million. I can't stand that I wasn't there with you, Ari. That I wasn't by your side."

I kissed his cheek and said, "Amano did the right thing. Even if he'd told me you were alive and I came to see you because you couldn't get to me, I could have easily been followed. We could have put the entire mission in jeopardy. So . . . All I can do is thank God that Amano was able to get you immediate help." I was beyond relieved, so very grateful. "And I'm just so happy to be here with you now. I love you so much."

He carefully set me on my feet just inside our bedroom. His hands cupped my face and he stared deep into my eyes. "I'm doing all of this to free us, Ari. But I know how painful it is for you. It's killing me, too." He brushed away my tears and softly kissed my lips. "It'll be over soon. I promise."

He stepped away, raking a hand through his hair. His shoulders bunched.

"Dane?"

With his back to me, he glanced around his shoulder and said, "I've made a lot of promises to you, haven't I? And I'm not keeping them."

Now my heart wrenched. His pain lanced through me. "We're not living under normal circumstances, Dane."

I closed the gap between us and wound my arms around him from behind. I'd missed the feel of his hot flesh and hard muscles beneath my fingers, against my palms.

His hands covered mine for endless moments. Then he unraveled my arms and turned to me. His head dipped and his lips glided over mine. My eyelids fluttered closed and I absorbed all the tingles skating along my flushed skin. A sigh fell from my slightly parted mouth. The bliss I'd lost when I'd heard Dane hadn't made it out of the Lux slowly returned to me.

He had made it out. And he was here. With me. No matter how temporarily.

He's alive. He's here.

I focused on that.

I carefully eased his shirt over his broad shoulders and down his arms, letting it drop to the floor. My fingertips skimmed along his strong forearms, up to his bulging biceps. Across his collarbone and down to his defined pectoral ledge. All the while, I gazed up at him. His eyes blazed with desire; his jaw worked rigorously.

I leaned toward him and gently kissed the scar on his chest. His fingers threaded through my hair.

"Ari." Need tinged his low, sensual tone. It had been months since we'd been together, and my own need mirrored his. The raging of my pulse and the pounding of my heart made my breath quicken with anticipation.

I whisked off my long tight gray sweater and tossed it aside. As much as Dane making love to me slowly and sexily held huge appeal, there was no way I could survive the *slow*.

"I want you," I told him as I ripped apart the button fly of my Levi's. "Fuck me."

He let out a primal growl.

"Don't be polite or apologetic about it," I added.

His gaze held mine as he deftly worked the fastenings of his belt and pants. He toed off his boots and shoved his clothes down, sweeping everything from his long, powerful legs so that he was gloriously naked.

My pulse stammered. "Oh . . ." I breathed heavily. "God."

I hadn't forgotten how magnificent he was—of course not. Yet the reality of him standing before me, so perfect even with scars, made the blood pump heartily through my veins.

He reached for me, pulling me closer. He knelt and divested me of my jeans, shoes, and socks. His fingers grazed over my bare calves, along the backs of my knees, and up my thighs, igniting fiery sensations.

His head bent and his tongue flickered tantalizingly along my pussy lips, the lace of my thong adding a hint of friction.

"Dane." I trembled.

He stood, not quite as fluidly as normal, I noted. Taking my hand, he guided me to the bed. He pulled back the covers. I sat on the mattress, then scooted farther back to lie down, sprawled at an angle. Never breaking the eye contact.

A riot of emotions competed with exhilaration. I desperately wanted to feel him inside me, but the thought of him touching and tasting every inch of exposed skin was equally enticing.

His fingers hooked in the sides of my thong and he peeled off the material. Then he reached around to my back as my spine bowed and he released the clasp on my bra. He flung it over his shoulder, the lingerie likely landing on the heap of clothes we'd built.

His eyelids closed as he kissed my jaw, my throat, my chest. Lower still to my aching breasts, kissing the inner swells. He palmed the heavy and ultra-sensitive mounds. I'd gone much too long without his hands on me, making my body respond quickly and vehemently. My nipples puckered tighter than ever before, and the ache intensified.

"Dane," I said again. My fingers plowed through his thick hair. "Suck my nipples." I needed it like nothing I'd ever known. Urgently. Frantically.

His tongue fluttered over one taut peak before his mouth closed around the bud. I let out a sharp cry of relief and pleasure. Then everything turned frenetic as I gripped his biceps and rubbed against him.

"I need you inside me. *Right now.*"

I felt his thick shaft along my dewy folds, sliding easily. His tip pressed to my opening and I raised my hips.

"I love how wet you get for me," he said in a low groan.

"Now," I repeated.

He thrust deep, and I cried out again. The sensation of him filling me, stretching me, was intense and spectacular.

"Oh, God. Dane."

"Yeah." He slipped a hand along my thigh and slung it over his hips. He drove deeper, in long, full strokes.

Throaty moans escaped my lips as I watched him fuck me, his movements strong and skilled, quick and exciting.

His tongue teased my nipple before he suckled again, with just the right amount of pressure to send wicked shock waves through me.

"Just like that," I murmured. "God, Dane. I'm going to come." So fast. And hard.

His pelvis gyrated and mine met his insistent thrusts, equally greedy.

"Christ, I need you so much," he said against my breast. His hand cupped my ass cheek and he lifted my hips, angling them as he pumped into me.

I clung to him, drowning in the heat coursing through me, the love and lust I had for him. My fingertips pressed against his rippled muscles. I kissed his neck, nipped softly.

He bucked with more force and all I could feel was the erotic thrill of him pushing me to the edge.

"Yes. Oh, God, yes." I couldn't hold on a second longer. I came on a flood of emotion and sizzling undercurrents as I cried his name.

"Ari!" He came with me, his hot seed flowing, his cock pulsing. I clutched at him and tremors continued to run through us both.

I wrapped my arms around him and held him tight. His breath was harsh against my throat as his face burrowed in my hair. Tears pooled in my eyes once more, but I fought the pain of the past couple of months and instead embraced the feeling of him inside me, alive and throbbing. Radiant and still hard.

This was real and beautiful.

Dane was mine. Despite the odds we'd faced from the beginning—still faced.

He was mine.

The sun streaming through the window woke me in the morning. Dane was wrapped around me, spooning me, holding me tight to his hard body.

He'd made love to me twice more during the night, and as I stirred against him, he murmured, "I want you again." Proving his virility and stamina were fully intact.

Of course I couldn't deny him.

After we'd showered, Amano came for me. The prospect of leaving Dane was unbelievably painful. I dragged my feet but knew he had important work to get back to.

"When will I see you?" I asked as I lingered in his strong embrace.

"I can't say. Hopefully soon. Amano will call."

I wasn't a fan of this clandestine stuff, but I'd take what I could get. "Please be careful. Safe. Like, really, *really* safe."

The corner of his mouth lifted in a sexy grin. "I will. But I ask the same of you."

"I have Kyle, remember? He's not inclined to let me get away with much."

Dane sighed. "I don't like leaving you with him. He gets too many ideas in his head—I can see it in his eyes and on his face."

"I'll admit he's not too happy you're alive. Nothing personal, but—"

"I'm sure he latched on to the opportunity presented with my supposed demise," he commented dryly.

"Still just a friend," I said to placate him. "*Always* just a friend." My lips pressed to his. "I am very, very, deliriously, happily married."

He grunted. "Not exactly what you'd expected. Or deserve."

"As long as I have you, that's all that matters," I was quick to say. To reassure him.

Dane kissed me passionately. I melted against him, instantly ready for him to take me back to our bed and make love to me once more.

But Amano awaited me in the SUV. So Dane unraveled from me and eased me away, as though needing to break free of the temptation before he succumbed and never let me go.

I wouldn't have minded.

"I'll try to be back soon," he said. His fingers swept over my cheek. "It's so hard to stay away." His head dipped and he kissed me once more.

This time, I was the one to employ a little restraint. I broke the kiss and said, "If I don't leave now . . ." I never would.

He nodded.

I turned to go.

"Ari."

I glanced over my shoulder. "I know," I said with a soft smile. "You love me."

"So much." And all that love and desire glowed in his beautiful emerald eyes.

With a nod, I told him, "I trust you, Dane. I believe in what you're doing. And I love you, too. So much."

It was hell to leave him. More excruciating than I'd let on. But I joined Amano in the garage. He opened the passenger door for me and I slipped into the seat, latching the belt.

We drove a ways in silence. I wasn't surprised. That was his nature.

Yet eventually he spoke. "I owe you a very personal apology that's just between the two of us. What I did—"

"No," I told him, twisting a bit so I could face him. "You don't owe me an apology, Amano. You've been with Dane his entire life. You know his secrets and you know how to protect them—how to protect *him*. I'm grateful for that."

His broad shoulders bunched. Those same shoulders that had borne the brunt of familial and professional obligation—and which had saved Dane's life.

I reached over and rested a hand on his biceps, covered in his usual impeccable business suit. "You've done so much, Amano, for a really good cause. I would have been selfish and demanded he stay with me, rather than risk his life further."

The bodyguard's gaze slid to me. "Maybe not." His eyes returned to the road.

I considered this. I hadn't exactly pitched a fit when I'd walked away a few minutes ago. I knew what Dane had to do and I knew why he had to do it.

How it impacted me—or even our child—was part of the sacrifice he had to make in order to curb the corruption, keep another economic downfall from profiting the extremely wealthy and hurting everyone else.

In a sense, Dane had given up 10,000 Lux—his ultimate dream—for justice. How could I not be proud of that and supportive of him? Even if it broke my heart to not be with him.

I said, "You had a chance to walk away after his parents died. Why didn't you?"

"I had a responsibility to the entire family."

Exactly as I'd expected. The familial tie. "Lara included."

He flashed a dour look.

"Yes," I conceded. "Dane told me."

Amano was quiet a few minutes. Then he said, "I stayed on as head of estate security because of Dane. I didn't feel comfortable leaving a newborn who'd just inherited billions of dollars high and dry. Anything could have happened to him."

"Did things almost happen to him? Things you thwarted?"

He didn't jump on my question, clearly not liking the line of questioning. But then he told me, "There were plenty of threats, from the beginning. I felt it was my duty to protect Dane and his aunt."

I already had immense respect for the man and eternal appreciation for how he'd taken my safety to heart, for Dane's sake. But I also admired that he saw the big picture. What could happen, what needed to be done, how to achieve the most important goals.

"You're really very amazing," I said, emotion tingeing my voice.

Again, he didn't speak for a spell. I didn't push.

Finally, he said, "I wasn't happy about what happened with you and Vale."

"You couldn't have prevented that, Amano. You needed to be with Dane, and I had Kyle. It's not his fault, either," I hastily added. "No one's to blame. Vale found the perfect ploy, the perfect . . . lure. My love for Dane."

I gave a half snort. Amano shot me a look.

"So maybe *I'm* to blame because I can't resist him."

"Ari, that F5 was the spitting image of Dane's—and there are only thirty in the whole damn world. Those are not circumstances under which you chastise yourself."

"Yet *you* still hold yourself accountable," I challenged. "Even though you weren't even on-property, because Dane needed you elsewhere."

"I *should* have been on-property. I should have been wherever you were."

"Amano, you have to pick your battles here. Dane's the priority."

"That is *not* how he sees it."

"But you know better."

Our gazes held for a second or two before he focused on the road. We headed down the red-dirt path to the rehab retreat. When he pulled up to the entrance, he cut the engine, left the vehicle, and came around my side to open the door.

He said, "I understand what Dane has to do. But neither he nor I are the least bit comfortable leaving you on your own—even with Kyle. Even here with all this security."

So, he'd staked the place out. Mr. Conaway must have given away my location, because I suddenly realized that I hadn't provided Amano directions.

He added, "It's not easy determining who we can trust with your safety. But we're working on it."

I frowned, taken aback. "What does *that* mean?"

"Just stay put for now. Don't venture out unless I specifically call you. Can you do that?"

It would be more difficult knowing Dane was out there somewhere and I wasn't with him. But I said, "We stream Netflix here. My queue is about a hundred selections deep. I'm good."

I didn't mention the need to continue my holistic healing to keep the morning sickness at bay and the fact that my body had never felt stronger or more balanced, because of Gretchen's excellent pre-natal yoga lessons. The retreat, in general, was a lifesaver.

He walked me to the gate, then waited until I'd entered the house to leave.

Kyle was finishing breakfast with his aunt when I came in. He grabbed his landscaping book and headed out back with nothing more than a slight nod in my direction.

I gave a heavy sigh and slid into the chair he'd vacated.

"Problem?" Dr. Stevens asked, her tone light, nonassuming.

"What'd he say?"

"Nothing," she told me. Her eyes glowed with earnestness. "And you don't have to tell me, either."

"I just needed to take care of some things," I said of my overnight absence. Added a dismissive wave of my hand for good measure.

"You don't have to explain or justify, Ari. You can come and go as you please. But how are you feeling?"

"Better. *Much* better. Famished, actually." It suddenly dawned on me. I hadn't eaten at the house, mostly because I feared it coming up on me while I was with Dane. How would I have accounted for that without revealing my pregnant state?

"You're in luck. Oatmeal and breakfast potatoes are part of the buffet. I know they settle a little easier in your stomach than most other foods."

"Perfectly strange combination though they are." I loaded up a plate and returned to the table where she sat.

"Another month and you'll be able to discern the gender of the baby. If you so choose."

I smiled. "I keep thinking about that. Do I want to know, or do I want to be surprised?"

"Depends on if you prefer to plan in advance—nursery colors, clothing, and the like."

"Which is what's so bizarre, because I'm one-hundred percent a planner. And yet . . ." I shrugged noncommittally. I'd been fairly certain I needed all the facts up front when it came to having a baby. I'd devoured every parenting book I could get my hands on and had endlessly quizzed the doctors and moms I came in contact with, using every resource at my disposal.

Still, there was something intriguing about the unknown.

If I were to dig a little deeper, I had a feeling I'd discover that was one of the many things that made me so addicted to Dane and the life we led. I never knew what tomorrow would bring—I never knew what the next ten minutes would bring. And that was exciting, challenging, empowering, motivating . . . Scary, too, but only in the sense that I had to remember I couldn't control everything, not even my own reactions or emotions. He'd proven that to me long ago and it was a lesson that repeated itself.

I couldn't say it all worked out smashingly for me now that I'd confirmed he was alive. Everything about us remained derailed. But our current predicament did leave me with that sense of optimism weddings always inspired. There was a chance things would fall into place for us. The potential existed and that was what excited me the most. What I held fast to.

Naturally, the possibility of it all falling horrifically apart again still lingered in a threatening, ominous way. I did my best to avoid that reality.

In fact, I instantly decided that I'd wait to find out whether we were having a boy or a girl. I wouldn't prepare without Dane, and I'd be surprised about the sex of our child right along with him. Because even though he didn't yet know I was pregnant, we were in this together.

For better or for worse . . .

chapter 14

Worse seemed to be the name of the game for us, for the time being. As February rolled into March, I waited anxiously for Amano to call. A week into the beginning of our spring season, Dane and I had a secret rendezvous at the house for a few brief hours. Two weeks later, we had even less time together.

I tried not to be greedy, tried to accept whatever precious moments I could steal with him.

In the meantime, I helped more around the retreat, working in the kitchen in addition to assisting with the landscaping so Kyle could concentrate on some maintenance issues that had cropped up. I'd also caught him on numerous occasions quizzing the security staff on *what if* scenarios he'd concocted. He was definitely into being prepared, though the security guys clearly had no idea what he wanted to be prepared for—I did, of course.

Macy, as she'd insisted I call her, had cut my invoicing substantially with all the work I'd been doing. I told her it wasn't necessary, that I chose to be involved, needing to stay active and occupied.

Though I still encountered dehydration symptoms periodically, which she vigilantly monitored because severe cases could be life threatening, I finally felt a bit more stable, much less round-the-clock nauseous.

We weren't quite sure why I had trouble, since I drank plenty of fluids during the day, so I succumbed to Macy's tests and combated the headaches with some of her natural remedies.

In late March, Amano texted me to meet at the house and I breathed a very loud sigh of relief. From my last discussion with Dane, he felt confident justice was about to prevail when it came to the last two corrupt members. I expected good news and an idea of when he thought this might all be over.

I quickly dressed in jeans and a lightweight pale-pink sweater. Kyle drove us to the house and punched in the gate code. We pulled up to the garage, while I attempted to contain my excitement over seeing Dane—and the anticipation of a positive progress report.

I felt things were looking up. Could literally feel the winds of change in the air.

So much so, I squirmed anxiously in the seat next to Kyle. Who cut into my happy thoughts.

"Hey," he said. "The garage door's not up."

I followed his gaze to the end stall, which Amano always opened for Kyle to drive his Rubicon into so it didn't sit outside for anyone to notice.

"Maybe Amano didn't come this time." I hopped out and entered the garage. I hit the button for the appropriate door and Kyle eased in. At the same time, I surveyed the stalls. Motorcycle, McLaren, no Escalade. No Amano SUV.

Had he just dropped Dane off? Did he have other business to attend to and he'd pick me up later? Or did he need Kyle to collect me?

I frowned. I wasn't sure if I should tell Kyle I'd need a return ride this time—and I was reticent to do it. He was always a bit on-edge when I got back to the retreat after being with Dane.

We started toward the house, but nothing about this situation sat right with me. My gut clenched.

I drew up short and turned to Kyle. "Amano texted. He usually calls."

"So?"

Was I being paranoid?

"So . . . nothing, I guess." But I didn't continue toward the patio.

"What is it?" he asked, suddenly catching on to my consternation.

"I don't know. Why isn't Amano here? And don't you think if all he planned to do was drop off Dane he'd still open the garage door, as he's done every other time? I mean, it's almost like a signal when he does that."

"Which would make this a—"

"Trap?"

Kyle shook his head. "Not on Amano's watch."

"Yeah. One guy trying to do everything he can to keep a hell of a lot of people safe." I just didn't feel right about this. "Let's backtrack. Play it cool."

I didn't have to suggest it twice.

"Oh-kay," Kyle said. "If you're going to pass over a hookup with the hubby, I'm going to freak out just a little bit."

He followed me to the garage. But as he made his way toward the Jeep, I told him, "That's not the vehicle we want." I grabbed the keys to the McLaren and tossed them his way. "We might need this car."

"Oh, hell yes." His eyes nearly popped from the sockets.

"Just going on instinct here. I could be wrong."

"Let's hope you're wrong. Still, it wouldn't suck to squeal the tires on this baby. That'll piss Dane off."

"Try not to get too much pleasure out of this. We could be in serious trouble."

"Not with me behind the wheel." Kyle grinned confidently.

I settled into the passenger seat and hit the remote for the stall door. Then I pulled out my cell and called Amano, the only number that ever came through to me. He didn't answer. As Kyle barreled through the gap in the gate at the entrance of the drive, I studied the numbers from the few calls I'd received and compared them. All the same.

What the fuck?

Why did I feel so off about this?

Our jaunt along the dirt road was a rugged, jarring one, but I barely noticed because we'd picked up a tail. I gazed into the side mirror first, checking out the silver Chevy Camaro that moved in behind us.

"Now would be a good time to speed it up," I told Kyle.

"On this road?"

"Yep."

He threw a glance my way as I twisted in the seat and peered through the back window. My nerves prickled.

"Well," Kyle said, "the good news is that this is not *my* million-and-some-dollar car."

We wound our way through the forest toward 89A. As we approached the main road, I tersely said, "We don't want to stop. Not with whoever that is following so close behind us."

"There's a bit of traffic, if you haven't noticed."

"And we can't go back to the retreat. We'll lead them right there." We reached the split in the road. "Hard left. *Now!*"

Kyle punched it and my heart leapt into my throat as the McLaren shot through a small hole of traffic that caused the slamming of brakes and a lot of blaring horns.

"Oh, Jesus," I squeaked out as the sports car fishtailed and Kyle worked to get the vehicle under control. "Not good."

Shifting in the seat again, I watched as the Chevy pulled almost the same move, three cars behind us. "This is going to get ugly."

Kyle passed two trucks ahead of us, but he couldn't shake the Camaro. We started up the switchbacks, a long, winding road cut into the craggy mountain and rising over four-thousand feet to the Mogollon Rim. At most points, there was no more than a sliver of a shoulder to our right—my side of the car—then the steep plunge into the oak- and evergreen-pine-covered canyon.

The speed limit was thirty-five. Kyle pushed fifty as he wove through the light traffic.

In a strained tone, I reminded him, "This is hardly the road for passing." Hence the No Passing Zone signs and the double yellow line.

"We need some distance from this asshole," he ground out.

Our first hairpin turn came at us—or we came at it—a bit too fast.

"For God's sake!" I cried. "Slow down!"

The McLaren handled the sharp navigation beautifully. Kyle, however, didn't have complete control again as we barreled down on a Toyota Prius barely creeping along as the driver likely took in the sights.

"Fuck," Kyle grumbled, then dropped the hammer and swerved sharply into the other lane.

"You see that truck ahead of us, right?" I shouted, my eyes wide.

He had to pass two vehicles to clear ours if we were going to get back into the correct lane.

My pulse raged in my ears. I raised my forearms in front of my face, unable to watch, knowing we were about to be the bug on the four-by-four's windshield.

Kyle cut back onto our side of the road and I felt the car shudder from the force of wind the truck created as it whizzed by us, horn wailing. I'm sure we were flipped a few fingers from all parties concerned.

I lowered my arms. Tried to breathe.

Kyle continued taking on the traffic and the treacherous turns as though we were stuntmen on a movie set where all the action was perfectly choreographed and timed.

But we weren't on a movie set. And every narrow escape left

me wholly regretting having suggested we take this route, not to mention fearing for our lives.

"This next turn is really sharp," I warned him. "You've got to slow down a little."

He didn't. We squealed our way around it, the ass end of the car shimmying.

"Kyle, you can roll us!"

"This car is built for these corners," he said between clenched teeth as he concentrated on driving.

"Maybe, but last time I checked, NASCAR wasn't beating down your door for the Daytona 500."

"Their loss." He shot out and around another small group of cars.

"Kyle, no!"

He couldn't make it this time. He veered off to the shoulder of the ongoing traffic. I screamed. The McLaren bounced along the rough edge. The shoulder that had flared briefly now started to narrow.

"You have to get back on the road."

"No shit."

"Kyle, we're losing the shoulder!" And headed straight toward the side of the mountain about to jut out in front of us.

The last car coming our way flew by, more honking ensued, and Kyle jerked the car back onto the road and crossed over to our lane, ahead of the vehicles he'd wanted to pass.

My head whipped around as I tried to gauge how much distance we'd put between us and the Camaro. That driver had made his own daring passes but lagged several cars behind.

I would have breathed a sigh of relief, had I not caught sight of a black object in the sky. I squinted my eyes.

Was that a—?

"Holy crap," I choked out. "There's a helicopter."

"Someone must have called the police."

The aircraft gained speed, flying toward us. Kyle crested the

canyon and blew past the scenic overlook. The curves were grad-
ual, not hairpins. Kyle shifted into fifth and hauled ass. We couldn't
shake the copter.

"That's not a police helicopter," I said. "Or a news crew. Solid
black, no logos. Looks pretty high-tech." My heart thundered. "Son
of a bitch! These guys have *helicopters*?"

Kyle took a few less risky passes on a straightaway, but I still
couldn't catch my breath.

"We have to ditch this car," he said.

"Impossible. Once we hit town, they'll catch up to us."

"We can jump onto I-17 instead of staying on the back road,"
Kyle offered. The interstate ran parallel to this neck of the woods.

I gave his idea some thought but then shook my head. "The
guys in the air will see the move. That totally puts us out in the
open."

"Well, I'd love to hear *your* suggestions," he barked.

I didn't have any. Except . . .

"Slow down," I demanded.

"Not a chance."

"Kyle, Fort Tuthill is up ahead. Take the turnoff on the left."
It was marked with tall signs screaming ARTS & MUSIC FESTIVAL.
Perfect.

There was another line of traffic coming our way. We didn't
have much time.

"I don't see how this is a good idea. We—"

"Just do it. Now!"

The razor-sharp veering of the car made the tires whine again.
We caught the outer edge of the turnoff onto the asphalt, sputtered
a bit, then Kyle corrected our overshooting the corner and put us
securely in one lane. Not ours, but we were the only ones on the
road, so I didn't mention the issue.

Heart still pounding, I said, "All these campgrounds . . . we have
to be able to hide the car somewhere. Sooner rather than later,
because at the end of this path is a wide-open clearing into the

fairgrounds and parking lot. We'll be screwed if we dead-end in plain sight."

To our current advantage, the tall, full ponderosas offered a bit of coverage and, were we to drive into the forest, we'd be beautifully concealed.

"That looks like a decent spot," Kyle murmured as he surveyed the south-end thicket. He peeled off and we bounced our way along underbrush and dirt, dodging fallen trees and crunching limbs beneath us. The scrapes of branches against the sides and roof of the car made me cringe. Not to mention the lava rocks we drove over. Dane would have a conniption when he learned we'd destroyed his expensive ride. Though for a good cause, so . . . I tried not to think about how I was going to break this to him.

"Here's a nice little cave." Kyle slid the McLaren to a stop, nestled in a collection of downed trunks and piled-up limbs, as though the Forest Service had started cleanup work for a seasonal controlled burn.

Kyle had to climb over the stick shift and follow me out on the passenger's side, since the protective shell was so slim, the car barely fit. We dragged a few more branches with layers of pine needles over the back of the Mercedes for added camouflage.

Then he took my hand and helped me through the rugged terrain as we made our way to the grounds.

We stuck to the boundary of the woods while assessing the situation. The helicopter hovered over the parking lot to the north. Ahead of us were the outbuildings for arts and crafts, vendor tents, and the grandstand with a stage. Music from a Country and Western band blared from the sound system.

"Now or never," Kyle said, because the helicopter started to move toward us, the guys inside obviously convinced we'd never made it to the parking lot.

We raced toward the picnic tables around the food court area. Kyle tossed the keys to the McLaren, with its flashy emblem on the ring, in a metal trash barrel. Then we disappeared under a vendor tent. He peered around one side of it before tugging my hand again and leading me to another tent, this one selling straw cowboy hats.

"Put your hair up," he said as he selected a hat for me and placed it on my head. He chose one for himself, then added aviator glasses, though the sun was setting.

He whipped out his credit card from his jeans pocket and then we hit another tent and slipped on Western shirts over the clothes we wore.

"Your evil dudes in the Camaro might stake this place out," he told me.

"*My* evil dudes?"

He slid his sunglasses down his nose and glared at me.

"Okay, right. My evil dudes."

This was all a little too edge-of-the-seat for me. I still couldn't catch a solid breath.

"So now what?" I asked.

"I don't know."

We left the vendors and walked cautiously to the grandstand. Couples two-stepped in front of the stage and kids danced in conglomerations. Others sat in the bleachers to watch and listen. Plenty of people milled about. We could get lost in this crowd, but how would we sneak out?

"Are we going to steal a car?" I asked. "Just so you know, I'm really not comfortable with that."

"Maybe we can bum a ride."

"Yeah, because we don't look shady at all, wearing sunglasses at night."

He groaned. "I don't fucking know, Ari. I'm not the one who's part of a goddamn secret society. I don't associate with stalkers and kidnappers and assholes with helicopters."

I winced at his under-the-breath outburst. "I know. I'm sorry. I'm sorry I got you into all of this."

He pulled his hat down lower on his brow and shook his head. "You didn't. I sort of volunteered, didn't I?"

"And you can un-volunteer at any time."

"Right," he scoffed. "Leave you to fend for yourself?"

I smiled, despite the tense moment. "You just can't resist being a hero, can you?"

"Well, someone's gotta be."

Since that fated day at Meg and Sean's wedding, when Dane had swooped in to save the day—for me and the groomsmen—Kyle had been trying to prove he was a good guy. And continually did a great job of it.

I squeezed his hand and said, "You're pretty awesome."

"Regretting marrying the Terminator?"

"I think of him more as the Bruce Wayne/Batman type."

"You would," Kyle said wryly.

"Anyway, that's currently neither here nor there. We have to find an escape that doesn't put anyone in jeopardy, so I don't think asking for a ride is an alternative."

"Then I guess we're stealing a car."

I sighed. "There has to be another way."

He glanced around our immediate surroundings. My gaze followed. He paused. I did as well.

"What?" I asked as we both stared at two officers clearly focused on crowd control.

Kyle put his hand at the small of my back and guided me away. "Just play along."

"Okay."

I had no clue what he was up to. We wound through the large groups gathered about, everyone laughing and drinking, having a great time. A part of me envied them, looking so carefree and . . . safe.

We strolled casually toward the food court, not drawing any real attention, thankfully. Then we passed through plastic white-picket gates and I halted abruptly.

"The beer garden?" I stared up at him, incredulous.

"Play along," he reminded in a quiet tone.

I huffed a little but followed him to the booth. We stood in line for a few minutes while I apprehensively glanced about. Not that I would know whom to search for—I had no idea who'd been in the Camaro. I kept my eye out anyway.

When we reached the front of the line, Kyle ordered two beers and paid for them. We stepped away and I said, "I can't drink this. I'm pregnant."

"You don't have to drink it. Spill some on your jeans. Your shoes."

I didn't know, but the plan did as requested.

"Slosh a little over the rim of the cup," he added, "onto your hand."

He did the same. Then he snaked an arm around my waist and pulled me close to him. I tensed, uncomfortable with the intimate contact.

"Relax," he whispered. "Act drunk."

I laughed emphatically. Gave a half snort, as though he'd muttered something hysterical.

"Good," he said. Then he started talking loudly about the music, the band, the dancing. Gesturing obnoxiously with the cup in his hand.

We made our way back to the grandstand and he literally plowed into a skyscraping broad-shouldered guy from behind, Kyle's beer splattering against the stranger's flannel shirt.

"Hey!" The mountain of a man whirled around and glared at us. I gulped.

"S'rry, dude," Kyle said. "Didn't see ya there. Which is, like, so weird, right? Because you're . . . *Damn*. Seriously tall." He craned his neck. "They call you Treetop or something?"

My gaze widened.

"What kind of prick are you?" the lumberjack demanded.

"One who works out every day." Kyle relinquished his hold on me and lifted his arm, flexing his biceps. "You, however, look like you could use some extra weight on your dumbbells."

Oh, fuck.

Dark eyes narrowed on Kyle. "You are one serious asshole, man."

Kyle staggered a bit—and spilled more beer on the guy. "Sorry," he grumbled. "It's just that . . . you take up a lot of space."

"And you need to shut the hell up."

"Wanna make me?" Kyle challenged as he swayed a bit.

"You need to learn some manners, buddy." The big lug took a swing and it connected. Kyle hit the ground. I screamed and dropped my beer.

"Son of a bitch!" I yelled, then sank to my knees to check on Kyle, who bled from a split lip. Crimson dotted the front of his new shirt.

"Maybe I should have picked a smaller dude," he mumbled.

His eyes rolled in the sockets. He likely saw stars. And birds.

"Jesus, Kyle." My stomach clenched.

"Hey, what's going on over here?" A new voice.

I glanced up to find the two officers closing in on us.

Time to play *my* part.

One of them reached for the assailant, but I clumsily got to my feet, stumbled as though tipsy, and declared, "Isnot 'is fault." I waved a finger toward Kyle. "'Is drunk. I mean . . . *heeee's* drunk." I cleared my throat. "He's drunk." I forced the enunciation as though it were challenging.

"Great," the second cop mumbled. "So are you."

"Is not." I shook my head. "Am not," I corrected.

"Come on," cop number one said as he helped Kyle up.

"Whoa," I called out, pressing a palm to the officer's chest.

Cop number two warned, "Don't touch him."

I kept my hand where it was. "He has to drive me home. I have someplace to be."

"*He's* not driving anywhere," I was informed.

Turning to Kyle, I said, "Then gimme the keys."

"Yeah, right. Let you behind the wheel of my pickup? Shit, not a chance."

Cop number two took my arm and said, "Let's go."

They led us to the emergency/security building and cleaned Kyle up while attempting to administer a field sobriety test on me. I knew now the trick was to get them to haul us off to jail. That would involve them putting us in the back of the police car and escorting us out without the Camaro driver or the helicopter backup knowing we'd even left the grounds.

I'd already failed the walk-in-a-straight-line test. Told the officer I'd fall over if I closed my eyes and tried to touch my nose—on account of having a problem with equilibrium. Which I pronounced incorrectly.

Finally, he instructed, "Say the alphabet for me. Backwards."

I laughed and wagged another finger at him. "I always wondered about that one. Most *sober* people can't even recite the alphabet backwards."

He groaned. "There's always the Breathalyzer."

"Which I can refuse." I defiantly crossed my arms over my chest. I might land in jail for some time, but it was safer than what awaited us if we tried to leave here on our own.

"You're right," the officer said. "We can do this the old-fashioned way. I can arrest you, take you to the station, book you for drunk and disorderly conduct, and get your alcohol level from a blood test."

"Sounds like a plan."

And that's precisely what happened.

"Watch your heads," cop number one directed as Kyle and I were helped into the back of the cruiser, our hands cuffed behind us.

As the officers climbed into the front, I shot my friend a look. He grinned, then grimaced. His lip and one side of his jaw were swollen, for which I felt horrible. But we'd gotten what we wanted. Safe passage into Flagstaff, where we could figure out what the hell to do from there. . . .

chapter 15

Yeah. Jail.

So not the place for me.

I was in with a couple of other rowdies from the music festival, a prostitute and a woman who claimed to be a meth addict and kept screaming that if she didn't get some crystal in her soon she wouldn't be responsible for her actions. Needless to say, I didn't dare close my eyes.

In the morning, cop number one came for me and put me in a room with Kyle. We sat opposite the officer, who pushed a file across the table and demanded, "Care to explain this?"

I stared down at a legal-looking document with "Negative" stamped across the top portion. "Neither of you were drunk last night. Not a trace of alcohol in your systems."

Kyle and I exchanged hopeless looks. We really hadn't thought this through. *Now what?*

Time to make it up as we went along. "See . . . it's just that we're, um, you know . . . Uh." I wracked my brain. Then blurted, "We're twelve-steppers!"

He gave me a blank stare. "You're *what?*"

"You know, like AA," Kyle joined in.

"Right," I said enthusiastically, so glad we always ended up on the same mental track. "We were with our friends last night, and they just can't handle that we don't drink with them anymore and it makes it kind of awkward, you know? We pretended we were drunk so they wouldn't think we were . . . well . . . lame."

Oh, but we were. I resisted the urge to roll my eyes—at myself.

"Uh-huh," the cop slowly said. "Twelve-steppers."

"I deserved to be arrested for picking a fight," Kyle confessed.

"But you didn't take the first swing," the officer pointed out. "Are you planning to press charges? Because we have the other guy's name and info as well."

Kyle pretended to debate this, then shook his head. "Nah. Bygones and all that." I could tell it hurt to speak, but he bucked up. "Will you let us go now?"

"Yes. Go back to Sedona"—obviously the officer knew where we lived based on our IDs—"and don't come back for a while, all right? Try to stay out of trouble. I don't want to see you two again."

We were given our cell phones back. I stared at mine, knowing it needed to be destroyed. Kyle turned his on, but I wouldn't let him make a call.

I asked a desk clerk, "Would it be okay for me to use your phone? My battery's dead and his doesn't have much of a signal up here."

She eyed me skeptically. We weren't exactly in a box canyon or in the boonies, so of course he had a signal. Still, she pushed the phone my way. "Dial nine to get an outside line."

I called the only person I could rely on at this point and very cryptically said, "Can you please pick me up at the police station in Flag?"

Mr. Conaway arrived an hour and a half later. Kyle and I settled into his Cadillac CTS, me in the front seat.

"This ought to be interesting," my lawyer said by way of casual conversation. I didn't miss the disapproval in his tone. Or the crinkling of his nose.

"Sorry for the stale-beer smell. We actually weren't drinking," I told him. "We were followed. Set up at first, then followed," I amended.

He shot a look my way. "Tell me everything."

I did, from start to finish. I wrapped up the eventful story right around the time we reached the scenic pull-off on the rim of the canyon. Mr. Conaway parked the car and we all got out.

"Give me your phone, please," he said to me. I handed it over.

He checked it. My guess was he was curious about the text message and did the same thing I'd done—compare that number to the few others that had come through from Amano.

"You've been hacked," he informed me, disgruntled.

"I didn't think that was possible with a disposable phone."

"Anything's possible, my dear." He handed the cell to Kyle. "Send it to the bottom of the canyon."

Kyle climbed over the protective ledge and made his way carefully to the precipice overlooking the canyon. He stretched his throwing arm way back and hurled the phone like a pro quarterback into the gaping mouth of Oak Creek Canyon and the rapids running through it below.

My stomach tightened. My heart constricted.

There went my only connection to Dane, via Amano.

"Now yours," Mr. Conaway told Kyle.

He flashed the older man a look over his shoulder. "I haven't been hacked."

"You don't know that. And really, it's only a matter of time."

Kyle's gaze flitted to me. I gave a small shrug. "Sorry?"

"Oh, for God's sake." He chucked his as well.

We returned to the car and I tried not to agonize over how all of this changed our game. Of course Mr. Conaway would tell Dane and Amano what had happened to me and Kyle. He'd likely already been on the phone to Amano. If my former bodyguard wasn't lying in a ditch somewhere.

I shuddered. Then asked, "Are you sure Amano's okay? No one had a gun to his head when that text came my way?"

"He's perfectly fine. I spoke briefly with him on the drive up. He's destroyed his cell as well."

I breathed a sigh of relief that he was alive—and not tied up somewhere.

Kyle chimed in, "Any idea who lured Ari to the house?"

"Not as of yet. However," my lawyer said to me, "you won't be returning anytime soon."

I squeezed my eyes shut for a moment, then gazed at Mr. Conaway. "Dane can't—*won't*—come to the retreat, for fear someone will tail him and we'll put everyone in jeopardy. The creek house is the only place we can meet, the only—"

"Actually, it's not." He didn't elaborate.

Great. More secrets.

I slumped against my seat, exhausted.

Closing my eyes, I was out in an instant. Didn't wake until Kyle's voice cut into my subconscious as he said, "You missed the turn to the retreat."

"Neither of you are going back there right now."

My eyelids fluttered open. My head rolled on the rest and I gazed at Mr. Conaway as I asked, "Where else would we go?"

"You remember the house where Vale held you hostage?"

My stomach lurched. "Absolutely not!" I declared, alarmed. "I am *not* going back there!"

"Relax, Ari," he said. "Please. Trust me. It's not the same. That house is . . . gone."

"Gone?" My brow crooked.

"Yes. There was all that blood, remember? From what Vale did to you. From what Dane did to him." I'd also gotten in my own solid blow to Vale's head, initially. When I'd tried to escape.

Mr. Conaway continued. "It seeped into the wood. We couldn't clean it all, so I offered the owner cash—twice the amount he'd paid the year before for the property."

I wasn't the least bit surprised.

He said, "Dane had the house mowed down. Even the foundation was ripped out. He started from scratch. The new manor is finished. Amano just recently approved the video and high-voltage security system."

I gaped.

From the backseat, Kyle tentatively ventured, "High-voltage?"

"Yes. Don't touch any of the wiring that tops the twelve-foot walls around the perimeter and you'll be just fine."

I couldn't help but snicker. My very formal lawyer had a sense of humor.

He added, "This is a better alternative than the retreat. And, obviously, the creek house has been compromised as a meeting place."

"Damn," I said. "I love that house."

"You can go back to it when this is all over."

"And when, exactly, do you think that might be?" Kyle inquired in a sharp tone.

"Hey." I didn't want him taking out his gritchy mood on Mr. Conaway. He could save it for me. "Let's be thankful we have someplace to go."

Regardless, Mr. Conaway spared a glance at Kyle in the rear-view mirror and said, "I'm afraid I don't know the answer to that question. But Dane and Amano—and others—are doing everything they can to bring this to a successful resolution."

Kyle grumbled under his breath. I kept my mouth shut. I didn't know what else to say at this point, anyway.

We drove through Sedona and headed west toward the outskirts of town, then north again. The long road led to 10,000 Lux. I'd not been out this way since the day that bomb blew the resort sky-high, three months ago. We weren't traveling directly to the Lux, however.

Several miles before the decimated hotel, we reached the patch of asphalt with the familiar, though faded, tire marks of the F5 used to kidnap me veering into a narrow opening of a red-dirt road. I prayed Mr. Conaway was right about the new abode. Not just that the security was top-notch but also that the entire property looked nothing like it had previously.

I'd had too many nightmares that had taken place in the partially constructed house to try to sleep in it.

We wove through the sycamores and brush, farther back toward the wall of the canyon.

A thought occurred to me. "There's no cell service here."

"You won't need cell service. There's a landline. And Amano will be with you from now on."

That provided a huge amount of relief. Except for one thing. "Doesn't Dane need him? Shouldn't he be protecting Dane?"

"Dane has the FBI. You have no one."

"I beg to fucking differ," Kyle spat out.

Mr. Conaway grinned contritely. "I didn't mean to offend you, Kyle. You and Ari have worked quite well together. I was referring to Amano's skill with security measures, monitoring, tracking, and the like."

"And the fact that he could kill King Kong with his bare hands," I added. "At least, that's what I think."

Kyle harrumphed. "Yeah, but can he take a punch from someone a foot taller than him?"

I couldn't help but laugh. "You baited well and received well. Seriously, you should have picked on someone your own size."

"Had to go for the gold," Kyle said, his chest puffing out a bit.

"And it saved our asses." No denying it.

We approached the property and everyone fell silent. *Property* was actually the wrong word in so many ways. *Fortress* was more like it.

The smooth terra-cotta walls were, indeed, topped with wiring. The large, circular barbed type you might see at correctional facilities. Or . . . surrounding a prison. The entrance was a solid gate. Not offering even the slightest glimpse of what lie beyond.

"Is that a . . . *guard tower?*" Kyle asked as he leaned forward and peered through the front window.

"Yes, as a matter of fact." Mr. Conaway spoke so calmly, this seemed like an everyday occurrence for him. "The manor sits on ten acres, all under constant observation. Patrolled twenty-four-seven. The interior is monitored as well."

Not the bedroom, I hoped. . . .

"In addition," Mr. Conaway said, "there are only three people allowed through this gate, aside from Dane and Amano—and security, obviously. We're it."

The gate slowly slid open and we passed through. The dirt path turned into a rustic yet elegant cobblestone drive that circled around an enormous fountain. We parked under the fancy porte cochere. The landscaping was lush and manicured, with striking bougainvillea in purple and fuchsia accented by vibrant leaves.

A long, deep patio ran the width of the main portion of the house, with trimmed pillars and archways. There was a wing on each side of the primary living space that sat at a slight angle—likely where the bedrooms and studies were housed.

This was definitely not the same place I'd been held captive six months ago.

The Mediterranean style was gorgeous and inviting. As we entered, I was stunned into silence. It was open and vast, with tons of tall, arched windows, warm hues, indoor/outdoor seating, alcoves, fireplaces, rich wood accents, plenty of gorgeous plants, and soft, glowing lights.

"Wow." Kyle let out a low whistle. "Nice digs."

Mr. Conaway showed us around the estate. There were seven bedrooms and ten bathrooms. An indoor pool and spa, and outdoor ones as well. A gourmet kitchen both Kyle and I salivated over. Formal and informal dining areas, a library, theater and fitness rooms, and so much more.

"It's like a mini Lux," Kyle said.

My stomach roiled as I thought of the devastation just a few miles down the road. "Let's not call it that."

"Well, there's a pool table, video games, and a shitload of other things to do," Kyle mused. "Something tells me we won't be too bored with no cell phones, apps, or Internet."

There was no Wi-Fi, but I knew it was better this way.

Though one distressing thought did pop into my head. "What about my dad?" I asked Mr. Conaway. "He can visit, right?"

"Oh, that." He gave me a placating smile. "Your father won a two-week first-class trip to the private Augusta National Golf Club. You should give him a call. I'm sure he was very excited when the package was offered to him."

It took a few seconds to process what he'd said. "You arranged for my father to play the club where the Masters are held?"

"Yes. The club's GM called him personally."

My dad had not made it that far in his professional career. This was . . . over-the-top.

Even Kyle appeared taken aback. "Unbelievable."

"So," Mr. Conaway mused. "He'll be enjoying himself and will, of course, be well looked after."

I blanched. "You don't believe—"

"No, absolutely not." The lawyer quickly picked up on my line of thinking. "He's perfectly safe, Ari. Kyle would have been as well, if you two hadn't shown up at the creek house together.

Therefore, the most important thing now is to sit tight while Dane finishes his work. Amano should be here in four or five hours. He booked a flight as soon as we hung up."

"From where?" Kyle wanted to know.

I sighed.

Mr. Conaway told him, "I'm not at liberty to say."

"This is really crazy and . . . whacked," Kyle announced. "I'm not the only one who realizes that, right?"

My heart twisted. "It is, yes. But there's nothing we can do about it, except . . ." I spread my arms wide. "Enjoy the estate."

He glared at me.

"Or skulk about," I mumbled.

Mr. Conaway said, "I'll have Eleanor buy you clothes and I'll bring them over this evening."

"Thank you," I said. "For everything. I'm so sorry for all the trouble."

He smiled. Patted my hand. "This is hardly your doing, Ari. And yet . . . you have a very interesting outlook on all of this."

"I knew what I was getting into from almost the beginning," I admitted. "Dane never once lied to me. Well . . . other than some farce about beavers chewing through wires at the Lux when the security system went down." I'd meant that statement as a joke, but something about it lodged in my brain. "Anyway, thankfully we're safe again." I eyed Kyle. He merely shrugged.

Mr. Conaway left us to a fully stocked kitchen and wet bar. Kyle offered to make omelets and I jumped in the shower in a master suite—there was one in each wing. My selection looked out onto the pool area, with a breathtaking rock-trimmed waterfall and a huge hammered-bronze cauldron-style fire pit.

I wrapped a plush robe around my naked body and joined Kyle.

"I'll get the plates and silverware so you can shower," I told him. "Take the other master suite."

When he returned, we settled at the kitchen island. We didn't have much to say over breakfast. The past twenty-four hours had been a bit surreal for him. Unfortunately, not so much for me. Terrifying, sure. But not exactly out of the ordinary these days.

As I rinsed the dishes and put them in the washer, Kyle finally spoke.

"Aren't you worried about the baby, Ari?"

I glanced at him, also dressed in a robe. "Of course I am. Dane doesn't know I'm pregnant yet, though, and I intend to keep it that way a little while longer. Until it's absolutely evident I haven't just gained a few pounds." I'd packed on some weight, but it was evenly distributed over my body, making even the tiniest hint of a baby bump just seem like I should spend a couple of hours in the gym every week. Or cut back on the oatmeal and breakfast potatoes.

Kyle lifted the towel I'd left on the counter after drying my hands and he snapped it absently, restlessly, against the marble. "Why haven't you told him?"

"Because he has extremely important work to do. And he'd stop if he knew about the baby. In fact . . . I'm afraid this latest episode is going to have him second-guessing what he's doing."

"It should."

"No, it shouldn't." I placed a hand on Kyle's arm. "You heard what I told Mr. Conaway. I knew going in that this would not be a normal relationship, that my life with Dane would not be normal."

"Or safe."

"He's doing his best. So is Amano. If it were any other caliber of people they were dealing with, my safety wouldn't be an issue at all. But these guys . . . Christ." I moved around to the upholstered stools at the island and slid onto one. "It's like they're everywhere at the same time. I don't get it. And it's downright eerie."

Nerve-wracking, too.

Kyle said, "You really don't have to be a part of this, Ari."

"Yes. I do. I'm Dane's wife. I'm about to be the mother of his child. And you can't deny that he, Amano, and Mr. Conaway have done everything in their power to keep us *all* out of harm's way when it comes to the corrupt members of the society. But Jesus.

They're like cockroaches or something. They seem to multiply instead of go away."

"This is such bullshit."

I pinned Kyle with an earnest look. "You can leave, you know? They won't come after you if you disassociate yourself from me. Hell, I don't even think they know about the retreat, because they never fucked with anything there. They needed me at the creek house to get to me."

He appeared to give this some thought.

"You have a choice, Kyle. I love you as a friend," I told him in a heartfelt tone. "And I'm eternally grateful for all you've done. But you're not bound by sacred oath here. To tell you the truth, it'd probably be best if you—"

"No," he said with conviction in his voice, his gaze locking with mine. "It wouldn't be best if I just walked away. Because *I* want to protect you, too. If Dane can't be here, if Amano has secret-society business to deal with . . . I can be here. For you. And for your baby."

I saw this for what it was—Kyle's defining moment. A decision that could be the one to give him a bit more purpose in life or . . . one that could be detrimental.

I understood the pros and cons, the reward versus the challenge— or, rather, the danger.

"Kyle, you need to be absolutely certain."

"I'm here, aren't I? I just spent the night in jail, didn't I? I nearly sent us over the edge of a canyon that plunges forty-five hundred feet, right?"

"Put like that," I said with a crooked brow, "you might want to seek your own mental health counseling. I think you're nuts."

He laughed, albeit gruffly. "Certifiable, without doubt. Then again . . . It's not like I had anything better to do last night but hang out with newlyweds and their brand-new baby. Guess I'm cursed."

I'd sent several items to Meg and Sean from their gift registry but hadn't yet made it to see them. I'd stuck close to the retreat of late, in the event Amano called and there was a chance to see Dane.

"I need to visit them," I confessed. "Unfortunately, Meg will likely figure out I'm pregnant because I'll be all googly-eyed over the baby and asking a million questions about what to expect when you're expecting."

"Yeah, that could be a problem. Anyway, they're sort of into the whole family unit thing at the moment, so you have time to make it up to them."

"I suppose." I stared at him a few seconds longer, a tormenting thought gnawing at me. Finally, I asked, "Do you really believe you're cursed?"

"No." He set aside the hand towel and said, "Since we're stuck here in paradise, I'm going for a swim."

"You don't have trunks," I mentioned over the sting of guilt I couldn't shake.

"So?"

I frowned. "That guard tower is manned, and there are guys patrolling these ten acres."

"Not my problem. They don't have to look, now do they?" He sauntered off.

Above obsessing over Kyle's angst and unwavering sense of duty, I prayed Eleanor Conaway would buy us swimwear. Given the latest disaster and my new criminal record, Dane had enough to contend with to put his blood pressure in the red zone without knowing Kyle was skinny-dipping in the pool fifty feet from me.

Yeah. That'd make for fun conversation.

chapter 16

Kyle and I wore new jeans and shirts and were in the middle of a Wii bowling tournament when Amano arrived. Sauntering in behind him was Dane, his gait evened out now that his leg had fully healed and he no longer needed the walking cane.

My heart swelled. Kyle scowled beside me.

Dane did not look pleased—and I was sure I knew why. Amano had told him everything, the details no doubt relayed by Mr. Conaway after he'd left us.

I wrapped my arms around Dane's neck, despite his tense, broody appearance. "I've missed you."

He was dressed all in black, and my fingers instantly itched to unbutton his shirt so I could touch him.

Holding me tight, he said, "This isn't getting any better, Ari. Not any safer, not any saner."

"Kyle and I are okay. And we *are* safer. This place is more secure than Fort Knox. Now that you're here, it's perfect."

He kissed my temple. "You find the silver lining in everything, don't you?"

"I love you."

With a low groan, he said, "I love you, too. Which is why I'm so damn pissed off."

"Wait'll you see your car." Kyle just couldn't resist.

I unraveled from Dane and said, "We had a little trouble and had to take the McLaren off-road." To Amano, I explained, "I can tell you where to find it, if the Forest Service hasn't towed it away already."

"Seriously, a sweet ride." Kyle poked a bit harder. "But you'll likely need a new undercarriage. Definitely a new paint job. Tires are pretty much shot to shit now, too."

I could feel Dane's temper flare. I placed a palm on his chest and said, "We're really very sorry. It was necessary."

"I don't give a damn about the car, Ari. I'm pissed off that you were in danger again." His gaze shifted to Kyle. "I'm sorry you were involved. But . . . thank you for taking care of her."

"I'm getting good at this James Bond stuff," Kyle said with a cocky grin. I suspected the split lip and bruised jaw made him feel tougher, more rugged. To Amano, he added, "Maybe you should teach me some bodyguard moves. Since I'm the one here with Ari."

"That won't be necessary," the stoic Amano said. "I'm here now. And will be until this is over."

Latching on to that segue, I asked Dane, "Any progress?"

"We'll talk later." He took my hand and led me out of the room. "Which suite is ours?"

I directed him down the long corridor. "I only get you for the night, don't I?"

He didn't say anything, just closed the door behind us. I turned to him. Wound my arms around him again.

"It's hell not being with you," he whispered in my ear. I heard his torment, his quiet fury. "I steal a few hours, then Kyle gets you

the rest of the time. I turn my back and you're in danger. I'm livid,
Ari. So worried about you. And so ready to just say fuck it all and—"

"No." I pulled away and stared up at him. "You can't quit now.
Not after everything we've all been through. Not when you're so
very close to finishing this, Dane."

He stepped around me. Raked a hand through his hair. "This
isn't getting any easier. In fact, it's much more convoluted. These
last two members . . . They're in deep, Ari. This goes beyond tax
evasion and blowing up the Lux. They've manipulated the global
network the society uses and they'll be the catalyst for another
massive recession—while *they* prosper. Creating all of that influence, wielding all of that power . . . To achieve that level of su-
premacy has required them to leave plenty of casualties in their
wake."

I sank onto the mattress. "Are you saying they . . . *murder* people
to get their way?"

"Whatever it takes," he said with a sharp edge to his low voice.
"That's how these people operate. You saw what they did to the
Lux. Every one of my employees—my *wife*—could have been inside that building when it exploded. Did they care? No. Because
to them, they're above reproach. Untraceable, untouchable."

"But *you're* tracing them, touching them. Helping to send them
to prison."

He paced along the bench that ran the width of the bed. "At
what cost?" he mumbled, agitated. "You could have been killed,
Ari. *Again.*"

I wrung my hands a moment, understanding how this tore at
him. But there was so much at stake. He couldn't walk away from
this now.

"Look," I told him. "I won't sit here and lie to you, say I haven't
been terrified—terrorized. But what you're doing is too significant
to turn your back on. Especially at this point. After all you've in-
vested in bringing these guys down, after all we've suffered. You

have to see this through. No matter what. These people must be stopped, Dane."

He drew up short and stared at me. "It's not worth the risk, not worth putting your life in jeopardy."

"Yes, it is." I stood and crossed to him. My palms splayed over his hard pectoral ledge and I gazed up at him unwaveringly. "I'm one person, when countless others suffer because of what the society has been allowed to get away with. You could have died. Amano, too. Easing up on them now is *not* the answer."

"And what about Kyle? His life is in danger, too, Ari. Now that they know about him."

My hands dropped to my sides. "I asked him to reconsider. To disassociate himself from me. Go back to his safe life."

With a grunt, Dane said, "Let me guess. He told you not a chance in hell."

"Pretty much."

"Fool," Dane hissed out. Then he whirled around, stalked over to the sliding glass doors, and glared out at the waterfall. "I should have never hired him at the hotel. Goddamn it."

"Maybe, but that was my fault, remember?"

"And how the hell would you ever look me in the eye again if anything happened to him? How would you ever forgive me?" he quietly demanded.

I really hadn't considered all of this. It'd been such a roller-coaster ride for us all, so many ups and downs, that I tried to catch my breath before the next potentially devastating hurdle came our way, not really giving such deep thought to the consequences of our actions.

"I can tell him to leave," I said. "I can tell him we're not friends anymore, that I don't need him or want him around. He won't buy it, though. He'll stick, Dane. He's already proven that."

"So I'm supposed to accept what might happen to him as *his* choice? The way I'm supposed to accept the same with you?"

"Yes."

I didn't like the implication of that one word for Kyle, myself, or our baby. But given the circumstances—the real and impossible-to-hide-from reality of the situation—and the fact that Dane, Amano, Kyle, and I had committed to that reality and knew what we were in for . . . I'd be a hypocrite to say the blame for anything going awry landed anywhere other than at the feet of those who chose this path. That meant *all* of us. Kyle and me included.

Unfortunately, the baby didn't have a say in the matter. And no, I certainly never intended to be careless with my life, thereby putting our child's life in danger. But this had started long before I became pregnant—long before I'd learned I was pregnant. It wasn't something I could extricate myself from now that I did know.

This was about our family. Other people as well. There were a lot of lives at risk, so much at stake, if we didn't continue on this path. More so than if we put a halt to this in an effort to save ourselves.

I joined Dane at the doors and wrapped my arms around his waist. "There's no turning back, because this is what needs to be done. You said yourself that this is bigger than what happened at the Lux—one of the world's premier luxury hotels. That's a huge statement. Yet, Dane . . . Though you won't be able to forgive yourself if anything happens to me, you won't be able to forgive yourself, either, if you give up on this in an attempt to keep me out of harm's way."

His hands covered mine and he squeezed them.

I continued. "That day when you almost killed Vale . . . You had every right to be furious, and I know it wasn't just about the secret society. It was about me. That he'd hurt me. You were completely enraged. Then you tried to convince me you weren't the bad guy. I had to walk away from you because everything surrounding you was too dark, too dangerous, too sinister. But it's never been your fault. That was why I came back. Because I realized you were right. You're *not* the bad guy."

He released my hands and turned to face me. Brushing strands of hair from my cheek, he said, "The worst part about this is that I want you too much—*need* you too much—to do what you did with Kyle. To tell you to leave."

"Doesn't matter. You could tell me. I won't go. I lost you the first time after Vale and it was pure torture. When I thought you were dead . . . ?" Tears pricked my eyes. "I honestly had to find something to live for—a reason to not want to be dead myself. Everything about our life together was—*is*—that reason, Dane."

His emerald eyes clouded. His jaw set in a hard line. "I don't know if I could do it, Ari. If the tables were turned. I don't know if I could find a reason to—"

"You would," I interjected. "But you won't have to, because I'm going to be just fine. I'm going to stay here and not venture out without Amano or Kyle. I will do everything I have to in order to be safe. You have to trust in that. And trust Kyle the way you do Amano. He's been strong and loyal. He's committed to being by my side."

"A little too much," Dane said in a dour tone. Then added, "But you're right. And I do trust him. Believe me, he'd need stitches if I thought he'd purposely put you in a hazardous situation."

"He didn't. It was a trap, Dane. And I was very, very lucky he was there with me to help me out of it."

Dane pulled me close. "You must have been so scared."

"Petrified." I shuddered at the thought of those hairpin turns and the helicopter looming on the horizon. But I said, "We might not come up with the savviest or classiest ways out of a mess—the way you would—but we manage."

"Drunk and disorderly conduct," he said with a half snort. "My wife, the town rowdy. I'll have to do something about burying your mug shot before it hits the Internet."

"Kyle's, too."

Dane was quiet a moment, then conceded. "Kyle's, too."

I snuggled closer. "Are you done being upset? Pissed? Worried? All of the above?"

"Not a chance."

"Hmm. That's too bad." I tugged the shirt hem from the waist of his dress pants and slid my hands under the material. His abs flexed beneath my touch. I grinned.

"You really don't know how to keep yourself out of trouble, do you, Mrs. Bax?"

My stomach flipped. "I like all your references to me being your wife."

"I like what you're doing," he murmured against my hair.

I worked the buttons on his shirt and spread the material open. Both palms glided over his hot skin and hard muscles.

Gazing up at him, I said, "You're too damn tempting." Even the scar on his chest and the one cutting across his chiseled abs, both just faint reminders of the disaster at 10,000 Lux, added to his edgy perfection.

I left kisses over his tanned and sculpted torso while he stripped off his shirt. Then his strong arms encircled my waist and he lifted me slightly off the floor and walked us to the bed. The backs of my legs hit the mattress and he eased me down.

He quickly peeled away my clothes, then stretched alongside me.

One of his hands skimmed over my shoulder, then down to my breast, cupping it and squeezing gently. I wondered if he noticed that I filled his palm more than in the past or if he'd comment about my slightly curvier figure and the low rise of my belly.

But then I recalled how I'd gained weight during all of the food sampling at the Lux before Thanksgiving, and suspected he didn't see or feel a difference. After all, he hadn't been with me when I'd lost weight in the hospital and when the severe morning sickness had left my stomach concave.

I relaxed, certain he had no idea I was pregnant. Not that I wasn't dying to tell him—what woman, wife, mother-to-be, wouldn't be? But following our discussion and his fear over how his work impacted me. I knew I had to keep my own secret.

Conversely, I was presented with the opportunity to be completely selfish. If I told Dane about the baby, he'd never leave my side.

But just as he'd never forgive himself if something were to happen to me, I'd never forgive myself for pulling him away from what needed to be done.

It was all kinds of fucked up, in the hopes justice would prevail. Given all I'd lost and succumbed to this far, I was in too deep to let it all slip away now, just to keep him close.

So I bit my tongue, even though every fiber of my being screamed to share the joy of childbearing with my husband.

Sacrifices.

I'd never made so many before, but once again, I thought of the greater good. Not just me, Dane, the baby, and Kyle. Though the reason I was likely capable of this approach was because of the protection surrounding me. And the fact that I wanted to safeguard my family just as fiercely as everyone else did.

I tangled my fingers in Dane's lush hair and said, "I'm sorry you had to drop everything to come back."

"I'm sorry I have to be away so long."

"I do miss your hands on my body." I winked. Tried to keep things light so I didn't spew my guts and tell him how painful it was to be without him. How much I wanted him learning everything about our child along with me. How I craved him each and every night that we were apart.

His lips grazed mine. Then he murmured, "You are so very beautiful. I lie awake and think of how soft and flawless your skin is. How perfect you are."

I groaned. "Not so flawless or perfect." I had my own scars.

"Hmm," he groaned sexily. "You never see what I see."

His finger and thumb toyed with my puckered nipple, tightening it more. His head dipped and he suckled softly before fluttering his tongue against the sensitive bud. My breasts grew heavy with desire. Need coursed through me, hot and bright.

He lavished the other nipple with the same delicious attention and I writhed beneath him, my back bowing to press myself against his mouth, my breasts aching for everything he offered. Every sinful touch.

"You taste good." His warm breath blew against the taut peak, making it impossibly hard. "And feel so incredible." His hand slid over my rib cage and belly, lower to the apex of my legs.

I parted my thighs just as his fingers whisked over my slick folds, a feathery sensation meant to tease and tantalize. My hips rose greedily as I offered myself to him.

"Dane," I whispered.

His emerald irises glowed seductively. "I think about this, too," he mused as he stroked me slowly. "How wet you get for me."

The pads of two fingers moved in a leisurely, circular motion against my clit as he stared into my eyes. The intensity of his gaze heightened my arousal.

The sweeping blades of the ceiling fan overhead sent a slight breeze skating over my skin, but it didn't cool me down. My internal temperature flared. A fire burned through my veins.

I wanted Dane to make love to me, but I couldn't break the eye contact, couldn't say anything that would cause him to deviate from the excitement he evoked with his masterful touch. My hips rolled with his sensuous rhythm. Everything in my head and all the danger and drama melted away as he maintained the eye contact and gradually picked up the pace between my legs, turning the leisurely stroking into a quicker fluttering that made my breath catch.

"You're going to make me come," I said on a heavy breath.

"That's the plan."

"So easily. You barely even touch me. . . ."

"I'll touch you more, then." Two fingers eased into me, filling me.

"Oh, God." My eyelids drooped, then closed. I let the feeling of him massaging my inner walls, pushing deep, stroking slow and sexy, consume me.

"Ari," he whispered against my cheek before kissing it tenderly. "All I want in the world is to make you happy."

The corners of my mouth quivered. A smile that competed with emotion. "You do."

His thumb rubbed my clit as his fingers pumped expertly, with just the right tempo, the right pressure. Lowering his head again, he flicked his tongue over my nipple, then sucked hard as his fingers drove deep.

Everything inside me erupted and I cried out his name, coming on a powerful release that raged through me. My fingers tightened around his hair. The other hand gripped his biceps, my nails digging in.

"Oh, God," I whimpered as the sensations flamed over my skin, ignited in my belly.

Dane let out a low growl as I clutched his fingers inside me, my hips still raised as I savored every second of the fiery orgasm.

"Ari," he whispered against my neck. "You make me so crazed with wanting you."

"Then fuck me. Dane, now. *Please.*"

I'd always needed him in a dark, frenzied sort of way. That need had grown into a relentless, insistent ache that made me desperate for him. Especially when I'd suffered weeks without him.

His fingers withdrew from me and he flipped me onto my stomach. Over my shoulder, I watched as he yanked the top button of his pants and shoved the zipper down, then pushed the material— along with his boxer-briefs—to his hips.

He thrust into me from behind, making me cry out from sheer pleasure.

His hand sought mine, our fingers twining above my head. My free hand curled around the comforter while he pumped solidly and fantastically into me.

"Oh, yes," I said in a throaty moan. "Just like that. Fuck me hard."

I could tell his need mirrored mine. He plunged deep with quick, full strokes.

His ridged abs pressed to my back. His chest sealed against my shoulder blades. With his head bent to mine, he whispered, "Tell me you know that everything I do is for you—for us."

I knew instinctively he spoke of the indictments. "Of course, Dane."

"Because I wouldn't be away from you for a second, wouldn't give up having you every night of my life. Forever. If it wasn't absolutely necessary. Imperative."

"You don't have to justify, Dane. Just fuck me."

I wanted him that much. Conversation, rationale, *nothing* mattered. Just him, inside me.

All that registered was the insane rush of adrenaline through my veins. The thundering of my heart. The racing of my pulse. My hyperawareness of Dane. A vibrant, powerful presence that surrounded me, permeated every inch of me.

He thrust deeper and hit that perfect spot until I was panting and whimpering and dying for more.

"Dane. Oh, Christ." He had all the right moves and knew exactly how to use them to push me so high up I couldn't stop the swelling and subsequent eruption inside me. "Yes, God, Dane!" I cried out.

Every sensation converged and burned until I couldn't think straight, couldn't feel anything other than my magnificent husband filling me as I clenched him tight.

"That's perfect, baby," he said in a lusty voice. He thrust heartily, keeping me aroused. I wasn't sure when one orgasm stopped and the other began.

"Fuck, Ari!" He surged and convulsed and exploded within me. So hot and searing that I came again.

chapter 17

I was sore the next morning, but oh, did it feel good! My inner thighs burned with the sensation of a really great workout. My pussy throbbed from the way Dane had filled and stretched me, the way his thick shaft had thrust in a confident, commanding way.

I clung to the tangible proof he'd made love to me the night before. Because I already knew he'd left me. The bed wasn't as warm. That strong presence of his had vanished.

Opening my eyes, I rolled toward the side of the bed he'd slept in, noting the indentation still in the pillow. Along with a long-stemmed white rose from our garden. I lifted it to my nose and inhaled. There was no note. As though he couldn't even take just the tiniest risk by leaving physical evidence behind that he was alive.

With a sigh, I hauled myself up and showered. Fought the tears that came with the heartache of not being with him. I focused, instead, on the cherished moments we did spend together. The man certainly didn't waste what little time we had on these rare occasions.

Still, it was like being married to a phantom. A seriously hot, sexy one, but an apparition all the same. A husband who could very easily be a figment of my imagination were it not for the soreness of my inner thighs.

I joined Amano on the back patio for breakfast while Kyle lifted weights in the fitness room.

Amano handed over a slim box with a coy grin.

"What's this?"

"Dane wanted you to have it."

Okay, maybe he did feel the need to leave some proof of life behind.

I opened the lid. My heart stammered—not in a good way. Carefully removing the ID bracelet, I said, "He wanted me to have his wedding bracelet? Why?" Panic seized me. "Is he not expecting to . . . come back? To survive this?"

"No, no," Amano was quick to say. "It's not his. It's one similar to his. Since you don't have the diamond bangle he gave you, he wanted you to have something as a symbol of your marriage, your union."

"Oh." Relief washed over me. "Jesus, that was scary."

I rubbed my thumb over the smooth platinum surface, happy for the material confirmation that, although my husband might be a phantom, I was, indeed, married.

Flipping the bracelet over to inspect the clasp, I got another surprise.

"What is this?"

"Inscription," Amano said. "It's on Dane's as well. You didn't know?"

"He never takes it off."

I studied the markings.

DB 51027211 AB

With a frown, I said, "I don't get it."

"Dane Bax, the date of your wedding, Aria Bax."

"Huh." My brow dipped. "Why's the date backwards?"

Amano shrugged. "Apparently, that's a secret-society ring decoder kind of thing. I don't know all the details."

"Something tells me that's a good thing."

I stared at the inscription a few seconds more, a curious thought clawing at my brain.

Amano noted my consternation. "What's wrong?"

"I've seen a number sequence like this before. But I can't remember where." I closed my eyes, envisioned the date of our wedding, and then tried to visualize the sequence I'd seen . . . and wondered why it made me think of Dane. Finally I shook my head. "All this intrigue is clearly messing with my mind. I'm going to do a little yoga. Thanks for bringing me the bracelet."

I collected our dishes and took them into the kitchen to load in the washer. Then I grabbed my mat and went out by the pool. Gretchen had already told me not to do any poses on my back or that would stretch my abdominals too much, now that I'd started my second trimester. So I took it easy, really just working on my breathing and light stretching while my mind churned with the mystery of those eight digits.

It took all day for one very ominous thought to click in my head. I was in the middle of slicing veggies for an appetizer platter before dinner when I dropped the knife. It clamored on the marble counter and Amano jerked to attention, having been engrossed in a magazine.

"Are you okay?"

"I don't know." My blood ran cold. Numbers that weren't quite defined but rather a bit blurred flashed in my mind. They were red. Blood red. Then they vanished. Next, I heard Dane's voice.

Digits? Do you remember what they were?

I hadn't written anything down that night I'd viewed the Lux's Web site to see what sort of jobs for the Events department were posted, wanting to get an idea of the positions that would report to and support me, were I to take Dane up on his offer to run the show.

Suddenly the site had turned a deep onyx and the words *Under Construction* had flickered on the screen, in crimson. Along with numbers in the bottom right-hand corner.

I closed my eyes again, attempting to make a distinct determination of what I'd seen before the Web page had gone blank, solid black.

I could see the five and the one. I concentrated harder, and though I couldn't recall the exact numbers after those two, I could for sure say there'd been eight digits total.

My lids snapped open.

"Who, besides the secret society, would know about the backwards writing of dates?" I asked Amano.

He looked a bit perplexed by the line of questioning but shook his head. "I can't say. I only learned about the society when Vale kidnapped you. And Dane didn't tell me much."

"It's supposed to be generational," I mused, not really certain in which direction my jumbled thoughts ran. "So if Vale wasn't the sharpest tool in the toolshed, but could still prove his worth to the society—namely the five corrupt members—he might get a seat at the table. But he'd really have to pull off some spectacularly masterminded schemes. Like . . . gently fuck things up at the Lux, initially, to get Dane, Ethan, Qadir, and Nikolai to consider bringing the original investors back into the fold."

As I ruminated over this, Amano joined me at the island, sliding onto a stool, obviously intrigued.

I said, "When that didn't work, Vale had to come up with a more insidious plot. Kidnap me and hold me for ransom, basically twisting Dane's arm until he cried uncle. But that didn't work, either. And Vale nearly got the life kicked out of him. Which wouldn't go over well with Daddy and the others, so his only saving grace would be to take the ultimate, drastic approach. Not just to save face and secure his seat at the secret-society table but also for personal revenge."

Hadn't I been thinking of that a lot lately? And understood how it affected people such as Vale?

Amano said, "I'd warned my security staff about Vale after he'd kidnapped you. They all knew what he looked like—there was no way he could get on-property without being seen by a camera, monitored by my guys."

I didn't doubt that. Amano was very thorough—especially after what had happened to me. Still . . .

"Vale wasn't doing the dirty work, remember?" I said. "It was Wayne Horton. And he knew every square inch of that property, every nook and cranny of those buildings. He had experience with IT, the security procedures and access points, the camera locations and angles. . . . And let's face it, he's one sneaky bastard."

Wayne's devious smile flashed in my mind. I cringed. The last thing I really wanted to think about was that terrifying day right here on this land. All similarities had been cleared away and a new house and grounds replaced the old, and yet this was the very spot where Vale had brought me. With Wayne Horton's help.

"It's impossible, Ari. I fired Wayne after you told me he'd purposely distracted you when you got into the F5, so that you didn't look over to see that it wasn't Dane driving the vehicle."

"Yeah, there is that. . . ."

"All of the access codes were changed. Every employee badge was reprogrammed with different rule sets. He wasn't privy to any of that. He couldn't have gained access to the lobby to plant the bomb."

I understood what Amano was saying. But the clicking in my mind happened again. "That you know of. He's a hacker, Amano. He hacked the Web site, taking it offline at the most critical point of hiring for the Lux. He deactivated my badge so that I couldn't get out of the stairwell, where he'd planted a diamondback on the landing below me. He was responsible for the damaged security wires. Not beavers. *Wayne*."

Amano's eyes darkened. Took him mere seconds to jump on-board with me. "He could have figured out how to hack your cell phone. Mine as well."

"I did try to call you when we were in trouble."

"No calls came through."

"So, he . . . what? Jammed or blocked me somehow?"

Amano smacked his hand on the counter. "Damn it, he proba-bly hacked Kyle's phone, too."

"Mr. Conaway thought of that. He had Kyle pitch it into the canyon, along with mine."

"That wily bastard," Amano said of Wayne. "He must still be working for Vale."

"And planted that bomb at the Lux." My blood chilled.

Amano got to his feet. "We need proof."

I groaned. "That's impossible. First of all, the guy's a wraith, like Dane. He's all over the place, but no one sees him. There's no evidence of him being here, there, or anywhere. And it's like he just . . . *knows* things."

"Chances are good he discovered you were meeting Dane at the house and it was him in the Camaro that chased you and Kyle."

"And what? Vale was in the helicopter?"

"He certainly has the resources, now doesn't he?"

"He, who?" Kyle asked as he came into the kitchen, a towel wrapped around his neck, perspiration dotting his skin from what had apparently been a rigorous workout. His muscles bulged and he breathed heavily.

"Vale," I said. "We're thinking he was in the helicopter and it was Wayne Horton in the Camaro."

Kyle scowled. "That lowlife asshole? Someone should shoot him and put us all out of our misery."

"Kyle." Appealing as the idea was, I didn't condone violence.

"Just sayin'." He crossed to the fridge and yanked on the han-dle. While he selected which variety of Gatorade he wanted, he added, "Look at what he did to you, Ari."

"And to the Lux," I said in agreement.

He pulled out a bottle of orange and downed half of it before asking, "So is someone going after these two thugs?"

"Not you," Amano asserted.

I drummed my fingers on the counter, then ventured, "What about me?"

Both sets of eyes burned into my skull. Seemed I was back to having flashes of crazy.

Amano said, "That's not even worth answering."

"Why not?" I insisted. "I mean, come on. I'm harmless. If I tried to get a confession from Wayne, he'd never see it coming. My life was destroyed, remember? I can play the lost little lamb to his big, bad wolf."

"Absolutely. Fucking. Not." This from Kyle as he stared incredulously at me. "He's willing to kill you, Ari. Did you not learn *anything* on those switchbacks? If we had gone over the edge, it would have been *sayonara and good riddance* on his part, and he would have simply washed his hands of you."

"It's not an issue, Kyle," Amano told him in a tone that held crystal-clear finality. "Dane would never stand for it." His gaze shifted to me. "Neither would I."

Planting my hands on my hips, I ignored the *case closed* voice of reason and reminded them both, "Dane is working with the FBI. Wouldn't they help us? They'd want to bust Wayne—they'd want his confession. We need to find him and get it!"

"Simmer down there, Lara Croft," said my bodyguard. "You might be right, but that doesn't change the answer. It still is and will always remain *no*."

I glared at Amano. Didn't faze him in the least.

Kyle piped up. "I could do it."

I gaped but recovered fast. "Put yourself in even hotter water? Did *you* not learn anything on those switchbacks?"

"Hey, if the FBI is involved, isn't it just a matter of them wiring me and then me engaging Wayne in conversation that leads to my suspicions about everything that's happened at 10,000 Lux and how I think he and Vale are behind it all?"

"Not a chance," I said. "He'd never engage with you—you're way too threatening. I'm the grieving widow."

"He already knows that's crap—he lured you to the house. Besides, he might not even know you're married."

"None of this means he knows Dane's alive," I reasoned. "He could have suspected, and he and Vale could have been attempting another kidnapping to draw Dane out, to confirm whether he really was behind all the evidence being provided for indictments."

"He will chew you up and spit you out," Kyle scoffed.

"And you'll push too hard from the beginning, not getting any of the information we need."

Amano stalked out of the room as though Kyle and I were bickering children and he couldn't take it anymore.

Kyle grinned. "I'm threatening?"

I rolled my eyes. "We aren't any good at this!" Throwing my arms up in the air, I said, "I'm no help to my husband at all!"

"Well," Kyle mused, "it's not like we really need the FBI wires. Cell phones have recording devices embedded."

"So, we just give Wayne a jingle and ask him to confirm he blew up the Lux—oh, and by the way, we swear we're not recording this conversation?"

Kyle let out a snort. "You are amusing. I meant that they have voice-recording apps—no need to be on the phone. We could do it in person. Accidentally bump into him somewhere."

"Because I'm sure he's spending his mornings enjoying a Grand Slam at Denny's."

"All right, stop." Amano had returned. "There's no point in continuing this, because you two are *not* getting involved."

I eyed him curiously. "You can't deny that chances are very good Vale is still in the game—regardless of family shame when he couldn't pull off the kidnapping—and that means Wayne is likely still his go-to guy. Which also makes Wayne a contender for Lux bomber."

"You're a bit better at this than you give yourself credit for," Amano admitted, albeit reluctantly. "Both of you. But I still want you to drop it. Forget about Wayne and Vale, except to keep an eye out for them."

"Yeah," Kyle said with a sudden hint of concern. "That high-voltage wiring won't mean dick if they realize this is where we're hiding out. They can rappel into the backyard from the helicopter."

I shivered. "Thanks for blowing all sense of security I was feeling."

"That's not going to happen, Ari," Amano assured me. "Watchtower, remember?"

"And what's the guard going to do if the helicopter gets too close?" Kyle asked. "Shoot it down?"

"Let me take care of that. Jack Conaway told me about the aircraft when he called in the details of the chase. It's already in my contingency plan."

Kyle and I exchanged a look. Amano had a contingency plan?

And . . . yeah, I was pretty sure that plan was to shoot the helicopter down.

Who would have known launching a luxury hotel could turn so dangerous . . . deadly, even?

With the dark cloud hovering over us, we all went about our day. Kyle opted for a swim. Amano conducted whatever business it was he conducted on the landline, since his cell wouldn't work out here. Occasionally, I stole a peek at one of the phone consoles and there'd be three or four lines lit at once. He had his own network of people—I hoped like hell they were more loyal than the ones in the society network Dane plotted to take down.

A couple days passed, and Kyle grew restless. He wanted to go to the retreat to do some landscaping and maintenance. One of the security guards picked him up in a rental—nothing flashy.

A pale-blue Prius. *Disposable* was the word that popped into my head, yet again.

I guessed they'd drive it once and then it'd disappear. They'd likely use a different one to return Kyle.

It made for boring times not having him around, given that Amano was always deep in secret-service mode. Playing Wii solo wasn't all that thrilling, and I didn't want to overly exert myself because of the baby.

So it was an even more pleasant surprise and relief when Dane came strolling into the living room, from the back patio, while I read.

Peering at him over the top of the book, I said, "Please tell me you're not a mirage."

He joined me on the sofa, lifting my curled legs onto his lap and stroking my bare skin. "Not a mirage."

"Thank God." I set the novel aside and pulled my legs from where they rested, sliding my butt onto his lap instead. I wrapped my arms around his neck. "To what do I owe the unexpected honor?"

He kissed me softly. One arm circled my waist. His free hand combed through my long, plump curls. "Aside from the fact that it's impossible to stay away?"

My fingertips grazed the side of his neck, down to his collarbone. "I think about you nonstop. I'll never get through this book, because my mind keeps wandering to you and then I have to go back and reread. Nothing but you registers."

His lips tenderly tangled with mine. Then he whispered, "I'm dying a very slow death."

Tears stung my eyes. "Don't say that."

He grunted painfully. "This needs to be over."

My gaze lifted from his tempting mouth to his clouded green eyes. "Amano's been on the phone to you all this time, hasn't he?"

"Not all the time. I've had meetings, depositions to give, more evidence to turn over."

"What did he say?"

"We talked about Vale Hilliard and Wayne Horton. I have to stop them. But they've both covered their tracks well. Vale because of his money—he can easily create a layer of anonymity. Horton's like—"

"A ghost. I know." I sighed. "But at the end of the day, doesn't someone with that sort of brilliance want people to know how clever he is? That he could sabotage a world-class, multi-billion-dollar business venture?"

Dane nodded. "It wouldn't be out of the ordinary. A lot of criminals get caught because they brag to friends or family, post something incriminating and stupid on Facebook, whatever."

"Like Walt on *Breaking Bad*."

"What?"

"A show Kyle and I streamed when we were at the retreat and had WiFi. So this guy is a meth cook and he's like, the absolute best of the best. When his brother-in-law DEA agent tries to help find this 'best of the best,' Walt gets sort of jealous that someone else is going to get credit for his recipe. Even though that guy would go to prison, not Walt. His ego takes over his sensibility."

"And that's why you think you could get a confession out of Horton? That he'd want to brag to you about everything he's pulled off?"

I shot a look out the open patio doors, wondering if my bodyguard was out there. "Amano tells you everything, doesn't he?"

Dane nodded.

My nerves jumped. It was only a matter of time before Amano discovered I was pregnant. I hid the pre-natal vitamins in my bathroom—wholly off-limits to him. I'd already devoured every book and magazine I could get my hands on when it came to parenting, so I didn't keep any around the house. I had gradually begun wearing looser clothes, subtly, so as to not draw attention. But eventually, the baby bump would give me away. And I'd need to see my OB-GYN soon. Not to mention, I wanted to start planning for the nursery. Though . . . I wasn't sure where that would be set up. Here? At our creek house? Somewhere else?

My life with Dane and plans for the baby were pretty much in limbo. Not a comforting position to be in when you were a planner who needed every detail nailed down before any big event. All of my details hung in the balance at the moment, making me antsy.

Really, I needed to rethink my strategy on keeping my pregnancy a secret. If Dane's visits became more frequent—which I would love—then any day he'd notice I wasn't just arbitrarily putting on weight, no matter how toned I stayed from yoga and genetics.

Getting back to the topic at hand, I said of Wayne's potential bragging, "It would sort of be an in-your-face for him, where I'm concerned. I'm sure he'd love to torture me with stories of how he's destroyed everything I love—whether he knows you're alive or not. Vale hadn't hesitated to tell me who he was and what his role was when he kidnapped me. He was just fine telling me he worked for the bad guys. He was proud to be their henchman."

"Still is, apparently. I thought for sure they'd cut him out when he fucked up so badly."

"Maybe they did. . . . Then maybe he came up with the plan to bomb the hotel. And had the perfect accomplice to make it happen."

Dane's jaw worked as he mulled this over.

I reiterated what he'd said, because it had merit. "Even the most meticulous criminals get caught because they do something absurd. They believe they're beyond reproach. That's when they fall."

He studied me a moment, then said, "You are not going anywhere near Wayne Horton, Ari. Do you hear me?"

I sighed. "Dane. Honey." I brushed my lips over his. He let out a low, sexy growl. Then returned the sensuous kisses, his lips twisting with mine.

Unfortunately, he seemed to realize something and his head

jerked away. "You've never called me *honey.*" His gaze narrowed. "If you think for one a minute you're going to sweet-talk me or se-duce me into letting you take a crack at getting a confession from Horton, you're seriously mistaken."

Toying with the button on Dane's shirt and peering at him from under my lashes, I said, "The sooner this is over, the sooner you can come home. For good. We can be together every night. And I promise you'll enjoy making up for lost time."

His eyes rolled and his head fell back against the top of the sofa. "Jesus. You don't play fair. My body aches for you every day and the thought of this being through so that I can get naked with you again anytime I want—" He let out a sharp breath.

I smiled.

But I'd only baited him so far—not hooked him.

He said, "These guys are going to turn on Vale, anyway. Put all the blame on him for anything related to the Lux to try to wash their hands of the blood—and get out of attempted-murder charges. I just need to finish what I'm doing."

"But you have to rope in two remaining guys from the society. I only need one. And he's here, Dane. Somewhere under my nose. Looking for me, I suspect."

His head lifted and he pinned me with a grave expression. "The answer is no. You've been in jeopardy enough. There is no chance in hell I would willingly allow you to—"

"What if you were there with me? Amano, too? The FBI? Close by. And we met in an open spot, someplace public where he couldn't grab me and drag me off?"

"He'd see it coming a mile away, baby. He's been setting traps—he'd recognize when the tables were turned on him, trust me."

"Not if it was an accidental run-in. Somewhere he frequents."

"Like Denny's?" Dane smirked.

I glowered. "Does Amano deliver verbatim reports, or what?"

"Pretty much. And while I found your reasoning sound, it was still amusing."

"I'm so happy you like my sense of humor." I tried to slip from his lap, a little peeved he didn't take me seriously.

But his strong arms caged me. "Ari, just try to understand that I love you too much to let you do anything dangerous."

"Marrying you was dangerous," I countered.

His expression turned even grimmer. I hadn't thought that possible. "I take full responsibility for the trouble I've brought to your life. Trust me when I say it keeps me up at night. But, Ari, needlessly inviting that trouble in will make this worse for both of us."

"I wasn't blaming you," I said, my tone softer as I tried to smooth the crinkle between his eyes with my fingertip. "I just want to help, Dane. And I want to be done with all of this, too. I want you back. Not every now and then, but all the time. Permanently."

He pulled me closer and held me tight. "I know, baby. I want the same. But this is not the answer."

"I disagree. It could work, Dane. It's worth a try."

"No. It's not." He kissed me. "No more discussion." He stood, with me in his arms, and carried me off to bed.

Dane returned a week later. He couldn't seem to stay away. I didn't mind.

He didn't bother with pleasantries this time, just came into the living room, took my hand, and led me down the hall to our suite. He kicked the door shut behind him, not turning on any lights, so that the only illumination came from the reflection of the rippling water against one wall from the pool lights.

Whirling me around so my back was to the door, he clasped my wrists with one of his large hands and raised my arms above my head. He kissed me hard, passionately, somewhat angsty, even. As though all the pressure and separation had finally gotten to him.

I returned the kiss with equaled fervor, silently demanding more.

His tongue swept over mine, twisting and tangling, delving

deep. His other hand cupped my breast and squeezed almost roughly. For once, I didn't worry over it dawning on him that the mounds were bigger, swollen in his palm. It felt too good to have him aggressively massaging and then teasing my nipple with his thumb through my tank top and lace bra.

He broke our kiss just long enough to gruffly say, "I need to make you come."

Excitement shot through me. I had no idea what brought this on, and I certainly wouldn't complain.

He gave me another sizzling kiss that nearly had me incinerating at his feet. But he continued to hold me with my arms pinned above my head and part of his hard body pressed to my side.

His hand slid down my belly to the button on my denim shorts. He pulled it apart and pushed the zipper down. Then his hand was inside my panties and his fingers glided over my already slick folds. His kiss and assertiveness made me instantly, ridiculously wet.

A tremor ran through my legs as he caressed my pussy lips, then targeted my clit, rubbing aggressively. With the exact amount of pressure and just the right tempo to send pleasure coursing through every inch of me. I was restless and hot, so fast. Needing the release as much as he apparently needed to give it to me.

He ripped his mouth from mine and kissed my jaw, my throat, nipping in a thrilling way, teasing my senses further. His head dipped and he tongued my nipple through my clothes as two fingers slipped inside me and he stroked wickedly.

"Oh, God," I moaned. "Dane."

"Come for me," he murmured. "Come all over my fingers."

"Yes. Oh, God, yes." My wild pants of air filled the quiet room. My heart pounded in my chest. Heat and exhilaration rushed through my veins. "Oh, Christ." The erotic sensations blossomed as the heel of his hand massaged my clit and his fingers pumped deeper, with determination.

I writhed against him, loving the muscles that pressed against me, the smell of him, the feel of him. My eyelids fluttered closed.

I shattered, crying out his name.

The climax was vibrant, radiating brilliantly as I clung to it. Savoring the pleasure he brought me, as always.

Dane dropped sweet kisses over the tops of my breasts, along my collarbone, up the side of my neck. His tongue pressed to that ultra-sensitive spot just below my ear, keeping the shock waves running rampant.

He nipped gently at my earlobe.

Then he whispered, "When were you going to tell me about the baby?"

chapter 18

I stared up at him.

Dane's eyes locked with mine. His jaw was set and his devilishly handsome face was a mask of hard angles. I couldn't read him—tell if he was okay with me being pregnant . . . or monumentally pissed off.

"I, uh . . ." *Huh.* I wasn't sure what to say.

"How far along?"

"Nineteen weeks."

He released my arms and stepped away. As he shoved a hand through his hair, he said, "You look sort of . . . balanced." His brow furrowed as though he wasn't sure that was the correct word.

It was.

With a nod, I told him, "I seem to slowly be filling out every-where. The boobs are keeping up with the bump. And the hips . . . Well. Let's just say I'm going to be a bit voluptuous when this is all said and done."

He spun around and started to pace. Unfortunately, I couldn't discern his source of consternation. He'd mentioned children once before.

Of course that had been long before the devastation that was now 10,000 Lux and the perils that ensued.

I said, "How'd Amano figure it out? I didn't tell him."

"He's pretty observant."

That was certainly a fact. I couldn't exactly be surprised or mad at Amano. I knew he'd catch on eventually, even if he'd never spent much time—if any—around a pregnant woman.

"So, I know this is a shock—a total accident because I skipped some of my birth control pills when I was wrapped up in Lux planning." I took a deep breath, let it out gradually. "Good news or . . . bad news?"

He sat on the bench at the end of the bed and dragged a hand down his face. "Good. Bad. Fantastic. Awful. I don't fucking know."

"Let's try initial, gut reaction," I tentatively ventured, my stomach knotting.

"You just got it. I couldn't arrive fast enough. My private Learjet can get me here from the East Coast in just under four hours, and that was still too long."

My stomach uncoiled. To help lighten the mood, I asked, "We have a Learjet? How cool is that?"

"Ari." He smirked. The supersexy one that totally did me in. My knees weakened. I crossed to the bed and plopped down on the edge.

Dane said, "I paced the aisle the entire way. Thank God no one else was in the cabin. I vacillated between soon-to-be-new-dad jitters and hell-yes-I-knocked-up-my-wife excitement."

I grinned.

"Then I saw you and all I could think was that I had to have you. Immediately."

"So, we really shouldn't waste time talking." I wagged my brows. "And P.S., pregnant sex is pretty awesome—at least from my side of things."

He grunted and went back to attempting to wear a hole in our hardwood floor.

"Okay," I said, my spirits sinking again. "Now that gut reaction is over. What are you *really* thinking?"

"That this is the absolute worst timing imaginable. I am a co-lossal idiot. And, let's see . . ." He shook his head, clearly angry. "I've put not only my wife's life in jeopardy, but also our baby's."

"Ah, yes," I said. "Hence the reason I didn't mention that we're with child." I stood and interrupted his path, forcing him to stop. "I knew it would worry you incessantly to not be here, to not know every second of the day how I'm doing, feeling, et cetera. You have to finish what you started, Dane. You don't need the distractions I pose."

"Ari." He gently gripped my upper arms and stared deep into my eyes. "You are everything." He grinned a bit impishly. "You and our baby," he amended, "are everything."

I flung my arms around him and held on tight. "I know that. And the baby knows that, too."

He harrumphed.

"Okay, well, he or she *will* know that."

"You haven't found out yet?"

"No." I pulled away. "I wanted to be surprised right along with you."

His head inclined to one side as he contemplated this. "How are you going to plan . . . colors, clothes . . . whatever?"

"I guess I'm not."

He gave me a long look and then asked, "You're okay with that? Because, come on, you have to be prepared for everything. I know you."

"Yes, you do." I kissed him. Then said, "But I want us to do it all together. So . . . I'm curbing my planning tendencies with meditation and yoga, and I'm basically driving Amano crazy with all manner of chitchat and making Kyle regret he's living here with us by challenging him to pool and bowling, since they're not strenuous and I'm of the ultra-paranoid mind-set when it comes to hurting the baby."

Dane's chiseled-to-perfection features darkened. "Then we shouldn't have been having sex these few—"

"Oh, no!" I cut him off. "I already checked, read, double-checked. The baby is well protected inside. Sex is okay."

He eyed me skeptically.

"Really, seriously." I gripped the material of his black dress shirt and said, "*Truly.*"

He finally cracked a real grin. "If you're sure."

"My OB-GYN confirmed it."

The grin faded. "Christ," he groaned. "You even have an OB-GYN that I didn't find for you and whom I've never met, and I haven't given you any sort of support or—"

"Dane." I held his gaze unwaveringly. "I chose to keep this from you so that you could do what you have to do. The reason I was at Kyle's aunt's retreat is because she's an M.D. and she contracts with really great specialists. I like my doctors—they're all wonderful. Trust me when I say I have been well taken care of and that everything with the baby is just fine."

"Except that you're going through this alone."

"I'm not alone."

His jaw clenched.

I blew out a breath. *Oops.*

He stepped around me and stalked to the door.

"Where are you going?" Though I already knew. . . .

Panic seized me.

He flung the door open and I chased him down the corridor. Before we reached the main portion of the house, though, he whirled back around. I followed him as he returned to our suite. He slammed the door shut behind us.

I jumped. "Please don't do that. I experienced enough slamming doors when growing up to last a lifetime."

"Kyle knows," he simply said. But his eyes told me he had much more to say on the subject. They burned with torment.

"Of course Kyle knows," I said in a quiet voice. "He was the one to suggest the retreat when I was so sick."

"When you were sick."

He was so twisted with guilt, it made my heart hurt. I rested a hand on his arm and said, "You made some choices independently of me. I did the same. We had no choice. Neither of us did it in a conniving way—we did it to protect each other. We did what we thought was right. Okay, yes, I'm pregnant. I'm sorry I didn't tell you sooner, but if I had . . . The FBI wouldn't be *this close* to busting apart the secret society that only intends to do more damage for the sake of their own bottom lines."

"I'm supposed to be in control of what happens with us, Ari—with your safety." His agitation mounted.

"Dane, I could slip and fall on wet tile, hit my head, and die tomorrow. You can't *control* that. As much as you want to contain the environment in which I'm in until the danger passes, there is never going to be a one-hundred-percent guarantee. That's not how life works, no matter how much money, influence, or power you have. We learned that with the Lux, didn't we?"

I could see how torn up he was about all of this. Ready to spit nails if I gauged accurately. His fists clenched at his sides and I knew he was all kinds of pissed off.

Searching my brain for some way to placate him was futile. I didn't blame him for the way he felt. I was pissed off myself. With the situation and with the fact that the urge to confront Wayne and get him to admit to all the damage he'd done practically burned a hole through my heart.

As I thought of this, there was a knock on the door. I was instantly taken aback, pretty certain Dane had told Amano not to disturb us—ever—when we were in the bedroom.

That thought, of course, made my cheeks flush.

Dane called out, "Yes?"

"It's urgent. A call you're going to want to take."

Tenderly gripping my biceps again, Dane said, "I couldn't be happier that we're having a baby. I hate the timing and the circumstances. But I love you. More than anything. And I want this baby."

I opened my mouth to speak. He cut me off.

"Ari, anything could go wrong at this point. You have to realize and accept that. And if things go bad for me, you have to stay strong for our child. The way you have so far." He kissed me fiercely, then added, "You truly amaze me. And I know I have to do everything I can to put an end to all of this so that I can be with you from here on out."

I smiled weakly as tears crested my eyes. "I'm glad you're happy about the baby. I'm . . . so happy. All I want is to protect our child, Dane. But I need you to not be distracted. We have Amano. And Kyle is a huge help. We're okay here. You can't think about us when you walk out that door."

He stared at me for endless seconds. I knew that what I said was literally an impossibility, but I needed that pledge from him.

"You want to keep a promise to me?" I asked. "Don't think about what you're leaving behind. Do what you have to do so you can come back to us."

I nearly choked on my words but did my best to deliver them as succinctly and calmly as I could.

"I love you, Ari." His hands cupped my face. "You're strong. So strong. Our baby will be just like you."

"Or you." I gazed at him through watery eyes and said, "I can't tell what I'm having, but a beautiful boy who looks just like you would be perfect. Just do me a favor."

"Anything."

"Make sure he has a father." More tears rolled down my cheeks.

"Ari."

"Be safe. That's what I'm asking."

He kissed me again, then stepped away. Turned to go.

I felt a strange wrenching inside. None of this was right, but it was inescapable.

I watched him pass through the door.

Wondering, as always, if this would be the last time I saw him.

I splashed cold water on my face, fixed my slightly mussed hair, and joined Kyle in the kitchen for dinner.

"Quick conjugal visit?" he quipped.

I glared.

"Ew. Not a nice look for you," he said.

Snatching the box of linguine from the counter, I opened it and poured the pasta into the water boiling in the stockpot.

"What are you making, anyway?" I asked. "Smells amazing."

"Pesto chicken to go with the linguine."

"Your mom must be one hell of a cook."

"She is. I had no choice but to watch and learn, since I was always taking care of the baby while she was in the kitchen."

"And your dad was on the road?"

Kyle pulled open the door to the double oven set into the wall and said, "Selling computer equipment. Good at his job but never home."

"Not even now?"

Kyle shrugged. "I think he likes the idea of home, marriage, family, but he's not exactly accustomed to actually being at home to deal with his marriage and family."

"That's too bad. And something I can no longer comprehend. Ironic, given my messed up childhood."

"Don't get me wrong," he said as he mixed dipping sauces for the bread. "He's a great dad. I mean, football was really his first calling and he helped so much when I wanted to play. Because of his mentoring, I was recruited onto the varsity team when I should have been playing JV. He would have made a great high school coach, but he went where the big bucks were and, again . . . I think he's always liked being on the move with his job."

I stirred the pasta. "I guess I can understand that. I mean, we've been restless here. I wasn't meant to be a full-time housewife."

"Does your husband know that?"

I laughed. "Come on, Kyle. You can be annoyed with him all you want. He made me an offer I couldn't refuse to work at the Lux and manage galas and weddings and fund-raisers that were meant to impress. I worked nonstop and loved it."

"So who's going to look after Bax Junior?"

With a shrug, I admitted, "I haven't thought that far ahead. I mean, I want to do it, of course."

"But you still want to plan your weddings."

"Sure. The good thing about that, however, is that the majority of work can be done from a home office. And we have Rosa." She'd been coming to the Fort Knox house twice a week, in addition to keeping up with the dust at the creek house. "Anyway, what about you?" I countered. "There's only so much maintenance to do at Macy's, and the landscaping is really just in the trimming stage at this point. We pruned and planted in late winter. What do *you* plan to do? Get another marketing job?"

"Kind of makes me sick to say this, but once you've had a marketing job at a place like 10,000 Lux, everything else is anticlimatic."

I laughed. "I can see how you would feel that way. But your credentials are awesome and you really built up your portfolio. Maybe you ought to consider another resort here in town. Or in Phoenix. Although . . ." I stirred some more, then said, "Here's an even better idea. What about marketing and design for one of the pro teams? The Diamondbacks, Cardinals, Suns . . . oh, my God. The Coyotes!"

He looked taken aback. "You're a hockey fan?"

"Big-time."

"I never would have guessed."

"My dad turned me on to it." I thought of him and frowned. "I need to see him."

"And tell him Dane's alive?"

I wasn't all that sure Dane would approve. Not that he wouldn't trust my father with the truth, but the fact was, the fewer people who knew Dane had survived the bombing, the better. The safer the secret would be. The more good he could do.

That meant I couldn't even let Mikaela in on the miracle that Dane was alive, which left me with a dismal feeling. Not that we'd become true gal pals, but I could certainly understand—relate to— the pain of losing someone she was so close to, someone she'd known her entire life.

But too much still hung in the balance for me to upset the ap-plecart. Plus, I had no desire to travel to Scottsdale again. It wouldn't surprise me to run into my mother while she was shopping in Old Town, and that would incited all-new levels of drama. She currently had no way of contacting me, no way of finding me.

I intended to maintain the disappearing act as long as possible. Especially while I was pregnant.

Breaking into my thoughts, Kyle said, "My aunt mentioned that your dad called the retreat after he came back from the vacation he'd 'won.'"

This made my heart jump. "What did she say?"

"She told him you decided to go on vacation, too."

"What? Why on earth . . . ?"

"Because that's what I told her." Kyle shrugged. "What other ex-cuse was I going to give? You went off the grid. I had to let her know why."

"I'll have to come up with a good vacay story, because I'm due for an ultrasound and a visit with my doctor."

"I don't know what you're going to tell your dad," Kyle said as he turned off the oven, slipped his hand into a mitt, and grabbed the chicken dish. "But you can tell everyone at the retreat that you spent a few weeks visiting family in Flagstaff and Prescott. Close drives from here. Nothing hazardous. No flying. Whatever."

"I don't have family in Flagstaff or Prescott."

"You do now. At least, for this purpose."

I drained and rinsed the linguine and poured it into a bowl. We set everything out on the patio and waited a few minutes.

"No Amano?" Kyle asked.

"I don't know."

"Well, I'm starving." He dug in.

I was hungry, too, so only waited a bit more out of respect for Amano and then enjoyed Kyle's awesome cooking.

When I was a bit less ravenous, I said, "I've noticed you've been studying Amano of late. What are you trying to glean? Bodyguard 101 through osmosis?"

"He's been tracking Wayne Horton."

That caught me off-guard. "What?"

"Yeah. I've been eavesdropping." He gave me a smug look.

"Oh, please. As if he wouldn't know you're listening in on his conversations. Come on, Kyle. The man's a professional. By a lot."

"And I'm learning from him. Do you know that he's a black belt in karate and that he once took a bullet for Dane's dad?"

"How do you know?"

"He told me. Showed me the scar on his shoulder. There was some scuffle—a protest—at a global economic summit being held in Mexico and revolutionaries popped off a few shots."

"Doesn't he wear a vest?"

"Sure. That doesn't protect the shoulders, though."

"True."

Kyle said, "He carries a Glock. I'm going to get one and learn how to shoot."

I stared at him, incredulous. "Why are you going all Rambo?"

"I don't know. Because buildings we're in get blown up and badass guys in Camaros and helicopters chase us?"

I took a few sips of my hot tea, hoping to calm my suddenly

rioting stomach. Then I said, "You shouldn't be getting so into this, Kyle. I mean, it's almost like you're thriving on the danger."

"I kind of am," he admitted. "And face it, Ari. Wouldn't you prefer to have a little extra protection for you and the baby, since your husband's not around?"

"Dane does everything he can to keep us all safe." I didn't really have to defend him. All I had to say was, "Look around this place."

Clearly, Kyle couldn't dispute the obvious. We were tucked away quite securely.

"I will admit, if we're going to be sequestered, it's nice to have the whole Club Med experience."

I smiled. "The pools are definitely a bonus."

"So's the workout room. And the kitchen . . ." He whistled under his breath. "If I had your billions, that's what my kitchen would look like."

My smile faded.

Kyle was instantly alarmed. "What?"

I sipped some more, dread seeping through me. "I haven't really thought about all the money. I've only been preoccupied with the baby and Dane's safety."

Kyle took a drink of his beer, then asked, "So what about the money?"

"Well, it's just that, I now know what people are willing—and capable—of doing to get their hands on Dane's fortune. Even when they have their own."

"Yeah, I can see where that might be of concern to you."

"Dane once told me it's like a drug for some. They're addicted to amassing wealth. They can't get enough—what they accumulate is *never* enough."

"And he associates with these guys." Kyle made a sarcastic chastising noise.

"He didn't know, going in, that they were corrupt. In fact, in the beginning, they really were effecting positive change. That was their oath, their mission. They used their influence and knowledge for political and economic improvements. It was an invaluable undertaking." I sighed. "That went horrifically wrong."

"And then some," Kyle mumbled. He shoved back his chair and stood. Gathering up the dishes, he carried them into the kitchen. I finished my tea and cleaned everything, since Kyle had cooked.

Then I wandered down the wing that housed the enormous office Amano had claimed as his private space, with a bedroom off one side. The door was closed. I wanted to knock, see if Dane was in there with him. I hoped he was still in the house, that he'd stay the night. But I couldn't even hear the slightest hint of muffled voices inside, and that made me curious as to whether they'd both left.

Feeling restless and a little lost, I went into the living room to occupy my mind with a book. It didn't work, of course. I curled up on a sofa and absently rubbed my stomach. I thought of Dane's reaction earlier to learning I was pregnant. I knew he was deeply concerned about the timing, and he had every right to be. But I could also see that it ate at him to not be here with me, especially during one of the most important periods in our marriage.

Worse, *Kyle* was here during this most important period. That had to kill Dane.

I let out another long breath. Dane really had ended up taking on so much, so quickly. The problems at the Lux, falling in love with me, the threats, our marriage, the explosion, the indictments, and now . . . a baby.

If we ever got around to the honeymoon we'd once talked about, I wouldn't be surprised if Dane slept through it.

"Hey, Ari," Kyle said in a tentative voice, interrupting my thoughts. I had no idea how long I'd been ruminating, but it was dark outside, stormy.

"What's up?" I asked.

"I think you're going to want to come see this."

I didn't like his ominous tone any more than his grim expression.

I slipped from the sofa and followed him into the den with a large flat screen mounted over the fireplace. The news was on. A Phoenix station. But I immediately recognized the backdrop as downtown Flagstaff, where they reported from tonight.

Kyle reached for the remote and turned the sound up. The reporter stood in front of the train depot, on the south side of the tracks, as a light mist fell. The streets were wet. Flashing red and blue lit the surrounding area and there were crowds gathered about.

The newswoman said, "The FBI has confirmed their involvement in a high-speed chase through downtown Flagstaff this evening that lasted only minutes and ended in tragedy."

My stomach wrenched. "Oh, God." I gripped Kyle's forearm to steady myself. "Dane," I whispered as terror ripped through me.

I could not do this again. I *could not* live through this once more.

"Wait," Kyle said. "Just listen."

The reporter continued. "We've learned that a person of interest, wanted for questioning related to the explosion at the luxury hotel, 10,000 Lux, in Sedona, attempted to outrun federal agents when they cornered him in a vacant lot along Steves Boulevard. The suspect fled the scene in a black BMW, weaving his way through light traffic along Route 66 toward downtown."

The camera panned to the left, where a train sat on the tracks. The lit sign for the famous Hotel Monte Vista rose in the background.

Then the camera zoomed in on a car—the black BMW. The roof had been torn off and the windows were shattered. There was no driver's side door and the entire front of the vehicle was smashed in. Really, it was all just a mangled, crumpled mess of metal.

"The suspect attempted to cross the tracks to elude the FBI," she said. "A train struck it and sent the car flying over the fencing and into the parking lot of the Lumberyard Brewing Company. The driver was pronounced dead on the scene."

"What was left of him," Kyle muttered. "Holy hell."

I felt queasy.

The reporter added, "The suspect is believed to be Vale Hilliard of the Caribbean country of Curaçao."

Kyle let out a strangled sound. "Notice she didn't say he was *identified*. There can't be anything to ID him with but his teeth— and good fucking luck finding those."

"I need to sit down."

He helped me into a chair as the wooziness took a strong hold of me.

"How about some water?" he offered.

"Yes, please."

Kyle grabbed a bottle from the mini-fridge at the wet bar and poured some into a glass. My hand shook as I sipped.

"Hey," he said. "This is good news. No more public enemy number one."

"Yeah, it's just . . . really gruesome."

And where was Dane? Had that been the call Amano insisted he'd want to take? Had the FBI closed in on Vale and wanted Dane to identify him or somehow be involved? Where was he now?

Kyle's thoughts must have run in the direction of mine, because he asked, "Is this why Dane came back tonight? Had the FBI alerted him that they'd located Hilliard?"

"Not that I know of," I said. "He came back because Amano figured out I was pregnant and told him."

"Shit, that's low."

"No." I shook my head. "That's loyalty. Amano might have some toward me, but his priority will always be Dane."

"He could have at least asked you why you hadn't mentioned it to anyone."

"Come on, Kyle. He knows why I've kept it a secret. He probably thinks he did us all a favor, and he just might be right. I mean . . .

In the long run, I wouldn't want Dane to die not knowing he left a legacy behind."

Fat drops rolled down my cheeks.

"Ari." Kyle put his arm around me. "Hey, he wasn't in the crash. He's probably just fine. Unfortunately."

"Kyle."

"Just sayin'. And you should know that if anything happens to him, I'll be here for you. I'll help you with the baby."

"Over my dead body."

My head snapped up at Dane's voice.

"That was sort of what the discussion was all about," Kyle said defiantly. Though his arm around me slipped away.

I got to my feet, a little shakily. "You're okay?"

"Yes." He crossed the room and took me possessively into his arms. Not before aiming a lethal look at Kyle. Amano did not appear pleased, either.

I said, "Won't Vale being dead make it more difficult to pin the explosion on him?"

"He was just the mastermind," Dane explained. "The one pulling the strings. Wayne Horton is the key to the bombing. And the fact that Vale is Byrn Hilliard's son will help with that side of the case. It'll be easy to prove he acted on behalf of the family—and that part of the society."

"Asshole got what he had coming to him," Kyle said.

"Yes," Dane concurred. "And with him out of the picture, Horton will be running scared. Too scared to do more damage. There won't be anyone to protect him—and no one to bankroll him."

"He's been hanging out in casinos," Amano told us. "Burning through cash playing poker and blackjack. He's at Cliff Castle in Camp Verde three times a week. Down in the Valley at Fort McDowell or Talking Stick on the weekends. Made a few trips to Vegas and Laughlin, but he lost big there and hasn't gone back."

Relief washed over me at the news regarding Vale and how it would release us from the threat of Wayne Horton as well. "No more looking over our shoulders."

"I wouldn't go that far," Amano said. "Yes, we're all pretty much in the clear. Dane just needs to wrap up these last two indictments."

"I haven't been able to get to my data," he admitted. "My hard drive's in a safe-deposit box in a Swiss bank. Hard to get to when you're a well-known dead man."

"What about Amano?" Kyle asked.

"He's the one who delivered it there, when I was laid up. But I haven't wanted him to return." Glancing down at me, Dane added, "I want him here with you."

"I can handle that," Kyle insisted.

I cringed.

Dane scowled. "Yes, I can see that's your plan. But I feel much better with the current arrangements, thank you."

Kyle shrugged. "I think she's safe with me."

"That's highly debatable," Dane shot back. "The switchbacks in my car? You could have killed—"

"Boys," I said, exasperation in my tone. "It's a little late in the day to be fighting over me. And no need to fight amongst ourselves." I gave them my best pointed look. Then asked, "So, why can't the FBI send someone for your laptop?"

Dane simmered a little but told me, "I don't want it directly in their possession. I can't risk them deconstructing the evidence I've gathered. I need it as-is for trial purposes."

I tamped down the *argh* welling in my throat. "Why does this have to be so damn difficult?"

"Because we're not simply talking about tax evasion the IRS can invariably prove. This is potential economic disaster of epic proportions. Billions of dollars, many empires, countless lives at risk. The stakes are too high, Ari."

"So Batman's got to save the day," Kyle said to me, making me smile. For all his angst and the fact he still poached on Dane's territory, it was quite evident Kyle had reluctant respect for my husband.

"Batman, hmm?" Dane mused.

"I kinda like it." I grinned up at him. "With the exception of the danger, of course. And the long absences."

"Which we shouldn't have to suffer through much longer," Dane assured me. "This is so close to being over, now that Vale is dead. Horton will crack under the pressure and the lack of protection. We'll get my data and then . . . everyone goes down."

I squeezed him tight. "Those are exactly the words I want to hear."

I yawned, now that the adrenaline had drained from my system.

Dane said, "You need to rest." He swept me up in his arms. Kyle rolled his eyes.

With a soft laugh, I told my friend, "A Glock is definitely out of the question."

chapter 19

Dane spent the weekend. I hadn't been so perfectly content since our wedding night. Though I knew not to get used to the feeling of normalcy, of us being a couple who filled their days with each other's company and spent their evenings together.

It was temporary.

For now.

That latter sentiment was what made it possible to lose myself in the time I had with him. I didn't let the word *temporary* penetrate my euphoria.

He made love to me on Saturday morning, and I cooked him breakfast. We ate on the west patio by the pool and waterfall. Kyle and Amano made themselves scarce, which I thought was sweet. Except for the fact that Amano had mentioned something about taking Kyle to the shooting range in Phoenix to see if he could aim straight. Given his quarterback's arm and training in hitting his target, I suspected he'd do just fine.

Which would have worried me all the more, had I not been thoroughly distracted.

Dane suggested a leisurely day of swimming and lounging. I didn't doubt relaxing was something he currently cherished, since he'd been on the move since December. We settled into the square, elevated alcove where two chaise longue chairs with thick cushions sat in shallow water.

Dane didn't really want to talk about the FBI and the case they were building, but I grilled him anyway, my curiosity running rampant.

"If the members of the society claim they had no involvement with the bombing—that Vale acted strictly on his own—how will it be proven otherwise, so that they're held accountable?" I asked.

"That's where Horton will come in handy. And honestly, Ari, with all the tabs Amano has kept on him lately, it's just a matter of days, hours perhaps, before the FBI picks him up. Once they've dealt with the aftermath of Vale's death, he'll be at the top of their list."

"I hate to say this because it's so evil, but I'm glad he's dead."

"Not more than me."

I glanced over at him. Got a little sidetracked with my thoughts as I admired his gorgeous body. Not as tanned as usual, since he'd spent a bit too much time the past couple of months cooped up with the FBI. By the afternoon, he'd have his normal color back, I was sure.

Regardless, he was mouthwatering. He clearly hadn't missed a workout. In fact, I thought he appeared a bit buffer. Maybe he'd taken out his aggression and angst weight lifting. I didn't know. All I could say was that he was sinfully delicious and it was almost impossible to merely sit next to him—not climb all over his hunky body.

Curbing the urge for the moment, I said, "It's a wonder Amano hasn't taken matters into his own hands when it comes to Horton.

He was the one to hire him at the Lux, after all. He must be furious. And he's so dedicated to you, Dane. This must be eating away at him."

"Precisely why I issued a strict order for him to leave Horton be. I don't want anything to interfere with the legal process. Or I'd kill him myself."

I gaped.

"Come on, Ari," he said, deathly serious. "You can't be shocked that's exactly what I want to do."

"Dane." Dark and Dangerous was back. It set me on-edge. "We talked about this. We agreed."

"He's still alive, isn't he?"

I drew in a long breath, let it out slowly. "Yes."

"I'm not blowing any of this on technicalities. I'm doing exactly what the FBI tells me to do. Everything is by the book. And when the axe drops . . . Trust me. It'll drop swiftly and destructively."

His stone jaw and the burning need for revenge in his eyes were telltale signs that he and the agents he worked with had this on solid ground. No room for errors or any slipup that would skew the entire justice system.

I breathed a little easier. Not just because Dane was so certain this would all work out as he wanted but also because my husband resisted his vigilante nature, which I knew took great effort. I'd seen him defend what was his—and knew the compulsion to do it again still raged within him.

Even walking into the den and seeing Kyle's arm around my shoulders had sent Dane into that dark place in his mind where I didn't want him to linger.

"Enough of the dreary," Dane said as he stood and took my hand. "Let's swim."

Amano and Kyle returned late afternoon. Amano handed over a garment bag, and I eyed him suspiciously.

"Eleanor took a guess at your size," he said.

I crooked a brow. "She knows I'm pregnant?"

"Yes. I had Jack set up more trusts for the baby."

"Oh. Thank you." Turning to Dane, I asked, "Why do I need a new dress?"

"Because we're having a party tonight."

My jaw slacked. "I haven't cooked anything, prepared anything. And Kyle's been out all day so—"

"Not here," Dane said with a coy grin. "Go get ready."

Excitement shimmied down my spine at the intrigue. And the opportunity to get all fancy for the evening.

As I headed toward the hallway, I noted Kyle had a garment bag as well. What, exactly, was Dane up to?

I showered and did my hair and makeup, again trying very hard not to get overly exhilarated about how right this all felt. Dane here with me, Amano appearing just slightly less like throttling a bad guy, Kyle still looking for that perfect chance—which would never exist—to convince me he was the better choice, yet still wanting to be a part of all of this.

I understood he came from a dysfunctional family, as we all had. Maybe that was why this particular unit worked for all of us. We might not be related by blood, but we were certainly bound by life-and-death situations. Bound by blood in a different sense.

We each had the option to scatter, to walk away from the intensity and the high-stakes game we played.

Apparently, none of us were willing to do so. That spoke volumes. Regardless of our differences and our points of view, we were committed to each other.

I donned a pretty halter-styled dress with graduating hues in sapphire that led to a fluttery, layered handkerchief hem. Eleanor had excellent taste. She'd sent dainty silver sandals as well and I felt like royalty after months spent in yoga clothes and slippers.

Dane joined me in the bathroom, his arms sliding around my

waist. "Baby, you look gorgeous." His lips pressed to the side of my neck. "You smell great, too. Maybe I should have made this a private affair."

"You can have me all to yourself later. In the meantime, why don't you tell me what you have planned for the evening?"

"Not a chance." He disentangled himself and turned the shower on.

I assumed Amano had brought him clothes, since Dane never showed up with anything more than a black backpack that likely only housed the absolute necessities.

I left the room so the humidity from the hot water didn't wilt my blowout. I found Kyle and Amano in the living room.

I whistled in appreciation. "So handsome. Aren't I the lucky girl?"

Kyle straightened his tie and said, "We clean up nice."

Amano poured sparkling water for me, champagne for everyone else. Dane sauntered into the room and I lost my breath.

He wore a charcoal-gray suit with a black shirt and tie. His hair was a tad longer than usual but still sexily mussed. His emerald eyes shimmered against his bronze skin. I realized I didn't need a party tonight—didn't need to be anywhere or with anyone else but him. I could just lie on top of him and admire him all night long. And be the happiest woman on the planet.

Obviously, he had other plans for us.

Extending his hand, he said, "Come on."

Our fingers entwined and I walked with him to the foyer.

"Where are we going?" I tried again.

"It's a surprise. But it'll be secluded. Safe."

I gazed up at him and smiled. "Okay." Despite my desire to simply be alone and naked with him, I got a little thrill from the prospect of an outing.

Knowing Dane and how we were all dressed, I suspected it'd be a stellar evening.

Amano drove us to the airport and we entered a private hangar.

I got my first glimpse at the Learjet Dane and I owned and the breath escaped me on one full rush of air.

"Holy shit," Kyle said from beside me, incapable of containing his shock—or the hint of awe.

"Yeah," I agreed. "Welcome to my world."

Dane took my hand once more and we walked toward the red carpet, where a flight attendant handed the gentlemen a flute of champagne and me more sparkling water.

"Thank you," I said. An SUV pulled into the hangar and I asked Dane, "FBI?"

"No. Another surprise."

Eleanor alighted, followed by Mr. Conaway and Ethan Evans, whom I hadn't seen since his visit to the hospital in December.

"A very nice surprise." I greeted them, accepting their kisses on my cheek. Beaming up at Dane, I said, "This is perfect."

"Almost." Mischief rimmed his green irises. He glanced back at the SUV and my gaze followed.

My dad climbed out, impeccably dressed in a navy suit with a crisp white shirt that had thin blue pinstripes.

"Yay," I said as I clapped and bounced softly on my toes.

He offered his hand to someone else inside the SUV, and Tamera emerged, stunning in a one-shouldered little black dress.

She crossed to where I stood and gave me her careful hug and air kisses. "Darling, you're radiant."

I was sure she had no idea I was pregnant, especially given the cut of my dress, but if she looked closely enough she'd figure it out. I said, "Thank you. You look sensational."

"So does your dead husband," she said, a hint of *what the fuck?* in her lovely British voice.

"Long story. I'll explain later. For now, please just keep our secret."

"Of course."

"And this one." I stretched the material against my stomach to reveal the baby bump.

"Oh, Ari!" She gave me another hug. "Congratulations, love!"

"Thanks."

"Well, this is all so very clandestine," she said. "I'm drunk with intrigue."

"Make it more fun and have some bubbly," I told her. The attendant had glasses for our five additional guests.

Tamera accepted one, but while we were still off to the side, away from any eavesdropping, she said, "I see you're still palling around with the very sexy Kyle Jenns."

"I couldn't help but notice you admiring him at Meg and Sean's wedding. At mine, as well."

"He's very easy on the eyes, love. Where do you find all of these delicious men?"

"I have no idea. But why don't you wander over and strike up a conversation with Kyle? I think he'd like it."

She didn't need additional encouragement. My dad sidled up to me after Tamera left.

"So," he said in a low voice. "He's alive."

I smiled brighter. "Yes, he is. Thank God. Sorry I couldn't tell you sooner. He's working with the FBI. They're going to nail those responsible for the Lux bombing. And other criminal activity."

"Ari—" His tone was tinged with warning.

"Dad, don't worry about it tonight. Let's all enjoy ourselves."

I could see it was a bit challenging to accept the reality standing before them. Even Ethan was taken aback. He clasped Dane on the shoulder and said, "You'd better have one hell of a good explanation."

"I do. But . . . I'll save it for later." He lifted his flute in the air and announced, "Thank you all for joining us once again. I regret it's been so long since we've all gotten together, but I do appreciate you spending the evening with us."

We all clinked rims. I noted Ethan's curious glance at my clear, carbonated drink, obviously not champagne. He didn't say a word, though. Didn't quiz Dane further, either, on his absence of late. No one mentioned his unexpected reappearance. Shock lingered in the air, regardless.

After polishing off our drinks, we all boarded a Gulfstream jet in the same hangar with the Lear, though this one was much larger to accommodate our group. I wondered if we owned it, too.

No one knew where we were headed, and Dane didn't elaborate. He didn't even tell me. Then the Grand Canyon came into view, and we approached the landing strip. I still didn't know what he had up his sleeve, but the location was spectacular, especially at sunset.

I glanced over at him and smiled.

He whispered, "I want to make you smile like that every day. Of course, that's not all I want to do to you every day."

Heat, and likely pink, crept over my cheeks.

Dane said, "I want to make you blush, too. And come."

I sucked in a sharp breath. Luckily, no one could hear it. We were in the back of the plane, not fully engaged in the animated conversations.

I said, "You should behave."

"That's not at all what you want me to do."

He had me on that one. "I'd say you win"—because I knew how much he liked to—"but we're about to touch down, so we're sort of at a stalemate."

"Hmm." His lips pressed softly to my temple. "For now."

I brimmed with excitement and lust but tried to keep myself composed as we all exited the plane and took SUVs—one driven by Amano, the other by his new protégé, Kyle—to the famed El Tovar Hotel, which sat a mere twenty feet from the rim of the canyon. The vistas were astounding. So breathtaking, we all absorbed the wonderment in awed silence. Twilight provided enough of a glow to accent the sedimentary layers of the canyon walls and sprinkle golden light over the mesas.

I hadn't been here since I was a kid. My sixth-grade class had hiked a portion of the canyon and we'd learned all about the wildlife and plants. I appreciated the grandeur much more as an adult.

Dane guided us to a private deck that was set for our dinner of nine. Lanterns and candles added to the gorgeous ambience. Music flowed from hidden speakers. Appetizer stations were set up, as well as a wine bar, with scotch and brandy in decanters. Dane played host, and I realized that was his way of keeping his appearance to a minimum—he didn't want even the servers at El Tovar to get a glimpse of him.

Everyone in our group seemed to grasp this, even my dad, though he was still stunned. I joined him at one point and said, "Again, I'm sorry I didn't tell you. Warn you. Whatever."

His gaze slid from Dane to me. "When did you find out he was alive?"

"A couple of months ago. We have to keep it quiet, Dad."

"Does this have anything to do with last night's car wreck in Flag? With the FBI involved?"

"Yes. Vale Hilliard was responsible for the bomb at the Lux. Though it was likely just his directive. Someone else did the dirty deed, we suspect."

"Jesus."

"It's really bad, Dad. Dane's helping to sort it out. The bottom line is that few people know he survived the explosion and it has to stay that way."

"So, I'm guessing the all-expenses-paid vacay to Augusta wasn't just luck of the draw?"

"You catch on quick." I kissed his cheek. Then I told him, "I swear I'll explain it all to you as soon as everything's settled."

"I don't know, sweets. This doesn't sound healthy for you or the baby."

"Dad." I understood his concern. But I didn't want anything—reality included—raining on my parade tonight.

He fretted a bit, then asked, "Are you doing okay?"

"So much better," I said with conviction. "Kyle's aunt and her specialists worked wonders. And then I found out Dane didn't die at the Lux, and everything with the baby is going great. I feel fantastic, I promise."

"Well, you sure look fantastic." Finally, he grinned. "Tamera is right. You're radiant." He studied me a few seconds more, adding, "You know, your mom never glowed, but sweets, you positively shine."

"I am married to an amazing man and having his child. So, literally, I could swing from the chandeliers."

My father was wonderful enough not to mention the time Dane and I spent apart, the way I'd freaked because I'd thought he was dead, and so on. My guess was, his sole focus remained on the fact that Dane was here, we were together, and I had a baby on the way.

We had a sensational dinner under the stars with the moonlight streaking over majestic Grand Canyon. The food was incredible, the company even better. And what pleased me more was that no one was in a hurry to end the evening. We lingered over dessert and cocktails. Kept the conversations flowing with no need to hastily wrap it all up.

Midnight came and went. Dane finally said, "We should get you all home."

No one jumped on the offer. We continued on. I was basically curled against Dane on a comfy patio sofa when Eleanor eventually said, "Ari, you're exhausted."

"Oh, keep enjoying yourselves," I told them. "Don't let the pregnant chick spoil your fun."

Everyone laughed.

Dane said, "You should rest. Let's not overdo it."

I hated to end such a wonderful evening. These types of get-togethers were much too few and far between. And would continue to be until this was all over.

But I couldn't deny I was wiped out. I crashed against Dane's shoulder again on the flight to Sedona. I was barely cognizant as

I said good-bye to everyone at the hangar and we made our way home.

Before I drifted off on the drive to the fortress, I whispered in Dane's ear, "Thanks for tonight."

He was lying next to me in the morning when I woke. I rolled toward him, my lids fluttering open. He gazed at me and I smiled.

"There it is again," he murmured. "All I want is to keep you happy."

"You gave me so much last night," I said. "It was incredible. I know it was risky for you. But you did it for me."

"Everything I do is for you."

Emotion welled within me. I ran my fingers through his hair. "Bringing everyone together gave me a sense of family. Thank you."

He leaned close and kissed the tip of my nose.

I smiled again. "We're perfect together. You know that, right?"

"*You're* perfect."

"Dane—"

"Baby." He looked deep into my eyes. "I love you more than anything."

"Trust me when I say the feeling is mutal."

And then he made love to me.

chapter 20

"This is heaven," I said with a contented sigh as Dane slid a fat, wet bath sponge lathered with lavender-scented body wash up my arm to my shoulder. I was positioned between his legs in the huge tub in our suite, my back pressed to his chest. I'd piled my hair on top of my head and his lips grazed my neck as he eased the sponge along my collarbone, over my breasts, and down to my belly.

He rubbed my stomach slowly, sweetly, practically making me purr.

"You have just the right touch," I murmured.

"I'm guessing a foot massage might be in order after this, given that you haven't been wearing high heels lately."

"I sat most of the evening." He'd pretty much seen to it. "But, yes, I am out of practice with the sandals. They were just so lovely. I couldn't resist."

"Back to your slippers."

"Gladly."

He asked, "Does the lavender help?"

"Immensely. It's very calming, soothing. I ran out of the frank-incense."

"I'll get you more. Qadir will send it."

"So he knows you're alive as well?"

"Yes. As does Nikolai. I contacted them last night. Like Ethan, they were a bit put out that I'd kept this from them, but understood the circumstances and what needed to be done. Also, I think they'd already begun to suspect, when the indictments started coming."

"It must have been difficult for you to maintain the secrecy. Especially with Ethan. I know how close you are."

Dane let out a short, hollow laugh. "It was damn near impossible to keep this from him. I hated every second of it, but it was necessary."

"He must have been shocked to hear your voice."

"Even more stunned to see me in person, though he hid it well. I know he feels slighted that I didn't trust him with my plans, but I also know that, were the shoe on the other foot, he would have likely done the same. Amano was smart enough to set it all up flawlessly. The only regret I have is that he didn't tell you from the beginning."

"You can't obsess over that, Dane. He did what needed to be done. We all have. And we've pulled through. Although . . . I do feel bad that Mikaela doesn't know."

He was quiet a few moments, then told me, "As much as I hate how this has affected her—and I know she orchestrated my memorial service—I can't tell her just yet. Not that I don't trust her completely. She's just so . . . exuberant. I wouldn't want her to accidentally blurt out that I'm alive. Or let it slip to Brizio."

"I understand. In the long run, all that will really matter to her is that you are, indeed, alive."

He kissed my temple.

Setting aside the sponge, he reached for a tube of sugar scrub. "What's this?"

"Exfoliates the skin."

"Huh." He removed the lid and squirted a little onto the pad of one finger, inspecting it.

I found his curiosity about all my girly stuff endearing. He'd grilled me endlessly as we'd cuddled in bed this morning, our legs tangled, our fingers entwined. He'd wanted to know all about how I felt in general and as a result of being pregnant. Had a number of questions about the baby and an infinite list of potential dos and don'ts he thought he should know about. It was really very sweet and charming. Such a nice change of pace from the dark and tragic drama we'd been embroiled in.

Beyond the fact that his inquisitiveness and genuine concern touched my heart, it had felt so fantastic to finally share all of this with him. We even talked baby names, but nothing jumped out at us as a definite possibility.

The only subject we hadn't broached was where we'd live after all was said and done with the indictments. The fortress was growing on me, as long as I didn't give too much thought to the look of the high-voltage wall. It wasn't as though our friends would find the impenetrable security out of the ordinary, knowing what we'd been through. Well, Meg and Sean would. Then again, perhaps not, since Meg's father was a global communications tycoon who had employed his own level of security to keep his family safe.

I assumed that was why Kyle hadn't wigged too much over all the gates and guards and even a watchtower. He'd been exposed to Meg's family before he'd ever met me.

Still, I hadn't lost any love for the creek house, despite being away from it for so long. In fact, I missed it. So I wasn't sure where we would reside in the future. For all I knew, Dane might want to leave Sedona completely. There was no Lux to bind him here.

As I considered this, and leaving Kyle and my dad, Dane gently rubbed some of the sugar scrub on my shoulders and over my chest, using the sponge. My eyelids drifted closed as the slightly grainy, partially creamy texture worked its magic on my skin. The light vanilla aroma mixed with the lavender to create a lovely scent, and I inhaled deeply. I was thoroughly relaxed, though acutely aware of Dane.

His muscles and presence surrounded me. His heat felt soothing against my lower back, which ached a little from the previous evening's exertions. He left feathery kisses along my throat as my head rested against his shoulder. I felt his erection and grinned.

"You can't seriously want me again," I softly joked. I'd lost count of the number of orgasms I'd had in the past forty-eight hours.

"Of course I want you again." His sexy voice rumbled against my neck. "The question is, do you want me?"

"That never has been, nor will it ever be, a legitimate question. Certainly not one worth posing."

He chuckled. "I always have enjoyed your bit of sass, Mrs. Bax."

"I've always enjoyed how hot you get for me."

"More than you know." He stroked lower to my breasts. The water only reached the top of my rib cage, since I'd complained it'd take half the day to fill the enormous tub and I'd been itching to get in.

He swept the sponge over my already pebbled nipple as his teeth tenderly bit my throat. I moaned at the sensations he evoked. His mouth on my skin turned me on as much as the tiny granules he rubbed against the taut peak, making it tingle.

"Feel good?" he whispered as he shifted the sponge to my other nipple.

"Awesome." I sighed. "They're very sensitive and the sugar adds friction."

He tossed aside the sponge and squeezed more of the scrub onto a palm and rubbed his hands together. Liquid heat flared through my veins before he even touched me—the mere thought of what he was about to do excited the hell out of me.

He cupped my full, aching breasts and massaged gently. "You always worry too much about your figure, but honestly, baby, you pregnant is the sexiest damn thing."

"I have a lot of competition," I noted. "I see how women look at you. Gorgeous women."

Mikaela.

"None more gorgeous than you."

He carefully rolled my puckered nipples between his fingers and thumbs. The sugar was a delicious stimulant, sending shock waves to my core. I writhed against him, pressing my thighs together as my pussy throbbed.

Opening his hands, he used his palms against the sensitive points of my breasts, caressing in a circular motion. The erotic tingle against my nipples from the micro-beads turned me instantly restless, so aroused.

"Dane," I whispered. "Let's get out of the tub."

His hands dipped into the water, washing off the sugar before he quickly rinsed my chest. Then he climbed out and helped me. He laid a towel over the marble vanity and lifted me onto it.

My fingers curled around his wide shaft and I stroked him slowly. His emerald eyes blazed.

"Ari," he murmured just before his mouth sealed mine. He kissed me passionately, deeply. A searing lip-lock that conveyed lust and longing. And love.

I wasn't sure if it was the pregnant hormones, all we'd been through, or the fact that I now considered every single moment we stole together the most precious of time—or all of that combined. But this kiss was so much more stirring than ever before. That was saying something, of course, because I'd always found Dane's kisses soul stirring.

This one took me to all new heights of unrelenting desire and irresistible affection. He hooked a forearm under my knee and spread my legs. Our lips and tongues continued to tangle and taste as the head of his cock nudged my opening.

I wrapped my fingers around his neck, keeping him close, keeping him kissing me. The other hand flattened against the vanity and I lifted myself slightly, angling my hips.

He barely pressed into me. Electric currents ran through my body. His tongue toyed sensually with mine as he moved a breath deeper, just an inch more. Taunting me, torturing me in the most seductive, provocative way.

I wanted him desperately, but the intimate teasing was sinful, playful. Downright exciting. As much as the urge to beg him to fuck me rose in my throat, I kept quiet as he dragged his mouth from mine and kissed my jaw, my neck. I luxuriated in the slow burn.

My lids closed and I dropped my head back. I concentrated solely on how he felt, pushing gradually in, filling me inch by glorious inch.

"That is so amazing," I gasped. "I love how you feel inside me."

"You make me come completely undone," he said as he pumped slowly, pushing deeper and deeper with every measured thrust. "I can't ever get enough of you."

A smile twitched at the corners of my mouth. "You know you're driving me wild."

"I just like taking my time. Staying buried right here as long as I can."

"No rush," I whispered against his lips. "My doctor's appointment isn't for another hour."

"I'm going with you."

"I figured you'd say that."

He continued to move within me, gliding slickly, stretching me. He kissed me again, and I reclaimed all my bliss from the nights at the creek house when he'd made love to me, held me, made me feel cherished and protected.

Like those exciting interludes, he picked up the pace now, stroking confidently. His kiss turned demanding, territorial.

I loved it when he got so caught up in the moment that he seemed desperate to have me—desperate to make me come.

I returned the kiss with equaled passion and possession. Because he was mine.

The bliss consumed me and the erotic sensations coursing through me erupted. I tore my mouth from his and cried his name.

"Oh, Christ, Ari." He groaned.

I knew I squeezed him exceptionally tight. I couldn't help it. I literally clung to every inch of him.

"Baby," he murmured before he thrust deep, his body jerked, and he came inside me while letting out that carnal growl that made all my nerve endings go haywire. Nuzzling the side of my neck, he said, "I have absolutely no control when it comes to you."

I smiled as euphoria flooded my veins. "Let's keep working on it."

We *all* drove to the retreat. An uncomfortable scenario in that I was there to see my OB-GYN for an ultrasound. I was thrilled Dane wanted to come along. I also understood that Amano preferred to chauffeur us for our own protection. And Kyle wanted to see his aunt and Chelsea.

Still, it was a bit awkward.

Regardless, it worked in our favor. Kyle cleared the way for us with Security and made it so that no one was around as we came through the door and entered Macy's office, Dane with a ball cap pulled low on the brow and his head down—the fewer people identifying him the better.

Amano waited in the hallway while I surmised Kyle went to greet everyone on the back patio, since it was a typical beautiful Sedona day to be outside.

Macy gave me a hug. "I've been worried about you, but Kyle said you've been doing some traveling."

"Yes," I perpetuated his excuse for my absence. Then I said, "I'd like to introduce you to my husband, Dane Bax."

He removed his cap and extended his hand.

Her jaw dropped.

I continued. "Dane, this is Dr. Macy Stevens, Kyle's aunt. She owns and runs the retreat. She's been a huge help with the baby. And in general."

"Then I'm indebted to you," he told her in an earnest tone. "I'm afraid our situation has been less than ideal. Complicated. And very difficult on Ari. But necessary." His jaw clenched for a moment. "Regrettably."

I could see we'd stunned her. Obviously, from her expression, she knew who Dane was. Who he'd been. I had no idea of the appropriate connotation, since he was supposed to be dead yet stood here in her office.

Ever graceful, she recovered quickly. "It's a pleasure to meet you." They shook. "And I'm so happy the two of you are together again."

It was evident she didn't know what to say. I didn't blame her.

"It's a rather long story," I explained. "I didn't know for some time that Dane had survived the explosion at 10,000 Lux. He was severely injured. Now he's working undercover with the FBI. So I'm sure you can understand how imperative it is to keep his . . . existence . . . quiet."

"Of course." She gave a slight smile, still looking a little confused and flustered but clearly trying to grasp the full scope of the situation. At any rate, she added, "Rest assured, both of you. Doctor-patient confidentiality is of utmost importance to me, but aside from that, as a friend, I certainly know how to keep a secret."

"Thank you, Dr. Stevens," Dane said. "We don't want to put you in any sort of compromising position, but I really wanted to be here today for my wife."

"I can imagine this hasn't been an easy scenario for either of you. Please, have a seat."

Dane pulled out a chair for me at her small conference table.

Macy told us, "We received a very generous donation this week, from your new foundation."

My brows rose. "Already?" Mr. Conaway certainly knew what he was doing. The man was quite the miracle worker.

"Yes," Macy confirmed. "Enough to bring in one more specialist for Chelsea so she has round-the-clock care, and all of her bills are covered for the next two years."

Dane shot me a curious look.

"Chelsea is autistic and absolutely adorable. So loveable. I'll tell you all about her later. Tell you why I did this."

"You don't have to explain or justify," he said, a hint of awe in his eyes. "It's your money to do as you please. And if establishing a foundation to help autistic children is what you want to do, I'm one-hundred percent behind you. Proud of you, actually."

"Thank you." I smiled.

Macy clasped her hands in front of her, resting them on the table. "Her mother, Abby, would really like to see you soon, Ari. She's so happy to be able to leave her night job and have some breathing room. She's extremely grateful."

"I can't imagine how challenging it must be, financially and emotionally, to have to rely on others to care twenty-four-seven for your child. I'm glad we could help."

"Chelsea would run away," Macy said. "If Abby turned her back for even a second, Chelsea bolted for the door. She'd run right out into a busy street. It's a wonder she was never hurt. And Abby lived in fear every day, every night."

I shivered. I couldn't fathom that, either.

"Clearly, Chelsea's safer here," I commented. "And seems to be doing so well."

"Much better. And now maybe Abby can get a little bit of her sanity back. Plus visit Chelsea more often with the freed-up time."

"I'll be sure to hook up with her soon. For lunch, perhaps."

"She'd enjoy that." Macy spread her arms. "Now, I understand you have an ultrasound awaiting you."

My stomach fluttered. I was thrilled Dane was with me today. "Yes, we do."

We all stood. Macy and Dane shook hands again and he thanked her profusely once more for all she'd done for me. I gave her a hug and apologized for the secrecy. She didn't seem to mind. Seemed relieved, in fact, that I was no longer a single mom. Or alone, though she'd never known I was married until now.

Across the hall, we went through the same thing with Dr. Preston. She didn't quite regroup as fast as Macy, but I got the sense that that had more to do with her shock over my very gorgeous and rich husband. I couldn't blame her for that, now could I?

She slid me a look with big eyes and I grinned. "I know," I simply said.

Composing herself, she directed me to the exam table, and I lifted my shirt to reveal an ever-growing belly. Dane positively beamed. Lovingly and with great pride. He appeared to get a kick out of knowing our baby was making his or her presence known.

"Everything looks fantastic," Dr. Preston said at the conclusion of her exam, though she broke down some details for Dane's sake, which I appreciated.

He was thoroughly fascinated with the image on the screen. Riveted. As though seeing the baby inside me truly brought home the fact that we were having a child. He was utterly mesmerized.

I laughed softly.

Dr. Preston asked, "Would you like to know the sex?"

Dane tore his gaze from the monitor and stared at me.

"Makes planning easier," I ventured.

"We'll need a nursery."

"Among other things. Many other things."

His emerald irises glowed with wonderment. He was a beautiful sight. My heart nearly burst with love.

"I think I'd like to know," he said.

I smiled. "I think so, too."

"Okay, then," Dr. Preston announced gleefully. "Congratulations, you're having a bouncing baby boy."

My stomach flipped. Tears sprang to my eyes.

An heir. Our firstborn would be a son.

"That's perfect." I stared up at Dane. "So very perfect."

He reached for my hand, brought it to his lips, and tenderly kissed my fingers. Then he splayed my palm over his heart and said, *"You're* perfect. And I love you so very much."

chapter 21

My bliss was short-lived.

Later in the afternoon, I met FBI agents Daugherty and Strauss. They came for Dane.

I fought back the anxiety and the angst. He'd done so much already. I was pissed that they wanted—*needed*—more from him. Even as I thought of the hard drive in a safe-deposit box in a Swiss bank, I resisted the urge to say he'd given them all that he could and it was their job to do the rest.

I resisted the urge to beg him to stay.

Especially when they said it was too dangerous for him to return here until this was finally put to rest.

"What does that mean?" I asked Dane.

His hands cupped my face and he gave me a valiant grin. "It means soon. So just stay put, with Amano and Kyle. Because I'll be back before you know it. For good this time."

Tears welled in my eyes and I tried to push them back, for his sake. He thought I was strong. I thought I was about to crumble at his feet.

We'd had an entire weekend of normalcy. A longer, saner span of time than we'd had since last Thanksgiving, five months ago.

A lifetime ago, as far as I was concerned.

He kissed me and then said, "Just remember how much I love you and how much I want to come back to you—to our family."

The agents gave me their obligatory apologetic smiles. I turned away and walked out onto the patio.

Kyle followed.

"At the risk of sounding like a tool," he said, "this blows. For you. I'm sorry."

"You're not a tool. You're stating the obvious." I swiped at more tears.

"Okay, at the risk of sounding like an asshole . . . you really could do so much better."

I laughed. "And now you're a tool."

He chuckled along with me. "Had a feeling that one would get you."

I sank into a sofa and pulled my knees up to my chest, resting my arms on them. "I don't begrudge him this duty. I just miss him every single second. Like . . . *every single one.*"

"Yeah, that figures." Kyle let out a long breath.

I said, "You know he's doing the right thing. No matter how painful it is for me or the bullshit it's brought into our lives."

He was silent for a couple of minutes, then told me, "This is going to sound crazy, but when this is done . . . I'm not exactly sure where I'll go from here. I mean, even the marketing jobs we talked about don't hold much appeal. I'm used to being on my toes now. I spend all this energy being prepared for anything, and the adrenaline rush is pretty sweet. How am I supposed to clock in to an eight-to-five desk job?"

I contemplated this, both alarmed at my best friend thriving on danger and comprehending it at the same time. The best advice I could offer was, "You're young and feeling invincible. Something you lost when you blew out your knee and had to take a pass on a pro football career. That doesn't mean you *are* invincible. But I will admit, you don't suck at the bodyguard stuff."

"So maybe I have a higher calling than marketing."

My stomach clenched nervously. "Call it best-friend worries or new, maternal wariness, but I'm not really liking the sound of that."

"And yet you know I make a good point. Ari, I could sit in a cube all damn day photoshopping designs on a computer, or I could save a life or two. Maybe even yours."

"Not at the risk of *yours*," I insisted. "Look, Kyle, I didn't know Amano when he started shadowing me. It was his job, and he's so loyal and dedicated to Dane that he clearly took on the assignment without a second thought. Unfortunately for him, I came with a bull's-eye on my forehead because of my association with Dane. But as I've gotten to know him . . . I'm not all that whippy over the fact that Amano puts his life on the line for me all the time. I'm most certainly not happy that you want to do the same."

He stuffed his hands in the front pockets of his jeans and shuffled around a bit. Then he asked, "How do you really feel about your husband being all warrior-ninja-like?"

"Similar to Amano, he's good at what he does. He seems to know how to blend and hide and be all-around stealthy to get the job done. Do I like any of this? Hell, no. Do I trust him? Absolutely. But would I wish this on anyone?" I stared unwaveringly at Kyle. "Not a chance. And I don't want you, one of the closest people to my heart, to do anything crazy, over-the-top, *dangerous*."

He opened his mouth to speak, but I interjected, "Don't mistake Amano or Dane for being warrior-ninja-like and get some high off of it. They do what they have to do in order to stand up to the society and to protect me. The baby. Even you and my dad. I don't want you putting yourself in that line of fire. For me or for anyone else."

He walked away. I debated the situation. Then I leapt to my feet, an idea popping into my head. I followed him into the kitchen. Amano was there, too, sipping espresso.

"Perfect," I said. "You're both here. Let's take a field trip."

They eyed me suspiciously. Kyle with a bit of angst brewing.

Because I didn't put him on par with Amano's mad skills as a bodyguard?

"Hey," I said, raising my hands in the air. "Trust *me*."

We drove down the street. As the wrought-iron fencing, lovely columns, and now-defunct lanterns came into sight, Kyle demanded from the backseat, "Why the hell are we here?"

"Method to the madness," I contended. "Give me the benefit of the doubt and work with me."

Amano pulled up to the security booth and lowered the window. "Hello, John."

I stifled a sigh of relief. I'd hoped John would be at the gate, knowing it would make this much easier. Relatively speaking. Only gaining access to the drive into 10,000 Lux would be easy. The rest would be monumentally, excruciatingly difficult. Painful.

Amano gave a little song and dance about wanting to check on the property for purposes of comparisons related to insurance matters. John didn't question the boss. He did make mention that he was glad to still have a job and that Amano had been right—it was a good idea to have the security gate manned to keep the lookie loos and media at bay.

As we rounded a grove of sycamores and entered the wasteland that was 10,000 Lux . . . I couldn't breathe.

I wasn't the only one.

"Jesus," Kyle muttered. "Holy fucking shit."

Amano parked the SUV where the valet area once existed. Right in front of the lobby of the Lux . . . that had once existed.

I stared up at the gaping hole. I'd seen something similar

before—the whole world had. I was instantly reminded of the huge void in the Pentagon after a plane had struck it on 9/11.

It was the creepiest, eeriest, scariest damned thing just like the Pentagon. This massive destruction in the very center of a once-amazing hotel.

We were lucky at the Lux, however. No one died. That did not take away from the devastation we stared at.

I climbed out. Amano and Kyle followed.

"I don't understand why you wanted to come here," Kyle said.

"I just needed to see it," I told him. My gaze didn't waver. I took in the scene before me. Shattered glass, splinters and chunks of wood, exposed metal, mammoth pieces of jagged-edged stone and marble, wrought iron, scorched land . . . I shuddered. A lump of emotion swelled in my throat.

To the west was the wing that had housed the executive offices. The very end still stood—where Dane's suite was, right by the stair-well.

My gaze shifted and fell closer to the destruction. Part of the gaping hole was my office. The beautiful one. So meticulously, thoughtfully decorated by Dane. The gorgeous space I had wanted my whole event-planning career and which I had loved fiercely.

It was now obliterated.

I thought of how wiping out brick and mortar, material posses-sions, and memories could shatter spirits as much as it could lives. So much so that it'd almost made me forget . . .

The beauty of this place.

The hard work we'd put into it.

The dream that had been Dane's.

I let out a slow breath. Couldn't pull in a full one. Tears crested the rims of my eyes.

I turned back to the SUV. What *had* been the point to coming here?

My hand lingered on the door handle of the passenger's side.

Something had compelled me. And I'd brought Amano and Kyle along with me.

Facing to the ash and burnt grounds again, I wondered what the hell would ever become of something once so painstakingly tended to, something so magnificently built.

"What are you thinking?" This from Kyle.

I slid a glance toward Amano. He gave me an empathetic look. I asked him, "What will he do with this?"

Amano seemed reluctant to say. It took him a few moments to answer, in fact. Eventually he told me, "Mow it all down and sell the land."

"But there are still buildings intact," I pointed out. "The aquatic center and its two restaurants, the conference center and ballrooms, the spa and fitness center. What about the five golf courses and all the private casitas?"

"Ari," he told me, "if there's no Lux for Dane, then none of this will exist for anyone else. Do you understand that?"

"Yes, I suppose so." I shook my head. "No. Not really."

Kyle repeated, "Why'd you want to come here?"

"I don't know," I confessed. "I just wanted to see it again. I mean . . . haven't you been curious?"

He shrugged. "Sure, a little."

I returned to the SUV, again reaching for the handle. I still didn't open the door. Glancing over my shoulder at the now-faded grandeur that had once held me spellbound, in complete awe, I said to no one in particular, "This wasn't just some arbitrary place where we came to work. It was Dane's vision and it became our vision. It was beyond comprehension in so many ways. He created something that inspired all of us. He built a legacy."

"Yes," Amano agreed. "But clearly, this wasn't a dream or a legacy that was meant to last. There were forces working against him. Now it's all over."

Finally, I yanked open the door and climbed into the passenger's seat. I felt sickened by what was left of so much hard work. And my husband's dream. The rubble that lingered in the wake of our extravagant plans for pre-launch and grand opening activities.

More than that, I hated that everything Dane had sweated over and bled for when it came to the Lux was now reduced to debris. The palace I'd considered more stunning than any other.

Honestly, I wasn't sure what had urged me to come here. There was nothing to gain from it, nothing to glean. Literally, it was what it was. A dream lost. One stolen, really, but devastated all the same.

We drove back to the fortress and I changed into yoga pants and a tank top. I couldn't sleep, though. I was restless and agitated. Maybe because Dane was gone again. And because I had no idea when I'd see him. *If* I'd see him.

I hated the variables. But they remained constants in my life. Nothing I could change.

With a heavy heart, I wandered into the living room, the reflection from the pool flickering over the inner walls of the archway-lined patio. It was quiet and peaceful. Tranquil. I liked the serenity because it reminded me of the retreat.

I tried to not feel so lonely, since Amano and Kyle were there with me, though they were engrossed in whatever secret-service stuff Amano now allowed my best friend to participate in.

I didn't see the point of self-pity—I had a bit too much on my plate to wallow in lonesomeness.

Still . . . There was a peculiar emptiness that crept in on me because Dane wasn't there. And because of what I'd encountered earlier at the Lux. A gnawing pang I couldn't shake.

Gazing up at all that nothingness that had once been something spectacular served as an agonizing and ominous reminder of how fleeting life and its significant pieces were.

I made a mug of tea and opened the patio doors to let in the cool evening breeze. I inhaled the scent of jasmine Kyle had planted, a soothing complement to my tea.

In the back of my mind, I told myself I only had days, maybe weeks, to endure the separation from Dane. Then we'd be together. All of this would be behind us. Life would go on.

I smiled, forcing out menacing thoughts.

We were so close, I convinced myself. *So very close.*

I crossed to the pool to turn off the waterfall for the evening. The sound of the sprinkler in the quiet night air made me draw up short. My gaze flashed to the edge of the pool. A second rattle went off.

I stared at the diamondbacks, coiled and hissing. Warning me of their deadly presence with the rapid-fire rattle of their tails.

My heart leapt into my throat.

One snake was random danger. But two?

Another nightmare come to life.

The mug slipped from my hand and I jumped back several feet. Then I whirled around and raced across the patio to the doors. I slammed them shut. And screamed at the top of my lungs.

Amano barreled into the room, followed by Kyle.

"What?" they both demanded at the same time.

My pulse raged. I couldn't tear my gaze from the uncoiling snakes.

Pressing a palm to the glass pane, I wanted desperately to put my hand through it and use the shards to sever the never-ending torment.

Resisting, I spoke slowly, a haunting chill in my voice.

"Vale's still alive."

epilogue

KYLE

Who are *these people?*

I'd done some research online when the first indictments had rolled in and Ari had figured out that Dane was alive. Like him, these guys were experts at controlling their global exposure.

They didn't decorate society pages or have their PR people post photos of them holding million-dollar checks written for charity. They were mysterious and operated in the shadows. That shadow had darkened our doorstep one more time.

Any day now, DNA samples would prove that it hadn't been Vale Hilliard in that high-speed chase in Flag. That car crash was pivotal to this whole insidious situation. To the depths of my soul, I believed it was Wayne Horton splattered across the front of a freight train.

With him dead, I wondered how easy it would be for the corrupt members of Dane's secret society to claim they knew absolutely nothing about the bombing and that Horton acted alone. Certainly

Vale would corroborate that story and attempt to wash the blood from his hands, too.

Ari's blood.

If Vale could never be placed at the scene of the crime, if there was no evidence of his connection to Horton, would they all get away with this? Would tax evasion and whatever crimes Dane helped the FBI to unearth be enough to keep these assholes in prison for the long haul?

Or would their vast wealth and influence have them walking the streets, untouched, exonerated?

Free to continue coming after us if they chose to?

I had to find a way to talk Ari out of all of this. Wasn't she convinced by now that being married to Dane and living in his world was too damn dangerous?

If I couldn't do that, then I needed to track down Vale myself.

And seek my own revenge.

For her.

read on for a preview
of the final book in the trilogy

coming fall 2016

burned

hearts

Danger lurks behind every shadow for Dane and Ari. . . .

"Remember all that's at stake, Ari."

"Yes, of course. I really am sorry. I didn't mean to make either of you worry—or piss you off. It just felt like too good a setup to let slip by. And it was."

Even Dane couldn't dispute that. Yet his scowl deepened.

"You don't seem to understand that this family doesn't work without you."

I sucked in a breath at his intensity. "It doesn't work without you, either."

We stared at each other for endless moments. Finally, Dane nodded.

"Okay, then," I added. I stood and crossed to where he'd stopped pacing. Fury still oozed from him, but I surmised it had more to do with circumstance and the big picture than what Kyle and I had done about Wayne Horton.

I splayed my hands over Dane's abs and stretched on tiptoe to kiss him. A tentative gesture, to gauge his mood. When I pulled away, he smirked. The sexy, bad-boy one that made my insides sizzle.

"Really?" he challenged as he crooked a brow. "*Now* you play it safe?"

"Just testing the waters. You can be very intimidating when you want to be. Which is, like, all the time."

A heartbeat later, he swept me into his arms and marched off to the bedroom.

The baby wasn't in his bassinet, so I figured Rosa had him nestled somewhere close to where she worked. Her current vice was sewing clothes for him. Given her creativity and skill set, I was on the verge of offering to help her financially launch her own clothing line, if that was what she wanted. I didn't even bother shopping for my child, because he had a new outfit or two every week, thanks to Rosa.

Dane kicked the door shut behind us. He set me on my feet and then swiftly pinned me against the wall, his hard body pressed to mine. Gripping my wrists, he raised them above my head. His eyes burned with heat, rage, need. The heady combination made my blood sing, my body tremble.

"Don't defy me again," he said in a low, territorial growl.

Exhilaration rode magma through my veins. "Promise."

"I can't live without you." His green irises were piercing, hypnotic.

"I can't live without *you.*"

With his jaw set in a hard line, he said, "I'm seriously pissed, Ari."

"You have every right to be."

"I love you too much to lose you. We can't take chances like this. *No more.*"

"Understood."

His mouth crashed over mine, claiming me in a possessive kiss filled with lust and fury.

A mix I found thrilling. Scintillating . . .